The K Code

Lorna Makinen

The K Code
Copyright © 2014 Lorna Makinen
All rights reserved

ISBN-13: 978-1495381935
ISBN-10: 1495381935
Also available in eBook

Cover Image Credit: Harewood Castle, Yorkshire, ©Risto Hurmalainen, rhurmal1@welho.com
Cover Design: Elizabeth E. Little, Hyliian Graphic Design
Interior Book Design: The Author's Mentor, www.theauthorsmentor.com

PUBLISHED IN THE UNITED STATES OF AMERICA

This book is dedicated
to those who encouraged me
to finish the thing after forty years
of toying with it.
Thank you for pushing me.

Cast of Characters
(in alphabetical order by first name)

1. Admiral John Benjamin: American navy commander also referred to as the Admiral, John or Benjamin.
2. Alex: an inspector for Scotland Yard is also known as Alex McGraw and Alex Wyndgate.
3. Arthur: a former British navy seal is the valet and close friend of Robert Braun.
4. Bertha: former navy seal nurse and nanny to Kimberly Braun.
5. Bishop: a former British navy seal, minister and a member of Robert Braun staff.
6. Bobbie: photographer and inspector for Scotland Yard. Also known as Inspector Barbara Grantwood.
7. Charlie: inspector for Interpol. Also known as Charles Donnohue.
8. Charles Gunther: Secretary to Robert Braun, also known as Gunthie.
9. Chief O'Doul: Head of Scotland Yard division of inspectors. Mostly known as Chief.
10. Defense Minister James O'Bryan: British defense minister and friend of Robert Braun.
11. Dennis Ross: Inspector for Scotland Yard. Also referred to as Ross.
12. Doctor Ann Brokaw: Botanist for the London Botanical Gardens.
13. Doctor Edward Edse: Braun family doctor. Also known as Eddie, Doctor, or Edse.
14. Doctor John Lewis: Psychologist and member of the Braun staff.
15. Doctor Mathews: American doctor aboard the USS. Bainbridge and good friend to Robert Braun.
16. Dream Team: Inspectors, Carroll, Linda Severance, Karen, Burr, Hennessy, Theresa Crough or Theresa. A special unit at Scotland Yard.
17. Duke: German shepherd. Robert Braun's dog and closest friend.

18. George Gabriel: Attorney for Robert Braun and family. Good friend to Braun family.
19. Gretchen: served in the British navy. Maid to Lucille Braun.
20. Gustov: Member of the Braun staff and works out of Austria.
21. Harriet Gunther: wife of Charles Gunther and aunt to Lauren Woodgrieves.
22. Herr Dietrich: Former navy seal and chef for Braun family.
23. James: Head of the Braun estate security.
24. John: One of the security guards at the main entrance to the Braun estate.
25. Kimberly Braun: niece to Robert Braun. Also known as Kim, Miss Kim or Kimberly.
26. Kurt Rollins: Head of the lab at Scotland Yard. Also called Kurt.
27. Lauren Woodgrieves: Niece to Charles and Harriet Gunther. Assistant to Robert Braun.
28. Lucille Braun: Wife of Robert Braun and mother to Windsor.
29. Marian Atwood: Formerly in British navy and secretary to Kimberly Braun at R & K Plastics Company.
30. Mark Woolsley: Chauffer for Lucille Braun. Son of Mike Woolsley, who was one of the navy seals and staff member of the Braun team.
31. Martin: former British navy seal. Chauffer for Robert and Kimberly Braun.
32. Peter Ghent: Member of Interpol and partner with Charlie.
33. Richard: Communications expert and electronics guru for Robert Braun.
34. Sheila Jones: freelance photographer. Lesbian partner of Lauren Woodgrieves.
35. Windsor Braun: Son of Robert Braun and cousin to Kimberly Braun.

Windsor Braun, in a wing back chair by the fireplace reading The London Times, was startled as Charles Gunther entered. "Windsor, have you no shame? Your father may die at any moment."

Windsor lowered his paper and glowered. His normal reaction would have been to respond with an indignant remark but his father's longtime secretary looked so pathetic it wasn't worth the effort. He continued reading. *It would be a better fucking day if that old man would get in bed with that asshole and die with him.*

Charles labored to sit down at the desk. He pulled out his pocket watch. It had gone past eight thirty in the morning English time and there would be a five hour difference in America. He struggled several times to dial the number of Robert's niece, Kimberly.

After the third try, he choked up. "Kimberly, child. You must come home immediately. Robert..."

"Gunthie? Are you all right?"

He cleared his throat. "Robert has had a severe setback."

Leaning on the desk his brow resting in his hand, he strained to talk over the tears. "Go to the airport. We'll make all the arrangements with British Airways." He slipped the receiver into its cradle.

Charles sat for a few minutes to catch his breath. He wiped his eyes and then dialed his business partner and Robert Braun's attorney, George Gabriel. "George, this doesn't look good at all. I've called

Kimberly. Book an emergency flight for her on British Airways. Buy out the plane! She must get here to be with Robert! I think he is hanging on until she does. He keeps calling her name…"

Charles hung up and sat quietly. He held his handkerchief up to his mouth. The tears welled again. *This room holds so many wonderful memories of my dear friend. Robert's favorite room and mine.* He surveyed the detailed wood moldings, huge floor to ceiling book cases, mammoth fire place, and wall tapestries. *This was the magic room for him and Kimberly.*

Roused from a trance, Charles jerked a bit to see Windsor almost in his face.

"I'll check our schedules, but I'm pretty sure Mother and I can be available for a funeral this week or next." Windsor sashayed to the door and sighed. "I hope it won't take longer than that…There're some parties I'd hate to cancel."

"Windsor, you're despicable!"

Gunther's heart pounded. "Someday, you wretched man, you'll pay for those ugly remarks! May I remind you, you're not even allowed in this room! Should I call Arthur?"

Windsor gritted his teeth. "That would make my day, *Gunthie!*" He opened the door as the elderly man shuffled past. "Isn't that what my dear cousin calls you?" He mocked. "Here *Gunthie.*"

Windsor stood in the hall for a few moments until the old secretary was out of sight. He went into the game room, another room off limits to him. *We need to celebrate!*

He took from the bar a bottle of vintage scotch and put it inside his newspaper and left the room. *I'll be the Master of the house and will get rid of those motherfuckers! The first to go will be Arthur!*

Windsor and his mother's suite of rooms were at the rear of the mansion. At first this arrangement provoked his mother's ire, but they soon found this to be very acceptable as their comings and goings were not, as far as they knew, noticed, or scrutinized. He strolled up the main stairway taking in his prize. *What kind of deal did she make to keep this? Whatever it was made her into a bitch, a drunken bitch at that.*

2

He arrived at her rooms and knocked. "Is my mother up and dressed?" Gretchen, his mother's maid, showed him in. "Yes she is, Mr. Braun."

Thank God, no slurring her words. At least she'll understand this is good news.

He walked over to the mini bar in the living room. "Would you ask her if I might see her? Tell her I've some wonderful news."

That same day, Thursday 1:45 pm London

Helping Kimberly on with her coat, the flight attendant smiled, "Miss Braun, the Captain said you can proceed without delay through Customs and your car will be waiting outside.

Kimberly went numbly through Customs and hurried to the waiting limousine. When she saw Charles Gunther, she relaxed into the leather car seat and gripped his hand.

"Kim, my dear child, I'm so sorry."

"Gunthie, what happened?"

The old secretary's eyes got glassy. "There isn't much time left, Kim. We've asked Dr. Edse to stay at the house to keep him comfortable until the end." Gunther started to cry.

Kimberly held her gloves tightly between her hands, "I can't understand this at all. It doesn't make sense to me. A week ago I talked with him. He told me how great he felt. We even talked about getting in some skiing before the season ended. I can't fathom any of this."

Gunther wiped his eyes and sat back in his seat. "He was feeling well, seemed very happy that you were able to come home for a long visit. Then something happened. Two days after your call, I went out to discuss some business with him and he about bit my head off about some trivial stuff. When I asked him if there was something wrong, he accused me of prying, and sent me off."

Kimberly frowned. "We all know he's got a temper, but he's never talked to you that way ever."

"Well, whatever it was, he couldn't cope with it. That evening, the doctor called to say that Mr. Braun had suffered a heart attack."

Tears in her eyes, Kimberly looked at Gunther. "Why didn't you call me then?"

"I wanted to but he responded so well to the treatment, he told me it would only frighten you and spoil your trip. When I asked the doctor, he said that with plenty of rest and proper diet he would be fine. Then when I drove to the house this morning, the doctor's car was parked out front. At first I thought he had come to make another check-up, but when I went in, Dr. Edse told me he had had a severe setback, and there wasn't anything he could do. He had gone into heart failure. Before I went to his room, I called you. Whenever he is conscious, he calls for you. He is holding on until you get there. There must be something he needs to tell you."

Kimberly wept quietly but soon regained her composure. As the car reached the stone archway of the Braun estate, Secretary Gunther squeezed her hand gently, "I don't want to alarm you, but the rest of your aunt's family is present, and there is an atmosphere of......"

Kimberly nodded "You needn't worry, Gunthie, I'm prepared for those parasites. I thought about it on the plane. I decided to keep my distance whenever I can and no arguments."

Arthur, her uncle's valet, helped Kimberly out of the car.

"Miss Kim, I'm so glad you're here. Dr. Edse has asked that you go to your uncle's room right away."

Handing her gloves, bag and coat to the maid, Kimberly followed quickly up the front stairway. Pausing at the bedroom door, she turned as she sensed someone looking at her. *I wonder who she is. Is she new?"*

As she opened the bedroom door, Kimberly turned again to look at this stranger whose head was slightly bowed. She glanced at Kimberly and smiled as if to give reassurance. Kimberly smiled weakly and entered her uncle's room. *Her smile is so very tender.*

5

The same day in the Customs Office

As the door closed to the Customs Office, the English Inspector Dennis Ross turned to his fellow officer. "What do we know about Robert Braun?"

The officer went to the file cabinet and began looking. "I've heard of the name, Sir. I know he's American and has a large estate in the country side near Berkshire County. Would you like a report made up for you?"

"Yes, that would be good."

That woman seemed distraught about this trip but what seemed more mysterious is we were ordered to pass her through without question. Ross dialed a friend who worked at the Home Office in London.

"Alex, listen, I'm a bit in a rush here. What can you tell me about Robert Braun?

As Ross listened to his friend, the officer came in with a large file and laid it on his desk, pointing to a label in bold letters Level Two

"My aide has just given me a file on the man marked Level Two. Hmm, interesting, he's a chemical engineer and has a company here. It can't be very big. Right now, I'm going on a gut feeling, nothing more. But if I think there is cause to look further, I'll call for an appointment with the Chief Inspector. *I wonder if he's known at the American Embassy...* Okay, let me look this file over and I'll get back to you. This could simply be an exchange of a courtesy between our governments. Good to talk with you, my best to Jane."

Mulling over what he had been told, he packed the tobacco in his pipe. *Wonder what kind of chemicals Braun works with for a Level Two.*

The Braun estate: Mr. Braun's bedroom

Waiting for the doctor to let her move to her uncle's bedside, Kimberly gazed at this aging man who was once a giant in his field.

"Miss Braun, your uncle is awake now. You may speak to him, but for only a few minutes."

Kimberly sat on the side of the bed and gently took hold of her uncle's hand. "I'm here now, Uncle Robert."

Her uncle's eyes opened and he smiled tenderly at his beloved niece. "Kim…"

"Uncle, you don't need to talk. I'm here now and won't leave you. Rest for a while, and then we can talk later."

She bent down and kissed him on the forehead.

The doctor brought a chair for her. Kimberly moved to the chair carefully, not letting go of her uncle's hand. The room was empty save for Charles Gunther and Duke, a huge German shepherd who never left her uncle's side.

Kimberly laid her head on her uncle's hand.

As if having a bad dream, he began to thrash about calling out to her, "Kim, Kim!"

"Yes, Uncle Robert, I'm right here."

His grip tightened to bring her forward so he could whisper. "Kim, before I leave you, you must remember... to... use restraint, to be ...cautious, and... always, alw..ays ..in control."

He opened his eyes and squeezed her hand for a moment. "Please believe me I would not hurt you. You're my world. Look for my help; you'll find it when you take my ring. The ring is for you, it will help you... I'll...always be with... you."

Saying these few words, he became listless and drifted away. She called for the doctor, who asked them to leave the room.

Kimberly gently touched Duke on the head, "Come on boy, and let the doctor help your dad."

At first, Duke resisted a bit. He even growled as the doctor approached the Master's bedside, but he calmed when Kimberly hugged him.

Kimberly and Duke reluctantly left her uncle's room. They somberly moved down the long hallway to her room. Duke stopped and started back to the room. "Duke, come on boy. You can't go in."

She dropped her head holding her sides. *Poor Duke must know something awful is happening or is terribly confused. I certainly can share that feeling. I can't bear the thought those might be his last words to me.*

She and Duke went to the big bay window seat. From this window she saw her life as it started there and now the world her uncle made for her and shared with her would be ending. Tears streaming down her face, she saw the tree outside of her secret garden that had a swing she and Uncle Robert had put up together. *My very own garden was the first and most special present from him.*

She clung to Duke. "He would read to me and your grandmother, Duchess, before going to bed and the day he showed me my special garden he gave me the story book The Secret Garden." Smiling between her tears*, he read that story over and over until he didn't need to look at the page.*

A knock at her bedroom door interrupted her daydreaming. Arthur entered. With a soft but cracking voice told her, "Miss Kim, your uncle has passed away. You may go to his room now."

She turned back to the window, the tears again streaming down her face. "Thank you Arthur. We'll be along in a few minutes."

Her world had come to an end, but then she heard his dying words, Restraint, Caution, and Control. That he would never hurt her and would always be with her. *But you never taught me how to live without you.*

She took a few minutes to freshen up and then she and Duke went back to her uncle's room. At the door, she hesitated to compose herself against the voices crying inside. She quietly entered and moved to the foot of the bed. It disturbed her how dark the room had become. *Uncle loved the light and said only in a blackout would he close a shade or drape.* Not only were the drapes pulled, but a lone lamp by his bed cast a dim glow.

Kimberly shuddered at the performance she saw developing. The unfriendly faces she wanted to avoid were standing next to his bed, crying? Her body stiffened when her aunt became hysterical and sobbed and her cousin was so attentive to his mother's needs. *Why is this conniving and twisted woman doing this? For whose benefit is she putting this act on? Windsor is Being Nice? How much money is he getting for this scene? Thank God Uncle Robert isn't here to see this. He would throw Windsor out of the window in a heartbeat.*

Kimberly bowed her head as she couldn't look another second at this travesty. She touched the bed post and her hand trembled. In the darkness she felt a soft hand lift hers. She turned to see who made this kind and loving gesture. It was her mystery woman she had seen earlier. As she turned to speak, the doctor asked if he could speak with her. No words were offered when her hand was again squeezed gently, only a sweet smile. Then Kimberly followed the doctor out of the room. *I wonder who she is. Twice now she has come to my rescue.*

The doctor held the door for her. Kimberly walked over to a set of French doors to look out. The doctor approached. "Miss Braun, please accept my condolences for your loss. I'm very sorry to bring this up but as the presiding physician, I've determined that your aunt is in no condition to make any decisions right now. Therefore, I must ask that you assist in making the funeral arrangements. Mr. Braun's secretary told me this morning that your uncle's Will is explicit and covers his interment. This is more a formality than anything else, but a family member has to see that the deceased's wishes have been followed."

Another play area she had as a child with yet another little swing distracted her for a few moments until she heard the doctor say Windsor needed to take care of his mother in their time of grief, and wouldn't be able to handle anything else.

Just then the uncle's door opened, as Windsor, gripping his mother's arm, muttered, "You can stop now…I think you've…"

Kimberly looked over at them startled... *What hypocrites!*

They were across the hall face to face with Kimberly and quickly Windsor pushed his mother toward her apartment.

With disgust she replied, "Yes, of course. I'll assist wherever I can."

Dr. Edse left her to return to the grieving family members. Kimberly wheeled around and headed toward her room. When she reached the main stairway, she had a quick change of mind and bolted down the staircase, grabbed her coat, cigarettes and dashed out the side entrance to her secret place.

She tried several times to light her cigarette and failed. *Why am I acting so stupid over this news? Is this a surprise to find out how irresponsible, uncaring, conniving, and loathsome those two are?*

Kimberly struggled with her emotions, wanting so very much to hear her uncle's footsteps and the sound of his voice calling her name. Her heart almost stopped at the sound of footsteps. She had sat down on a stone bench behind one of the many bushes in her garden, when around came her mystery person.

"I'm terribly sorry; I didn't mean to startle you."

Kimberly wiped her eyes and stood up quickly. "Not at all… I got caught up in the moment, emotions you know. Actually I should be used to certain members of this family but..."

She wiped her eyes again and extended her hand. "I don't even know your name, but, under the circumstances of the last half hour or so, I think I'm still Kimberly Braun."

The stranger smiled so beautifully. "Yes, I know. We've never met; I'm Gunther's niece Lauren Woodgrieves."

Kimberly replied with surprise. "That explains it. I only know

Gunthie's wife Harriett, who would be your aunt."

Lauren laughed. "That would be correct."

Kimberly got out her cigarettes and offered them to Lauren.

"The first time I saw you, I had a strange feeling that I should know you. Now I see the resemblance."

Lauren blushed, as her aunt was a beautiful woman. "Thank you for the compliment. My aunt and mother are identical twins." Lauren leaned forward for Kimberly to light her cigarette, "You wouldn't know this, but this is my first cigarette in six months."

Kimberly pulled her lighter back. "Terribly sorry, I hope I haven't caused a setback."

Lauren chuckled, "No, no, it was getting so very, should we say tense in the house that I think this cigarette is probably a little less damaging than having a few stiff drinks, which I don't do either."

Kimberly nodded in full agreement. "I've you to thank for saving me twice; once in the hall and the other at Uncle's bedside."

Just then Arthur walked by the hedge of the garden.

Kimberly stood up. "Are you looking for me, Arthur?"

"There you are, Miss Kim. I hoped I'd find you here." He walked inside the garden.

"Is everything all right?" Kimberly saw a very sad face.

"No Miss Kim. Mr. Gunther asked if I could find you and ask that you go to the library. I believe Mr. Gabriel has arrived." He paused a bit and then whispered to Kim, "The hearse will be arriving shortly for Robert's body. Would you mind if I went with them?" He fought back the tears.

Kimberly put her arms around him." You're more like a brother to him than a valet. I know you'll miss him. You do what is best for you. Right now, I can't watch that happening."

Arthur hugged her back and whispered "Being alone with him will mean a great deal."

Kimberly wiped her eyes. "Well, it seems we aren't meant to have a conversation. Gunthie wants me to come to the library."

"That is quite alright, perhaps another time after things have settled."

Kimberly paused outside of the hedge. "Will you be staying here

12

tonight with your uncle?"

Kimberly's remark surprised Lauren. "Actually, I didn't think I'd be here this long today, but now we have met..... Besides, I didn't bring a change of clothes and I don't have a car and I really must be at work tomorrow. So I should go back with his driver."

Kimberly scuffed at the sod a little. "I don't want to put you on the spot, but, there are six cars in the garage, plus the limo. I'm sure you could use one of them. And as far as a change of clothes is concerned, I've a complete wardrobe you could choose from."

That made Lauren laugh heartily....Kimberly was at least a foot taller, and maybe twenty pounds heavier. "You wouldn't happen to have a tailor in the closet too?"

Kimberly smiled, extending her hand to Lauren. "You have a great laugh, very genuine, and I needed to hear that. Thank you for being here. It really has been a help to me. Now I must go. I bet you know that neither of our uncles liked to be kept waiting. Hopefully you'll want to stay."

Back in the mansion, Kimberly handed her raincoat to the maid. Not having any time to freshen up, she stopped in front of one of the beautiful antique mirrors mounted on the walls in the main hall. Her eyes were red and a bit swollen from all the tissue wiping. She adjusted her blouse collar to the outside of her suit jacket, fluffed her hair and entered the library to meet with George Gabriel and Gunther.

She didn't have the same relationship with the attorney as she had with Gunthie; however, she still had a feeling of trust and ease with him.

"I can see you've had a difficult day, and you have my deepest regret that I've to extend this hardship by asking you to fulfill this obligation."

Kimberly shook his hands and sat next to Gunther at a small conference table toward the back of the library. "Yes, it has been a nightmarish day."

She looked at both of the men who served her uncle for all the years she could remember. "I can't believe any of this has happened. It has to be a bad dream. I think I'm more torn up with the degrading exhibition my aunt and cousin put on, and for whom? Perhaps it was

13

their way of clearing their conscience."

Gunther patted her hand. "Trust me, Windsor has no conscience."

George handed them a schedule. "We can go over this in the morning if you wish, but, I do need you to sign the papers that need to be sent with your uncle's death certificate. Arthur will be going with his body and he can hand them to the authorities. I must admit, Charles and I were surprised Robert wanted the local mortuary to handle the interment."

She frowned. "Why the surprise?"

"To avoid red tape in a foreign country, the American Embassy recommended Rutherfords in London."

Charles shook his head. "I know we had it set up that way but I sure don't recall him changing it…It's there so he must have."

His eyes welled. "Maybe I'm getting too old."

Kimberly signed the papers. " Gunthie, don't be ridiculous."

Handing them to the attorney, she faintly smiled. " If you can stay the night, we can go over your schedule in the morning at breakfast. I feel saturated and would like to rest a bit."

The two gentlemen agreed. The attorney then excused himself to give Arthur the needed paperwork for Robert Braun's embalming.

Kimberly went to her uncle's desk and called to tell the staff to have an early night. "Yes, if you would prepare the usual rooms for our guests. There might be three staying… Oh, she did. That will be all for the night. Thank you. I'll be fine."

She hung up the phone and stood for a few moments. *I wonder why Lauren feels it is so important to finish her work at the lab for Uncle Robert. It was nice she gave Bertha a message for me. At least she will be at the funeral. I would like to get to know her before I go back to the States.*

Gunther put his arm around her. "It will take time for us all to handle his death."

She looked down at him. "I know Gunthie. " She hugged him. "I was just thinking that I need to book my flight back to the States. When is the funeral?"

Gunther stepped away and looked at her in shock. "What did you say?"

She looked at him rather peculiarly. "I just asked when the funeral is."

George Gabriel walked in and saw the strange look on Gunther's face. "Have I missed something?"

"Yes, I think you need to hear this, Kimberly tell George what you just said."

Kimberly frowned. "I remarked that I needed to book my flight back to the States and asked Gunthie when the funeral would be. Have I said something terrible?"

Gunther looked at George with a raised eyebrow. "Why on earth do you feel you must leave so quickly?"

She stopped from opening the library door and turned to face them. "Gunthie, Mr. Gabriel, do you really think I would stay in this house a minute knowing my cousin had become the *Master of the estate*?"

The attorney gave Gunther a little nudge in the side. "Kimberly, we understand how you feel, and after this is all over Gunther and I'll handle booking the return flight for you. Won't we Gunther?"

George Gabriel opened the library door for them and motioned to Gunther behind Kimberly's back to say something.

"Absolutely… we'll do just that. Not to worry, child. Now you go up to bed and George and I will have a little night cap."

She hugged them both and left for the main staircase. "Remember, breakfast is at 6:30 am sharp."

Where's Duke? I'm sure he didn't go with Arthur. I won't sleep if I don't know where he is. She went to her uncle's room. Lying by the bed, Duke whimpered. Her eyes welled "Duke….you're so pure with your devotion. Come with me. I don't want you to be alone."

Kimberly knelt as Duke sat up for his hug. "I bet no one has told you that you come from a special stock. The fact is, Duke Braun, you are the third generation of that stock."

They strolled down the hall. "Yes, that's a fact. Your grandmother Duchess the First was here when Uncle Robert brought me. She took care of me until I was about twelve. Sadly she passed but not until your mom was born. Uncle called her Duchess Braun. She was so smart and so very close to us but died having her last litter.

Heartbroken, Uncle Robert said no more dogs and he sold all the puppies but you. You were the runt and no one wanted you."

She paused in the hall and looked at Duke. "I was working on my Master's degree at Oxford and came home unexpectedly. I hadn't seen any of the litter but gosh, when I saw your little face, it was love at first sight."

Kimberly smiled. " I can tell you know I'm talking about you."

Duke threw his head back and barked.

They continued walking to her room. "It was some doing but we won Uncle Robert over, didn't we."

Her bed had been turned down and on the pillow was a little envelope. It was from Lauren saying she had to go back to the city not only for work the next day but to handle some personal business. She promised to be there for the funeral. Kimberly smiled at Lauren's signature, "the little knight.""

The management of the Braun estate could easily be compared to the operations aboard a Navy ship. Kimberly woke to the sound of the bedroom door opening. She knew it had to be five o'clock and nudged Duke, who was sprawled over her bed. "Duke, Bertha is here. Get up; you have to go out now."

After his usual stretching and yawning, Duke jumped down and left. Bertha put Kimberly's tray on a little table near the bay window and then opened the drapes showing the moon that hadn't set. Normally this would be a happy time for the two. Her uncle had nurtured her to love getting an early start, to love learning, to be organized, to be thoughtful and kind, to be honest and persevere. Bertha had been Kimberly's maid since she was three and this bit of time they shared was always special.

Kimberly warmed her hands with the tea cup, looking out at her swing. "Bertha, you've taken care of me for thirty years. Did you work for Uncle Robert before he brought me here?"

Bertha had made the bed, and was about to enter the closet. "No, the fact is, I had just left the navy. I was on my way back to the States when the unit I was in had a layover in the UK. I met Arthur and

Martin somewhere in London. We'd been on the same base in Korea. Anyway, they told me about Robert wanting to care for his niece as the parents had been killed in a crash. Since I was a Navy nurse, they begged me to come out here to interview for the Nanny's job. You'd been here for a day or two when I came in. It was love at first sight. You came up to me with your little arms open to give me a hug. And, I've been here ever since. Though, I think that will be changing."

Kimberly got glassy eyed. "Would you consider coming back to the States with me?"

Just as she asked the question, there was a knock at the door, and it opened. It was Gretchen, the maid for her Aunt Lucille. "Good morning, Miss Kim. I'm sorry to interrupt, but your aunt told me to tell you she'd like to see you right after your breakfast. She knows you'll be working with the attorney."

Kimberly looked at her watch. "Seems she has gotten past her grief. I'm sorry I didn't mean to put you in the middle. Tell her I'll be up to see her before I leave for the funeral home. Now I better get a move on it."

ৡ৵ৡ

Dressed in a navy –blue double breasted suit with a white silk turtleneck blouse and navy heels, Kimberly walked into the breakfast room at six thirty. Voices drifted down the hall as she poured herself a cup of coffee and took her usual place at the table.

"Good morning, Gunthie, Mr. Gabriel. I wish I could believe it was a good morning. I hope you slept comfortably."

Gunther squeezed her shoulders and kissed her forehead. "The sun is at least shining, my dear Kim. You know Robert would want you to realize the positives."

"You're right, Gunthie. Unfortunately, I won't have you with me to remind me of this."

Gunther and George Gabriel looked at one another a bit confused.

George had his brief case with him and took out the papers that covered the funeral arrangements her uncle outlined in his will.

"While Gunther and I had a night cap last night, we made up a schedule for you today and one for next week."

Kimberly laid the papers down next to her plate and read as she continued eating her breakfast. The two men carried on with their comments about the schedule. Gunther poked his colleague and chuckled, "They are like two peas in a pod. She ignores us while she is reading, just like Robert did."

She finished eating and reading about the same time, took the last swallow of coffee, laid her napkin on the table, "Well, that sure is a full day. But I've to take care of one item you aren't aware of." She pushed her chair back. "Aunt Lucille's maid came very early this morning, to tell me Aunt Lucille wants to see me before I leave the house."

At the door she turned. "I meant to ask you, Mr. Gabriel, if you're planning to make a statement to the press? I think one should be made but I don't want a lot of information given out. I would prefer you leave my name out of it."

The two gentlemen stood by the table and the attorney pulled out of his brief case a copy of his announcement. "I have it made out if you'd like to read it. I know what you mean. Robert guarded his privacy and we'll continue that practice."

She looked at him strangely. "Continue the practice?" Then at her watch. "I better get up there before she sends Gretchen again or Windsor to fetch me. I'm sure whatever you and Gunthie think best to say to the press is fine with me."

She whistled and Duke appeared from nowhere to make the long walk with her. She chuckled. *Even though he is out of sight he really is not far away. He is always there to take care of me. Now I've to make sure he is safe. I wonder if I could take him home with me. I can't bear the thought that he would be left in this house with Windsor and Lucille. God forbid.*

As they came around the corner of her aunt's wing of the house, Gretchen was leaving and had just shut the door.

"PST, PST, Gretchen, is my aunt ready to see me?"

Gretchen jumped a little, being taken by surprise. "Oh... Miss Kim. Yes, she is up and is even dressed."

Kimberly was amused that her aunt was already dressed.

She knocked on the door and went in.

18

"Good morning, Aunt Lucille."

Her aunt's smile faded when she saw Duke. Kimberly told Duke to sit by the door.

"Come in Kimberly, my dear. Come and sit next to me."

Now what is she up too? Just keep your wits about you. Remember, restraint and control. "Is there anything I can do? I'm sure this is hard for you."

Sitting down she caught a whiff of J & B. *Ugh, nothing has changed in that department.*

"I know you have a lot to do today, so I'll come right to the point. There are a few things you must do."

She reached over and handed Kimberly a little ring box.

"Have the people at the funeral home put Robert's rings in this box and bring them back to me. They can leave his wedding ring band on. He doesn't need to be buried with his watch either, so you can bring that back too."

Kimberly lit a cigarette, *obviously she isn't very observant. Uncle Robert hasn't worn his wedding band for years. Just his father's ring and the ring he had made especially for us.*

"Aunt Lucille, I've just read the portion of Uncle Robert's Will regarding his interment and it specifically states he's to be buried with his rings on…I can have Mr. Gabriel make a copy of that segment for you."

Her aunt's eyes almost bolted out of her face as did her voice. "I don't give a damn what he put in that Folly of his. I want those rings and watch. I'll be damned if they're going to be in that casket only to rot…..Besides, they belong to Windsor now!"

Duke sat up and growled. Kimberly motioned to him to settle. A confrontation was the last thing that Kimberly wanted at this time.

Her adrenalin pumped. "I can understand your desire to give Windsor at least one of those rings; however, I can only suggest your request to Mr. Gabriel."

"Suggest! Suggest! God dammit, you tell him! Did you hear me Kimberly?"

Kimberly stood up and Duke moved quickly by her side. *I'm glad you're here with me because I'm not ready to take her on.* They walked to the door while her aunt continued to shout orders at her.

Angered even more that Kimberly had turned her back while she was speaking, Lucille followed her to the door.

"Kimberly, I expect you to hand me those rings and watch the moment you return from the funeral home or….."

Kimberly reeled around and looked sharply at her aunt. "Or you'll do what, Aunt Lucille?"

"You'll see! And take that damn dog out of here."

Kimberly and Duke left without another word. *That's it. We're done here. I'm booking the flight today and there is no way you're staying here another minute with that woman.*

Kimberly burst into the library where Gunther and George were discussing the funeral plans.

"That woman has got to be the biggest *bitch* on this earth."

Gunther and George were shocked by her language and entrance. "Whatever happened between you and Lucille?"

"My God, Gunthie, she couldn't even wait for his body to get cold. At least when he was alive, she was more subtle getting what she wanted, but *now*! She no longer stands on ceremony, she just tells you to jump. Well, she has got the wrong person to push around."

Kimberly grabbed her purse and brief case.

"Kim dear, you still haven't told us why you're so upset."

"I'm sorry; she is determined to have Uncle's rings and watch. She claims they are to be given to Windsor. Well, you know that is a load of... Especially when Uncle Robert told me the ring was to be mine because it was the mate to the one he had made for me.

What's troubling me most is that I'm acting shocked that she isn't wasting any time in grabbing anything and everything she can get her hands on, and why?"

She opened the library door. "She should be relaxed and planning all she will be doing to alter this place like she wanted to do years ago. Why can't she wait? Next Tuesday, I'll be back in New York. She won't have to worry about dealing with me any longer."

Gunther's mouth dropped. He took Kimberly by the hand. "Kim dear, we don't have to leave just yet. Come back and sit for a moment.

She followed them. "Gunthie, we need to get going. We have a full schedule."

George shut the library door and they moved to the couch by the fireplace.

"Kimberly, as your uncle's attorney, I must insist that you're present for the reading of his Will, which, I would imagine your aunt will want done as soon as it is socially acceptable. The funeral will be Sunday afternoon, and I would think within the next two weeks she will ask for it to be read."

"I'm sorry, Mr. Gabriel and Gunthie. The funeral will be about all that I can handle. Let me take Duke, uncle's ring and I'll have all that I want. I've wonderful memories and that's all I need. As far as I'm concerned Uncle Robert is alive in my heart. I don't need to be in this house another minute. I can't bear this ugly and hateful behavior."

Gunther patted her shoulder. "Kimberly, we certainly can't make you stay; however, I know Robert would be dismayed if he knew you had ignored his wishes. He made a video tape he wanted you to have – his last wish- but we can't release it until the day of the reading of the Will. He felt this video would be something you would have of him for the rest of time. Please reconsider."

Kimberly picked up her things. "Not to make matters worse I'll stay on until the Will is read… Now, can we get on with it and leave?"

In the limousine, Kimberly continued. "Gunthie, you know this is only the beginning. Do you know she had the nerve to say bring these things to me or else! I'll be damned if she thinks I'm going to be her puppet. As much as I love this place, I really can't wait to return to the States.

"Kim, my dear, Lucille Braun thinks she has the power now to wheel and deal. Her act can be quite convincing, but you must see this through."

Kimberly, staring at the sun's rays filtering through the trees along the long driveway of the Braun estate, clutched Gunther's hand. "I just don't understand. She knows they're getting everything of any importance. Why, then, does she want to strike out at me?"

Gunther gently squeezed her hand. "Perhaps, she isn't as confident as you are in your assumptions. At any rate, you'll have to be firm at all times until this whole matter is settled. Trust George and me. As for Lucille's demands for the ring and watch, I'm sure George will know what to say when he talks with her this afternoon. He won't be overjoyed to handle it, but he's had to confront her in the past over Windsor's indiscretions."

When the funeral arrangements were completed, the director of the funeral home handed Kimberly a small box that contained her uncle's ring and watch. She looked at Gunther. "I can't and I won't give these up. I would die if Windsor had them."

Gunther put his arm around Kimberly. "Most definitely, these are yours. It says it in Robert's Will… George and I will handle Lucille."

As they got into Gunther's limo, the driver reported Lauren had called suggesting they meet for lunch. Gunther nodded. "Good idea!" *We all need a break from this sadness.*

After the meal, the three walked out to Gunther's car.

"Before I retire for the night, I'll have had conversations with the Bishop about the eulogy and George about the funeral plans. I'm sure they will do their utmost to have everything go smoothly."

Gunther got into his car and rolled down the window. "Goodbye my dears. Lauren, do you suppose you could stay at the estate with Kimberly tonight?"

Kimberly was startled at Gunther's suggestion. "That's all right, I'm sure I'll be fine and I'll be busy with a lot of little things to be checked on."

"You're right, Uncle; I'll stop at my flat and pick up a few things on our way back to the estate."

"Were you able to talk to Sheila?"

Lauren was surprised by her uncle's question.

"Why no, I believe she's on the Continent."

"You believe? Strange, how you can live with someone and not know where they are. What is she doing there?"

"She's probably there on business."

Gunther dropped his head. *Damn it, I've embarrassed her. Harriet tells me I should think first.*

Lauren's face had blushed quite noticeably.

"Well…" He cleared his throat a couple of times. "You know what I want to say about it. Anyway, your aunt and I will see you both tomorrow."

Kimberly refrained from making any comments or asking any of the many questions that Gunther had raised with his niece's scolding. The two women walked in silence to Lauren's car. Lauren looked up at Kimberly as she unlocked her door.

"I don't live far from here if you'd like to walk some more."

"That's fine with me. It's certainly a beautiful day for walking." *Wonder what Gunther meant? He came down on Lauren pretty hard. Who's Sheila? I've never seen him so agitated.*

They started up a cobblestone street probably sixteenth century, a beautiful quaint area.

Lauren took hold of Kimberly's arm. "I hope you're going to give me a chance to explain my uncle's sudden outburst."

Kimberly didn't know how to act. She was in a sea of confusion. "I must admit I've not seen this side of Gunthie before. I get the notion he doesn't like your roommate very much. Doesn't she do her fair share?"

Lauren stared at Kimberly. *One hundred percent naïve!* "I'd like to talk about it sometime."

Kimberly offered Lauren a cigarette. "Not now, I really want to quit and this is a good test of will power."

"Well, I guess if you can quit, then I can too." She walked over to a trash can and threw out the pack.

"Are you sure this is the right time, with all that's going on."

"I have to start sometime. Maybe this is a new beginning."

Lauren smiled. *Maybe for both of us.*

They turned the corner and Lauren pointed to an old, very old, but well-kept apartment building.

Kimberly was impressed with the architectural lines. "This is fascinating. Bet there's history behind this."

"No, I don't think it has other than it was built around the eighteenth century. The landlord told me once that he is related to Lord Mountbatten. He also said one of the early Churchills lived here, not Winston. I guess that is some history."

A light came on in a window on the second floor. She got out her key but hesitated at the door. "Do you still want to come up?"

"Is that Sheila who turned on the light?"

Lauren nodded. "I really thought she was on the Continent."

They entered to a beautiful marble stairway. Kimberly turned about to take it all in. Lauren took hold of Kimberly's hand to redirect her attention. "Will you understand, that I too am starting a new beginning and that my returning home the other night was with that in mind? You remember the note I left for you?"

Kimberly squeezed her hand. "Yes, it is still on my dresser. I must admit, Duke and I read it about five times."

They both laughed while Lauren unlocked the apartment door. Kimberly chuckled looking at the hallway. "Wow, what an alteration. It's like walking through a time capsule"

Lauren looked confused. "What do you mean?"

Kimberly walked up to the pictures that were different sizes and mostly black and white. "Sorry, I was thinking out loud. Passing through the door, I was thinking the idea of the Old versus the New or Modern."

The wall was a brilliant red wall paper that went tastefully with the black and silver frames. The intense lighting, directed to the walls, allowed each picture a unique presentation.

Kimberly loved photography and studied the pictures on both sides of the hall.

"While you browse, I'll see where Sheila is and then I'll get some things together for tomorrow."

Lauren returned with Sheila. Kimberly didn't know they had been watching her looking at the details of the photos.

"I'm sorry; I didn't hear you come back." She smiled at both of them. Lauren's roommate was about her own height and weight with similar features.

Lauren made all the proper introductions. "Well, what do you think of them?"

She handed Kimberly her overnight case while she put on her coat.

"Are all of these yours? These are beautiful. Really like the black and white instead of color. It gives such a different perspective."

Lauren and Sheila were amused. "Yes they are ours. Sheila's work is on the right side and mine over here. Sheila is a freelance photographer for a magazine. They send her all over the world."

"You'll have to show me your equipment and give some lessons."

Sheila leaned against the wall. "I think Lauren would have the time to do that for you. I'm not around that much, am I, Love."

Though Sheila and Lauren smiled at one another, Kimberly wasn't quite sure how to handle that remark.

"Well, we best be on our way. I still have quite a lot to do this evening. It was nice meeting you; I hope we can meet again under better circumstances."

"Oh, I'm sure we'll see each other. By the way, I'm sorry about your uncle." And she left the room.

Lauren stood for a moment pondering Sheila's remarks.

Kimberly could see Lauren's hesitation and touched her arm, "We better go."

Walking back to Lauren's car, Kimberly asked Lauren how she met Sheila.

"About three years ago Windsor had a huge party at the estate. Your aunt and uncle were in Washington."

"They would have to be away for that to happen. According to Uncle Robert, Windsor gave the staff two days off and…"

"Now let me finish…" Lauren put her hand up to Kimberly's mouth "Shush."

Kimberly beamed at Lauren's tenderness.

"Windsor had overheard my uncle telling your uncle that he and my aunt were flying over to the States to attend the graduation ceremony for my doctorate. Well, then I moved back here. Windsor had this party and invited me. I still haven't figured out why since we never were in the same circle of people. My uncle and aunt thought it would be a nice change from all the studies before I started my job at your uncle's company… which is another story. I really don't know how Windsor knew I was a lesbian but he evidently did and introduced me to Sheila. We left the party before it got out of hand."

Lauren pulled out of the parking spot. *Maybe I've said too much.*

"We've never had a meaningful relationship. Sheila acted as if she had to be my lover rather than wanted to be. It's all been very trying and I ended it last night."

"You did?" Kimberly responded awkwardly.

Lauren glanced at Kimberly. "Are you okay with this?"

Kimberly nodded "Obviously Gunthie knows about it?"

"Oh yes... he and Aunt Harriett are very unhappy with my choice."

"Not that you're a ... "

"No, not at all. They just want me to be happy, and feel this relationship has put a strain on me."

Kimberly listened while she watched the sun's ray dance in and out of the trees as they sped by. *I wonder how obvious it is that I haven't had a relationship of any kind. Now what do I do?*

The outline of the estate in the distance reminded her that some ugly moments were still to be dealt with and soon. Lauren could see tension returning to Kimberly's face as they drove through the gate. She pulled up to one of the garage doors. "Kim, you know I'm here for you." She took hold of Kimberly's hand.

"Yes, thank you. You've been a big help to me already and it's reassuring to know that I'm not alone."

She was getting a bit tongue tied with her explanation as she knew too well she had her uncle's staff who helped bring her up and loved her very much. "I mean it's nice to have someone of my own age near me. Am I making any sense or does my naivety show?"

Lauren, seeing Kimberly's unsettled feelings, replied. "I understand completely."

They used the servant's entrance. Kimberly wanted to get a feel as to what had gone on while she was away and thought her allies might still be in the kitchen. At any rate she didn't think her aunt would be looking for her there. It would be beneath her dignity to be seen in those areas of the household.

Duke met them in the kitchen with tail wagging.

Arthur grinned. "Duke gave you away, Miss Kim. He certainly knows your footsteps."

Kimberly hugged her ward and made a fuss over him while she

and Arthur talked.

"Well, what kind of day have you had? I hope Mr. Gabriel was able to talk to Aunt Lucille. Has she been looking for me?"

"No I don't think so at least she hasn't called this evening."

Then Arthur chuckled. "She may have been distracted. The staff and I were talking about your aunt's explosive temper at dinner."

Kimberly looked at Lauren. "You're not referring to Mr. Gabriel, are you?"

Arthur quit smiling. "I really shouldn't make light of it, but, your aunt did get a bit crazy and I'm not sure, but she may have fired a gun at George Gabriel."

"What! *A gun!* Was he hurt?"

Arthur shook his head. "No, nothing like that. But it did sound like it, from here at least."

Bertha dashed into the kitchen, "Oh, Miss Kim, You missed it! Gretchen came screaming for us to come and help! Your aunt went bonkers at Mr. Gabriel. The poor man, I don't know how he got out of here alive!"

"Come on Bertie; don't be making a drama out of this."

Arthur called on the staff phone for Gretchen to come to the kitchen, while Bertha told Kimberly and Lauren what she knew about the incident.

Bertha poured them some coffee as Gretchen came in. "Miss Kim, Arthur said you wanted to know what happened today."

"From what I'm hearing I'm almost afraid to ask, where is my aunt now?"

"I'm not being unkind, but, I do believe she has passed out from over indulging."

"At least I don't have to confront her tonight. Where on earth did she get a gun?"

"No, Miss, it wasn't a gun."

"Why don't you start from the beginning?"

Kimberly motioned for Gretchen to sit with them around the kitchen table and handed her a cup of coffee.

Seeing the five of them around the table, Duke left eating his dinner and sat next to Kimberly. She scooted over to make room for him. "Who ever said dogs aren't smart?"

"I guess you can start, we must all be here now." She petted Duke's head.

"Well Miss Kim, I had just served your aunt a late lunch when Mr. Gabriel arrived. They seemed to be conversing okay while I was there. I left the room to get some cleaning done in her bedroom, when I heard Mrs. Braun shout some bad words. The F word was one of them."

Knowing how shy Gretchen was, they couldn't help but be amused with her explanations.

"I stopped to listen. She shouted more bad words at him. He told her that Mr. Braun's Will went into great detail and couldn't be altered or contested. Mr. Braun had made certain of that and she had to wait for the reading to find out the contents... that's when Mrs. Braun started throwing things at him. Miss Kim, I thought she was going to kill the man. I ran into the room to stop her hitting him with the bellows from the fireplace. The room was a disaster. He had food all over his suit coat! He tried to get out and she just kept grabbing things and throwing them at him. He had slipped to the floor and she was just about to crown him with one of her antique French vases when I grabbed her arms. Mr. Gabriel struggled to his feet and left the room. She wormed her way out of my grip. I was afraid to hold her too tight. She wheeled around and hit me in the head with the vase."

Gretchen showed Kimberly the large bump she had on the side of forehead. "Maybe you should have that looked after."

"No, Miss Kim, I'll be fine…. Then she pushed me aside and ran after Mr. Gabriel. That's when it sounded like a gun shot. She still had that vase and must have thrown it just right to hit the wall and it sounded like a blinking explosion. I ran down the back way as fast as I could to get Arthur."

Kim shook her head. "I better call Mr. Gabriel and see if he is alright and find out if we still have an attorney…"

Kimberly turned around at the kitchen door. "I'm wondering now how you'll manage after she and Windsor take over the estate. I wish I could take you all back to the States with me but I live in a New York apartment. I can't imagine living here with them. Not for a minute."

28

She and Lauren left the kitchen. "If it is alright with you, I want to get out of these clothes into something more comfortable."

"Mr. Gabriel, I've just heard. Are you okay? Nothing broken, I hope. Thank goodness! I hope you can get some rest ….. Yes I was worried that you might have left the country to avoid dealing with this insane behavior." Kimberly hung up. *My God, what else can she do?*

Arthur came in. "Miss Kim, I left some messages there on the desk for you and would you like a late dinner served?"

"Thank you, but you all can call it a day. If we get hungry, I'm sure we'll find something to take the edge off. I do want you all to attend the funeral and would like it very much if you, Bertha and Gretchen would ride in my car. We can pass on breakfast. Just set up some coffee and scones and let all of us help ourselves. Don't you agree?"

Arthur smiled. "That's very thoughtful. I know the rest of the staff will appreciate the extra time to get ready for tomorrow. If that's all, I'll say good night."

They both left the library. Duke met her at the top of the main stairway wagging his tail as if to tell her that he had beaten her. "You have to know how many times you've brightened my day, saved my sanity and made me feel loved."

Duke stood on his back legs, put his paws on her shoulders, and made some whimpering sounds as if to assure her that he understood. She hugged him and they went to her room.

At her dresser, she took the ring box out of her pocket. She looked in her jewelry box for a gold chain long enough to hide her uncle's ring around her neck. *Now it's safe.*

When they got back to the library, she found a note on the door. "I'm in the kitchen."

"Well, I wondered if I left enough clues for you to find me." She had set up the kitchen table with a couple of plates and a tray of sandwich makings in the middle. "Tonight we have DIY."

Kimberly's questioning expression let Lauren know how pampered her new friend had been. She motioned for Kimberly to sit down while she poured their coffee. "Miss Kimberly, that means 'Do It Yourself.' "

Wide eyed Kimberly popped up. "Wait a minute, you forgot something. I'll be right back."

She made a beeline for the dining room. *I can do DIY.* She grabbed a crystal candle holder and ran back to the kitchen. She came in and lit the candles from the stove. "Now we can eat in style."

She put the candles on the table and turned off the overhead lights. They burst into laughter.

A half hour passed. Kimberly put her napkin on the table, "That was fun, and your DIY food was excellent."

Lauren offered Kimberly more coffee. "Don't worry, it's decaf."

"It won't be the coffee that will keep me awake, I can assure you. If anything it will be the worry to get through the funeral tomorrow." She looked at the clock over the sink. "It's getting late. I better take Duke out for his walk before we turn in."

Lauren's smile and her eyes glowed in the candlelight. "Would you mind if I tagged along?"

"I don't think Duke will mind, what say you fella?" *This is a strange feeling.*

Duke knew the words "out and walk" and stood waiting at the kitchen entrance. Kimberly took a couple of jackets off the coat rack and helped Lauren on with one. It was a moonlit night. They walked out through a little gate. Lights flickered in the distance. "We don't need to walk in that direction. Men are finishing the final preparations for uncle's interment."

Kimberly visibly stiffened. Lauren took hold of Kim's arm "You know a day didn't go by that Dr. Braun didn't talk about his wonderful niece one way or another. In fact, I really think he thought of you as his daughter rather than a niece."

They walked toward Kimberly's secret garden. "Did he tell you how we met?"

Lauren took hold of Kimberly's hand, "I don't know if I heard the whole story, but I do know that he had a very difficult time dealing with the death of your parents. Once I heard him say softly, he felt responsible and would have done anything to have saved them. Then he remarked how worried he had been that the court wouldn't award him custody of you. I'm sure that is why he married Lucille, who was his secretary at the time, to sway the judge, who according to your uncle was a bull-headed ass hole."

Kimberly smiled. "That remark isn't foreign to me. The way he said it always made me giggle. I remember once when I was playing in my garden with Duchess, his first shepherd. I didn't know he was there with Arthur and I mimicked him. Boy, did I catch it! I think Arthur walked away so he wouldn't get into trouble for laughing."

"It's wonderful you have those memories to look back on."

"Those were the most wonderful years of my life. I owe him everything..."

Lauren stopped walking to face Kimberly, "I'm sorry, I don't mean to cause you more pain thinking about all of this."

Kimberly wiped her eyes. "I appreciate your concern. Perhaps it will take a while to sink in, but I truly don't believe he's gone. Call me crazy, but I feel him around me. What is disturbing is the behavior of Lucille and Windsor. It just tears me apart and I can't wait to leave this place. I want to take Duke and leave."

Just then Duke appeared. "We better go in now. Truly, I'm sorry I showed my anger."

Lauren clutched Kimberly's hands. "I'm glad that you feel free to show your emotion and not bottle it up."

As they stood in moonlight, Kimberly tingled all over. *This is so unreal. I just can't get involved. In a few more days I'll be back in New York. She is so beautiful and so loving.*

They strolled back to the house without conversation. Both relished the simple glow of that moment. Kimberly hung up their coats and turned off the kitchen light. Lauren and Duke continued to the front stairway. They turned and waited for Kimberly to catch up.

At the top of the steps Lauren turned to Kimberly and kissed her sweetly on the cheek. "Good night. I hope you can get some rest," and went on to her room.

Heathrow Airport Customs Office

The Chief Inspector for the Heathrow Customs Office walked into the office reading an article on the front page of the London Reporter, when the phone rang. "Inspector Ross here."

He put the paper down on his desk and reached for his pipe. "Good morning Alex... Yes I was just reading the article in the Reporter. Interesting. Very unassuming... The man is close to being a billionaire and who knew it. I see the estate is in Berkshire county, beautiful countryside. I don't ever recall seeing it from the road. That would be a good reason, a *ten foot* wall around *one hundred twenty-five acres!*" Ross chuckled.

Ross lit his pipe. "If you need a hand, I'll be wrapping up the assignment here at Heathrow today. The funeral is tomorrow... Interesting... The Navy is involved... Hmm... Sure... glad to help... I'll see you at Home Office in the morning at seven. It will be like old times."

Ross stood at his office window watching a plane land. *Interesting, funeral for Robert Braun be without incident? No press? No local police? Why the American Navy?*

His aide interrupted his train of thought. "Sir, I think this might be of interest. I did some more searching on the Braun family and found this in our Frequent Departures to Designated Places File. It seems the Braun son likes to go to Austria."

Ross glanced at the file and then at his aide. "This man is always travelling. Does he have an occupation?"

He read further. "Oh, I see why there is a file on him... Drunk, disorderly conduct... foul language... striking an officer."

Ross tossed the file on his desk. "Here's a case of those who have it versus those who don't. Anyone else with those charges would have their ass in jail. Seems Mr. Braun and I would have a difference of opinion on how to raise children..."

Their conversation ended and the aide left.

At ten o'clock his aide knocked on his door.

"Enter."

"Sir, you asked to be reminded of your meeting this morning with the Head of Operations."

Ross looked at his watch, "Thank you, Gerald. By the way, while I'm gone could you make me a copy of these two files you've shown me about the Brauns? I'm not sure if the Home Office has any of this information." *Something's amuck.*

The day of the funeral

Shaken out of a deep sleep, Kimberly sat up in bed. She could have sworn she heard a noise. The sun just pushed over the horizon. *At least it will be a pretty day. I feel like I've been running from someone or being chased by something. I need a shower.* Stretching her arms above her head, she was startled by Bertha opening the door.

"Excuse me Miss Kim; I wanted to get Duke before I brought your tea. I didn't think you'd be awake yet."

"That's alright Bertha; I'm still having a difficult time sleeping. Actually, I could have sworn I heard a noise like a wheel squeaking in my room…"

Bertha frowned a little and pulled the drape back from the bay window. A little more light came into the room, "No squeaky wheel in here. Come on Duke. Arthur is waiting for you."

They were amused by Duke's yawning and stretching on Kimberly's bed.

"Great protector you are, you big baby." Kimberly ruffled up his hair as he walked to the door.

"Oh, don't kid yourself, Miss Kim. I would bet he heard me come down the hall and knows all of our footsteps. Don't you boy." Bertha petted Duke on the head and they left.

By the time Bertha returned with the tea, Kimberly was already in the shower. Bertha made the bed and then laid out a couple of outfits she thought appropriate for the funeral. Kimberly came out of the bathroom in her bathrobe, drying her hair in a towel.

She smiled at Bertha and headed for the tray. "I've decided not to wear black today."

Bertha raised her eye brows.

"I know what you're going to say, but I really don't think my uncle would want me to look drab dressed in black."

"Miss Kim, I do understand. Why don't you pick what you think Mr. Braun would like to see you dressed in."

"I won't be having breakfast this morning, so you can get ready for the funeral."

"Your aunt didn't issue any orders allowing any of us to attend the funeral. Arthur told Gretchen and me that we were to ride with you. That was very kind of you."

Kimberly hugged Bertha. "I know Uncle would want that as much as I do. You better get ready."

A half hour later, Kimberly walked into the library dressed in a light blue silk dress suit with a beige silk turtleneck blouse and heels to match. At the window she watched the limousines pull up in front of the house. The chauffeurs stood at the side of each car waiting to take the family and invited guests to the grave site.

Lauren got into her uncle's car.

Just then Arthur knocked and entered. "Your car is waiting, Miss Kim; I think we should be leaving, if you're ready."

As Kimberly walked out with Arthur and Bertha, Gretchen sped around the corner a little out of breath. "I may get fired for this but I couldn't miss showing my respects."

Kimberly put her arm around Gretchen. "You'll always have a job even if you come to the States to work for me."

As they proceeded to the car, voices raised in argument rang from the upstairs hallway.

Kimberly stopped. "Now what's going on?" Her shoulders

stiffened. "Let's go, I don't want to know*!" I refuse to let that woman ruin this day.* She motioned for them to go ahead.

She wanted to have a word with Gunther. "Good morning Harriet, Gunthie," and then smiled at Lauren.

Gunther patted her hand. "Is everything all right, Kim dear? I can see something has happened."

"As well as can be expected, Gunthie. We were coming out and we heard Aunt Lucille lashing out at someone in the upstairs hall. Her voice resonates to the core of your body, and it is so full of hate."

Gunther motioned for Kimberly to look. Kimberly's aunt and cousin rushed from the house to their car.

Kimberly returned to her car. Her uncle's last words RESTRAINT, CAUTION and CONTROL jumped into her thought. She took a deep breath and got into her car parked behind her aunt's. She opened the window half way to catch the breeze and closed her eyes.

George Gabriel charged out of the house with a very red face, his hair all askew, carrying his overcoat. Lucille Braun's window rolled down as he passed. He stopped to listen. "George, my orders will be carried out today, or I assure you this matter can and will be handled in another way. Do I make myself clear?"

The browbeaten attorney looked livid, "Yes Lucille, you have made yourself quite clear."

He stomped to Gunther's car and got in. "Charles, that woman will be the death of me yet. She is so callous….It's all I can do to keep from punching her in the face. Pardon me Harriet, but Lucille Braun is a wicked Bitch."

Charles handed him something to drink. "No apologies are needed my friend. What demands did she make this time?"

George put his glass out for a refill. "You'll be happy to know that she has insisted that the Robert's Will be read right after the burial. I mean today."

"What?" Charles Gunther and his wife exclaimed loudly.

Gunther's driver, not prepared for this eruption, jumped in his seat. Lauren told him not to worry, just follow the procession.

Charles offered George another swig. "No, getting hammered

isn't the solution. Not now. As much as this is in such bad taste, she does have this right and we have to honor it. I feel dreadful having to break this news to Kimberly."

"Robert wanted to share this moment with her using his video to give solace. I'm afraid all hell is going to break loose."

The ten minute drive to the crypt located on the estate was not long enough to lower the emotions of the morning.

Lucille Braun remained in her car until her husband's casket had been placed inside of the crypt. Dressed in a black suit and wearing a veiled black hat, she walked down an aisle with her son and sat in front of the rest of the family and invited guests.

Bishop Rutgers' eulogy lasted about thirty minutes. His very moving words revealed he was dear friend and confidant of Robert Braun. He finished with a prayer and then handed the grieving wife a rose. "Lucille, you're to put the first rose on the casket."

She glared and whispered back. "I hope you've started to pack!" She grabbed the flower and stood.

She and Windsor placed a rose then left the crypt to return to the house, without acknowledging anyone. Kimberly wasn't at all surprised by her aunt's actions but hoped people would think she left out of remorse rather than rudeness. She slipped in quickly to represent the Braun family in the wake of her aunt's departure, graciously accepting the condolences of the guests as they passed by her uncle's casket for the last time.

Bishop Rutgers put his arm around her. "I wouldn't need to ask anyone to point out Robert's niece to me. Let me look at you." He stood in front of Kimberly holding both of her hands. "The family resemblance is very evident, and from what Arthur has told me, you favor Robert in every way."

The Bishop, over six feet and like Arthur, very well built, had a twinkle in his eyes when he smiled.

Kimberly appreciated his genuineness. "I consider that an endearing compliment. My uncle has referred to you as his closest friend. He praised you in every way and told me I could come to you if I ever needed counseling."

"That is very true, Kimberly. I knew him better than anyone else, and I know he's still with you in spirit."

Her eyes widened. "You know, that's exactly how I feel. If anything it is all of this family turmoil that's upsetting."

The Bishop glanced around the room. "It looks as though we'd better continue this conversation at another time, but let me leave you with one more thought. Be selective with whom you confide. Please come and see me before you go back to the States. I'm sure we have a lot to share."

He shook her hand and turned to talk to others leaving the crypt.

Kimberly moved quietly away to sit on a bench very near the casket.

Lauren came back inside to find her. "There you are. Can I squeeze my bottom on this bench with you? Let me look at you. Are you okay?" Lauren turned Kimberly's face toward her. "Yes, I can see two beautiful eyes... maybe a little tired."

Kimberly blushed. "Are you saving me again?"

"No... Uncle Charles sent me to find you." Lauren took Kimberly's arm and lifted. "You still have the wake to attend to. How about we take care of that obligation and then after everyone has left, we'll come back here where it's nice and quiet."

At the cars, Gunther and George Gabriel were waiting.

"Well, how are you holding up, Kim dear?"

She hugged Gunther. "I'm okay. How about the three of you?"

Gunther's eyes got so glassy. "It will take time to get used to him not being around, not being awakened at all hours of the night."

Harriet gave him some tissues, put her arms around him, and led her husband to their car. "He needs to sit. We'll wait for you in the car."

Kimberly sadly watched. "I hope it isn't too late for them to enjoy some retirement. Uncle Robert told me Gunthie would never take a vacation. He was diligent at handling all of uncle's affairs which included me." She looked at George Gabriel. "I feel dreadful that the two of you have been subjected to such horrible circumstances."

"I wish I could say that this seeming nightmare is over...but...we have another situation."

Kimberly looked at Lauren and then over to Gunther's car. "What

38

do you mean?"

George pulled his watch out of his vest pocket. "Just before we left for the funeral, not even three hours ago, Mrs. Braun informed me she wanted to have Robert's Will read in the library following the interment…If you had been in the house, you couldn't help hearing her lash out when I told her I thought that would be tacky. Unfortunately, it is within her rights and I've to abide by her wishes. If not, she has threatened to take the matter to the Press."

Kimberly put her hands on her hips. "Of course, knowing full well Uncle hated any kind of publicity which my dear cousin has more than once contributed… Yes, we heard the noise and I wondered who… gosh I'm so sorry she got to you again."

"This time she wasn't armed."

Kimberly and Lauren couldn't help grinning.

Then Lauren advised. "Well, go ahead with it. Aunt Harriet and I can represent the family at the wake."

Gunther called to them. "George. Arthur has called to say that Mrs. Braun is waiting and is about to have another… drink. I think we had better get back to the house. Kimberly, get in the car. George and I need to talk with you."

"Are you feeling better?"

"Yes, my dear, I'll be fine. We need to know that you'll be okay."

"What do you mean? Of course I'm fine."

"Kimberly, you have to be at the reading of the Will. No matter what Lucille says or does… we are there with you and…"

"Okay, but, I told you before what I want I already have except I want to take Duke back to the States with me."

Arthur met their car. "Miss Kim, may I suggest that you use the balcony entrance to the library for your meeting with Mrs. Braun. There are still guests mingling in the main hall and I think you really want to get to the library before Mrs. Braun has more to drink."

"That's a good idea. Thanks Arthur." She took hold of Gunther's arm and gestured for Mr. Gabriel to follow.

The three entered the library. Arthur had set up a screen and projector to show the video that Gunther had told Kimberly about.

Charles Gunther touched Arthur's shoulder. "Don't leave, Arthur. Mr. Braun has a portion of his Will for the staff and you can represent them."

The attorney set his briefcase on the desk and pulled out a folder of papers. "After I read Robert's Will, I'll give you each a copy of the Will for your records and you'll also be required to sign off on the original."

Kimberly sat in a wing back chair near the fireplace. Her aunt and cousin sat on one of the couches across the room. *He better get on with it before she ruins another suit.*

Mr. Gabriel hurriedly addressed the group as Lucille grabbed another drink. "Now the bequests: 1. The servants are to remain permanently, unless they choose to leave. In addition each will receive pensions based on years of service and cost of living."

Not good, another drink. Poor George, he can't read any faster. Finally Windsor… It really isn't funny…..it's pathetic.

The attorney turned to face Windsor. "This may come as a shock to you, Windsor, or maybe you might be relieved to know that you're not my son. I'm sure you all have a look of total surprise."

Windsor looked at his mother. "What the fuck is he saying? You told me he didn't know!"

"Windsor, shut up! We'll *talk later*!!"

Kimberly put her hand up to her mouth. *Are you kidding me? Holy… Oh my …there truly is a God. Look at his face.* She looked over at Arthur. Not even a grimace in his face. *Arthur knew all along. Hmm… What doesn't he know?*

"Yes, Windsor, I'm claiming you even though I've known for some time that you're my brother Kurt's son. I wouldn't have known this had it not been for a letter I found in his belongings after he died ten years ago. For ten years I've known my brother Kurt was your father. The letter to prove this is in one of my safety boxes. In it your mother tells him of her pregnancy, and also of her undying love for him. The choices we make. I wanted to be successful and he wanted his bottle. It seems you're following in his footsteps. I'm overlooking the miserable life you've established for yourself and leaving you fifty million dollars, plus whatever you've already taken from me, which you thought I knew nothing about."

Kimberly leaned her elbow on the arm of the chair, looking aghast at her cousin. *That explains why Uncle Robert never had any pictures of his family around. He and I have one of my mom and dad holding me as a baby.*

Windsor jumped up. "Let me get this right. That bastard is claiming me as his son… and that's all I get?"

Lucille glared at him. "Windsor, sit down!"

Kimberly studied Arthur; *I think Arthur would like Windsor to do something stupid like go after Mr. Gabriel. That's all we need with guests in the house.*

"Lucille, you better get him under control! Windsor! If you leave without signing off on this document, you'll forfeit fifty million dollars."

Windsor stomped fuming to the desk. George Gabriel put the document down for him to sign, and then stepped back by Gunther.

"Windsor, don't you sign that paper!! My attorney should be here very soon."

"Lucille, I've explained this to you, the Will can't be contested. Robert has made sure of it. It is foolproof. Now, may I please continue?"

Windsor put the pen down and went back to the couch.

The attorney wiped his forehead, took some water. "Lucille, my devoted wife, for the past ten years and probably more, I have overlooked what you were doing behind my back not only with my brother, but with all the other men you've solicited. Yes, my dear, I've known about all of your indiscretions. How foolish I was to think that I caused your drinking because of my devotion to my work. I wanted to trust you rather than listen to my advisers that you were scheming to steal from me. Though I would have reason to do otherwise, I've chosen to take care of you the rest of your life and leave you seventy-five million and all of the real estate I've acquired in the States. I truly hope this doesn't alter your life style."

The library door opened, Mrs. Braun's attorney slipped in quickly. She motioned for him to sit beside her on the couch. She handed him the papers. "You'll have to wait. I want to watch this video Robert made for this bitchin niece of his."

Mr. Gabriel pulled out a video tape from his brief case. "This tape was made for you, Kimberly. Mr. Braun wanted you to have a lasting remembrance of him. I might add that this video is a legal document and would be accepted in any court of law. Please note that the video displays all the proper seals."

"Mr. Gabriel, may I watch this in private?"

"I'm sorry Kimberly; I have to follow the law. Since there are no transcripts of the tape, everyone must be present." The attorney pushed the button.

The screen showed her uncle sitting on a bench in her secret garden. "Kim, this video has been made so that I could read to you the portion of my Will which I've set aside for you. I also wanted to make this video as a memory we could share. What better place than in your little garden." Her uncle got up and Duke trotted up. They walked together as he continued.

"Before I begin I wanted to tell you some things that you aren't aware of. The loss of my brother was very painful for me. I never told you about my childhood only because my brothers and a sister endured hardships that most adults don't have to face. Suspecting the Gestapo would find our family had Jewish ties, our parents arranged for my siblings and me to escape from Germany to America. Your dad took care of me from the time we fled Germany until we were safely in America. Sadly, we lost our sister during this flight. I was the youngest of the four. Stewart vowed to our parents that we would all be good people and would be contributors. I know he passed the test, and I'm still trying. "

Windsor acted like an ass, and made some whimpering sounds behind Kimberly. She was so engrossed, she didn't even notice him.

Mr. Braun and Duke found a stone bench on the balcony outside of the library. Duke sat between his legs. As her uncle talked he showed more emotion than usual. His movements seemed tense. He held onto Duke's collar and then he rolled his hands around.

"You were three when Stewart and Monica were killed in that plane crash. I couldn't imagine parenting a child, especially being an older bachelor. All I knew or wanted to know was chemical engineering and nothing else. When I came to get you, as nervous as I was, my whole world changed."

Lucille Braun rose from the couch. "Jesus, Robert, when are you going to get to the punch line! Windsor, give me a drink."

Mr. Gabriel turned off the video putting his hand on Kimberly's shoulder. She was rigid beneath his touch. "Mrs. Braun, could you please be more considerate?"

Mrs. Braun's attorney stood up next to her and whispered, "Lucille, get a grip. These outbursts can't and won't help your case."

He poured coffee for her. "Now, drink this."

He walked over to George and Charles. "Please accept our apologies. Lucille is distraught over her loss and is not coping very well."

Charles nodded. *That was smooth......I wonder what else is going to happen.* "Perhaps you would like to have her sign off on her portion of the Will and then she can leave the room."

Lucille's attorney grinned, "You know as well as I do, that won't happen."

He asked Arthur to bring a straight backed chair for her to sit in. This put her behind Kimberly.

He then got her more coffee and stood next to her chair. He motioned to George that he felt he could resume the video.

George didn't say anything and pushed Resume Play.

"You were standing holding a stuffed animal with your hat and coat on. I stooped down and you wanted to share your toy with me. I looked into those little blue eyes and it was love at first sight. I knew you were the daughter I would never have. Now we have spent the last thirty some years teaching one another. The greatest gift you've given me is that I've learned how to be loved and more importantly how to love. Now my dear child, I want to pass on to you one of my greatest loves, my entire business...Kim..."

Lucille stood and threw her cup at the screen. CRASH! Hot coffee splashed on the floor, on Kimberly and all over the screen.

"What the FUCK is this? You conniving Bitch. You'll rot in hell before you get your hands on that business. My attorney will contest every last word. That money belongs to me! I didn't stay around that damn bastard all these years to watch you take over what belongs to me. Who the fuck do you think you are?"

George Gabriel looked down at Kimberly. She sat still, tears streaming.

"Lucille, please contain yourself. The Will is final. All that is required is Kimberly's acceptance."

She pulled away from her attorney's arm and went charging after her niece. "I've a few words for you. You fuckin Bitch."

Kimberly stood and faced her aunt. Lucille swung her fist at her. ..Kimberly caught her aunt's fist to stop her. "Aunt Lucille, I think you've made your point. There's no doubt in anyone's mind that you're a money hungry old fool."

Kimberly kept pressure on the hold she had of her aunt's hand. Every time Lucille started to pull back, Kimberly tightened the grip.

"You're hurting me."

"You've hurt me a lot more and I'm sure everyone in this room has been torched by your mouth. So now it's your turn... For your information my dear aunt, I had no idea I was in Uncle Robert's Will. I'm very satisfied with what I have. Mainly because I've earned it. I'm sure you and that spineless cousin of mine wouldn't know what that means. You're so consumed with greed; you don't even know what you have let alone be happy with it."

Kimberly loosened her grip, "You haven't a clue what I'm talking about do you? You're just seething with hate. Perhaps you'll understand this. I do accept my inheritance with the intent of running the company and not selling it to the highest bidder as you would. Now sign your paper and leave."

Kimberly let go of her aunt's hand with a small push and Lucille almost fell into her son's arms. Those in the room could have heard a pin drop on the carpet. Even Arthur looked surprised.

Kimberly asked George Gabriel for her copy of the tape, signed the paper at the desk and left the library using the balcony French doors. *I can't believe I did that. What in God's name have I done?* She started to run to her uncle's crypt.

George slumped in a chair next to his business partner. "You did hear all that or am I day dreaming?"

Charles laughed. "That was no dream, George. Utter brilliance. Robert would have been so proud of her."

"Though we know only too well, Lucille manages to have the last word. I had a word with Lucille's attorney and...."

"Don't mean to interrupt but what is his name. No introductions were made. He does look like we should know him."

"He is William Thornton the III. Ring any bells?"

Charles chuckled, "Oh, yes, I do remember. One of Windsor's many indiscretions we had to keep from the Press. Didn't Thornton II ship him off to another country until the gossip died down? Hmm. Now he is an attorney. Lucille must have turned in one of her chips!"

In the main dining room, Lauren walked over to her aunt. "I thought I heard some noise coming from the main hall. It's been over an hour and none of them have come in to join us."

"I did hear something... I do hear something now...Lucille! We better go check."

Lauren and her aunt made an exit into the main hall, to encounter Lucille Braun. "When you catch up to your friend or should I say your playmate, ask her how well received you'll be after I get done talking to the Press."

Lauren moved toward the stairway, but her aunt held her back. "Don't say anything; you'll only play into her hand..... I want to find Charles."

The two went to the library only to find that Kimberly had left.

"Lauren, my dear, maybe you should take a jacket with you for Kimberly. She went out the balcony door. She may be chilled after she settles down."

Arthur handed her his suit jacket. "This will fit her. I would bet she went to her uncle's crypt."

Harriet then told them of their encounter with Lucille in the hall. "She isn't happy unless she can make a scene. This time, notably, family and friends saw her in a drunken state..."

Harriet put her hands on her husband's shoulder. "Now I think I need to get you, Mr. Gunther, home!"

Charles looked at his partner who sat in shock. "First, George and I need a cup of tea. Then we need to talk to Kimberly and then I'll go home."

George nodded. Harriet asked Arthur if that could be arranged so they wouldn't have to go into the dining room.

Lauren drove her car along the path to the crypt. *Arthur guessed right. There's a light shining through the stained glass window.*

She couldn't see Kim from the doorway, but found her sitting next to the casket.

Kimberly looked at Lauren with teary eyes. "Sorry, I had to be alone."

Lauren helped Kimberly put on Arthur's jacket. "To save time looking for one of your jackets, Arthur gave this to me and said it should fit."

Kimberly tried to find her hand pulling the sleeve back. "That was sweet of him. It is nice and warm."

She sat next to her. "I can leave if you want to be left alone. I just wanted to make sure you're okay."

Kimberly smiled a little. "I'm fine. My mind is spinning searching for some logic. I can't believe all of this has happened in just three days."

Lauren held her hand. "I can only imagine the heartbreak and confusion you're feeling. I wish I could help you some way."

Kimberly stood up. "You already have. I've never felt that I was alone."

Lauren put her arms around Kimberly and held her. "You don't deserve this hardship." Lauren kissed her gently on the cheek.

"I... think we can go back to the house now."

When they reached the house, Lauren's aunt and uncle stood out front. Kimberly sighed. "Such a relief. I was worried we'd be confronted with guests or Aunt Lucille."

Mr. Gabriel had just come out the front door. "I hope we can talk before we leave. Are you okay? We were getting a bit concerned."

Kimberly looked around to see that all the cars had left. "Thank you. It's comforting to know and have your support."

"Kimberly, child, you needn't be concerned. Lucille and Windsor have left the estate. She came back into the library like one of the storm troopers. I think she expected to find you back in the house, so that she could attack you again. The disappointment was marvelous. She could see we were amused, which enraged her more. After she made a few more cutting remarks, not worth repeating, she stomped out of the room knocking over a few antiques that were conveniently in the way. Windsor came in and said his mother would have a moving company come for her things. That is some good news. Wouldn't you say?"

"As well as I know Aunt Lucille, I know she won't rest until she's had the last word, and for that reason, I know I haven't heard the last from her. Legal or not, she will have her day in court."

Mr. Gabriel shook her hand. "I'm glad to see you're not afraid of her, Kimberly. It's unfortunate this matter had to turn out this way, but it's all over with now. A day won't go by that we won't miss seeing or hearing from your uncle. Though rough around the edges, he was truly an honorable and good man. You get some rest and then call when you're ready to start your new career."

Kimberly hugged him. "I'll be in touch soon. Thank you for all your help."

He drove off and Kimberly walked Charles to his car. "It is such a relief to know that you and Mr. Gabriel will be here to guide me along. Being in charge of such a dynamic company is a scary proposition."

"Kimberly, I thought you said I'm to take Harriet on vacation, that it would be good that I retire and..." Gunther smiled like a Cheshire cat.

"Yes, I did say that... But, you see... Harriet, he isn't being fair!"

"Charles, you make it sound like a great sacrifice is being made here. Kim. The truth be known, he would be devastated if he couldn't be here to guide you. Charles, she doesn't need your sense of humor. Good night Kim."

Kimberly and Lauren kissed and hugged them as they got into their car and waved them off. They walked back to the front door.

47

"I really do want to start work as soon as possible."

"Are you sure you shouldn't take a little time for some R & R?"

Kimberly opened the door for Lauren. "It'll take some weeks to handle my affairs in New York, before I can give my full attention here. Maybe after that we could go away."

Arthur met them in the main hall. Kimberly rolled down the sleeves. "What do you think? Fits like a glove." She laughed out loud. "I'm sorry Arthur.....your remark to Lauren that the jacket would fit, was too funny.... It helped to break through all the ugliness that surrounded me."

Duke also made an appearance. "I've missed you." His tail swished to let her know the feeling was mutual.

"Miss Kim, would you like dinner sent to your room?"

"No actually.... We would like to have dinner with the household staff in the main dining room." She looked at her watch, and the grandfather clock chimed. "It is six o'clock. What say we all meet in the dining room at seven-thirty?"

Arthur stunned. "Are you quite sure about this?"

"Have I asked something so unusual? Are you saying it can't be done?"

"Of course it can be done, but I just think they might think something bad may happen. You know like their jobs might be in jeopardy."

"Well then, make sure all of them are on time." She and Lauren continued walking with Duke toward the stairway. "Arthur, it might be easier on Herr Dietrich if he made the meal buffet style."

Arthur stood for a moment. *This character change is most interesting.....it's almost like talking with the boss. But what could it lead too? Guess we'll find out at seven-thirty.* He went to the kitchen. *I better put the warning out...*

"I'm going up to change clothes, and then I want to watch my uncle's video. Would you like to watch it with me?"

"I may take a little longer. I've to call the lab for the results of a test I did the other day. Don't wait for me. I can watch it with you again after dinner."

Duke had been left alone for a good part of the day and wanted both of them to know about it and gave quite a chorus of barks. Kimberly laughed and hugged him. "Excuse me, would you like to watch the video with us." Duke yelped twice. "I'll take that for a Yes."

Lauren had almost made the turn at the end of the hall.

"Lauren, we'll be in the game room instead of the library."

She waved her hand. "Got it, Game Room. That's nice. Where is it?"

Kimberly and Duke stopped and walked back to where they could see her. Kimberly spoke louder. "At the foot of the staircase make a horseshoe turn to the right."

"You need to provide people with a map of this place."

They started back to Kimberly's room. She yelled. "There is one by your phone on the vanity."

Kimberly and Duke got to the Game Room first. This was her second most favorite room in the mansion because she and her uncle had decorated it together, as they did the library and kitchens. *Uncle Robert let Aunt Lucille do the rest of the place, mostly to give her something to do, if not keep her out of his way. No frills to be concerned about in their special rooms.*

Though all were large, their rooms still had the touches of soothing comfort. A big open fireplace took up the whole outside wall. She looked around the room at the floor to ceiling bookcases. Books everywhere. *He loved to read, especially for scientific research. Any questions? The answers usually were here.*

Sports plaques dotted one of the walls. She smiled at a set of original golf clubs used by Harry Vardon. *I helped him hang those. Hours in here, even when I was little… Lucille would never come into the rooms, making them more special.*

She put the tape into the VHS player and sat in her uncle's oversized chair. She pressed the remote when Lauren came in.

"I'm sorry, I took a lot longer than I expected on the phone."

"Were the test results what you expected?"

Lauren sat in a similar chair next to her. "No, there seems to be a glitch somewhere in the formula. I'll check it tomorrow. When you start your new job, I can show you the world I shared with Dr. Braun."

Kimberly started the tape over and paused it. "Lauren, this next part I watched while you were changing, and I'll be interested in what you think." She pushed play.

"Now, Kimberly, my beloved child. I want to pass on to you one of my greatest loves, my entire business. Kimberly, you must keep in mind everything has two sides. This will help you determine the directions you need to take with the formulas I've developed."

Mr. Braun sat without a word for what seemed like a long time. He fingered his ring many times and then petted Duke and held onto his collar. "Kimberly, everything I ever taught you or gave to you had a reason. The reason is for you to find and develop. Remember I told you to work with caution, use restraint and always, my dear, be in control. I'll always be with you."

The tape ended as Arthur entered the room. "Miss Kim, it is seven-twenty nine and your guests are arriving."

She leaped off the chair. "Oh, thank you Arthur. I got involved with uncle's tape and didn't realize the time. Gosh, I hate to be late. We'll be right there."

At the stroke of seven –thirty, they rushed into the dining room, came to a screeching halt, and looked embarrassed.

Bertha laughed with some of other staff members. "That entrance sure brings back old memories when you were little. Your Uncle Robert wouldn't tolerate tardiness of any kind. We of course couldn't let on he wouldn't hurt a hair on your head."

"I get so involved with what I'm doing. Guess I'll never change."

Kimberly and Lauren greeted everyone.

"Arthur, is everyone here?"

"No, not everyone Miss Kim. We had to keep someone in the monitor room and at the main gate. Mike's son Mark is now your aunt's chauffeur and will be living wherever she is until she gets a replacement. Maybe ten are not here."

No one showed any interest in the beautiful display of food the family chef had prepared. Instead, the staff hung back and watched

Kimberly. *I've an idea how to handle this…* She took off her shoes, pulled out a chair and stood on it. She whistled between her teeth. "Ladies and gentlemen. May I have your attention, please?"

She turned around pointing to the huge buffet behind her. "To avoid any loss of appetite and waste all of this delicious looking food, I would like to say a few words."

She then read the portion of her uncle's Will pertaining to them. Protecting their jobs, salary increases, excellent pensions and benefits were among the items included.

"I've known most of you since I was a little girl and unless you really want to leave or retire, I would very much like you all to stay and continue to run the Braun estate for me just as efficiently as you did for my uncle. Now enjoy this family dinner."

The staff applauded. Arthur stood by Kimberly. "Before you move, I would like to propose a toast to you, Miss Kim."

"This is the first time I can see over your head… I'm sorry but you're the tallest man I've ever seen."

They all laughed.

Red faced, Arthur began again. "Miss Kim, on behalf of all of us, thank you. We loved your uncle. He was an honorable man. He treated us with kindness and respect. As the Bishop said earlier, outwardly he wasn't a religious man, but, he had three great loves. First his great love and devotion for you, second for his work, and third for mankind, through his work. What better role model could one have? We salute your decision to continue his work and follow in his footsteps. May God bless."

All the glasses in the room raised and a chorus of "Hear, Hear" rang out.

Kimberly squeezed Arthur's hand as he helped her down. "I don't know that I can fill those shoes."

"We're here to help and guide."

Interesting, how could he help unless he was more than a valet?

"Arthur, would you and Bertha start the line? You've been here the longest…By the way, just how tall are you?"

"I'm only six foot-eight, Miss Kim."

"Only!"

"Both of my brothers are over seven feet."

"I see what you mean. It's all relative, isn't it?"

As they wandered to the back of the line, Lauren commented. "After all that went on earlier, this lovely evening has to be a relief."

"You have no idea how much weight has fallen off my shoulders."

By nine-thirty the last of the staff had left. Kimberly and Lauren gathered up dishes until Herr Dietrich came in with his daughters and told them not to worry they had it all organized.

Kimberly hugged him. "That was a wonderful meal. You're a genius."

Out in the main hall by the stairway, Lauren looked up at Kim. "You're thinking about your uncle's tape."

Kimberly shyly smiled. "You know me already....but, you're right. Something Arthur said makes me wonder about him."

"You have me confused a little. First it's about your uncle's tape and now about Arthur. Why do you feel there's a mystery here?"

Kimberly led Lauren back to the Game Room and shut the door. "I'm sure people are still about and could hear. I don't want them to think I'm going off my rocker, but I think there's something very strange about this video."

"What did you see that makes you feel this way?"

Kimberly went behind the bar to get some bottled water.

Arthur knocked and walked over to the bar. "Miss Kim. Will you be resuming the regular morning schedule?" He saw the bottled water on the bar and took it. "Are there any more of these bottles in that refrigerator?"

Kimberly checked. "No, that seems to be the last one."

"That refrigerator has just been replaced and the service company must not have thrown out everything. I'll have that restocked tomorrow."

As Arthur started to leave, Kimberly cleared her throat. "To answer your question, we will keep to the regular schedule. Nothing will change around here. That is what you wanted to know or is that bottled water more important?"

Arthur intently looked at her. "Yes, of course. I'll advise the staff." *Hmm, I think we've made a big mistake...*

Kimberly stared at him as he left. *How does water go bad?*

"Kim, tell me what you think is so strange about the tape."

Kimberly turned the tape back on. "Okay, this is the beginning. You see him very calm. He calls me Kim." She speeds the tape forward to where he and Duke have moved to the balcony from the garden. "Now, first he calls me Kimberly and then he sits there fidgeting with Duke's collar and then his ring."

"Lauren, the only name I've ever known or heard my uncle call me is Kim. Three times in that video he called me Kimberly. Why is he calm in the beginning of the tape and restless at the end? The man has given speeches all over the world, to governments for that matter. I think he's telling me something." She ejected the tape. "You think I'm chasing rainbows, don't you?"

Kimberly sat on the arm of the oversized chair.

Lauren put her hands on Kim's shoulders. "No... I don't think you're going around the bend. Not yet. I think... well I know you don't want to believe your uncle is dead. He trained you to think using deductive reasoning... and...." Lauren put her hand over Kimberly's mouth. "Let me finish. Your sense of reason has been challenged seeing something out of the ordinary in this video. But remember, Dr. Braun made this because he knew he would be dying soon. Maybe he suffered an attack while this was being filmed. Kim, I don't want you to become a victim of your loss."

With that Kimberly began to cry in Lauren's arms.

"You poor thing, you've had to cope under a lot of strain. This is going to take time to get over. You'll have good days and bad ones. Eventually the good ones will win over the bad ones."

Lauren gave her a tissue to wipe her eyes. "I really think you should give some thought to getting away even for just a week-end."

Kimberly got more tissues. "I feel so very foolish."

Lauren led Kimberly from the room. "Don't be silly. I know you want to do right and get started at your new job, but anyone with any sense about them can see how stressed out you are. Take some time out for yourself. End of story. I've said my piece."

Lauren stopped short. "Did you hear any of it?"

Kimberly just smiled and nodded.

They walked the main hall quietly.

Kimberly helped her on with her coat. "What kind of week-end would you have in mind?"

"Well, I love to ski and Arthur told me you've skied all your life, so I had the idea maybe before the season is over we could fly to Austria for a week-end. There's a resort he mentioned you liked."

Kimberly's eyes enlarged, "The Kitzbuhel! That is a wonderful place. Uncle would take all of us there for Christmas holiday."

They walked out to Lauren's car.

Kimberly continued to reminisce. "I almost forgot there was a period of time when we lived happily around here. I think it all changed when Lucille became pregnant. Anyway, after Windsor was born, she went less and less, but we continued going."

"Ok, then if you're game, I'll check my schedule for say tomorrow through Thursday? We could get an afternoon flight and still get some skiing in before bedtime."

Kimberly shut Lauren's car door. "That sounds like a plan. It's getting cold, better put your top up."

"The fresh air will keep me awake."

The moon flickered through the movement of the trees. Lauren sat looking up at Kimberly affectionately.

She is so beautiful. Okay, Kim, this is where you're supposed to be romantic and say goodnight. I don't know what to do. I really hope she'll understand. How dumb can I be?

Kimberly kicked at the sod on the driveway. "Drive safely. I'm sorry Lauren….I…"

Lauren put her hand on top of Kim's. "Kim, don't be sorry. I do understand. Your innocence is very sweet, not at all judgmental. Actually this attraction for one another is..."

While Lauren talked, Kimberly leaned down and kissed her sweetly. "Thank you for all you've done for me." She stood back and waved a little.

"Very refreshing. Yes, the cold air will be very helpful. Good night."

Lauren drove off. She waved and watched in the mirror. *That was so tender. I hope she didn't feel pushed into kissing me. I would feel awful. She truly is so wonderful. I can't wait to tell Uncle Charles and Aunt Harriett.*

When Lauren's car reached the trees, Kimberly went to find Duke for his walk. She whistled. *Maybe Arthur did the honors. Or Uncle Robert's bedroom. I can't believe I did that. I've never kissed anyone like that. How do I apply Caution, Restraint, and Control to a feeling I've never had before. Would Uncle Robert approve or be disappointed? Now where is Duke?*

She walked around the back of the grounds giving short whistles to make sure her chum wasn't out having a good run. *I'm sure he heard me whistle. I wonder. I won't be able to sleep unless I find him.*

She went in the house through the staff entrance and no Duke. She went up the back staircase. The wall sconces had dimmed for the night. Sure enough she found Duke lying outside of her uncle's bedroom door. He sat up quickly and whimpered at the door. "Duke, I've been looking everywhere for you. Why do you need to go into Uncle's room so badly?"

Duke scratched at the base of the door.

"Okay, just for a while." The knob didn't turn. *Hmm, it's locked. Maybe the door is stuck.*

She wiggled the handle and pushed a little on the door and nothing. She then knelt to peer through the key hole. *I can't see through. Obviously the lights wouldn't be on, so I really can't see if there's a key in the lock.* "I'm sorry fella, I can't help you out tonight, but I'll ask Arthur about it first thing in the morning. You stay with me tonight."

They walked down the hallway together. "Besides, you shouldn't be by yourself."

The day after the funeral

Six o'clock came all too quickly for Kimberly as she was awakened by Bertha coming into the room with her tea. Bertha pushed at Duke to get him off the bed so Arthur could take him for his walk. "Miss Kim, wouldn't you like to sleep in a bit longer this morning? You really need to rest, child."

Kimberly sat up quickly and stretched her arms accepting her cup of tea. "And change our routine? With all I've got to learn, having the day organized is half the battle."

"Just take it a day at a time. You'll do just fine, Miss Kim."

The phone rang as she had one foot going into the shower. She grabbed a towel around her to answer. "Well, good morning. You're a step ahead of me; I'm in the shower mode. What's up? I'm sorry to hear that. Maybe dinner tonight. I'll give you a call this afternoon." *That must be quite a project for Lauren to postpone our trip. Could be a contract or something Uncle Robert developed? Get started on the job. Maybe I can watch the tape again before I see her.*

She finished dressing and as she walked along the main upstairs hall, she decided to use the back stairway and have her breakfast in the kitchen instead of the dining room. As she neared the kitchen door, she heard Arthur talking firmly on the phone. *I feel sorry for the soul*

56

who's on the other end of that conversation. I've never heard Arthur talk so sternly before. She listened.

"This is way too much for her. I don't feel it is fair nor is it safe! You have to change your point of view, R..."Arthur turned to see her standing there and hung up the phone without another word.

Arthur curtly directed her. "Your breakfast is waiting in the dining room Miss Kim."

After eating, she returned to the kitchen to get a jacket and hoped Arthur was in a better mood. "Do you have a minute?" She looked at him with a questioning smile.

He had cooled down and started to apologize. "I truly am sorry, Miss Kim. There are times when I lose my patience with the outside business district. *" I'm not good at this. I hate being the fall guy.*

She stopped and looked at him as if he had just spoken to her in a foreign language. *Don't pursue this. How does what I heard relate to the business of ordering groceries, or stock for the place? Drop it.*

"Well, I wanted to tell you that my plans with Lauren have been changed as she has a problem with a test at Uncle's lab. Maybe next week we'll go skiing. So, today, my schedule will be to first take Duke for a nice long walk. I've already called the London office and asked Gunther and George to come out for lunch. They have papers for me to sign and I've questions for them. I'm not sure about dinner. I may go over to the lab and check things out there and take Lauren out for dinner."

She whistled and laughed hearing Duke thundering down the back stairway. *I wonder why he was upstairs.* Then she remembered. "By the way, last night when I came in Duke was outside of Uncle's bedroom scratching to get in. When I tried the door, it was locked. Can you explain that?"

Arthur's face flushed. "We've had problems with that lock before. I thought it had been taken care of, but I'll certainly look into it. "

"Yes, please do. Right now that is the only place Duke has close to Uncle's scent. I'm sure he's grieving too. Come on, boy. Let's go play."

Duke went to his toy box and picked out a soccer ball and ran out the door with her.

He put the ball down. She got behind the ball and bent down. "Are you ready?"

Duke had moved backward about ten yards anticipating the snap. So excited he didn't miss any movement she made.

I'll act like I'm going to kick it straight and then kick from the side of my foot. Maybe that will confuse him. Kimberly booted it off the side of her foot way up in the air for him.

"Well, so much for that plan. You're just too good, Duke."

She marveled at his agility. *He's just too smart. I can't bluff him.*

They ran all around her garden. She got her bicycle and rode around to the front of the estate.

Duke put the ball down in front of her and then backed up a few yards in a crouched position waiting for her to say the word Ready. She looked out to where she would kick and saw a person walking around near her uncle's crypt. Kimberly stopped playing and said to Duke, "Look!"

The game was over! Duke immediately took a guard point in front of her. No panting, all ears, listening for her next command for action. Kimberly pointed in the direction of the crypt. "Who is that? Check it out!" Duke took off. She got on her bike and still couldn't keep up with him. She relaxed a bit when Duke greeted the man.

"Bishop Rutgers, I'm so relieved it is you. From the house, I couldn't tell who Duke would have to deal with."

The Bishop tried to hold Duke to keep him from going into the crypt, but... Duke wasn't going to let him have his way and bolted inside.

"Kimberly, you startled me; I was working on this week's sermon. Robert always encouraged me to come here to work as it is so beautiful and peaceful. He would say he had many of his ideas here."

While she smiled and listened to him, Duke quickly disappeared inside the crypt. *Maybe I better see what Duke is up to. I wonder if they have lowered the casket into the vault. Oh, what is that?*

Kimberly moved out of the path of the sun to look at something on the ground.

"Kimberly, this would be a good time for us to get more acquainted."

Out of respect, she sat with him on a marble bench away from the crypt entrance. "I used to love this area too. Uncle brought me here to play while he did his calculations. Now, I don't like it here."

The Bishop frowned. "My goodness child, nothing has changed. It is still so beautiful."

Kimberly looked to the entrance. "You see I can't believe he has died. Coming here changes that vision for me."

He touched her on the arm. "I know how you feel. It has been hard on us all as well."

She looked at him inquisitively. "Are there others close to him whom I haven't met?"

This poor child is devastated and is on a mission. The Bishop folded his hands and looked at her with a bit of a smile. "I almost told this at the eulogy, but, your aunt told me to cut out all the ... well, you know what she would call it. Anyway, I want you to know something very special about Robert."

"Back in the nineteen fifties, Arthur, Martin, Michael, your uncle and I met for the first time in Korea. We were British and American Navy Seals assigned to a special task force. Robert commanded the unit. I can't go into a lot of details, but I can say that none of us would be here today had it not been for your uncle's brilliance and bravery."

The Bishop watched Kimberly's eyes softened. She hung on every word. "It is hard to convey the bond between you and your men, especially when your life has been saved. Anyway, as time passed we were able to work and stay together, until Michael passed away."

"Uncle Robert called me about Michael's accidental death. I know he'll be missed. Michael told me once how he dreaded being the temporary chauffeur for Aunt Lucille. Poor man, he loved gardening and had such a gentle way about him. "

The Bishop smiled listening to her. "You can be sure that Michael is missed every day. Actually, Michael's son, Mark, asked to take his father's place." *I wish I could tell her that Michael's death wasn't accidental and that Mark is here to help us catch who's responsible.* "Robert hired him thinking it would help the family. Michael's wife died some years back and left him to raise two boys. So Mark now is the breadwinner. Robert made sure we were to watch over Mark."

Kimberly nodded. "I thought I knew everything about him, and now I've a ton of questions and it isn't fair that he isn't here to answer them."

Her eyes filled. The Bishop took hold of her hand. "You mustn't feel this way." He paused... looked over at the crypt for a few moments thinking and then back at her. "All any of us could tell you would be that we were there. That we served together... Our unit was Special Ops. To this day we can't reveal anything about the assignments we had... I'm very sorry."

She looked from the crypt to him in bewilderment. "This is like being in a maze. I think I've found a direction to follow and then something happens and I've to make another huge adjustment. Right now I feel like I'm at another crossroad. I don't know you at all. I've heard Uncle Robert mention you, but in all the years I've lived here, I've never once seen you, and yet at the funeral you advised me to be careful with whom I confide."

Kimberly looked at her watch. "I don't mean to be rude but I've a meeting with the attorney in less than an hour, and I'm still not prepared." She whistled for Duke and he came wagging his tail.

The Bishop saw her discomfort. "I know you have many questions and if you give yourself some time, you'll be able to work this out. Be patient. There really is a plan here for you to follow."

He walked behind the crypt and returned with his bike. "Also, through your childhood neither you nor Robert was ever out of our sight and that is still the program today. You can trust that." He smiled. "Maybe I'll see you on Sunday?" And he rode on a path that led into the woods.

Did he just say I've been watched all of these years? Be patient there is a plan!

Duke's bark startled her. "Okay, I hear you." She got on her bike and headed back to the house. *Why did Uncle Robert and I need to be watched? Still? Why me?*

☙~☙

She heard the vacuums and talking in the upstairs hall. Not wanting to get involved, she went to the library and called R& K

Industry, where her uncle's lab was located. "Is Lauren Woodgrieves in please? When she comes out, would you have her call Kimberly Braun. Yes thank you."

As she hung up, the monitor room rang to say that her guests had arrived.

As the two gentlemen walked in the phone rang. Kimberly answered and motioned to Mr. Gabriel. "Your office is calling." She handed him the phone and then greeted her uncle's secretary and now hers.

The attorney interrupted her. "Kimberly, is this the fax number on the machine? The office needs to send me something important for this meeting."

She nodded. "I'm so glad you could come out today, Gunthie. Though, I do feel a bit guilty, having you make the journey."

"My dear, I may be years older but I'm far from being disabled. Besides, lunch is a very good incentive."

She backed away laughing. "Oh…that's what I am to you," as Mr. Gabriel finished his call.

He printed out three pages of a fax and started to give them out when the phone rang again. The caller ID said the R&K Lab. She excused herself and took the call.

"Hi, I wondered if you would be able to call back. Now, I can't talk; Mr. Gabriel and your uncle are here to start my crash course."

Gunther could be heard in the background. "Talk as long as you want. We can wait."

She laughed. "He really is something. How about I drive over to the company around six. I could look around while you finish up and then we have a bite to eat at the Pub around the corner? This way, you won't have to change clothes and you won't have a long drive home. See you later."

❧❦

Kimberly observed Gunther beaming. *It's obvious that Lauren told her uncle Charles about last night.*

"Before we get started, read this fax. It's a letter from Scotland

Yard, and to be honest I'm totally mystified."

Kimberly and Gunther read the fax.

"George, this is preposterous. Why on earth would the US Government ask Scotland Yard to protect Kimberly?"

"Charles, read further, the request is to include all those involved with R & K Industry. That would mean the two of us, Lauren and the other chemists that work there."

Gunther looked flabbergasted. He tossed the letter to the table. "There has to be a mistake somewhere in all of this. We have worked for Robert since the first day he started this business. That was how many years ago. He had retired from the Navy several years before that. Now, after he has passed away, they want to protect the families. That is sheer nonsense."

Kimberly gazed out the French doors to the garden in bloom. *Okay, Uncle Robert, Caution, Restraint and Control. This letter makes no sense, but Bishop said I'm being watched...Clues to what?* "Mr. Gabriel, we have to find out what is going on. If you both don't know anything about this, and I certainly don't, then you must set up an appointment with Scotland Yard immediately. Have Charlotte schedule something for tomorrow afternoon. I'll see Lauren tonight and ask her to attend and bring anything she might consider important."

"Charles, Kimberly's right. We need answers. The only way to get them is to meet with Scotland Yard and right away."

"Well, then, that's settled. Let's have some lunch." She led the two men into the dining room.

After a delicious lunch, Kimberly walked the men to their limousine, and as she waved them off she noticed one of the gardeners and Arthur walking toward the mansion with Duke. *I've time maybe I could join up with them.*

She walked toward them and waved. *Wonder what's so important they don't even see me. How close do I need to get for Duke to be aware of me?* She quickened her step as they walked around the corner of the house heading toward the garages. *There's no entrance on that side so I should be able to catch up with them if I run.*

She got around the corner and they weren't there. *Maybe they saw me and ran. Could Arthur be playing with me?* She whistled for Duke but he didn't come. She walked across the grass to her garden. She started to sit on the swing but changed her mind. It looked fragile. She looked at her watch.

She skipped along the path, then ran back and into the house almost crashing into Arthur, Bertha and Gretchen in the kitchen. Her surprised, "Oh!" made them laugh.

She continued to run up the back stairway calling over her shoulder. "Arthur, I really wish you'd give me some of your time in the next day. I've a list of questions I know you can clear up for me."

She didn't wait for an answer. As she passed her uncle's room, she quickly tried the door and it opened. For the first time since he died, she went in. A sense of peace filled the room. Suddenly Duke appeared from the bathroom.

"You startled me. Where have you been?"

He woofed and wagged his tail. He stood up on his hind legs for his hug.

Kimberly hesitated for a moment. "Listen." Duke stopped panting and was very quiet. She looked at Duke. "Did you hear that noise?" He barked and went to the door. *That's twice now I've heard that noise. It sounds like a wheel moving or something.* "Another question... I'll leave the door open now so you can go in whenever you want."

At six pm., the Braun chauffeur opened the car door for Kimberly to get out at the R & K Plastics Corporation Laboratory. "Thank you, Martin. We made it on time, in spite of me being late getting to the car."

The security guard greeted her at the door. After a few formalities, the guard escorted her to the third floor where Lauren's office and the main laboratory were located. The security guard headed back to his post, once he had shown her Lauren's door. Instead of going into Lauren's office to wait, Kimberly amused herself by looking at her new surroundings. One room had an extensive library with computer workstations along the wall. Very strange, so very quiet, almost an eerie atmosphere.

The silence ended when Lauren came up from behind. "There you are."

Lauren, in her white lab coat, stood in the doorway and smiled radiantly at Kimberly. "Well, what do you think?"

Kimberly looked enthusiastically at Lauren. "This place has changed since I was here last, such a transformation! Can you show me the lab and what you're working on?"

Lauren took her hand, led her to a set of double doors, opened one, and stood back. "Come into my secret room, my inner sanctum."

Kimberly walked past. "Not very scary." She followed Lauren to a work table. "Were you able to figure out the problem with the test you were working on?"

Lauren smiled and nodded. "Yes, I think so. Take a seat by that microscope. I want to show you something." She went to the vault and took out a slide and put it on the plate under the lens. "Okay, boss, tell me what you think?"

Kimberly peered into the microscope, made adjustments, peered again, and shook her head. "What am I looking for or at? There's nothing there."

"Well, that's just the point. It is there, but we can't see it."

Kimberly sucked in her breath and stared. "Oh, my gosh..." She sank down onto the stool. "I'm no chemist, but I think you're saying that he has developed a kind of transparency, or am I using the wrong term?"

Lauren sat next to Kimberly. "In all seriousness, I can't be sure until I can look at the formula as a whole. You see, your uncle never gave any of us anything in its entirety. Even after he made me his assistant, I still got bits and pieces. Plus, he identified everything with a letter or a number, sometimes both. He was the only one who could put these together in a format that he alone understood. I can only speculate, but this last series of tests leads me to agree with you. I can't imagine what else it could be."

Kimberly rubbed her brow. "Lauren, there's got to be a correlation between Uncle's video and this test. I feel so sure about it."

Lauren took the slide out of the keeper and returned it to the vault. "We can talk about it at dinner." She stopped at the door. "You may have a point regarding the video ...At first, he did give you instructions. The only real visual of movement on the tape was..."

Kimberly pulled the chain out from her blouse. "He fingered his ring! Can this microscope look at my ring? Remember he told me that the ring would help me. I know it's valuable, but I don't need money. So what else could it be?"

Lauren took the ring off the chain and put it into a box. "This is a new machine where we can view three dimensional things from every possible angle without moving it." At the computer she punched in some numbers and hit the start button. "There you have it."

The ring appeared very true on the screen. Lauren rotated it very slowly. "It would help if we knew what to look for. Why don't we first look for writing of any kind?"

"He had our names engraved on the inside of the band."

"Okay, then, we'll zoom in just a titch and look at its design."

As Lauren very slowly rotated the ring, Kimberly frowned. "Is that a shadow on that side of the ring? Or is it a dot of some kind?"

"Wow, I thought I had good vision." Lauren zoomed in a little closer and made some resolution adjustments.

"Look, that's not a dot. It's a hinge, the top of the ring opens..."

She rotated the ring to the opposite side. "Sure enough, I think that mark is a hole and I bet some sort of a key fits it."

"Can you enlarge this anymore so we can see the shape?"

"I think we're pushing our luck now. That is pretty small." Before Lauren turned off the scanning device, she pressed another set of buttons and a list appeared.

She returned Kimberly's ring and chain. "I'm no metallurgist, but that list on the screen gives the breakdown of the ring."

She chuckled. "That sure must be important, because you'll never cut it open, burn it, or smash it. It's made from Iridium, the strongest and rarest metal in the world."

"I've never heard of it. I thought Titanium was the strongest?" Kimberly swiveled on the lab stool and frowned. "That settles it, until we find the key, we have to remain quiet and that means everyone! Not even your Uncle Charles! I could tell this afternoon that someone had mentioned a special incident to him." Swiveling back and forth, she half smiled squinting at Lauren.

"I totally agree! About Uncle Charles. I really didn't say anything to him. He must have guessed because he said I looked radiant." Lauren blushed telling Kimberly.

"I would agree with him."

Lauren took Kimberly's hand. "We better go to dinner before I get fired for fraternizing."

At the door, Kimberly heard a sound like a wheel turning. "Did you hear that?"

Lauren smiled, "Yes, I heard it the other day and mentioned it to one of the maintenance men."

"What did he say?"

Lauren raised her hand. "Oh, something to do with the heating system."

Kimberly frowned. "Heating system? Hmm. I've heard it twice now at the house… I'll ask Arthur, but I doubt very much the heating systems are…"

Laughing, Lauren pushed Kimberly toward the door. "At this precise moment, *I don't care* about the noise or the heating system. *I'm starved. Let's go!"*

Before they left the building, Kimberly asked Lauren to instruct the guards not to miss any of their inspections. Though the sun had reached the horizon, it wasn't too cold to walk to the Pub.

The barmaid took their orders and left to get their drinks.

Kimberly opened her brief case and gave Lauren her copy of the fax. "Well, to add more fuel to this conundrum… read this."

Lauren read it and looked at Kimberly with a blank face. "This would be absurd if we hadn't already seen the test results." Lauren stopped talking when she saw the barmaid approaching with their meals. "I've got to be honest; I thought your emotions were getting hold of you about the video. You were so close; he might as well have been your father. So your remarks seemed natural. But this puts a different light on everything."

Kimberly put the letter back into her brief case. "I told Mr. Gabriel to make the appointment as soon as possible, like tomorrow afternoon. Would that work for you?"

Lauren nodded as she took a bite of Shepherd's pie. "I don't mean to change the subject, but this is so good. There's nothing closer to home cooking than eating at a pub, and I didn't get any lunch today so this really is hitting the spot."

The barmaid filled their coffee mugs and left Kimberly the check.

"If it isn't too late, I'll call you later with the time for the meeting. I haven't a clue what these inspectors will want to know from us, but I think it wise we say as little as possible about his personal work."

"I wonder if they already know I'm his assistant. In actual fact I wouldn't be lying to say about the projects being numbered. Each test had a form to fill out listing the results. End of that story."

Kimberly held her mug, observing the others in the pub.

Lauren broke Kimberly's trance by poking her with her spoon. "Okay, you didn't hear a word I said. What have I missed?"

Kimberly put her mug down. "You're right. I'm having a hard time. I'm so used to solving problems with logic and especially having everything in order. Now I feel every step I take I'm confronted with another enigma. A week ago, Uncle Robert and I talked. He felt great and was planning all sorts of stuff for us to do. But two days later, Gunther calls telling me to drop everything, Uncle Robert is dying. Then we have the mystery of the will. He could have written all of this, but instead he made a video. Also we have my conversation with Bishop Rutgers. All of these surprises. Now we have your test results and the US Government. Where does it end?"

Lauren frowned. "Ah, back up. How did Bishop Rutgers get in all of this?"

Kimberly looked at her watch. "It's getting late. You need to get some rest."

Lauren pulled Kimberly down in her seat by her jacket. "Kim, tell me. What has Bishop Rutgers said that has caused you to be more concerned? You don't just drop his name out as if it is nothing when in fact it means something."

Kimberly paid the check. Outside the pub, she told Lauren of her surprise meeting with the Bishop at the crypt. "The way he acted, I got the distinct feeling that I had interrupted more than his sermon."

Lauren handed Kimberly her brief case. "That *would* seem weird.

Are you sure he wasn't really deep in thought?"

"No, Duke got to him first and I noticed he had hold of Duke's collar and really didn't want Duke to go into the crypt...He's a big man, yet Duke still won. Then we chatted and I know he wanted to be comforting and I truly believe his remarks were sincere, but everything he told me I knew nothing about. All of a sudden Uncle Robert became a stranger."

Kimberly told Lauren all she had learned about Korea. "I'm sure I showed my discomfort. I just wanted to leave. Luckily I did have an excuse – preparing to meet with Mr. Gabriel and Gunthie. On the way back, I recalled Uncle Robert words – things always having two sides...

They had reached the street ready to cross when Martin pulled up in the Rolls Royce. They got in and drove to Lauren's car.

"I'll call you later about the meeting. Get some rest. See you tomorrow."

8

London, the day after the funeral

In London at a Ritz Hotel, in one of the Penthouse suites, Lucille Braun slurred her words loudly into the phone making demands and threats. Windsor opened his bathroom door and heard this commotion. He looked at his watch. *Holy shit it's after nine, who is she yelling at now?* He finished dressing and could still hear her ranting.

"You fuckin bastard, quit telling me you brought up everything the movers delivered."

"Mother! Put that damn phone down."

He took the phone out of her hand. "Hello, who is this? ...Oh... well I was going to apologize for her, but now... I don't care who you were talking to! Let me remind you, you dip shit, she happens to own this fuckin place and I suggest that you look for another fuckin job!!"

Windsor slammed the phone down. "For Christ sake, can't you be sober once during the day."

"Oh, you should talk.... Have you forgotten, my sweet, all the times I had to save your ass at the airport? Perhaps you've forgotten all the times I lied to cover your ass at your school or should I say schools for all of your sordid acts?"

Windsor's eyes tightened. He wanted to take her bottle and beat her for that. *You bitch. You'll find out how indecent I can be…..* He put on his coat and held his hat.

She tried to sit up in her chair holding a paper. "Where the fuck do you think you're going?" She shook the paper at his face. "You can't leave until you find this!"

He grabbed the paper out of her hand. "I've an appointment." He sat in the chair next to her. "What are you looking for?" He looked at a list of items that had been delivered from the estate that afternoon. "So what's the big deal? There's a check mark next to each item."

She tried to sit up again. "Yes, but they didn't bring my iron men…they have a secret in them."

Windsor looked at the list and saw Viking fireplace irons. He got up and went to the fireplace and there were two Viking soldiers. He threw the paper at her. "Mother, you're not only a mean drunk, you're now hallucinating. What do you call these? I have to go, do me a favor and pass out."

"They don't have their shields. Windsor come back! They don't have their shields."

Windsor walked to a pub near Trafalgar Square on Cranbourn Street called the Cork and Bottle. Hardly the sort of place he would be recognized. His contact sat alone in a booth.

Windsor felt edgy in this new situation and motioned to him. "Let's do this outside. This noise is too much."

A few street lamps illuminated his contact. *Holy fuck, look at this guy. There's not a wrinkle or blemish anywhere. Talk about gorgeous.* Windsor cleared his throat. "Ah, sorry… I expected someone ….."

The stranger retorted. "Yeah, some form of lowlife that you wouldn't identify with. Be my guest but those are the dirt bags that get caught."

Touchy over this sudden attraction, Windsor handed the stranger an envelope. "I don't give a fuck what you look like, just so the job gets done. There are two pictures in that envelope. However, a third project has come up and I don't have a picture."

Windsor handed him a newspaper with his mother's picture all over the front page. "I've circled the picture and put the address where she's living."

"Is there any special order you want?"

"Yes, the first one should be the newspaper picture, then the other two."

The stranger looked at the newspaper. "*This* is your mother."

Windsor put his hands on hips. "Aren't I the lucky one. Do you have a problem with this?"

The stranger smirked. "No... Not at all. It's just money in the bank." *What a sick bastard.*

He put the newspaper in his coat. "You were told I don't work fast? My record is perfect because all of my hits are planned to the minute. I get ten K a pop with half down and the other half on completion. You realize this is going to take some extra planning with your mother being a celebrity." *Seems I should know that name.*

Windsor grinned and gave him another envelope. "I can wait. Here's five K. You'll get a nice bonus after each job."

The man pulled out an inhaler while they talked. "Don't get in a twist; this doesn't affect my job in the least."

Windsor handed him his business card with his private numbers on it. "Only call when it's really important. I don't want anything traceable back to you."

They shook hands. "I'll let you know when you should take a three day trip."

"I travel a lot to Austria on business. So that will work out just fine."

They went their separate ways. The stranger crossed the street and vanished in the dark. Windsor went back into the pub. He went to the bar and ordered three brandies.

Let us all drink to the demise of my dear mother, my dear cousin. And my cousin's future chemist… mate? Finally, some freedom!

9

The Braun estate, midafternoon

When Lauren pulled up to the mansion at two forty five, her uncle's chauffeur was playing ball with Duke off the main terrace. She tooted her horn and waved. Arthur greeted her at the door and showed her to the library where the others sat around a conference table.

Lauren sat next to Kimberly. "I'm sorry I'm late."

Gunther handed his niece some papers. "On the contrary, my dear, if anything we are early."

Just as Gunther pointed out things of interest to them, Arthur appeared with the two gentlemen from Scotland Yard.

They shook hands and made their introductions. The gentlemen waited for Kimberly and Lauren to sit and then they took places at the table.

Mr. Gabriel shuffled some papers and was about to speak, when he was taken aback, as was Gunther and Lauren when Kimberly, sitting very straight- backed, nodded to her guests. "Before Mr. Gabriel begins this meeting, thank you for coming on such short notice. You must realize your letter came to us as a total surprise and we hope you'll be able to either show us cause for concern or from the information we can offer, determine a grave mistake has been made and we can go about our business as usual."

Kimberly then motioned to George Gabriel to continue. "Kimberly, you have pretty much covered what I planned to say, so perhaps we should turn the meeting over to Scotland Yard and see what they would like from us. You said Inspector McGraw is the leader on the case." The attorney motioned for the Inspector to take over the discussion.

Alex McGraw shoved his reading glasses above his forehead. "Thank you. We share the same gratitude for this meeting....What I mean is, we don't always get cooperation from the private sector to make our job less stressful. As you'll note, I'm passing out two pages. This is a questionnaire we would like you to fill out. Not today. Perhaps in the next day or two you could fax them back to us. This is nothing more than a routine questioning. Today, my partner, Inspector Ross, and I would like to clarify the letter sent to you."

"Mr. or Inspector McGraw, all this claptrap is quite disconcerting." Charles Gunther shoved the two pages across the table to the Inspector. "What are you promoting here?"

Kimberly swallowed hard and looked incredulously at her secretary. "Gunthie! This isn't like you at all."

Gunther ignored Kimberly and continued. "You sir, have sent us a letter saying that our daily activities henceforth will be watched for our own safety, when, for the last thirty years that Robert Braun has been working in this country and abroad, there hasn't been the slightest notion of your concern." Charles pointed at George." Tell him we feel this is all rubbish."

George Gabriel sat next to his business partner and put his hand on Gunther's arm. "Yes, I must agree. Your letter made very little sense to us, especially when we haven't ever had any kind of business relations with any government except on one occasion. We had our staff go through all of Robert's business dealings and we found one invoice for the Navy dated 1968. I've the file here and will make copies for you if needed." George looked around and saw that coffee and tea had been put out. He looked over at Kimberly.

Kimberly was still amazed by the sudden exchange of words. "Oh, of course, please... help yourself."

Lauren jumped up and patted her uncle on the shoulder. "I'll get you something." She poured a cup of tea and added some whiskey.

Her uncle smiled after taking a swallow.

The other inspector with cup in hand walked back to the table. "Part of our department's question is that we weren't aware of Mr. Braun's activities in the plastics world. We know of the company, but not anything more." His remark got a wicked look from his partner.

Kimberly stared at him. "Then what is your point? Did you or did you not get a request from the US government for our protection?"

McGraw quickly responded. "Yes, we did Miss Braun......We aren't here on a witch hunt if that is where you're heading. We simply need to know if your uncle's death was..."

Wide eyed, Kimberly looked at the attorney and then at Lauren. "Sir, are you suggesting that he died from other than natural causes? You do have a death certificate, don't you?"

Inspector Ross felt the tension building as Alex continued. "I'm saying that we are here to do a routine investigation. Your uncle is an American citizen, living in the UK. Your government has shown concern and has asked that we investigate the entire situation. Perhaps one of you could tell us why Mr. Braun moved his home and business to the UK."

Kimberly stood at the side of the conference table with her cup of tea. "I can answer that. My uncle told me he moved here to get away from the attitudes and life styles that had crazed the eastern coast back in the sixties. He had developed some things after the war, and they sold, making him quite a bit of money. He told me that he had been to England once and loved the beautiful countryside, the quiet and the relaxed way of life.

Uncle Robert loved solving problems. He thought he could make a decent living solving chemical problems for companies. He told me he invested all that he had made from the formulas he had developed, buying this estate. Originally, he had the lab in the garage. Then as his business grew, he bought the property where R & K sits today."

Inspector McGraw had been taking some notes. "That's interesting... Now, I believe one of you is Mr. Braun's assistant." He looked at his list of names. "That would be you, Miss Woodgrieves."

His stare made Lauren uncomfortable. *This man is weird.* "Yes, that is correct. I'm Dr. Braun's assistant."

The inspector started another page in his note book. "Miss Woodgrieves, could you tell us what kind of work you did for Mr. Braun. Did you analyze formulas for him? Were they Dr. Braun's formulas or were they as Miss Braun said, from other companies?"

Charles Gunther interrupted. "Inspector McGraw, there is no secret here. If you want a list of the contracts we have, we can produce them for you now. Most of the companies R & K works for are in the US. We have contracts with Proctor and Gamble, Lubrizol, and General Mills, to name a few. Not one of these companies could be considered a government risk."

Lauren didn't like this inspector's attitude. She hesitated, glancing at Kimberly, who signaled discretion by showing her fingers closed together.

"In actual fact, I've been Dr. Braun's assistant for the last two years, though I've worked at his company for eight."

"I see you also have a PhD in chemical engineering." *She knows a lot more than what she's sharing. A few minutes alone, I could break her.*

"So being his assistant, you should be able to answer that question? Did you analyze Dr. Braun's formulas? Is there a reason why you're stalling, Miss Woodgrieves?"

Lauren gave McGraw a sullen look and took some papers out of her brief case. "Dr. Braun warned his staff about industrial espionage. His primary concern was to protect his client's product."

Lauren handed each person a paper that had numbers and letters in many columns. "My hesitation, Inspector... .McGraw... isn't to add intrigue, but to let you know this paper I'm passing around to each of you is exactly what accompanied almost every test. You may assume what you like, but I can assure you that only Dr. Braun would be able to tell you who the test belonged to and what part of the formula it fit. When the project was completed, he sent his findings to my uncle and the contract would be fulfilled."

McGraw sat staring at the paper. *Son of a bitch!! I can't believe what I'm seeing. All these fuckin years! My God, this is the K Code.*

McGraw whispered. *"Braunstein!"*

"Inspector McGraw, is there something wrong?"

McGraw flushed with embarrassment. "I'm sorry. I'm so…taken by the complexity. It looks mind boggling. Ah, Miss Woodgrieves, you said that a questionnaire would be attached to each test. Do you keep copies of your results?"

"The procedure is very exact. No more than one test can occur at a time. Each time a test is removed from the vault, it is automatically documented. The vault will not release another test until it has documented the return of the test that had been previously timed out."

"So, you're saying you've never or can't make any kind of a copy of your work. And, does that procedure apply to all the chemists or just *you?*"

Lauren bit her lip and clenched her fists under the conference table.

Kimberly jumped in. "Inspector McGraw, I find it a bit disconcerting that you seem to be on a fishing expedition using Lauren and I would like to know why."

The inspector stood up and put all of the papers back into his brief case. "I apologize; I sometimes get tangled up in things that I find interesting. Dr. Braun went to all of this trouble to protect a company's formula. Well I find that amazing." *We need to leave; I've got to make calls right away.*

He motioned to his colleague he was ready to leave. "However, I'll turn in these two documents to our lab at the Yard."

Ross stood up with his back to the rest of them. "Alex…what is the rush? These people still have more questions. Personally, I feel we owe them an explanation. They have been open with us and…"

"Dennis, just get your stuff together, we are leaving *now*!"

They all looked startled at the sudden end of the meeting.

Kimberly stood up with the others. "Inspector, you really haven't told us if we are restricted in our activities. I've made some travel plans for this coming week and I would like to know if I can proceed or must I cancel them?"

"Well, Miss Braun, as far as I'm concerned you should all carry on with whatever. I'll make my report to my superiors, but I'll get back to you with their recommendations."

With a jerk, McGraw turned to Kimberly. "Miss Braun, did your uncle serve in the Korean War?"

Kimberly shrugged and stared at McGraw. Then looked at Gunther and Gabriel who both nodded. "Yes, I believe so. Why are you asking?"

McGraw smiled a little. "No special reason. Just wondered." *It's got to be Braunstein. Come on, Ross, move your ass, we've got to get out of here.*

As Ross put on his coat, George Gabriel approached. "Inspector, among other feelings, I'm totally confused with this meeting. We certainly have accommodated your requests so what is the problem?"

"Mr. Gabriel, I apologize for this." Ross stared at McGraw. *What's happened? Alex has lost it.* He shrugged his shoulders. "I don't know what to say. Inspector McGraw is in charge and has his reasons for being abrupt." *How do I not make him look like a fool?* "I can assure you, we will get back to you with a full report."

Gunther lit his pipe in the main hall. He walked with Kimberly and Lauren.

Lauren grinned and then laughed. "Uncle Charles puffs like a train when he's mad or put off about something."

The inspectors walked out of the library and caught up with Kimberly. "Miss Braun."

They stopped and turned. Charles blew smoke almost in the inspector's face.

"Yes, Inspector McGraw."

The inspector used his inhaler. "Be reassured. You and your staff are not in any danger. I'll submit my report. If my superiors feel you have need of protection, we'll arrange it and you'll not even know it."

Kimberly frowned when he took a breath with the inhaler. "Not to worry, this doesn't affect my work."

Kimberly pursued her concern. "You certainly don't mean inside our homes."

She heard her name . Arthur stood off to the side of the hall. She walked over to him. "What is it Arthur?"

With his back to the others he whispered. "Miss Kim, your uncle would be very upset if you allowed any intrusion on the estate. I can assure you, you're protected wherever you go and always have been for all of your life here."

Kimberly said nothing. *First the Bishop tells me and now Arthur about my safety here. Why is this so important?* She looked up at him.

He motioned for her to go and tell the inspector. "Trust me."

Kimberly returned to the inspectors and showed them the estate monitoring room. "As you can see we monitor the entire estate both inside and out. During the day, to allow privacy, the system is off in the house. James, would you ask one of the staff to enter an area typically not used? Thank you."

The five staff members each had head phones on. Kimberly pressed a switch at the end of the long bank of screens so that the inspectors could hear the alarm go off the second someone walked in that area. "Bong, Bong."

Kimberly nodded for James to continue the test.

"*Stop* where you are! Put your hands up*! Do not move!*"

Inspector Ross gulped. "My, what an operation you have. How many acres surround the house? And this system covers all of that? "

Kimberly smiled, "Oh yes. We have a hundred twenty-five acres and there is a ten foot wall completely around it. Most of the acreage is kept as a sanctuary for the wild life. Anyway, as you can see, we are well protected. Plus we are plugged in with the local police and they are notified at the same time of the incident."

McGraw grinned. "Then they know of this test?"

James nodded to the inspector. "Yes, sir, they get notified first before the test begins."

The inspectors agreed that the Braun estate didn't need any outside protection from Scotland Yard and left.

Kimberly raced back to the library. She stood for a moment at the table shaking her head. "First that McGraw character cuts the meeting short and can't wait to get out of here and then I show him the security system and I can't get rid of them."

"I spoke briefly to Inspector Ross. He seemed very surprised by his partner's actions. I must admit, Charles, you shocked me when you shoved those papers back at McGraw and told him what for." George Gabriel tapped his pipe out in the ash tray, chuckling.

Lauren patted her uncle's shoulder. "For someone who is always so soft spoken, it sure amazed me!"

Arthur announced dinner would be served in ten minutes.

Kimberly swept the papers from Scotland Yard into the waste basket. "I think that is enough excitement for one day." She waited for the others to walk with her. "What do you think if I take a few days off and go skiing? Lauren thinks I should take some time before I start my new career."

An hour later, Kimberly and Lauren stood outdoors at the main entrance.

"Uncle Charles, this is one of those times I'm glad you're not driving." Lauren hugged her uncle and helped navigate him through the limo door.

George Gabriel hugged them both. "I think he's tired and a bit giddy." Bent down to get in the same car, he turned giggling. "He's so proud of his outburst to that pompous ass of a Scotland Yard man that it may have unleashed a new Charles Gunther!"

"Oh Lord, I hope not."

They waved them off.

"Well, I better get going as well. You'll take care of the plane tickets and I've already booked the hotel so we should be in good shape. Meet you at nine at Heathrow? Don't be late?" Lauren hesitated; *it's so hard to hold back.* Instead she said "Good night" and kissed her on the cheek.

Kimberly walked along the balcony almost in a daze and went through the library French doors. Another moment of my life I can't share with him. Her body sank in despair. *What good is all of this without you? These feelings! Am I going in the right direction? Uncle Robert?* She burst into tears.

After an hour, Duke startled Kimberly by giving her a big lick on her face. She had fallen asleep on a couch in front of the warm fireplace. She sat up and wiped her eyes. "I'm sorry fella. I let myself go to one of those pity parties. Look at the time."

She and Duke went into the hall.

Arthur had started dimming the wall sconces. His back to them, he only heard Duke's paws tap on the marble floor. "I'll be done in a minute and will take you out."

Arthur about jumped out of his skin when he saw Kimberly reflected in one of the mirrors standing next to Duke.

Kimberly would have been amused, but the stern look on his face scared her. "I'm sorry. I should have said something or made a noise."

He sighed and relaxed his posture. "I'm sorry too, Miss Kim. I thought you had gone to bed." Arthur saw that she had been crying, and avoided asking about it. He had two more lights to go. "Not to worry, I'll take his lordship out as soon as I'm finished."

She walked toward the stairway and stopped. "Arthur?" She turned back. "Is there a time we could have a conversation. I've questions and no one to talk to, and really feel at a loss…"

She saw strain in his face. "It doesn't have to be now. Maybe we could talk when I get back from my trip. It would mean so much to me, please."

Arthur dimmed the last light. *God I hate doing this to her. This is so unfair. I have to give her an answer! Damn, I knew this was going to fall in my lap. This is the last time I'm going to lie to her. He'll have to get someone else to do it!* He walked over to her.

Kimberly felt the warmth of his smile. "I promise. When you come back I'll try to answer all of your questions. Now, you get to bed. We'll work this all out." He watched her go up the steps. Then he scooted to get his jacket. He stopped in the monitoring room. "James, call a meeting right away." He went out the back entrance, got on his bike, and he and Duke headed for the crypt.

10

The meeting at the Crypt

Arthur put his bike behind the building. He got the lights on just as the Bishop rushed in out of breath. "Is everything okay? James's call woke me up out of a dead sleep."

Arthur nodded. "Wait till the others get here. We've got a situation."

Not even a minute later, Martin came in panting and then the youngest members Mark and James carelessly dressed.

Arthur looked at his watch. "I know it's late, but we've got a situation developing, and I hope we can handle it without getting him involved. Right now our priorities are to protect all those involved in this project. But, we now have a challenge. *Kimberly.*"

The Bishop put out his cigarette. "She startled me outside the crypt yesterday morning. She suddenly appeared with Duke. Duke got the Boss's scent and ran inside. I couldn't hold him back. Thank goodness the sun was so bright it helped block the tire tracks. She may have seen something-- she was looking. I got her to sit for a while. Poor kid has a lot of questions. The kind you can't answer truthfully without exposing this whole situation."

"Well, here's another twist. It seems Robert's death has caused the US Government concern about his formulas, and now the Pentagon sent a letter to Scotland Yard asking for protection for the Braun staff and family. George Gabriel set up a meeting, at Kimberly's request, with the inspectors from Scotland Yard in charge of this case. They had it in the library. I knew nothing about it until a few minutes before they arrived and couldn't tape it."

Martin broke in. "Well, I saw them leave and it sure could have been an excerpt from one of those old silent movies where the police go scurrying about. The taller one almost raced out of his knickers to get to his car and the expression on the other inspector's face could have won a prize."

"Seriously, Robert will want to know who is creating all of the interest."

The Bishop checked his watch. "We can't tell him about this now. He's still in a delicate condition. I think we'll have to keep her in the dark a bit longer."

"That's easy for you to say. She is so much like Robert. Kimberly will spot in a minute that I've lied to her if she thinks I've avoided answering her question. She knows how to get in your face even if she's across the room."

The men chuckled. "You think it is funny....well, I'll lose all credibility with her if that happened and I would have a hard time living with that."

"Arthur, quit beating yourself up. Keeping her in the dark is part of the plan and we have to stick by it."

The men started to leave. "There's one new development. Kimberly and Lauren are leaving tomorrow to go to the Kitzbuhel."

Martin took his address book out. "Who should I call for her tracker?" He looked at the updates. "I take that back, we only have Gustov. Heinrich has a broken leg."

The Bishop lit up a cigarette and made some smoke rings. He grinned knowing this would annoy Arthur.

"God, I wish you'd quit that awful habit" Arthur waved his arm at the smoke. He grinned back at the Bishop, knowing he had tried to get his goat. "Gustov is the man. He's a good skier and Kimberly won't know him."

"It's time to go. Is everyone on the same page here? Any questions?"

Mark's hand went flying up. "Yes, sir, I've a very important one."

The others said, "The answer is no!"

Mark put his hands through his hair. "Arthur, this isn't fair! You told me that being Lucille Braun's chauffeur would be a cushy job and *temporary*. I've been there six months now and I still haven't seen her totally sober, and the woman can't keep her hands off me."

Arthur tried to keep a straight face. "Mark, remember you don't start work there until eleven in the morning and you're back here by dinner. That's pretty cushy to me."

Martin put his hand on Mark's shoulder. "Seriously, young man, we wouldn't have found out about Sheila Jones' relationship with Windsor had you not been the driver."

Mark looked up at Martin. "I know…and I saw her give Windsor an envelope that maybe could be related to some of the missing formulas. That was only one time. My dad, however, kept a diary indicating various times he had, on short notice, picked Windsor up at the airport. He just put initials and I'm sure there were several SJ's listed. I know that bastard had something to do with his death. I think dad got close to finding something out and…Windsor and that Dr. Edse killed him."

"Give it another month and then we'll let James trade with you."

"Thanks a lot. Why do you pick on the new guys?"

"For your information, Lucille *hates* anyone who has a history with Robert. None of you served with him in Korea… We did and we are here because he saved us."

Mark and James frowned. "So why would she hate you? What was the big deal?"

The Bishop put his cigarette out. "She hates us because she knew Robert would give up his life for us and…almost did when he single handedly rescued each one of us from torture in a prison camp and hid us in a cave until we were able to leave on our own. This was in the dead of winter in 1953. He was our commander and he wouldn't leave without us. I won't even explain what we endured." The Bishop opened his shirt up and showed them a burned number on his chest like a cattle brand. The flesh still hadn't regained any quality. "This is just for openers."

Martin and Arthur showed them the same on their chests as well.

"She couldn't compete with that kind of devotion and her hatred only increased as the years went by. You're young, good looking and she can flaunt herself all over you. As a result, Mark learned of Windsor's association with Sheila Jones, who we found out later is living with Lauren. Is there a correlation? Yes. Can we prove a possible conspiracy or collaboration? No. We know we're on to something. Need I say anymore?"

"No sir."

"Okay, let's call it a night. Thanks for your quick response."

Arthur turned the lights out. "That was nicely put, Bishop. No point trying to explain our war experience. Even as well trained as they are, I don't think they would understand what we went through. Those memories don't leave, do they?"

The Bishop shook his head. " I wonder if Michael ever talked about the war or those last weeks of hell to Mark?"

They walked behind the crypt to get their bikes. Arthur turned his pant cuff up to put his clip on. Martin appeared with his bike.

"Arthur, how's the boss today? Bishop said he's out of danger now."

"It would appear so, but the doctor still hasn't been able to determine the extent of damage that poison caused. Robert still fades in and out of consciousness. The doctor thinks that poison will be out of his system in another twenty-four hours."

Martin got on his bike. "We know Windsor and the great doctor Edse did this. Why don't we just plan a nice execution and be done with it. Then Kimberly can be with him."

He said that so innocently, the Bishop and Arthur laughed out loud. Arthur swung his leg over his bike seat. "Well… for openers, we aren't vigilantes…and…"

Martin shook his head. "I know what you're going to say. Robert suspects Windsor is stealing his formulas and possibly the doctor is in on it as well. So, who gives a shit? You'd have them arrested, is that going to give Robert his appearance back? As far as I'm concerned the tortures I sustained in Korea don't even come close to what he's suffering. I can't even look at him!" Martin wiped his eyes.

Arthur looked over at the Bishop to say something. "*Martin!* We all feel the same way as you do, but this is *not the time* to get emotional. Robert has trained us to be in control. We can't mix the two. We are all Robert has to protect him as well as Kimberly, and... *You know this!* Plus, we promised him Kimberly would never see him in this condition."

Martin looked up and nodded. " I know we did. I'm okay. Thanks, I'm there for you." He smiled and rode off.

The Bishop shook his head. "I hated talking that way to him. Of the four of us, I think Martin's wounds were the worst. I know, after all those years I still have nightmares. I think he would die if Robert doesn't pull through this."

"I agree. I'm just so glad Robert detected something wrong and called his Navy buddy, Dr. Mathews. The doctor seems to think with time his skin will stop seeping that mixture of blood and puss. He told me the skin reaction was caused by a combination of the poison and Robert's latest development which had been sprayed on him. It's late. Can't talk about it. See you tomorrow."

"Later."

The drive back to Scotland Yard

After five long minutes of total silence, Inspector Ross studied his colleague and friend, who drove as if he were chasing a criminal. "Alex, I'm really troubled. I've never seen you act like this. Are you going to tell me what's going on?"

The trance broken, Alex slowed to the speed limit. *Why do I have to be stuck with him? Times have changed. We're no longer bosom buddies.* "Sorry. The situation wasn't at all what we were led to believe. Braun's company isn't doing any government work. He's not doing any research or development. So I don't see any need for further contact. The niece told us he irons out problems for other companies. So what's the big deal?"

The whole time Alex talked, he kept waving his hands up off the steering wheel.

"No, as far as I'm concerned someone has screwed up and sent us on a wild goose chase." *Jesus, I hope Dennis agrees with me.* Alex shook his head. *No he's showing that damn frown of his when he's deep in thought.* "Okay, why don't you agree?"

Ross had his brief case on his lap. He pulled out some papers. "I can see your point; however, my query is why does Robert Braun have a Level Two rating with both governments?" He showed him the file.

"I did mention it to you briefly when we talked about the niece."

They had reached the outer limits of London. *Damn, I forgot about that. Seeing that code again has knocked the bejesus out of me. He's right to wonder. Son of a bitch...how can I get him to agree there's no case here.* Alex felt his blood rushing through his system, his body tensed. *That code is worth millions. I almost had my hands on it once. Now that ass hole is dead...it is there for the pickings.* "Dennis, perhaps you've got a point."

Alex pulled into the garage at Scotland Yard and parked in his space. "How about we review your file over dinner? I really haven't had a chance to look at it. I'll drop off the papers the assistant gave us to the lab. You write up a report about our meeting at the Braun estate, and then I'll meet you at the Chief Inspector's office around five thirty before he leaves. I'll call Jane and tell her I won't be home for dinner."

"That sounds like a good idea. See you later."

12

The next morning in Alex McGraw's office

The next morning, after his dinner with Dennis, Alex sat at his desk studying Lauren Woodgrieve's page of project assignments. *There is something different about the identification of these projects. I can recognize the K code on some of these, but why isn't it being used on all of them?* Alex got up and poured coffee and sipped. *What and how does any of this have to do with his son? He's got to be selling the formulas.*

He stared at the papers another ten minutes when his secretary came into the outer office.

"I'm terribly sorry I'm late, sir."

She scurried to open the window shades, turned on the fax machine, the computer and started to pour her boss his coffee.

"No need I'm all set. Was the traffic bad this morning?"

His secretary's face looked very sad. "No sir. I'm late because of my youngest. I don't know what to do with him. I can't get him to eat what's good for him. I'm running out of ways to camouflage his food. Thank goodness he can't read yet. I've marked all the treat boxes that are for him, so that the rest of the family doesn't touch them."

Alex's eyes opened wide and he smiled, *Thank you Mrs. Logan.* "I'm sorry to hear that. I've some calls to make and then I'll be gone the rest of the day. Shut the door on your way out. Please."

He took up the project list. *Of course, that has to be it. Camouflaged the code. The projects that are either government or Braun's own developments he would protect with his code. The others have a look alike code that only Braun would know in a flash.*

Alex looked up a number in his directory. He then took a little box out of his drawer and hooked it up to his phone before dialing. "Is Charlie Ringle in? Yes, I'll wait. Charlie...Alex. I need you to find out if there are any formulas being sold on the black market. Call me at home...By the way, would it be possible to tap a phone at the yard?"

"Sure. It'll cost though."

"How much?"

"Thousand pounds...I know it's a lot, but, it gets done without a trace. You taught me to deal with only the best."

"I'll let you know when you call tonight."

He then cleared his desk, put on his coat and left the building using the stairway. *I don't want to run into Dennis. He's like a pit bull. Once he gets an idea he won't let go of it. I don't think he accepted the Chief's explanation that Braun's Level Two rating was due to his navy rank. Come to think of it, the Chief didn't say there was a change in his name. It has to be him. I know this is the code.*

Alex knew he couldn't chance making a call to Braun's son from his office. Instead he returned to the pub where they first met and found a phone booth. He dialed the number twice; perhaps Windsor would figure out that this was important. The second call worked. "Thirty minutes, pick me up at the Cork and Bottle. *Very Important.*" To the minute, Windsor pulled up, quickly Alex hopped in, and Windsor sped away.

As they drove to a little burg outside of London, Alex revealed that he was an inspector for Scotland Yard.

Windsor stared at Alex in shock, pulled his car off the road into an un-kept cemetery, and braked with a screech. "What the fuck are you telling me?"

He jumped out of his sports car and Alex followed. "Windsor, shut the fuck up and listen to me. I told you this for good reason."

Alex explained why he and his partner had been sent to the estate. "Now, look at this paper and tell me if you've seen it before or know what it is?"

Windsor, still hyper over this revelation, took the paper. "What the fuck is this?" He waved it at Alex. "You call me and get me to come out to a creepy cemetery, scare me half to death telling me you're an inspector, and then show me a stupid piece of paper! Are you playing with me?" Windsor pulled out a pistol. "What's so fuckin important about it?... It looks like gibberish."

Alex took back the paper and sat on a tombstone. *This man is mental*! "Windsor, just take a deep breath and calm down. Put that silly gun away. I'm not going to arrest you. I know you're selling your father's formulas. If anything, I want to help you."

Windsor fumbled with his lighter and then threw the cigarette. "Oh, I see. Now you're the comedian. Well, inspector, how do you propose to do that?"

Alex glowered at him. "Do yourself a big favor and quit being an ass. For your fucking information, this piece of gibberish could be worth a billion dollars in the right hands. Oh, now I have your attention."

Alex raised his eyebrows to Windsor and nodded. "After our first meeting I wondered why you wanted to get rid of your cousin, the lab assistant and your mother. I got my answer at the estate...your cousin got almost everything. That really screwed things up for you. Now, I'm wondering if Braun's death was from natural causes."

Windsor slumped down on a tombstone. His voice could hardly be heard. "That swine got everything that belongs to me. It took months of planning....His death was a masterpiece plan, and now you're telling me, I can't have what belongs to me, because of this fucking code."

Windsor glared at Alex, and then a frown appeared. "Wait a minute. That can't be true." He paced around running his fingers through his hair. He raced over to his car and opened the glove compartment and found his flask. He took a huge gulp. "Hmm" He shut his eyes to enjoy his swallow... " Now I can think better."

He offered Alex a swig.

"No thanks...I'm on duty" and smirked at Windsor. "What were you going to say before you needed that, and remember, you're the driver?"

Windsor strode some more. "Okay, let's just say that I have a way to get a hold of some formulas and a way to sell them. So far, we, I mean, I haven't had any complaints. No one has asked for money back. So that would mean …?"

Alex interrupted him and took his flask. "That doesn't mean jack shit, Windsor! Now, I know what I saw. This code was developed by Robert Braunstein. That was his name!"

Alex pushed his hat back on his head. "The name Braun just didn't ring any bells. He must have changed it after the war. Braunstein was known for being able to make a bomb out of almost anything and to protect his formulas, he developed this code which…today, buddy boy, no one has been able to crack it, read it or understand it."

Alex dangled the paper in front of Windsor. "I don't think Lauren Woodgrieves would have shown us this paper if she knew what it meant. So that tells me he has developed something really important! I'll bet he mixed up his research within other projects so that no one would ever suspect. One of these times, you're going to get a formula that you won't be able to open and if I were you,I wouldn't try to sell it because my guess is the person who buys it isn't going to be very happy. Put your plan on hold for a while until we can sort this out. Don't worry; I'll still get rid of the bitch."

Alex emptied Windsor's flask on the ground. "Oh, this should perk you up a bit. You can count on the first one on your list being gone by the week-end. I suggest you take a trip and leave tomorrow."

Windsor's eyes lit up. "At least something good is happening. I'll pay you extra if you would film it."

Alex shook his head. *I thought I had seen them all.* He thrust the flask in Windsor's face. "You know the cliché, like mother like daughter, well," He smiled and nodded, "like son!"

Windsor grabbed the flask. "We'll see who has the last laugh." *God I hate this man. He gives me the creeps.* "Are we done here? I've a plane to catch."

Heathrow Airport

Around eight – forty five the chauffeur dropped Kimberly at Heathrow Airport. She looked around for Lauren in the concourse for Lufthansa Airline. *Lauren likes to be prompt as well.* Not seeing her, she found two seats. Arthur had made all the flight arrangements. They just needed to show their passports for boarding passes. She went to the check in counter. "Excuse me; this is the gate for Austria. I notice you don't have it posted."

The flight attendant assured her she had the right gate.

Kimberly looked at her watch. *Nine o'clock and she's still not here.* Nine fifteen came and Kimberly paced a little, glanced at the clock, and went to the bank of phones. *Maybe I can catch Martin before he gets too far away.* Just as she picked up the receiver, Lauren went dashing by her.

"I wondered if you'd make it. They've just announced first class boarding."

Lauren stopped in her tracks hearing Kimberly from behind. She turned sporting a very colorful outfit in brown and orange and sunglasses to match. It amused Kimberly.

"What's so funny, you don't like my *new outfit?*"

"Oh yes, chic, sunglasses." Kimberly squinted. "They're not big enough to cover that shiner. Whatever happened?"

They boarded and got settled.

Lauren started to open her brief case. "If I tell you what happened, will that wipe the smirk off your face?"

"You can try, but I can't promise a thing". *Gosh, I wish I had a camera.*

"What were you just thinking? Your face is lit up like a neon sign; you're almost ready to burst." Lauren put her hand over Kimberly's menu the flight attendant handed them. "Maybe...I wish I had a camera."

Kimberly roared with laughter. "You're too funny. Am I that obvious?"

Lauren nodded. "Just a bit."

"So from what you're telling me, Sheila didn't strike you. It was an accident."

"Well, I'm sure had she not been so angry, she wouldn't have tugged at the photography case, lodged on the closet shelf, so ferociously. When the thing came loose, I was right behind her and Voila!"

Kimberly leaned on the armrest and squinted with pursed lips. "What on earth would make her that angry?"

"When I got home last night, I could tell by her actions that she hadn't taken me seriously about us breaking up. I told her we were going skiing and I wanted her to move out by the time I got back."

Kimberly blushed. *Gosh, this is too fast for me, what do I say?*

"Kim." Lauren put her hand on Kim's knee. *She's so naive!* "Relax...I need my space too. I really never had a chance to get settled after being made your uncle's assistant. The last two years have been mostly work and parties. Now I've the chance."

Lauren put her brief case on her lap. "Do you mind if I get some work done. I don't want any of this on my mind after we get there. We've another hour before we land."

Kimberly nodded opening her brief case. *Her devotion to her work is certainly admirable. I wish I could tell Uncle Robert what a wonderful choice he made.* She sadly smiled at the back of the inside cover. In the card slot she had a picture of her and her uncle in her garden.

She took out the notes she had scratched down during the meeting with the inspectors. *Interesting. My notes end after Lauren gives out her project assignment sheets to everyone.* She glanced over and Lauren had just finished marking some of the boxes and wrote some comments. "Sorry to interrupt you. Could you explain what you're doing with that coded sheet? I was just going over my notes from the meeting and they end when you gave out that sheet."

Lauren studied Kimberly's face for a minute. "Isn't that when that jerky inspector decided to call it a day?"

"JERKY? You mean more like rude. So, how do you know what or which one of the letters or numbers to mark?"

Lauren pointed to various squares. "This isn't going to make any sense to you unless I've a project for you to look at and then I can show you how each element of the formula has a place on this sheet."

"What about the project you showed me at the lab. Do you have that sheet with you?"

Lauren pulled out another sheet of numbers and letters. "No, I don't. That project and paperwork had a star on it which means that it can't leave the lab and must be vaulted. This sheet is used to evaluate all starred projects."

Kimberly held the sheets side by side. "Interesting, they almost look the same."

The flight attendant told them that they would be landing soon.

As they were putting on their coats, Lauren took hold of Kimberly's arm. "Kim, will you make me a promise?"

"Promise? What about?"

"Your mind is going ninety miles an hour regarding the last two weeks, and that is understandable, but I really want us to have a good time. So could you promise me that we'll ski during the day and then the evening we can discuss whatever is on your mind?"

"I hear you and I promise… Do you suppose our room will have a video player?"

"You didn't bring that…"

Kimberly smiled and nodded. "More for safe keeping than

94

anything else." She raised her hands a bit, laughing. "I honor all my promises, Miss Lauren."

The gleam on Kimberly's face seeing the resort made Lauren's day.

"You spent a lot of time here?"

Kimberly still glowed. "Oh yes, we didn't miss a season. I think it's just the last five or six years we only came three times. I was getting my doctorate and Uncle Robert had started to revamp the company."

Kimberly's eyes widened when the bell hop put their luggage in a room for two. He showed them all the amenities which included a TV with a built in video player.

After they settled in, they dressed and headed for the slopes.

As they went out of the hotel to the lifts, Kimberly looked twice as a car drove by. *Windsor's car? Can't be.*

"What's the matter, Kim? You look like you forgot something."

"No…I just saw that car speeding by and it looked like Windsor's. Why would he be here, let alone have a car here, especially that one? My God, the man hates skiing…Though, I did see a two after his initials. Maybe he bought another car or got his mother to get him another one. What's another hundred and fifty thousand dollars?"

Lauren gasped at the amount. "*That* car costs that much?"

"Yes, it's a toy for the rich and famous. I see a lot of them in New York."

They had a beautiful day for skiing. It had snowed the night before, all the slopes were still open, and the lifts weren't crowded. Perfect conditions!

They skied the rest of the afternoon and then stopped for a delicious dinner. Their waiter told them that the slopes would be open until midnight for the experienced skiers.

"That sounds like fun. How about it?"

Surprised that Kimberly was interested in more skiing, Lauren said, "The sky is clear I bet we'll have the glow of the moon too. Why don't we skip dessert and go now?"

At the lift, Lauren had to fix her boot and told Kimberly to go on and she would catch up. Kimberly rode to the top and waited for about ten minutes.

Concerned, she skied straight down missing the moguls.

Lauren was slouched on a bench flicking snow from her mittens. Kimberly released her binders, picked up her skis and rushed to her. "Are you okay? Is there something wrong with your foot?"

Lauren shook her head. "No, my foot is fine. I've just lost interest in skiing at the moment. Could we go back to the room?"

"Sure, that's fine. Let me take our skis." *Whatever could have happened for her to change her mind? I don't think I should pry. Hopefully she'll tell me.*

They walked in silence all the way to the room.

"Would you like to be left alone? I can get my shower."

Distraught, Lauren looked up at Kimberly. "Please, don't go. I want you to know what happened."

Lauren sat on the couch in front of the fireplace. "I had fixed my boot and then felt someone's hand on my shoulder. It was Sheila. She startled me so. I asked her why she was there, had she followed us? I couldn't imagine how she even found out we were here."

Kimberly lit the fire and sat next to her. "She didn't attack you again."

"No, no. She started to cry and apologized several times for causing my injury. She pleaded with me not to break-up."

"This sounds pretty personal and really doesn't involve me." Kimberly looked at the fire and then back at Lauren. "I'm not one to give advice as this is a totally a new world for me, but it seems Sheila wants to change her ways to save your relationship. Perhaps she should have another…"

Lauren's eyes glistened in the glow of the fire. A few tears streamed down her face. "Another chance?" She shook her head slowly. "No, not anymore. I'm truly glad this happened. I meant what I said before about wanting to sort out my life…."

She smiled at Kimberly.

Kimberly felt a tingling sensation that started from her toes. *I think it is time to start a new subject. Getting too awkward.* "Did you see the lifts open at six am.? How about a cup of tea." Her voice cracked a little when she said it. The cracking sound broke the trance and resulted in a burst of laughter for both of them.

Kimberly added wood to the fire. She cleared her voice. "Well, while you make the tea, I'll get a shower. I still feel a little sweaty from skiing." She went into the bedroom and shut the door.

Near eleven o'clock at night at the Kitzbuhel hotel

That night about eleven o'clock, in another suite, there was a loud knock at the door. Windsor stopped pouring a drink to open it. "Well, it's about time you got here. I've been waiting all day."

As he stepped back from the door, Sheila pushed past him, "Should that bother me?" She dropped her coat into a chair on the way to the bar.

Windsor shut the door. *She is such a bitch.* "Seems like you've had better days?" He poured her a double shot of bourbon. *Now, of all times, why does she have to be unmanageable!*

Sheila grabbed the glass before he added a chaser of pop to it, and swallowed it in a gulp. She slammed the glass down on the bar for a refill.

"All right, drama queen, it is fuckin obvious something is wrong. Are you going to tell me or are you just going to drink all my bourbon?"

Sheila took the second drink, topped it up with some cola. "Yes, I'm a bit upset. For openers, Lauren has ended our relationship and has given me this week to move out. That's not enough; she and your cousin are here on a skiing vacation."

She downed the drink and gave the glass back to Windsor for a refill. Windsor stood motionless. *I wonder if she knows about this code stuff that Alex told me about. Can't remember what he said. Something about not being able to…*

"Windsor, your little game is over. Got it? It's over." She stood with her hands on her hips.

He poured her another and glowered at her with contempt. "Like hell my game is over. Did you bring the rest of the formula?"

She reached for the drink but Windsor put his hand over it. "Well?"

"Don't be an ass! Yes, I've your *formula*. But, I'm telling you this is the last one I'll be able to get on a regular basis." She handed him a disc folder, shoved his hand away, and took her drink.

Windsor pulled an envelope out of his pocket and put it on the bar, not letting go of it. "Listen, I'll tell you when it's your last drop. Besides, how do I know this is the right duplicate, now that you say it is the last disc?"

Sheila glared at him, tore open the envelope and riffled through the bills. "Are you crazy? I check every disc. Only two wouldn't open."

Windsor's eyes widened. "You've never said anything about that before. Why wouldn't they open?"

"How the *Fuck* should I know! Should I have brought them? I can just see your screaming tantrum if your buyer bitched that they couldn't open it!!" Sheila laughed out loud over that visual.

"You just bring me all of it."

"Smart ass, just how do you propose I get what you want? Did you not hear me say that I've to be out of the apartment by the weekend?"

Windsor put the bottle away and moved from the bar. "Well then, I guess you have about four days to get the job done before Lauren gets back. I suggest you get on the next fuckin plane and get the fuck out of here!"

Sheila shrugged into her coat. "Listen up, you prick. The risk factor for these thefts has doubled, so you can bet your ass, my payoff has too."

Windsor stood in front of the door. "You're really pushing your luck now, you bitch."

Sheila snickered. "Are you threatening me? After all the money you've made from the formulas I've stolen. You really think you can scare me, you sack of shit."

Windsor raised his fist at her.

She grabbed his fist. "Don't push me! Being blond doesn't mean stupid. I've got everything documented. Anything happens to me, I'll hang you by the balls. If you want more formulas, buddy boy, you'll just pay more for them… I'm no longer at your beck and call. Now, if you'll excuse me, I've a plane to catch."

Sheila pulled the door open very deliberately and walked out.

Windsor slammed the door and screamed, "That Bitch! That Fuckin Bitch!"

She heard him from the hall and grinned, but, then she thought she heard him talk to someone. She went back to the door to listen. She could hear him screaming again, one of his typical temper tantrums he used on his mother.

She smirked and started to leave, when she heard another voice yell back, "Would you get a hold of yourself."

Sheila's heart stopped. *Son of a bitch, who's that? I don't know the voice.* She ran to the elevator to avoid being seen.

Windsor stomped into the next room. "Did you hear how that bitch talked to me?" He took off his jacket and threw it on the bed. "What do you think? Is she expendable?"

Edward Edse, dressed in a robe, sat in a chair by the balcony door, his back to Windsor. "Windsor, Windsor, you get so worked up."

The doctor swiveled in his chair. "We'll play her game until we have all that we want, and then I'll just have to prescribe the same medication I gave to your father."

Windsor stripped down to his shorts, went into the bathroom, and turned on the shower. "Don't call him my father. God I'm glad that bastard is out of my life once and for all."

He got into the shower and called out. "Eddie, I want to be there when you give her the drug. I want to watch that bitch die."

The doctor stood in front of the bathroom mirror to shave. "Have I ever not given you what you wanted? We do make an exceptional twosome." He lathered up his face. "What time is our dinner engagement with those two nuns?"

Windsor got out of the shower and started to dry off. He hadn't told Eddie about Alex McGraw. "The hell with them, cancel the fuckin dinner! I'm worried we may be losing control of Sheila." *I know he'll go ballistic if he finds out I hired someone to kill off mother and the others. These are my ideas and my money funding all of this. I'm done being told how to handle my affairs.*

The doctor smiled as he watched Windsor dry off. "Hmm, that's a good idea; we don't need to have dinner with them. We could have dinner for two here. I'm sure the menu is good because the dessert looks excellent."

Windsor put on his robe and threw his towel over the doctor's head. "Son of a bitch, Eddie, will you quit it. She's right; she does have us by the balls. We're being blackmailed."

The doctor finished shaving. "Getting hysterical over this isn't going to help, my dear. You've got to keep your cool." Eddie wiped his face and studied the after shave lotions. *This should do it. It smells luscious.* "You lost control by threatening her. Let her think she's right and keep to the bargain. If she wants more, then give it to her. Still complain as you usually do or she'll get suspicious. Can you do that, my sweet?"

Windsor sat putting on his socks. "You're right as usual." *All of this is my fuckin idea and I still can't run it my way.* He looked at his watch. *I wonder if Alex has finished the job. At least there are benefits from hearing Eddie bitch at me.*

The doctor came up from behind. "You realize we have to keep her on track. There are a few discs left to complete this formula and without them we lose the big money."

" Eddie, Sheila said there were two discs she couldn't…open."

Eddie had switched mental gears and no longer wanted to talk about Sheila. He fluffed up Windsor's thick blond hair. He knelt on the bed and kissed Windsor on the back of his neck. "Call the nuns and tell them we'll do it another time…tell them I've a severe headache."

☙◆❧

At five thirty a.m., Sheila hurried out of the hotel to a waiting limousine. As the chauffeur shut the door, she glanced up and saw Kimberly and Lauren looking out of the window. Sheila quickly moved away from the door. *So what if they saw me. I'm sure Lauren has told Kimberly what happened.*

"Is that Sheila leaving in the limo?" Kimberly moved closer to the window as Sheila looked up and then jolted back in her seat. "It looks like she doesn't want to be seen, either. Strange, you said she's here for a week's holiday."

Kimberly frowned at Lauren's sudden amusement. "Are you going to share that bit of humor you're enjoying?"

"It's not humor. Maybe a little sarcasm mixed in with realization. Hard to explain, but looking down and seeing her leave, I saw the whole picture of what she would typically do when she hadn't gotten her way! She would leave." Lauren's smile tightened. "I can recall several times when she left a party and I had no way to get home and had to call Uncle Charles."

Kimberly grinned. "Which would explain Charles's and Harriett's dislike for her?"

"To be fair, Sheila does have many good qualities and maybe that's why I overlooked the bad ones for so long." Lauren chuckled again. "She is not a morning person at all! So that scene suggests she realizes this relationship can't go any further and has gone to find out about the apartment down the hall."

Lauren paused. "Why are you frowning? You look confused."

"You're right, I am confused." Kimberly shrugged a little. "Perhaps it is coincidental. I know this resort is very popular and most of the experienced skiers come here, but Windsor? I realize I didn't see him but I know that was his car. Though the license had a two on it, what are the chances that someone would have the exact car, initials as well? Then, how did Sheila know we would be here? You did say that Windsor introduced you to Sheila. Is that a coincidence? I know none of this has any correlation to uncle's video, but the events have a way of stirring the pot."

Kimberly put her cup on the bar. She looked at her watch. "We better get a move on it, if we're going to have breakfast. The lifts will be opening in a half hour."

She waved a schedule she found inside the bar. "Did you see this posted in the bathroom by the Jacuzzi? They don't want people to forget why they came here."

Lauren chuckled. "Well I ordered breakfast in case…."

A knock at the door made them jump. "That must be breakfast. To save time, we can have breakfast while we watch the video. With all of my problems, we really haven't given it much time since we've been here."

Kimberly pushed the remote. "I've set the video where all of this ambiguity begins, the fingering of his ring and fiddling with Duke's collar. I haven't discounted your thought that he could have been having an attack of some sort during this filming, but I can't forget his last words to me were to be in control, to use restraint, and to be cautious. At the time he said it, he was without a doubt in control."

Lauren poured them more coffee. "Run the tape back to where Robert is with Duke. We know that there's a lock of some sort in his ring. Okay, stop it right there" Lauren pointed her fork at the video. "Isn't it odd that Robert would ask you to take care of Duke?"

"How sly can you be? Of course! He's telling me Duke knows something." *Uncle would speak German to Duke. I wonder if knowing what he said might help.*

"You have that look on your face. What's going on in there?" Lauren rolled up her napkin and threw it at Kimberly.

Kimberly laughed. "Nothing gets past you, does it? Okay, smarty pants, what was I thinking?"

Lauren went to the phone. "You were thinking that we should go back home and talk to Duke… Yes, could you tell me when the next flight to London is? Ten thirty." Lauren made all the arrangements. She hung up and looked curiously at Kim. "Strange, why would the manager be upset that he wasn't told that you were here for the weekend?"

Kimberly chuckled getting up from the table and tossed back Lauren's napkin. "It could be …. because Uncle Robert owns the resort!" She quickly went to the bedroom and shut the door as a couch pillow hit against it.

The chauffeur opened the door as they walked out of the hotel and got into the limo.

"Did you see the look on the concierge's face when you asked if your cousin skis on the big slope? I don't think he knew if you were kidding him or being serious."

Kimberly put on her sunglasses. "I couldn't think of another way to find out if that car is his. Interesting that Windsor is here almost every month in one of the penthouse suites. Wonder who's paying for that."

Lauren looked at the parking areas as the limo drove off. "I'm sure the stories the bell hops could tell would be priceless." Lauren asked the driver to stop. "Kim, look over at the end of that row. Isn't that Windsor's car?"

৵৵

The flight back to London gave Kimberly time to prepare the ideal schedule, knowing fully well it wouldn't even be looked at again. She amused herself watching Lauren's concentration in her work.

"I've a question, Dr. Woodgrieves."

Lauren giggled. "Yes, Dr. Braun." She turned in her seat to face Kimberly, took her glasses off, and stared at her with her eyes crossed.

"What kind of a look is that?"

Lauren laughed. "This is my studious, professional and consequential business look."

"Hmm, I think it best you stay in the lab." Kimberly laughed out loud.

"What's the question?"

"Have you thought how we can identify and or finish the projects you're working on so that we can bill the companies?"

"That's a very good question. I started to think about it the other day when you pointed out that the code sheets looked similar yet they were different."

She opened her laptop. "I didn't want that weird inspector to know I had all my projects with me, except for those in the vault."

She scrolled down the list, showing the dates of completion. "Fortunately, it appears the lab is only working on three projects. Interesting that two of them are in the vault and the third is on my lap top using the secondary code..."

Kimberly stared at the two pages of code. "So this first page is the one that gets locked up in the vault with the test and this second page is used on the tests you've got listed on the lap top. Is that right?" Her eyes widened. "Lauren, the list on the laptop, are any of those tests ever put in the vault?"

Lauren narrowed her eyes thinking. "No, I can't say that I've seen any of them in the vault. We have them under lock and key, but certainly not protected like those using the other code sheet." *I can't understand why Robert would want to have these codes so similar, unless. ...* "Kim, didn't Robert say something about things having two sides?"

Kimberly looked through some notes she had taken watching the video. "Yes, I wrote it down because it seemed too serious! He said, Kimberly, you must keep in mind everything has two sides. This will help you determine the directions you need to take with the formulas I've developed...... Those are remarks from a man I don't know. Uncle Robert never talked to me in riddles. Everything was matter of fact." She looked at her watch. "Sorry to interrupt our train of thought here, but I better call Arthur and have a car sent to meet us."

"Why don't we take a cab?"

Kimberly shook her head. "No, that is one thing I learned from yea high. You don't surprise Arthur or Uncle Robert. I'll just be a minute."

She returned to find that Lauren had opened up the billing of a company that she knew R &K frequently worked for. Lauren saw Kimberly's eyes widened over what showed on the laptop screen. "Several months back, Uncle Charles used my laptop at a meeting Robert had at the estate and when I was going through the hard drive, this came up. I don't think Uncle knew how to save it to a disc. Good for us, I recognized one of the accounts." She gave the laptop to Kimberly. "I found this more by accident but if you use F-3, it goes to another program that I think is structured to translate this second code sheet into billing information."

Kimberly grinned and nodded. *Oh, my gosh*! "This whole program is much of what my doctorate was based on." *I can remember the discussion we had picking a topic and...*

Lauren nudged Kimberly. "What is it? You get that glow on your face when you're reminiscing. So what do you remember?"

"You're right. Again. I had a hard time selecting a topic and Uncle Robert spent hours talking about it. I remember he asked me what I thought about Translation. The concept had been touched upon but no real documentation had been developed. My professors thought it was too far advanced. Uncle Robert told me to prove everything in a very basic way, and not worry about making it interesting. I did this and the department approved my topic and I got my *Hood*."

Kimberly pointed to an open square on the screen. "The right number or letter put into that box would open the entire program for this account. The program can be adjusted in many different ways."

She typed in some words and phrases and the screen opened to hundreds of coded lines. "The beauty of my design is it is idiot proof. I put so many backups that the program will not let you make a mistake." She studied the screen. "What he has added, or should I say omitted, is any discourse between the beginning and the end."

Lauren gave her the time out sign. "Sorry, you lost me with discourse."

"To maintain total control, he has designed the system to accept only the data you enter from this sheet, which is for you just numbers and letters. Then the program reads it and converts it into a language that the customer will receive, be satisfied and pay the bill. My guess is the main office never handles any of these projects once they have negotiated the contract."

"So there's no middle person to make a mistake."

Kimberly nodded. "I would be curious how he incorporated this second sheet of letters and numbers into my program." She sat back in her seat. "To do that, he needed to create a master translator."

Lauren had the two coded sheets side by side on her brief case. Kimberly smiled, leaned over Lauren and picked up the first page and looked up at her pressing her lips together. "How much do you want to bet that this first page is the Master Translator?   And no one would ever know."

She leaned back. "He said everything has two sides. On paper none of this means anything." *But in the right program this code becomes a whole new culture.* "I don't understand why all the secrecy? He didn't even tell me why he really wanted me to research and develop the topic." *Why would he do that to me?   All these questions and I can't get any answers.*

As Kimberly sank into her seat and closed her eyes, Lauren reached for her hand. "Hey, don't jump to conclusions before all the facts are in.   Isn't that a main rule in research?"   She squeezed her hand gently.   The "Fasten Your Seat belt" sign rang and flashed.

"You never did say if Arthur would have the car there for us."

"I thought maybe I had lost the connection after I told him we were on this flight.   I think I may have interrupted a major project going on at the estate.   I didn't get the feeling he would be delighted to see me back so soon."

"He is sending Martin?"

"Yes, of course.   When I chokingly said we would take a cab, he immediately said Martin would be there, and hung up.   Poor Arthur, I hope he isn't wishing for retirement.   I would be lost without him."

Lauren took off her glasses.   "Oh, I can sympathize with Arthur.   I can't tell you how many times I would be working on a project, deep in experiments, when your uncle would rush into the lab and want me to drop everything I was working on to do something with him."

Lauren shrugged her shoulders with a sigh.   "You couldn't get angry with the man.   You had to be in awe of his brilliance and energy.   Furthermore, beneath all that gruffness, everyone knew he was a very kind hearted man who dedicated his life to his niece."

She put her glasses back on.   "No one knew of course, what a wretched child you were."

Kimberly burst out laughing.   "Where did that come from…I was a dear little girl."

Lauren almost choked.   "Oh, and I'm sure you can prove that."

ॐ∽ॐ

Martin put their luggage in the trunk. "Sorry you had such a short vacation, Miss Kim. Skiing not good?"

He got in the car and adjusted his mirror. "Will we be going directly to the estate, Miss Kim?"

"No, we'll take Lauren home first."

Within a half hour the limo pulled up in front of Lauren's flat. "I shouldn't be terribly long."

Kimberly rolled down her window. "Lauren, please, none of this is to be told to Charles."

Lauren caught Martin's eyes move with Kimberly's remark. She whispered. "Kim, I think Martin's listening to our conversation."

Kimberly shut her eyes. "Hopefully he didn't hear much. I'll see you later."

15

Sheila and Lauren's flat on Cornwall St

C lose to ten am. Sheila hopped out of the cab outside of her and Lauren's flat. Throwing the money at the driver, she grabbed her bag and ran up to the apartment, two steps at a time. Inside, she dropped all of her stuff in a chair and went to Lauren's computer. She had just so much time to search everything of Lauren's in the apartment. Out of the corner of her eye she saw something move and shot up straight in the air to look. *Son of a bitch it's my reflection in the mirror.* She stood and peered at the image. *Look at yourself. Is this what you've become, a thief for that maggot?*

"RING, RING...RING" The sound of the phone scared her to death. "Hello, oh, it's you! There's nothing here...I just went through all of the discs. I'm headed over there now...What! How long ago did they leave? Did you see them? You realize of course, going to the lab is my last shot at this for a long time. So you're going to need money coming out of your ass to pay for this."

She slammed the phone down. *I hope he lost his hearing, big simple shit. God I hate that man. The desk clerk told him his cousin just left. If they knew what a prick he is, they wouldn't let him in the place. Okay, come on now get a plan going.* It was obvious Lauren had taken her laptop with her.

As she left Lauren's office, the door closed a bit, showing a case hanging on the back. In it she found a couple of discs she couldn't recall. She slipped one in the desk top computer, but it had a lock on it requiring a password. So did the other one.

What do I do now? This hasn't happened before. She paced back and forth. *Could she suspect that I've copied the others?* She sat on the corner of the desk. *No...she's too trusting and too involved in her work. Hmm. Maybe this is something very special. If I take them, will Lauren think I took them or will she think she misplaced them? I'll hide them and then I can always get them.* She took them into the bathroom and taped them to the back of the toilet tank.

She went back into the office to check that everything looked untouched, grabbed her purse and left. She stopped at the Manager's office on her way to her car. *At least something good has happened. The apartment is available and the Manager's son can move all my stuff for me while I'm at work.* She jumped into her car and lowered the convertible top as she flew out of the lot, to go to the Braun lab.

16

The Braun Estate

It was almost three in the afternoon when Martin passed through the gate at the Braun estate. Lauren had been dropped off at her flat with the idea that she would return later for dinner.

Happy to be home, Kimberly handed her coat to Arthur. "I truly hope I haven't caused you a lot of trouble by returning so soon." She frowned at Arthur. "Where's Duke?" Before Arthur could answer, she whistled between her teeth a loud screeching noise.

A galloping sound could be heard from the end of the hall. Duke thundered down the main stairway to share hugs with her. "My day is complete."

Arthur smiled briefly. "Miss Kim, you'll find all your messages and mail on the desk in the library."

"Thank you…Oh, I just remembered something. When you have a moment, like now, could you come to the library? I want to make a change in procedure." She smiled at him. Totally taken off guard by the request, Arthur raised his brows. "Is there something wrong, Miss Kim?" *I can't put her off again if she wants to collect on my promise.* "May I have about ten minutes to finish a project in the kitchen?"

Kimberly waved. "I'll be waiting." She and Duke played together on her way to the library.

"That was good timing. I just went through all the mail and messages you had out." She showed him a letter. "Scotland Yard has given me permission to travel, but would like to know if and when I should like to leave the country."

She grinned. "Why are you frowning? You look like you're going to be hung any minute."

Arthur sat down next to the desk. "I know I prom…"

Kimberly cut him off. "I want to make some changes in your duties."

"What?" Arthur gasped.

"Arthur, I need to change your job description. You already run the house, but, I don't think it wise that you be my Valet. Do you? Running my bath, picking out my clothes, like you did for Uncle Robert." Arthur tried to cover up a grin with his hand.

"Well, I don't, and I just wanted to let you know, and you can wipe that that grin off your face, that I would be making the change, putting you officially as manager of the estate and Bertha and Gretchen will manage my personal requirements. I'll let Charles know to make the pay increases. Perhaps you could do the same with Charles for the pay increases for the rest of the staff."

"Oh, I'm sure that will be fine with them, and yes I'll confer with Charles."

Rather than leave, Arthur waited for Kimberly.

"Have I missed something, Arthur?"

"I couldn't help notice the mannerisms you share with your uncle. I'll tell …I mean, I wish I could tell him not to worry, that you're doing just fine handling his affairs."

Kimberly squeezed his arm walking out of the library. "Oh, I wish I shared your confidence. I'd give anything to have a moment with him. I miss him so much."

Duke leaned on her leg and growled. "Okay, okay!"

They both chuckled at Duke's antics.

"This is where I get to tease Duke." Her jackets were in the kitchen on a hook by the outside door. "Which jacket do I want to go play with Duke?" She pointed to her blue rain jacket and Duke just looked around the room, but he was watching her. Then she took her blazer that had padded elbows and put it on. He stood up, got his ball and went to the door. "Oh, maybe I changed my mind." She started to take it off, Duke put his ball down and barked and barked at her. He picked up his ball and nudged her to get moving.

Arthur laughed out loud. "Which of you is well trained?"

"Isn't that a treat?" Kimberly looked up at the kitchen clock. "We'll be back in an hour. Almost forgot, Lauren will be coming out later for dinner. Tell Herr Dietrich not to make anything special. Just so we have orange sorbet and fudge sauce for dessert." She smiled, grabbed some apples and left with Duke.

Arthur went to tell the Chef. *He's one of the finest chefs in the country and ninety percent of the menus are salad and sorbet, poor man.*

Kimberly and Duke played kick ball all the way to the crypt. Kimberly sat on a stone bench to catch her breath. "That was some work out, Duke." Duke barked and got on the bench with her. She stroked him for a bit. *Interesting, on uncle's video he pet Duke while holding onto his collar. The thought of Duke leaving his side is absurd. So why the obvious?* She started to look at his collar when her eyes glimpsed the ground just behind Duke's head. "Hmm, Duke, what do you think that is?"

She squatted a few feet from the bench to look at some very narrow tire tracks. "I don't suppose you know anything about these, do you fella?" She could see the tracks headed to the door of the crypt. Duke barked a few times and then stopped to listen. His ears went straight-up. His voice changed to a low kind of growl.

Kimberly heard him. "You better find out who's here."

Duke took off and in a few minutes returned with Lauren by his side.

"I do hope I'm interrupting something."

Kimberly beamed, "A few minutes ago you would have observed a very serious game of kick ball."

Duke knew what she was saying. He barked and went for his ball.

"Yes, I'm sure you know which of us won." They both laughed. "How did you know we were here?"

Lauren sat on the bench. "The short version of my tale is I didn't

113

want to have a run in with Sheila so I grabbed some things and thought I could finish my lab work here rather than in the flat. When I arrived, a gardener told me you and Duke were playing in this direction, and drove me here. Now I can walk back with you."

"Good... you can help us investigate a finding."

Lauren's eye brows perked up. "That sounds like fun. What did you find?"

"We were taking a time out from our game here on the bench when I happened to see these wheel tracks." Kimberly pointed to them and then showed Lauren the direction the tracks led to the door of the crypt.

"Doesn't the width of the track look really narrow?"

Lauren squatted to measure the width of the track with a twig she found on the ground. "That can't be much over an inch."

"I would think a wagon wheel would be twice that. Though, I've seen carts with narrow wheels but the spread of the wheels would be a lot more than this. What do you think?"

"I agree. When I saw it, I immediately thought of a wheelchair. Can you remember anyone at the funeral being in a wheelchair? I couldn't so I dismissed it. Well, let's see where it goes."

They got up and went into the crypt.

Kimberly opened the iron gate. "I heard Martin telling Arthur that the electrical had been finished out here. There should be a wall switch near the door." Kimberly rubbed her hand up and down on the wall. "I guess I heard right."

They stood in the doorway. Duke squeezed by Kimberly's leg to run in. He went to the back of the coffin vault and sniffed around. Kimberly and Lauren stepped into a clammy chamber.

Lauren looked all around hugging herself. "Quite a difference the sun can make."

Kimberly looked back at the entrance. "Tell me if my observation is nutty. The wheel tracks end at the entrance. As deep as those tracks are out there, I would imagine quite a bit of sand would have been brought in on the floor. Granted, if work had been done and the crew was conscientious in cleaning up, but, would they have washed down the whole room? I can smell disinfectant. Can you?"

Kimberly walked over by Duke and found sand at the corner of the vault. "It looks like they missed some sand." She knelt down to look at it. "Why would they remove the sand inside and not outside?"

Lauren put her hands on her hips. "Maybe whoever thought it would rain and wash the tracks away."

Kimberly put her hands in her pockets as she walked around. "Lauren, look over here." She pointed to the far end wall. "Is this interesting or weird? A thermostat in a crypt?" *Why would you need to maintain a temperature in here?*

They both looked at it and suddenly they felt short blasts of heat in the room. "This is run by body temperature. Why? It is a crypt. Who would come here?"

"This is too weird! Let's leave." Kimberly turned off the light and they started back to the house.

Lauren looked at her watch. "It's nice the days are getting longer. Gosh, it's later than I thought."

Kimberly took hold of Lauren's wrist, "Can't be that late. Not to worry, Arthur would sound the dinner horn if we were really late."

Lauren grinned. "You're joking of course. Arthur sounds a horn?"

Kimberly frowned. "No silly, he wouldn't sound it if we had company. It was so I wouldn't be late. Uncle Robert ran a tight ship. I had a terrible habit of forgetting the time. I think I could have taught a course in Book Worming. Now with the new security system, the guards know exactly where we are, and if they want, they can talk to us."

Lauren looked around, "Yes, I see what you mean. Doesn't that make you feel... inhibited?"

"Not really. Privacy is highly respected around here."

Duke dropped his ball in front of Lauren. She stopped. "Do I kick it or throw it?"

"Either way, he loves to chase it."

"I might be a better kicker." She backed up a few paces, jogged forward, and then booted the ball and it rolled all of twenty feet.

The look on Duke's face to Kimberly bent her over into hysterics.

"I'm sorry Duke. I'll try again."

Duke mouthed the ball and ran back to the house. This made them both laugh harder.

"I think he's telling you, you didn't make the team."

Kimberly sniffed. "Kitchen window must be open. Ooh…It smells like we're going to have lamb roast for dinner."

Arthur gave them another half hour before dinner would be served. While Lauren got her things from the car, Kimberly went to her favorite room. *I've time to watch the tape before dinner. There's something I'm not seeing.*

After fast forwarding, she noticed on the remote that she could run the tape in slow motion. *This is great. The way uncle is holding onto the collar, there's got to be something inside or on it.* She stiffened her lips, curled her tongue and let out a piercing whistle for Duke.

Duke ran in licking his chops. "Were you eating your dinner? I just want your collar and then you can go back to the kitchen." She took his collar off and he left. *He's just so…human.*

She sat at the desk studying the collar. She checked the stitching. Nothing could be removed. She put the collar on the desk. Arthur entered and retrieved a key from behind the grandfather clock. As he wound each workings of the clock, Kim's mind whirled. *He's using a key to wind the clock, but, it doesn't look like a key.* She picked up the collar. *Okay, what on the collar could be a key? The only possible part would be the tongue or pin.* She took a magnifying glass out of the desk drawer and looked at the buckle pin.

She looked again and the tip was triangular. *Oh!... Is this possible?* She pulled her chain out from her blouse, took off the ring, and put the buckle pin in the tiny hole of the ring and it fit. *It fits. I don't believe it. My God, it fits.* She jumped up from the desk. "IT FITS! IT FITS! ARTHUR, IT FITS!" Arthur dropped the key to the floor with her sudden shriek. Kimberly ran out of the room and yelled for Lauren. "Lauren, come quick. It Fits!"

Lauren rushed down the staircase. "Are you okay? What on earth is wrong?"

Kimberly's eyes were as big as saucers. "Come. I've done it. Wait until you see this. You won't believe it." She took Lauren by the hand and ran back to the desk. "Look, watch!"

Lauren put her hand on Kimberly's. "Just *wait!* Kim, take a breath."

Kimberly looked up to see Lauren staring at Arthur. Arthur turned quietly toward the door but hesitated when Kimberly said, "Arthur, please don't leave."

Lauren dropped her eyes and Kim's hand. "You're making a mistake."

Kimberly shook her head. "Not at all! Lauren, no! I've known him all my life. No one is more dedicated to my uncle than Arthur."

She smiled and motioned for him to come closer.

Kimberly picked up the collar and her uncle's ring and put the buckle pin into the side of the ring and turned it. "Oh my, look! The top has lifted."

She looked over at Arthur who had moved across the room near the desk. "I couldn't get over the way Uncle Robert acted in the video. I knew he was telling me something."

Her eyes widened as she studied Arthur's face. "You knew about this all along. Didn't you?"

Arthur pressed something on the bookcase and soon a door opened. "Yes, I did, Miss Kim. No one realized you would be so observant. All I can tell you is that what is in that ring must be put in this vault right now. I can assure you, you won't understand what it is, but, it is very important."

Lauren snapped at Kimberly. "Why not use the vault at the lab? It's bigger and more modern! It would be safer!"

Kimberly took the ring to Arthur. He pressed another button and the inside wall slid open exposing a door with flashing lights that opened a safe.

"This will be very safe right here."

Arthur very gingerly took the cover off the ring and turned it over. There lay a piece of microfilm. He took a small box out of the wall safe. Using the key from the collar he opened the box and placed the piece of microfilm into it. After everything was locked up, he gave the ring and collar to Kimberly.

He whispered to her. "You have just prevented a breach of world security."

Kimberly stood back aghast. "I'm a stranger in my own house." She stepped back to sit on the corner of the desk. "IF this is true...then... Uncle Robert was murdered."

Arthur eyes flashed wide. "No, Miss Kim, you mustn't..."

Lauren looked startled as well. "How did you come up with that?"

"It has to be. Think about it. Someone is after this microfilm. What about the test you showed me in the lab. I bet that has something to do with it too."

Arthur moved closer to Lauren. "Have you got the test results for that experiment?"

Lauren became defensive. "Why would you want to know?"

Arthur stared back at her and spoke quietly. "Trust me. We need to know."

Lauren brushed past him. "Trust me, those results are in the lab vault and only Robert and I have the combination."

Arthur turned to Kimberly. "If you'll excuse me, I best leave."

Kimberly took his arm. "Please don't. I need to talk to you"

"Another time, Miss Kim," and he quickly left the room.

Kimberly sadly watched him. "Lauren, that was so unnecessary. Whatever made you so defensive?"

"*Defensive!* You've just given up a piece of microfilm to be put into a safe you don't have the combination to. What do you have now?" Lauren paced as she spoke angrily. "He wouldn't even stay when you almost begged. So who's in control now?"

Kimberly glared at Lauren. "Before this issue gets out of hand, let me talk with him. I know Arthur wouldn't cause a scene or want a confrontation." *Please don't make me take a side.*

"I see, you think I've put him in an awkward situation." Lauren shook her head and looked right up into Kimberly's face. "I hope you're not disappointed..." Her eyes glazed up. "I think you've got a keg of dynamite here and it's close to going off. Call me when you feel I can be trusted." She opened the door and looked back at Kimberly. "You can't judge loyalty by how long you've known a person."

With Duke beside her, Kimberly swallowed hard as Lauren's car sped away. They walked to her favorite spot where her uncle would help her solve all of her problems both big and small. She stood by her little swing and quietly reminisced, pushing the seat on the swing. Suddenly she turned. She had a strong sensation of being watched. It wasn't totally dark yet. She looked up at her uncle's bedroom windows that overlooked her garden. Arthur was looking down at her. She stared. *Is that someone sitting in a chair next to Arthur? They're gone. Maybe it was a shadow. I could have sworn it looked like someone....wheelchair?*

Kimberly made a dash for the house. She took the main staircase two steps at a time and abruptly halted in front of Arthur as he came out of her uncle's bedroom.

"Arthur! Who was in Uncle's room with you? Someone was sitting in a chair next to you!" She bent over to catch her breath. Then, searching for an answer, she started to go in her uncle's room.

Arthur looked at her strangely. "Miss Kim, I was standing at the window alone. The way you were pushing your swing, I knew you were thinking back."

"Then you don't mind if I look for myself?" She tried the door and it opened. She looked at Arthur and could see a sigh of relief on his face.

"We had it fixed, Miss Kim." *Thank God, it worked.*

She saw nothing different in the room and came out riddled with guilt and shame. "I'm so sorry that I acted that way, please forgive me."

She hugged him. "So much is happening, and all I want is Uncle to be given back to me."

Arthur, uncomfortable with this closeness, patted her on the back. "Truly, Miss Kim, I wish I could give you some peace of mind. Please be patient. We all handle grief differently and life always gets better when we can hold onto the good we have."

17

Scotland Yard

Three days after the interview at the Braun Estate, Inspector Ross arrived at the Home Office. Heading toward his office, he met the chief lab inspector, Kurt Rollins, getting on the elevator. "Kurt, it's been awhile."

Kurt smiled, and they shook hands. "Dennis, it's good to see you. I thought you had been given the Heathrow project."

The two men exchanged the usual cordial conversation as they rode on the elevator.

"By chance, were you able to decipher those papers Alex brought to you a few days ago? We wondered if it is a code relating to National Security or simply a code used for business."

The elevator door opened and they got off. Kurt frowned. "Papers?..." He pulled out a little day planner from his inside pocket, and grinned. "My years here are catching up to me. I've an entry for anyone that comes into the lab." He shook his head. "Sorry Dennis. His name isn't here. What kind of papers?"

Inspector Ross put his coat and hat down on a bench in the hall way and opened his brief case. "I should have a copy. Here, two sheets of a strange looking code of some sort. We just met at the Braun estate for a routine inquiry about Braun's death and the lab assistant gave us this. She said they're used to identify projects they do for businesses."

Inspector Rollins studied the papers and shook his head. "Nope, haven't seen these before. You say Alex was going to bring these to us for evaluation? Maybe he forgot? Gosh, I haven't seen Alex for at least a month." He handed them back to Ross.

Ross put his hand up. "No, keep them. I still need a report on them, but if it's all right with you, I'd appreciate it if we could keep this between us for the time being until I find out about the mistake." *If he'd seen how Alex acted when he was handed these pages, he too would think it very odd that Alex hadn't taken them immediately to the lab.*

They shook hands. "Just call and I'll come for the report."

Returning later from lunch, Ross heard his phone ringing as he dashed into his office. "Inspector Ross. Yes sir, I'll be right up." *I wonder what Chief Inspector is wanting. Strange we just had a meeting with him the other day.* "No, I haven't seen him yet today. No I won't say anything and will leave directly."

He threw his coat in a chair with his hat and went out the door. Chief O'Doul's secretary sent Ross right in. Ross waited for a signal to sit, while his superior studied some papers.

Chief O'Doul pointed his eye glasses at Ross and motioned for him to sit. "Dennis, we have a situation you aren't aware of."

The chief looked dead serious. "It is very sensitive, and...only a few of us have been assigned to the case."

The Chief put his glasses on and laid the papers he'd been studying face down in front of Ross. "In the next few minutes you'll be meeting two high ranking men and you'll be given information that can't leave this room. I felt you'd be the right man to help in this matter. However, I need to know that you're unequivocally clear about this. Otherwise you can leave and we'll understand."

Ross stared at his boss. "Yes, sir, I completely understand."

Just then Defense Minister James O'Bryan and an American Naval officer, Admiral John Benjamin, arrived.

The inspector's eyes almost leaped out. *Holy mother of Jesus.* Ross swallowed hard and stood up.

After introductions, the two men sat across the table from Inspector Ross and Chief O'Doul.

The chief continued. "Dennis, our first question is just how close you are to Alex McGraw?"

Ross hesitated, with his hands squeezed together. "I've known Alex for as long as I've been here at the Yard. That's about twenty years. We were very good friends at one time. We shared an office, partnered a lot of cases. Our wives were the best of friends, so we did a lot of things together, until my wife passed away. I lost her about eight years ago. That's when we seemed to drift apart. We still play golf on the occasion, but it isn't the same."

The two men across from him stared at him and listened.

"Dennis, turn the pages over in front of you. What can you tell us about them?"

He turned the pages over and saw they were the pages he had given to Kurt Rollins. His head dropped. He looked up frowning. *Now will he think I'm lying?* "You got these from Kurt Rollins." He bit his lip.

The chief asked him to explain. Ross gave a brief synopsis of Alex and his meeting with Kimberly Braun and her company staff. Ross raised the papers. "For whatever reason, these two pages caused quite a stir with Alex. He couldn't wait to get out of there and very sternly told me to pack up my stuff. I was put in a very awkward position and had to lie to the others to smooth the upset. I promised we would return to answer their questions."

James O'Bryan, the Minister of Defense interrupted Ross. "To come right to the point, we have reason to believe we have a spy within our ranks. A lot of unorthodox events have occurred and can't be attributed to anyone in the known crime circuit."

Ross cocked his head. "What kinds of crimes, sir?"

The Chief Inspector cut in. "Right now, it seems most of the crimes are gang related, almost like someone is testing us. There's no doubt whoever is committing these crimes knows exactly what they're doing, planting false leads everywhere. We've done sweep after sweep of our rank and files and all of our personnel are clean, until you asked Kurt about these papers."

Ross sat back in his chair staring wide eyed. "You think Alex may be the rogue cop? I'm sorry sir, but I can't see a correlation yet."

The Chief nodded to the Admiral. "Inspector Ross, have you ever served in the Armed Forces?"

"I was too young for the Korean War."

Admiral Benjamin pulled three folders out of his case. "I'm here for several reasons: First: To explain the Pentagon's interest in this case. Second: To explain the development and importance of the K Code. And Third: How all of this leads us at the Pentagon to find Alex McGraw a person of interest."

"Here is a shortened version of Robert Braun's background you can read at another time." The Admiral handed a folder to both Inspectors. "I think you'll find the information very interesting.

He pulled out another folder. "Quickly I want to explain my relationship to Robert Braun, who during the Korean War and before was known as Braunstein. All of this is covered in that bio. He was under my command in the Navy Seals. A brilliant chemical engineer, Robert created many explosive devices in the field that continually saved our butts, and I might add some of the bombs are still being used."

The Admiral took out pictures and laid them out in front of everyone. "These pictures show Robert and his team of six men."

Ross studied the pictures and pointed to one. "I saw this man at the estate. Actually he answered the door. I'm sure it was him. Older looking, but just as fit as he is in this picture. Kimberly Braun called him Arthur."

Admiral Benjamin grinned. "You're right. And, I'm sure if you met the rest of the staff at the Braun estate, you'd probably meet the rest of his team. Toward the end of our tour of duty, Robert noticed pieces of equipment moved. He had a box where he kept his formulas and felt it had been opened. Troop replacements had come into the camp when this started to happen. To make matters worse, our secret location was found out. Robert's men stayed to cover while we escaped with the equipment and his formulas. Unfortunately, four of his men were captured and one killed."

The Admiral pointed to the pictures. "To make a very long story short, we found another hiding spot. It was the dead of winter and we were totally locked in. In only a matter of days, Robert came up with this code. Then he burnt the formulas."

Ross, deeply involved with the Admiral's story, quickly asked, "What happened to the sixth man and the other four that were captured?"

The Admiral frowned remembering. He pointed to another picture. "These are the four captured. This Seal was killed and this one was able to track us and got to our location. Sadly he didn't make it. He'd been our translator and I think he held out until he could tell Robert he heard the Koreans say what camp the others would be taken to. Also, he whispered he was sure he'd been shot by one of the troop replacements."

The Chief Inspector shook his head. "I know very few got out of those camps. Those that did died soon after. I was there at the end." He looked at the Defense Minister. "He got them out, didn't he?"

Minister O'Bryan chuckled. "Still seems like yesterday." He looked over at Ross who sat amazed. "Benjamin gave Robert permission to leave the unit to go after his men. I don't know any of the details but he brought his team back with him."

Admiral Benjamin smiled and nodded. "I couldn't believe it either. There wasn't time to talk when I saw him. He and his men were in such bad shape they were air lifted to a ship. It didn't take Robert long to regroup. The four he saved were sent back to the States. He came to me with the name Alex Wyndgate. Before his team member died in Robert's arms, he whispered Wyndgate's name to Robert."

The Admiral opened his hands. "I can tell you, he went looking for that man. The weirdest thing is Wyndgate couldn't be found. It was as if the guy never existed. As hard as it was, he finally gave up the search. Then he went back to the States. The last time I saw Robert was at an awards ceremony at the White House. He was given the Navy Cross and the Medal of Honor for that rescue. We've talked on the phone but only about Navy business. I think you'd probably have to talk with one of his team to find out the details and even then I doubt if they would tell you."

Ross shook his head. "Are you telling me Alex served under an assumed name?"

Benjamin nodded with a very serious look. "Here's our file on Alex Wyndgate, which doesn't leave this room. That was his legal name at the time. He had been trained for a special ops task force. We thought he was a double agent, but again we couldn't prove it. All of this got lost in the shuffle, obviously for many years." He handed it to Ross.

"He looks so different with a moustache." Ross handed the file to the Chief. "Then, my giving Kurt those papers triggered this meeting?"

Chief Inspector handed the picture back to Benjamin. "That's one of the reasons you're being asked to be on this team. For lack of a better word... your integrity. Had you not followed up and been concerned about Alex's behavior, we wouldn't be having this meeting. You see, there's a red alert on this Code. As soon as Kurt notified me, I called Benjamin with Alex McGraw's and your names."

The Chief got up to get his lighter for his pipe, and puffed thoughtfully. *Mm, that's better...* "During the Korean episode, the Americans had already started using computers and had established quite a bank of information. Since they and the UK merged on this ops mission, the Americans wanted all of our personnel records as well."

The Chief leaned on the table and picked up the coded pages, looking at Ross. "When Kurt stated you left him these sheets, I asked him to identify any prints on them. There were yours and McGraw's. Then when I reported that these prints had been found, the Admiral ordered them to be sent to him. Nothing came back on you of course, but..." The Chief smiled. "They found a match with Alex Wyndgate, but they had no record of Alex McGraw." He then sat in a chair at the end of the table.

Benjamin nodded approval at his colleague, and then handed each another file. "That was a huge revelation."

Ross studied the next folder and shook his head.

"Inspector Ross, I sense that you're confused about this code business."

"Yes, sir, I am. I've a feeling you're getting into an area out of my league. I can track a lot of this, but I can't understand why seeing this paper would cause Alex to literally sweat."

The Admiral raised the coded page. "This page is known as the K Code. What's so remarkable is that in over forty years nobody has broken this code. For many years Robert allowed the US Government to use it for its highest level of secrets. By itself, this page really is useless. Robert told me he put his translator on microfilm."

The phone interrupted the Admiral and the Chief Inspector answered. "Yes, when did this happen? You have called for an ambulance. Rope the area off! Absolutely no press allowed. Tell the local police not to touch anything. Fax me a picture. I'll send Inspector Ross to take over. Until then no one gets near the area. Is that clear?"

The Chief Inspector dropped his head for a few moments.

"Chief, what's happened?"

"There's been an accident outside of London in the West end, of all places. Little burg called Dothan. A limousine went over the bank into a ravine. It was found by some joggers. Two bodies were found and one may be alive. The license plate was partially covered but the officer said they could read L Brau."

The Chief noticed Ross's eyes look sharply at him. *Hmm, that shook Ross up. Wonder why?* "What is that Americanism when it rains, it pours?" The Chief glanced at his watch. "Admiral, I'm sorry for the interruption. Please continue."

The Admiral pulled another folder of pictures out and spread them on the table face down. "I'll try to cover this quickly. We think Alex has a contact in the Russian Black Market." He turned over the first two pictures. "For your information, getting someone in that organization is as difficult as getting someone inside the Mafia. These two men are Black Market Agents. It took us almost five years to get them accepted."

He showed the other three pictures. These men aren't ours but we believe if Alex has a contact, he has heard from one of these three, as we have, that a formula using this code as a password has been sold for several million dollars."

The Admiral sighed. "At least we have time on our side, only because we know that formula can't be opened without the code translator."

Around the table eye brows lifted.

"I think you're realizing the magnitude of this situation. We know it's only a matter of time before someone will attempt to get that microfilm. Can you imagine what that microfilm could be worth? We at the Pentagon think Robert before his demise discovered something so important that he used his code to protect it. We're convinced someone knows about the Code and knows that a translator exists and we know they won't stop until they get it. The ramifications are unthinkable!"

Ross rubbed his chin and closed his eyes. "I don't want to believe that Alex is in on this."

"We don't know that he is....we just need you to realize the scope of this situation and also, Ross, we need to know if we can count on your help and support?"

Benjamin and the Defense Minister left the Chief Inspector's office with the understanding that all communications would come from the Chief Inspector O'Doul. Ross agreed to help and would continue to work with Alex.

The fax machine began printing as the Chief escorted his colleagues out. Ross sat again as the Chief put a picture on the table.

The Chief Inspector took more puffs on his pipe and nodded. "Look at the car registration and the names involved..."

Ross gasped. "Lucille Braun!" *I can't believe this. Is it possible?* "Sir, I've to tell you something else..." Ross took a deep breath. "After leaving Kurt, I went to Alex's office to confront him about all of this. He wasn't there. Looking around for a pad I noticed the name Braun on a crumbled piece in his wastebasket. Sir, Lucille Braun was written on it. I put it back and left."

The Chief Inspector nodded. "Interesting..." He sat for a bit. "All the more reason I want you to handle this. Check it out. It very well could be an accident. The police reports show a history of drunk driving for her and her son. But the car in the photo is her limo. Not likely she was driving. Take whomever you need to do the photo work. We need to close this up fast."

127

18

Sheila arrives at R & K Plastics Company

A twenty minute ride to the lab seemed like an eternity to Sheila, as she pulled into a space next to Lauren's car. She still had a copy of Lauren's security badge from when Lauren had been sick and she had to pick up reports for her. Lucky for her, Lauren had forgotten to ask her to return it. *You'd think this bloody place was the tower of London, with all these security doors.* She went up the back stairway to the main laboratory and Lauren's office on the third floor.

Before she opened the door into the hall, she stood silent for a moment to make sure a guard wasn't making his rounds and to catch her breath. Her heart was pounding. *Getting caught in the apartment is one thing, but being stopped by the guards would be scary. Well, here goes.* She slowly opened the door and peered up and down the hall. No alarms had gone off... *Oh God, I hope that's a good sign.* She had Lauren's badge hanging and carried a brief case to look the part of one of the devoted employees, should she be seen on the security monitors.

At the office door, she swiped Lauren's card and the light went on as she pushed down on the door handle. *This place reeks of perfection. If allowed, the dirt would be in alignment.* Luckily the shade for the window that faced the hall had been closed. *Where to begin?* She set her watch timer. *Five minutes should be enough time. I swear this is the last time I get involved in something like this, ever again.* Shrugged her shoulders and began. Quietly opening and closing one drawer after another. Flashing over notes between Lauren and her boss. *Interesting!* "The enclosed disc is a duplicate of my test results that I gave you on…" *This might be it. It is! Shit, who's coming!*

Sheila froze. She could have sworn she heard a voice or sound of some sort. She put the disc in her pocket and gently, but quickly, shut the drawer. Lab coats hung on a hall tree behind Lauren's door. Being skinny, she hid behind the coats as the door opened.

"No one is here, sir. Perhaps her car was left the other day."

Sheila leaned heavily against the wall and caught her breath! As she moved from the hall tree, the badge swung on the chain and caught onto a little box on a file cabinet. *What do we have here? Lauren, you're a sneak! More discs with Duplicate stamped on them. Windsor got his knickers in a twist when I told him about these weird discs. This is it. We are Done!* She gathered the discs, about six in all, into her pockets and then emerged from behind the hall tree.

Her search had exceeded her five minute allotment. *Here's the plan, kill Windsor and leave the country. Good plan…but…Think! Sheila!* She shut her eyes. *Okay, first we check the room, next we leave as we came in with confidence and then we breathe.* Wanting to run, she forced herself to walk to the exit door that now looked a mile away. She sped down the three flights of steps to the cars. Feeling safe and more confident, she took time to look in Lauren's car for her laptop. *Knowing Lauren, she probably took it with her. Doesn't matter. Whatever is on these discs will have to suffice that Ass Hole.* Just to make sure, Sheila had a set of keys for Lauren's car and opened the trunk. *I'm sure she's got it.* She slammed the top down and smiled. "Okay, job done. We are out of here."

Feeling quite proud, Sheila hadn't noticed two men come up behind her. "What is your name, please, Miss?"

She stiffened with fear and slowly turned to answer. " Ah… I'm Lauren Woodgrieves' flat mate and I came for some of her stuff."

"I asked you, what is your name?"

Her legs were weak at the knees as the men came closer. They didn't seem friendly and were huge, towering over her.

She tried to smile. "Oh, my name is Sheila Bannister Jones."

The two men stepped forward, took her by the arm. "You'll have to come with us. You're trespassing."

"But I've this badge and I…."

The men almost carried her into the building. As they waited for the elevator, one of the men called on his phone. "We're to take her to the interrogation area."

To her surprise, the man put his key in the elevator panel and another set of buttons appeared. Wow. *This building doesn't have five floors.* "Are you sure you've got the right person? You can call Lauren Woodgrieves and I'm sure she'll tell you…"

"Be quiet!"

The elevator went to Lower Level II. The door opened and she was escorted to an eerie looking room. They told her to empty her pockets on the table. They took her brief case and badge. They left her alone.

"Can I smoke?"

There's nothing in here. A chair a table very little light. She walked around the room several times and then sat in the chair. *Have to keep my head.*

She lit up a cigarette. Still no one came in. She walked around the room again. *I guess I can smoke, no one's complaining. They must have seen me in Lauren's room.* There wasn't any carpeting so she stepped on the cigarette and lit another. I'll bet they're watching me right now! She picked up the cigarette butt and put it in her pocket, and sat down again. *I can't appear afraid even though I'm scared shitless. Oh, for one moment with Windsor! What am I going to tell them? Those men are so big. One punch and I'll be dead!*

She sat with her head in her hands, when she heard the door unlock. Quickly she straightened up. One of her captors motioned for her. She followed him down an empty hallway to another room. *Maybe this is it and I've just had my last…everything!!*

"No more smoking! Go in and sit down in that chair by the table!"

Sheila did exactly what she was told.

A few minutes went by and another man came in and put a goose neck lamp on the table. He directed the light downward.

After what seemed an eternity, two men came in and she heard a noise behind them.

That sounds like wheels turning. She was very alert to the sound and tried to look above the light at the men.

"Miss Jones! Is this what you've been looking for?"

Out of nowhere a disc appeared on the table under the light.

"HOLY SHIT!" Sheila jumped out of the chair and stepped back by the wall. "What the fuck's going on?"

"Sit down, Miss Jones...now!"

She stared at the men in the room. They hadn't spoken or moved. *This voice sounds different. It is softer, not deep like the one that brought me in here.*

Very slowly she sat down. "What am I missing here? Is someone really here or are you watching me talking from another room?"

"I've simply asked you if this is what you were looking for."

With that the disc disappeared and then reappeared.

"Just take a deep breath, Miss Jones. This is the end of the road for you. You'll not be leaving here."

Sheila was terrified, her heart pounded. "You can't be serious! Please! I'll tell you anything you want to know. Just don't kill me!" She wiped her eyes and tried very hard not to cry. "What do you want to know?" She started to stand, and the two men moved toward her. She quickly sat. "Sorry, I wanted that box of tissues."

"Well, then, will you answer my question?"

The disc disappeared again.

"Sir, I've *no idea* what I've taken."

She slumped back and told her story to the invisible presence before her.

"That's it in a nut shell. Windsor Braun introduced me to Lauren and then later offered me *big* money to take a disc whenever I could. At first, it was easy to make copies of the discs Lauren would bring home to work on. Then Windsor became more insistent. I had to give him something every month and then every other week."

"What caused you to become so reckless?"

She dropped her head and then looked up straining to see something. "I suppose you could say the bottom fell out of the barrel. Lauren broke up with me and Windsor has gone totally crazy, threatening me. It's no longer a game. I thought I could give him all this stuff, get my money and leave the country."

She heard the wheel noise and it suddenly dawned on her. "I've a feeling that disc you've shown me has to do with why I can't see you."

"You're very smart, Miss Jones."

She retorted. "You mean foolish!"

The two men opened the door and stood to the side. Someone was leaving.

"I do have one request."

The wheels stopped. "Yes, that is?"

"Is there a chance that I could settle a score?"

The wheels started moving. "We'll talk again, Miss Jones."

Accident Scene

Inspector Ross left the Home Office and drove to the scene of the accident. The area was roped off per instructions, with many observers watching the tow truck get in position to pull up the car. Ross saw his photographer had arrived as well.

They walked toward one another; she waved and smiled. "I got here as soon as I could, boss."

Her name was Barbara Grantwood, but her badge read Bobbie. She had a reputation of going beyond thorough in her crime scene photos, and also had an excellent analytical mind. In addition, she always enjoyed working with Dennis as he did with her.

He smiled. "I truly am sorry to take you away from that case you were on, but the Chief told me to handle this case flawlessly." He grinned boyishly. "So, I needed the best and here you are!"

Blushing, she got her camera out. "Are we going to hike down the slope?"

He peered over the side of the ravine. "It looks like we can make it down. It may be slippery with all the rain we've had." He glanced down and saw her boots. *She's always prepared.*

Bobbie looked over as well. "I better take my back up flash. It's looking kind of dark down there. The cloud cover doesn't help. Shame they took the bodies. One of the police said the driver was alive and they rushed them both to the hospital."

With her camera case over her shoulder, they scrambled down to the scene. The officer at the bottom of the ravine showed where he and his men found each of the bodies.

"The driver was sprawled under the dash board and Mrs. Braun was in her seat belt in the back seat. Strangest thing, sir. Her hand was in a position as if she had been holding a glass. It could have been the one we found on the ground over here. My guess is the car rolled over and righted as you can see the roof is badly smashed in."

The first responding officer left to answer a call.

Inspector Ross and Bobbie continued studying the area. Just as Ross stepped over what looked like a handle sheared off the limo door, he noticed something round and blue. With rubber gloves on, he secured the piece and dropped it in an evidence bag. *Why does this look familiar to me? It's plastic and looks like it could be a ...*

"Ross, can you look at this?" Bobbie peered around her camera and pointed to the side door of the limo.

As the inspector walked over to her, she continued flashing away with her camera.

"Do you see anything weird about this door?"

Ross looked at the mud she pointed to. "Didn't the officer say the chauffeur was sprawled out under the dash?"

She carefully made her way around the car where he was standing. Ross lit his pipe as he studied the impression in the mud that could pass for a shoe scuff. "Yes, I see what you mean"

He scratched his forehead and then looked through the window where the body would have been. *If I didn't know any better, this would look like a body went into the car before ...or perhaps was put into the car after it was pushed into the ravine. Odd, that all the windows are open not broken.*

His thoughts were interrupted when Bobbie poked him a little. "Dennis, look down on the floor by the gas pedal."

She leaned through the window not touching anything and flashed a picture of the gas pedal. The flash revealed an object lodged between the pedal and the floor. It was shiny. "I don't want to disturb anything until the car is sent to the lab, but I sure would like to see what that is. I've a retriever tool in my car."

She whistled to an officer above and directed him to bring her tool.

Ross shook his head. "You never cease to amaze me." *Oh, to be ten years younger. Mm, she is something else.*

An officer brought her the tool. "We just heard from the paramedics that the chauffeur didn't make it and the bodies have been taken to the morgue."

"That's too bad. I thought we might be able to have a word with him."

With tool in hand, Bobbie leaned inside the car and secured the piece from underneath the gas pedal. "I love this tool."

Gingerly, she came out of the car window dangling the object in front of her boss. "Almost looks like a piece of jewelry."

She carefully laid it on Ross's rubber gloves.

Ross nodded. "It's heavy, almost too heavy to be a pendant. I don't see a loop for a necklace chain either."

Bobbie held open the evidence bag. "Dennis, did you notice that the windows are all open? Wouldn't that be strange in a limousine?"

"Yes, I noticed how easy it was for you to take pictures leaning inside. Usually there's broken glass to navigate."

"Dennis, if it's okay with you, I'd like to pursue this case and work with the lab."

He almost glowed approving her request. *Ross, how dumb was that, you've got to be five shades of red. You're going to scare the poor girl.* He cleared his voice. "Sorry, what all do you want?"

"With your approval of course, I think the car needs to be moved as is, without being touched." She looked up at him. "Could we have it bagged?"

Ross laughed. "Yes, we can." He then radioed for a crane to be brought out and someone to plastic wrap the vehicle before lifting. "Anything else, Chief Photographer?"

She poked him again for his teasing. "Yes, there is, and I know you're going to think I'm on a trip of some sort, but I would like the bodies put in place as they were found. I realize rigor mortis has set in and there'll be a stench, but the pictures could be invaluable."

Ross frowned. "Then I can assume you feel this may not have been an accident."

Bobbie glanced at him and raised her eye brows. "I've too many unanswered questions. Plus, I can tell you have some reservation as well."

Ross shook his head. "How can you tell?"

She smiled and started up the hill. "Oh, I've a special camera in my eyes."

They made their way up to see the crane arriving.

Ross glanced at his watch. "Do you want to supervise this operation? If I leave now, I can go over to the Braun estate and let them know about..."

Ross opened the chauffeur's wallet. "Mark Woolsley." He showed the picture in the wallet to Bobbie. "Nice looking young man." He stared off as he put the wallet in his pocket. *It's her car, how and why would Alex be involved? Why would he have her name? We never talked about her.*

"You're really bothered by all of this, aren't you?"

"What? No... I'm not bothered about it. I just hate having to break sad news to people." *Come on Bobbie, don't push.*

She knew how far she could push Ross. "Sure, go ahead. I would stay anyway to make sure it is done the way I want." *There's something he isn't telling. That's one of the reasons you have to love this man, Mr. Integrity plus.*

A half hour later, Arthur greeted Ross. "Inspector Ross, come in. I would guess you're here to see Miss Kimberly."

Ross entered and handed Arthur his card. "Yes, I would like to see her and Windsor Braun if he might be around, or perhaps you know where I might reach him."

Arthur saw this wasn't a social visit. "I'm sorry, sir, Miss Kimberly has gone into London to the Home office and Windsor Braun moved out with his mother almost three weeks ago. Is there something I can help you with?"

Ross stared at Arthur. "Well, you see there's been a tragic accident. Mrs. Braun's limousine was found in a ravine outside of London. I'm sorry to say she and the chauffeur have been killed."

Arthur dropped his head. "How tragic! Mark Woolsley was such a fine young man. His family and our staff will be devastated." His eyes were glazed and jaw clenched. "Mark took over his dad's position soon after his dad's passing."

"Yes, I know. Mike Woolsley was under Robert Braun's command too?"

Arthur frowned, "Oh! Why would you want to check out Mr. Braun's staff?"

Ross shook his head. "No special reason. I like to know everything about my cases even if they are accidents or natural causes. You say, you don't know Windsor's whereabouts?"

Arthur resumed his posture and looked dead straight at Ross. "No, Inspector Ross, Windsor would need an appointment to enter the estate."

"Then, I take it you're not upset or concerned about Mrs. Braun's death."

"I'll let Miss Kimberly know you were here, sir."

Arthur opened the door for him.

Ross persisted. "I would still like to have an interview with her. I just have some standard questions." He put his hat on and turned to leave. "Oh, I do have another question. Have you seen a gold medallion with a coat of arms on it? We thought it might belong to Mrs. Braun. It looks to be a piece of jewelry. We found it in the car."

Arthur frowned. "No, I can't say that I've seen Mrs. Braun wearing a medallion as a pendant. I could ask the staff if Mark was planning on giving a piece to his girlfriend.*" Somehow we need to get that medallion back. He's looking for a reaction from me.*

Ross smiled. "Thank you, Arthur. You've been a big help." *He's good. But I know this young man's death is tearing him up. That medallion means something.*

Arthur watched the inspector leave in his car. He shut the door and raced to the stairway. *First Mike, now Mark. Accident, I don't think so. The Bishop and Martin teased him about his cushy job. They'll...be shocked!*

Three strides and he got to the top meeting Duke. "Come with me Duke." *He's not going to be happy either.* They went toward the Master's bedroom. Almost to the end of the hall, Arthur pulled his gold medallion from his pocket and brushed the paneled wall. It slid open and they disappeared.

Trip to London

Kimberly left the dining room carrying the newspaper. Bertha met her in the hall with her coat and brief case. "I wondered if you had seen the news about Mrs. Braun and poor Mark."

Kimberly nodded. "Terrible shame! Arthur told me about it last night. I never really knew Mark. I remember his dad worked here when Uncle Robert brought me here." Her eyes got glassy. "Mike taught me so much about my garden. I came home for his funeral, and recall meeting Mark. That must have been such a shock to all of you."

Bertha sniffled as she helped her with her coat. "Mark was very close to his dad and wanted to follow in his footsteps. He did a beautiful job in the gardens until that...witch got her hands on him, and insisted that he be her chauffeur."

Kimberly put on her coat. "I can tell you I won't be attending that funeral. As far as I'm concerned, she let her drinking decide her fate."

She hugged Bertha. "We'll certainly take care of Mark's siblings. That's the least we can do."

Kimberly took her brief case. "Have you seen Arthur?"

"No, Miss, I saw him earlier with Duke."

She pressed her lips with a frown. "I'll check with James in the Monitoring Room."

"James, when you see Arthur, let him know that I've taken one of the cars and will be in London to check out the main office. I'll stop at Scotland Yard to answer their questions and, if it isn't too late, I'll stop at the lab."

James waited for her to leave then sent out an in-house alert that she was leaving the estate unattended.

Martin was polishing the Lagonda outside the garages in the huge turnaround. He glanced at her and kept working. "Good morning, Miss Kimberly."

She smiled at him. *Mark must have been very special to the staff. I would guess he had to be even younger than James. Looks like Martin has been crying.* "I'm truly sorry to hear about Mark. I only met him at his dad's funeral. From what Bertha said, he was a very good man and will be missed by all of you."

Martin didn't look up at her. "Yes, he will be missed." *I can't shake the thought that we razzed him about being Lucille's chauffeur. God, had any of us known she was an intended target, we wouldn't have let him go.*

"Martin, Mark's family will be taken care of. Bertha told me about Mark's autistic brother. I can assure all of you he will get the best of care the rest of his life."

"That's very kind of you. We could have avoided this, and I feel so very responsible. I'm having a hard time shaking it off."

Kimberly frowned. "Why do you feel this way?"

Martin's eyes got glassy. "He asked several times to be removed from her service. Instead, we teased him about the cushy job he had."

Kimberly looked down at the ground. "But, you can't blame yourself for an accident! If it had been intentional, that would be another story."

Martin's eyes opened wide. *That's exactly what it was....I've got to get control here, or she'll sense something is really wrong.* "You're right, Miss Kimberly. It's more because he was so much a part of our little family."

She leaned on his arm. "Can I be a member?"

She got him to smile. "You've been a member since the day you came to the estate."

Her eyes glazed. "That's sweet." Kimberly squeezed his arm. "You're all my family and we have to stick together."

He nodded. "I promise....now where are we going?"

"James told you I'd be taking a car!. Weasel How did you guess the Lagonda?"

Martin laughed heartily. "Well it could be because you grew up playing in this old car. Remember, I would drive up and down the driveway so you could stand on the running boards, or when you played cops and robbers you would jump out from the bushes to run and jump on the running boards as I drove by…. Or when…"

"Okay. You got me….Well, is she ready? It is such a gorgeous day. It's a perfect day for a divine ride into the big city."

 She looked to see if the keys were in the ignition. Then put her hand out. "Yes, please."

Martin shook his head. "Okay, I'll make you a deal. How about you chauffeur me up to the main gate house, and if you feel that you can handle this old beast, then I'll walk back and you can be on your way."

"That's fair enough." She tossed her brief case in the front seat. He handed her the keys and then stood still clearing his throat.

He stood and looked around, whistling to himself.

"I get it." She opened the back door and he started to get in. Out of nowhere, Duke leapt into the back seat and gave several loud barks.

She stopped at the main gate and looked in the rearview mirror. "Well?"

"Good job, Miss Kim, but you'll have to park this big old Puff."

 She grinned. "Seems like there's a plan here. Okay, I give up."

 They switched places except for Duke. He barked and growled and then barked.

 Martin adjusted the rear view mirror. "I wonder who he takes after."

His eyes twinkled. "Yep, he's pretty stubborn…. And spoiled like…"

"Thanks a lot!"

They drove through the gate.

"Don't mention it."

Thirty minutes later, Martin opened the car door outside of the corporate offices of R & K Plastics. Several people gathered to admire this beautiful vintage car from the thirties.

Kimberly and Duke got out. She looked down and chuckled. "We shouldn't be long."

The elevator opened into the lobby of the main office. Kimberly noticed Duke's change in behavior. *Uncle Robert would be so proud of this dog. He stays by my side without being told and I can tell he watches every move anyone makes.* She petted his head and whispered. "You're the best friend anyone could have." Duke whined a little but never lost his concentration.

She walked up to the receptionist and asked to see Charles Gunther or George Gabriel. The woman pointed to the dog and shook her head. "Ah, Miss, there is a pet restriction rule in this building."

Kimberly nodded. "I understand, but we won't be here long." *That rule's going to be changed! Though I can't blame her for doing her job.* Kimberly smiled. "If you would be so kind to call Mr. Gunther's secretary and say that K…"

The elevator opened and Gunther and Gabriel walked out. "Kimberly child!" Those in the lobby were stunned by the outburst and looked around wondering Who is Kimberly?

The receptionist shrank in her chair. "I'm terribly sorry Miss…"

Kimberly smiled and shook her head. "You were doing your job, and very well."

"Come, come, child . Charlotte! Charlotte, tea for everyone." Kimberly walked between the two gentlemen. Duke gave a small bark at the receptionist as he passed her desk following behind his mistress.

Gunther took her coat and moved a chair for her. "Sit, my dear. What brings you to the office?" He bubbled with a chuckle. "Checking up on us?"

"No, nothing like that. Well, first I came to see my office."

She opened her brief case and handed them a list of items. "Then if you could have your staff prepare these items for review, it will help me understand how the company works."

She laughed out loud at the blank faces and dropped mouths. "Have I said something wrong or don't you want me to participate?"

141

"No, No, No, child." Gunther sat down with papers in hand. "We weren't expecting Robert's twin so soon!"

They laughed. "This really is good, though a lot of extra work."

"Charles. Don't give the poor girl a hard time. We do need a little time to redo Robert's office. You see, he never used it. Once that lab got done, he lived there. The first five years we constantly wanted his approval and suggestions on the estimating of the jobs, what kind of jobs he would accept, especially foreign accounts. Scanning your items, I see you're asking the same. The company began in 1960. After thirty years, we were still asking the same questions because Robert had an "Exception" rubber stamp he used frequently."

"Obviously, that stamp won't be used anymore. According to Lauren, the billing is done on computer directly from the lab."

The two men smiled. "Yes, Robert told us that you developed your dissertation around Translation."

Gunther chuckled. "I'm sorry, Dear, but we felt he was talking in a foreign language. He told us he would be coding and decoding...whatever. After an hour of our looking stupid and he acting like a little kid in a candy shop...He convinced us the lab computers would handle the data from the tests and bill the customers directly. It works for us. We handle all the estimates and put the money in the bank."

Kimberly just loved their bubbly spirit. "Well, I need to understand it because if it should breakdown, who's going to fix it?" She bit on her lip and frowned at them.

"Well, then, your office will be ready in two weeks, if not sooner."

She closed her brief case. "I guess we're ready to go."

Duke sat up.

The men were awed by his intelligence. "What doesn't he know?"

Kimberly nodded and petted Duke's head. "By the way, how are you handling the news reporters and Aunt Lucille's death? I've not answered any calls."

Gunther nodded. "One of those would have been from me."

She shrugged her shoulders. "I'm sorry Gunthie."

"You realize we'll be attending both funerals."

Kimberly's eyes widened and stared at him. "What, are you dreaming? After all that woman said, you think I would even consider attending?"

Gunther put his hand on her shoulder and shook his head with a smile. "Kimberly, my child! The Braun family has never aired their laundry to the public, and you of all people cannot give the press an opening to probe. When Windsor was growing up, we had our hands full keeping him out of the press to protect Robert's growing empire. You see, you must attend."

She closed her eyes and tightened her lips. "I'll feel like a hypocrite."

She stood. "But, now there's Mark. Please make sure we take very good care of his family. I feel so bad that poor man was a victim of her ugliness. Bertha and Martin told me a little about the family. I guess Mike had another son who's autistic. When the mother passed away some years back, Mark really had to be the parent."

George Gabriel nodded. "According to Arthur, Mark was a very hard worker. Seems he has an aunt up in North Country near Scotland. Arthur is handling the funeral arrangements."

Kimberly and Duke walked to the door. Gunther helped with her coat.

"Well, that's fine with me as long as we take financial responsibility for the brother and aunt. You'll do that, today? Perhaps you could find out if she would move here to take care of the boy. Before the funeral, I'd like to know this was handled...Yes?"

The two old men nodded knowing fully well, she, like her uncle would not forget and would follow up on her request by the end of the day.

"Where are you off to now? You wouldn't be going past the lab, would you?"

Kimberly shook her head. "Gunthie...!" She shook her finger at him. "You, sir, are a trouble maker." She laughed and hugged him.

He squeezed her hand. "Don't let this get out of hand, my dear. Lauren was only concerned for your welfare. Your backgrounds are so different, but you've both learned to cope successfully. Stubbornness doesn't suit either of you."

She smiled at him and nodded. "I appreciate your comments. First we have to stop at Scotland Yard to answers some questions, and then..."

"They didn't call in here." The two men frowned at the other. "About Robert or Lucille?

"I've no idea what he wants. Arthur said that the nicer inspector, Ross, came out to report the accident. He was also looking for Windsor."

The elevator opened. "I'll let you know if it's anything important. But you'll take care..." the door closed.

The two men walked back to their offices. "She's determined to have that young man taken care of. I think she feels responsible for the family embarrassment."

"Well, I can certainly vouch for Lucille's treachery and abuse. I can just imagine what that young man had to endure."

George Gabriel looked at his watch. "It's been five minutes and you still haven't made the call. You're slowing down Charles!"

"I didn't want to be rude and shut my door while you were talking. But I'll do it right now!"

Outside, Martin posed with various tourists in front of her favorite car. When he saw her and Duke standing off to the side, he immediately dispersed the people and opened the car door for her. Duke hopped into a jump seat along the side of the car and Kimberly slid into the posh seat in the back. *That was good. Perhaps that helped to ease some of his pain.*

Martin drove to Scotland Yard Headquarters.

"Duke, you stay with Martin." She chuckled over the commotion they had made at uncle's building. "Here, we could get a ticket."

Kimberly was taken to the Inspector's office. His secretary paged him and he entered a bit out of breath.

"I'm sorry to disturb you. I'm here on business and thought I could save you coming out to the estate. Arthur said you wanted to see me."

Ross shut his office door and pulled out a chair from his conference table for her.

"I need you to identify some photos since we can't locate your cousin Windsor. I thought this would be better than going to the morgue. They still aren't the nicest." He put two photos in front of her.

She nodded that the pictures were of her aunt and chauffeur, Mark Woolsley. She then signed an affidavit for legal records.

"Miss Braun, I just have a few questions."

"I'm happy to offer any information I can."

"Would you know if either person had a drinking problem? Let me qualify that." Ross picked up a report, "The autopsy report indicated that both Lucille Braun and Mark Woolsley had alcohol content above the legal amounts by two and a half points." Ross scratched his head, "Why would the chauffeur be drunk? Was he also her escort?"

Shocked by this, Kimberly shook her head. "No... that can't be right, Inspector Ross. I know my aunt had a drinking problem, but...Mark! No way. I realize I didn't know him, but I can assure you he wouldn't be on our staff. My uncle had zero tolerance for any habits or addictions of any kind. Any of the staff would tell you Mark was exactly like his dad and had the very same set of values." *Martin said something that this would have or could have been avoided. I wonder what he meant by that.*

Just then Bobbie called. She was still with the coroner and in his examination he couldn't get the chauffeur's hand to open. "Dennis, do you remember at the crash site you picked up a piece of plastic and wondered if there was a connection. Well, the coroner just got the hand opened and there's another piece of the blue plastic. Here's another situation for you, remember the responding officer told us Mrs. Braun had the seat belt on and held a broken glass?"

"Yes, I remember."

"No alcohol stains could be found anywhere in the car. Is that interesting?"

Ross frowned. "What about on the clothes?"

145

"Nowhere!" Bobbie's voice blurted out. "When can you come over here? I want to send this bag over to the lab for fingerprints."

"Absolutely, send the bag over here at once. I can be there within the hour. Yes, that is very interesting. No, I can't right now. Yes, you're right."

Kimberly sensed his caller needed his attention and stood up to leave. "If there aren't any more questions, I'll leave now." *Whatever that call was about sure has him in a think tank zone. I wonder if it has anything to do with this accident. Do I dare ask?*

Inspector Ross walked Kimberly to elevator. "Miss Braun, would you have any idea how we can reach your cousin? It seems he travels to the continent on a weekly basis. Do you have any idea what his occupation is?"

Kimberly looked at him quizzically. "I truly don't have any knowledge of my cousin's business interests, or his social life. Technically we lived in the same house, but I saw very little of him. You see, Windsor was sent to private schools all over the world. I attended private school but Uncle wanted me to live at home. I was taken to school every day." *Now I wish I could tell you his occupation is Leech!*

When the elevator opened, Inspector McGraw stepped out. He looked from Ross to Kimberly in surprise. "Dennis! I was just coming to see you."

He nodded to Kimberly.

Ross slipped his hand on Kimberly's elbow. " Sorry Alex, I've a meeting right now. I've tried to reach you. Where have you been?" As the door started to close, "We have the Braun accident to handle." Ross held the door. "I should be back in a couple of hours."

McGraw waved. "I'll be in my office. Come as soon as you can..."

21

McGraw's office

Realizing time was short, Inspector McGraw went to his office and locked the door. *Well, I'll find out if all that money was worth it. Ross is acting strange. I know something is going on.*

Alex knew about the building surveillance and guessed he had three minutes at most before he'd be caught. He set a timer and then dialed a number to hear a recording of his partner's calls. *Hmm. Seems I've underestimated Dennis. He's in charge of the Lucille Braun case and there's evidence? There can't be! Whatever he thinks he has, has to disappear!* He heard enough before the timer went off and he quickly locked up the equipment Charlie had given him.

In a flash, the ideas came. *I wonder if I still have that make-up kit we took off.....*He opened a file cabinet drawer and there it was. He smiled...*This is from the bank robbery we worked on before Dennis was assigned to Heathrow.*

He scooted into a stall in the men's room. *I never looked in this kit before, there's even a mirror.* In a few minutes he opened the door and admired himself in the mirror above the sink. *Hmm. Not bad. I look pretty old.* Checked his watch. *Still fifteen minutes before people would be hustling back.* He casually crossed the hall to the stairway and then darted up two flights to the evidence room and lab.

Took a deep breath and opened the stairwell door. Just as he approached the room, the elevator door opened. McGraw's heart about stopped. *Holy Fuck not now!* He slowed and smiled as he took his key out. "Are you bringing me some bags?"

The courier smiled back. "I'm running late. There aren't many. Do you mind signing out here?"

He handed McGraw a box that had about ten large envelopes in it. *You're running on time in my book, kid.* "Not a problem." He quickly checked the name on the door to make sure he got it right. "How's that."

The courier left and McGraw rummaged through the envelopes and grabbed the one marked Lucille Braun. McGraw had rubber gloves on and wasn't worried about prints. He laid the box and receipt on the floor in front of the evidence room and walked nonchalantly to the stairwell. He had eight minutes to get back to his office.

Pouring with sweat, he locked his office door and dashed into the back of his closet. A loose panel, in the back wall, made for a great hiding place where he hid the bag. Before closing the wall, he glanced at the contents of the bag. *Blue pieces of plastic! Damn that chauffeur! He took my inhaler out of my pocket. What's this piece of gold?* McGraw juggled it in his hand and then looked at it closely, noting the coat of arms. He pulled his new inhaler out of his pocket to check the color and this one was red.

He closed everything, including his make-up kit, and went to the men's room to wash. *That was too close. That chauffeur fucked everything up. He said something to her about his notice. He screwed me up and a change of plans doesn't always work.* He looked in the mirror wiping his face. *Soon, this will all be behind me and I'll be worth millions. Now to initiate Plan B.*

22

A quick stop at the R & K lab

"**M**artin, would it be too much out of the way if we run over to the lab on our way home?"

Martin shook his head. "That's very doable." He pulled out on Victoria Street and headed for Trafalgar Square. He knew a short cut and within five minutes they were headed toward the lab in Burlington. This little town sat on the edge of Berkshire County.

The Braun estate was also in the county but further north. Kimberly learned the estate saved a lot of money in taxes by having the two in the same county.

Martin looked in the rear view mirror at her strained face. *Poor kid. Arthur said Kimberly and Lauren got into a spat over him. Maybe this meeting will help. Keeping Kimberly in the dark doesn't help either.*

Martin opened the door. "Duke, you stay with me fella."

Kimberly saw people looking out of the windows from both floors. *Oh, Lord, I can hear the remarks now. "Miss Goodie two shoes." Just keep your head down as if they aren't there.*

As she approached, one of the guards recognized her and opened the door.

The other guard hung up the phone and took her to the elevator.

She questioned him, learning he was in his forties and retired from the British Navy Seals.

He smiled as the door opened at the top floor. "I had this job offered to me the day I retired and I've been here five years."

Kimberly thought about his comment. *It is very comforting to know I'm surrounded by a strong defense, but why is that so necessary? When you think about it, there's not a person around me that is out of shape.* "That's interesting. Did you join the service right out of school?"

"Out of college, yes mum."

He unlocked Mr. Braun's office for her. Her eye brows rose. *Do I dare ask what his major was?* "I'm very impressed. What is your degree in?"

"Actually, all of us here were in a demolition task force. My degree is in computer science and I've a second degree in electrical engineering."

"And the others!"

"Oh, yes mum, they all have degrees too. Dr. Braun says no vegetables here!" He chuckled but his voice trailed off. "We miss working with him."

"Yes, I bet you do."

The door opened and Kimberly stood for a moment looking around at the spacious area. *This looks exactly as I pictured it when he'd call from here. Uncle described it perfectly. Everything I suggested is here. It is so beautiful.*

She turned to the guard with moist eyes. "You can leave now. I won't be long. I just wanted to see where I'll be working."

The guard hesitated frowning a little. "Miss Braun, we weren't informed that you would be working here. I've let you in the building twice now under Martin's approval. However, to have free access you'll have to be screened and given the proper badge allowing you to be in the building without setting off the alarms."

"Of course, I'll need that."

"I'll just wait for you out in the hall."

She smiled and nodded as he left the room. She stood behind her uncle's chair and tears flowed. *Kimberly there's no room for tears.*

Suddenly, she thought she heard that noise again. *Lauren said that noise had something to do with the heating system. That doesn't make sense. Could it be...?* She dropped her head. "Kimberly why can't you accept he's gone." She cried in her hands. *Stop this and get hold of yourself! If that guard comes in and sees you in this state, he will certainly tag you as incompetent! Is that what you want?*

She straightened, wiped her eyes, and looked around for a sink to freshen up before he came for her. Back on track, she adjusted her collar on her suit, fluffed her hair and left the bathroom.

The wall of windows showed a vista of the English countryside. *Who couldn't love this serenity? Hmm. I wonder who Martin is talking to. Someone in a lab coat. Might be Lauren.*

She opened the office door to find the guard waiting for her. "Oh, I'm sorry. I took longer than I expected."

She hoped he hadn't seen that she had been crying, and quickly returned to their conversation about the staff.

He led her to the security office to get her clearance. She was taken aback by all she had to do. *I can understand the fingerprints, but an eye scan and voice recording?*

She joked. "Now, am I a Navy Seal like the rest of you?"

The officer in charge chuckled. "No, Miss Braun. You're now one of the three people able to enter the vault in the lab and..." then he stopped talking as if he was told to stop.

She frowned and shrugged her shoulders. "Did I miss something?"

"No, Miss Braun, I caught myself. Only two of you, Miss Woodgrieves and you, can go into the vault at any time without permission. I'm sorry, we haven't made the adjustment."

Kimberly smiled. "Don't apologize; I'm having the same problem."

She wiped her hands. "When can I come and start working?"

"I doubt if we'll find that you've a record anywhere in the world, so I would say tomorrow morning should be fine or any time thereafter."

The person talking with Martin was Lauren. *From here, I know that figure, yes I do.*

Martin motioned with his eyes that Kimberly was behind Lauren.

Lauren turned with an engaging smile, dissolving Kimberly's concerns. "Hi."

Kimberly blushed to a crimson red. Martin hid a laugh and got into the car.

"I'm glad you're still here. The guard thought you had gone to lunch. We could go to lunch if you'd like."

Lauren looked at her watch. "I would love to but I've a test that will be out of the equalizer in another ten minutes. Actually, I was going to call you about something I think is very unusual."

They walked toward the building as Lauren explained her concern. Kimberly had her head down listening and stopped abruptly. "You're absolutely sure? There're two additional tests to be done, and this is since last night?"

Lauren smoothed her lab coat. "Yes, I'm very sure. That's one of the procedures before closing the vault to verify what has been done and what is to be done. Hence those sheets or code would be machine stamped. Believe me, the vault would tell me if I had forgotten one of the steps."

Lauren checked her watch. "I've got to get back. I can't imagine how anyone could get into that vault."

"Then someone has gotten the combination."

Lauren held the door open. "It's more than a combination, Kim. It requires hand recognition on the pad."

That's what that security officer meant. Kimberly stared at Lauren. "I know you have to go. For now, keep the tests going…Call me when you can take a break."

23

Scotland Yard testing facility

Inspector Ross drove to the rear of one of the Yard's inspection facilities, where Bobbie waited for him.

He was buzzed in at the door. He hadn't been to this building since it had been refurbished. *Wow, this is impressive.* He jumped hearing his name called over the loud speaker.

"Inspector Ross, go to station number six!"

The building was more than a hundred foot square. The facility was designed in the shape of a wheel. The center had elevated spokes connecting to each station. As he got closer to number six, he realized the spokes were raceways for all the technology provided. His escort told him the design was completely fire and explosion proof. "It's one of a kind and even the American FBI has asked to see it."

He was amused to see Bobbie's impatience. "Ross, I thought you'd never get here. You can get rid of that grin, too. I've got a lot to show you!"

She wheeled around and Ross quickly followed her through a clear glass or plastic walled doorway. *All of this is fire and explosion proof? I've a feeling Robert Braun developed this material. I wonder if she has a clue what's going on here.* Bobbie took him over to the Lucille Braun limo and began pointing to all of the noted places that prints and pictures had been taken.

"Dennis, wait until you see this machine."

She turned to the station operator. "Could you show him how you checked the outside of the car for prints?"

She took Ross by the hand. "We have to move away from the car."

After a few commands were put into a computer and the "Enter" key pressed, a lift hoisted the car a few feet and a clear plastic shroud lowered from above, boxing in the car. A large screen made a bleeping sound with each bleep marking a print.

Ross' mouth hung open in disbelief. He shook his head. "This is fantastic. My God, this was done in minutes!"

"Yes, and they should be able to identify the prints by tomorrow."

The car lowered and Bobbie pointed to the mud on the door. "I'll bet the lab will identify this mark as a scuff from a shoe. I'm really going out on a limb here, but I think the chauffeur was put in the car after the fact. I don't think this crash killed him and if it didn't kill him, then the obvious, it didn't kill Lucille Braun."

She stood with her hands on her hips. She shrugged. "I also think that evidence bag I sent to the lab will tell us something about those plastic pieces and that piece of gold."

Dennis stared at the car door. *The handle is missing on this door. I think Bobbie is onto something.* "Bobbie, have you developed any of the pictures you took?"

"I downloaded my digital card at my lab last night. My team is making enlargements for me, but I still have my digital card. They've a screen here if you want to look."

She gave her camera to the technician and he hooked it up to the computer.

Dennis shook his head and smiled. *To think I read about all this in comic books as a kid and now look! It's for real.*

"What are you chuckling about?" She handed him a remote. "Here, you can find the picture you're looking for."

Ross scrolled through the pictures and sure enough, he stopped on one of the first pictures she had taken of the ground around the car. He then walked over to the car.

154

"Bobbie, look. The mud is partially covering where the handle is missing. If you look at your picture, the handle and that piece of plastic are almost side by side in the mud under this door. Therefore, I think you've got an excellent theory. That handle didn't come off from rolling down the ravine, because if it did then we would have found it somewhere else."

Ross looked at the technician for approval. "Am I right?"

The technician got his clipboard. "If you like, Inspector, I can run some ideas through the simulator and prepare a report for you."

Ross and Bobbie raised their brows and smiled. "That's great. Bobbie, give him your ideas. I'll call the lab and see what they've come up with."

Ten minutes later, Ross came back looking like he lost his best friend. He thanked the technician and then told Bobbie he needed to leave. *I need to get some air. I just can't believe Alex is a killer. How much can I tell Bobbie? I need to convey all of this to the chief.*

"Bobbie, I need to leave." He took his coat and hat and rushed off.

"Dennis, wait up! Obviously, something is really wrong. Aren't you going to tell me?"

Dennis stood by his car and almost whispered. "The evidence bag never got to the lab."

Bobbie's eyes looked like saucers. *"What!"* Her voice echoed through the parking garage.

"Shush, keep it down….Listen to me. I really can't say anything at this time, but I need your help."

She took his arm. "Of course! What can I do?"

Ross dropped his head into his hands for a few moments. *Somehow, Alex or someone overheard our conversation about the evidence bag. The only one in the room was Kimberly Braun, but it can't be her. My phone is tapped.* He looked up. "Okay, I think I've a plan."

He pulled out his notebook and pen and wrote for several minutes. He folded the page and gave it to her. "Take this to Chief Inspector O'Doul. Bobbie, you must hand this to him personally and wait for an answer." *I hope I'm making the right move letting her help me. Two people are dead and I'm sure there's a connection with Robert*

Braun's death. Am I putting her in harm's way?

Bobbie smiled and squeezed his hand. "I can do this. Where will I meet you to give you his answer?"

Still frowning and staring off, he bit on his lip. "Here's the sticky part. When we get back to the Yard, I'm going directly to Alex McGraw's office. He's expecting me."

"So, you want me to bring the Chief's answer to you there."

Ross nodded. "Hand the message to me directly, regardless of what Alex says."

She nodded and rushed off to her car. Ross drove to the Home office.

24

Sheila was taken to another room on that same level beneath the ground. *Well, this is a little better. That bed over there gives one a feeling of permanence. Better than the alternative.* Just as she bounced on the bed, the door opened.

Another huge guard walked in with sun glasses on. "Miss Jones, follow me."

He took her to a room marked Testing Lab. *Oh, my God, what are they going to do to me.* "Are you sure we should be going in there? I promise I'll tell them what I know." Sheila hung back. "I've seen movies of what..."

The guard knocked and John the interrogator came out. The guard motioned. "Miss Jones is terrified. She's convinced your lab is a torture chamber."

Sheila sank to the floor, almost in fetal position. John knelt next to her. "Miss Jones, my name is John Lewis. I'm a psychologist and I've been asked to talk to you."

Sheila peered doubtfully. *He seems friendly, even sincere.* "Couldn't we sit out here and talk?"

The interrogator looked around. "I guess we could put a couple of chairs over in that corner. I've a better idea. We have a cafeteria for

157

the staff and breakfast is over. Why don't we go there?"

Sheila nodded with a slight grin. She allowed him to help her up, exhaled deeply and followed him.

The doctor interrogated Sheila for three days, eight hours a day with very few breaks other than an hour for each meal.

The doctor closed his notebook and leaned back. "I think we're finished. That wasn't the kind of torture you were expecting; nevertheless, this wasn't easy for you. You did a good job. I'm sure the Braun staff will be grateful."

Sheila nodded and grinned. "You're right. It wasn't a physical torture, but mental. I'm exhausted. May I go back to my room? I want to sleep forever."

The next morning Doctor Lewis met with Arthur, the Bishop and Martin to review the results of Sheila's interrogation. "Here's all we've done. The beginning of this project had its moments. Miss Jones became terrified when the guard brought her to the lab for interrogation. The first full day we used the cafeteria until we gained a trust between us. She did agree to a lie detector, the use of sodium pentothal, and a battery of tests."

The interrogator handed the results to each of the men. "I taped the entire session too."

Martin frowned. "Reason being?"

Dr. Lewis pursed his lips. "Mostly for field analysis in my work at the university. In this case, I believe you would gain more viewing her answers than reading them."

"We now have dates, times, and items taken. The meeting place was at a ski resort in Austria."

Arthur glanced up from reading. "Did she say which resort?"

"Yes, she did give me the name." He leafed through his notebook. "Here it is. Rather difficult name to pronounce, Kitzbuhel."

The Bishop chuckled. "The boss will love hearing this. I wonder how long Windsor's been going there."

Doctor Lewis raised his brow at the Bishop for more information. "Would that be important to this case?"

"Only that Robert owns the resort and may not be too happy to find Windsor has been staying there and perhaps with someone else. Definitely we'll check this out."

Arthur put a question mark next to the resort and Windsor's name. He nodded to the analyst to continue.

Doctor Lewis turned the page in his book. "Not too much later, Lauren became ill and arranged for Sheila to come here to get some of her work. That was a pay day for her. She was able to make copies of all Lauren's discs she could find. Two discs she couldn't open and left them. She can produce a complete list of everything she took."

Arthur raised his brow. "She told you all of this? And agreed to sodium pentothal?"

"In the beginning it was a bit scary for her, but after the first full day, she realized we weren't going to torture her. She said it was better than putting up with Windsor screaming like a hyena. Evidently, Windsor can get pretty ugly when he's been drinking."

"Here's an example of what I mean."

The Doctor pressed on his lap top a couple of numbers turning the screen for them to view…

"Sheila, you've said Windsor gets ugly when drunk, how was this last time different?"

Sheila's hands tightened as she stared at the doctor. "This last meeting at the resort, Windsor acted different, like his mission had changed."

She frowned. "He came on very strong. Usually he walks and talks like ah, damn queen. This time, to make a point he grabbed my arm hard and told me he didn't give a fuck if Lauren dumped me. He wanted any and all the discs by the end of the next week or else. That's when I got pissed off and told him about my insurance policy. The only thing that saved me is I'm as tall as he is and maybe a few pounds heavier."

She sat back in her chair and rubbed her arm. "He's never been physical before, but I felt he had some sort of time table now."

"And, what is this insurance policy you have?"

Sheila took a drink of water. "Have you ever met Windsor?"

Dr. Lewis shook his head. "No, I can't say that I've had the pleasure."

Sheila stared at him grinning. "Pleasure? Trust me, after you meet him, you'll want insurance too. He backed off when I told him I had copies made of everything he wrote down for me to steal. Doctor, he belongs in your chamber!" She pointed toward his lab. "He's a parasite. He gets his jollies from hurting others. He's ah, psychoshit piece of work who on your best day can't be trusted. I wouldn't be surprised if he didn't..."

"Didn't what, Sheila?"

She squirmed a bit. "Well, I've no proof, but I've heard him make some dreadful, really hateful remarks about his father and then the old man dies. Well, my guess is the old man had help in his demise."

The Bishop chuckled. "She's mighty astute. I think we need her on our team."

The door opened and the men stood up as a nurse wheeled in their boss's chair. They made room at the table for Robert Braun.

His hands, arms and head were wrapped in gauze. He uttered softly, "I'd like to hear your findings."

Arthur asked to him to play the tape again for the boss.

Arthur raised his hand a little. "Robert, this is the first we've heard about the resort and will be on it as soon as we finish."

Arthur hesitated. "Could we use her as an agent?" He looked to the others. "What do you think?"

Martin shook his head. "Arthur, you and Bishop caught her in the parking lot. I've not met her or seen her for that matter. I'll yield to your decision."

Mr. Braun pointed to the interrogator. He whispered to his nurse who said, "Mr. Braun would like to know your opinion of Miss Jones."

"Robert, she got caught up in a get rich fast ploy instigated by Windsor and then didn't know which way was up. Right now she really thinks she's making her peace before the ax falls. You've made her think she will be dying soon. There's not a shred of evidence that she is lying. In fact, I used the sodium only to verify what she gladly wanted to tell."

The nurse handed Arthur a list of questions. "He wants to know if we use her as an agent, do you think she'll just take off."

The interrogator leaned his chair back and crossed his arms. He frowned at Robert and nodded his head. "That's one of those yes and no questions. Without going into a lot of psychoanalysis stuff, I would say that the three days she's been here has caused her to reevaluate her life. She hasn't been mistreated here in any way. That has made a big impression on her. She sees the interaction among the staff, the dedication, the loyalty, the commitment and under her brazenness, she'd like to be a part of it."

He held up the second page with her test scores. "If you look at her totals across the bottom line, you'll see she's no dummy. All in all, she is a good person with exceptional skills."

He leaned forward. "Also, she hates Windsor so very much and wants to even the score. She'd jump at the chance to expose him."

He hesitated a moment and raised his finger. "There's something else she said last night and I didn't have time to get it typed. It's on the tape at the end."

He fast forwarded the disc. "Sheila, did anything else happen to make you think Windsor was different? Do you think he was acting alone?"

Sheila nodded. "Yes, I thought he'd organized this whole scheme until I left his suite."

The doctor remained calm and quiet. "Did something happen?"

Sheila leaned back on her chair. She laughed. "Oh yeah! Just when I was leaving, I dropped the bomb on him my prices had gone up as the risk was greater. That's when he started screaming and raised his fist at me. I laughed and told him he better make it good cause I had enough proof to hang him by the balls and left. How I pulled that off I don't know because I was scared shitless. Anyway, he slammed the door on me. I was so relieved to be out of there I stood in the hall to catch my breath and heard him screeching at the top of his lungs what a bitch I am. It made me laugh. That's when I thought I heard someone tell him to calm down."

The doctor paused the disc. "I'd like to add here, most people who come across as obnoxious, brash aren't that way by choice. I didn't go into her childhood very much, but I did get the feeling that she's not had it easy. In this case with Windsor, I think her smart mouth probably saved her life."

The Bishop leaned forward in his chair. "Did she recognize the voice?"

The interrogator shook his head. "That's all she can tell us."

Arthur stared at the interrogator. "Do you think she knows what's on the discs?"

He shook his head. "No, not before you captured her. She knew Windsor is making money off them. The day you caught her is when much of this made sense to her. Remember, I told you she isn't dumb. Hearing Robert's wheelchair, seeing a disc appear out of nowhere, talking to someone she couldn't see, is when she surmised that Mr. Braun developed something to do with some sort of transfiguration. She deduced that information is on the discs she couldn't open."

Mr. Braun motioned for him to approach and whispered. "Thank you, John; you've made a good report. Stay close by; we may need some profiles done on Windsor. We also may have another name for you to profile in the next day or two." The doctor nodded and left the room.

Arthur put his report on the table. "I know you want our opinions and I'll go first. I think she's the best we have. It sounds to me like she's relieved she's been caught."

Each of them agreed with Arthur.

Robert cleared his voice. "Bishop, go to the resort and find out who's been staying there that might be of interest. Show some pictures of Windsor and Doctor Edse. Then put some of our people on the staff there."

He became quiet for a few moments.

Concerned, Arthur asked the nurse to check Robert.

The nurse gave him a drink of water. "He's making good progress. His throat is mending nicely, but he knows when to rest. You can't see this because of all the gauze." She looked at the wall clock. "We better leave now. The gauze needs to come off so we can bathe the wounds."

Martin opened the door for them. Robert pulled on Martin's hand. He whispered. "I want to meet with the Jones woman tomorrow. We need to set the wheels in motion now."

∾∾

At six in the morning, a female guard woke Sheila. She was told to get dressed and report to the lab. There were a few areas she was allowed to roam freely.

This request came as a surprise. She became frightened. "Is everything all right? Have I done something wrong?"

The guard put her hand on Sheila's shoulder. "Calm yourself, Sheila. There's nothing to be frightened about. Another staff member would like to visit with you."

"At this hour?"

"Just happens to be how the scheduling runs. Now get ready. You need to be in the lab promptly at seven."

Sheila almost flew through a shower, dressed and rushed to the cafeteria. *God, I hope this isn't my last cup of coffee. Get hold of yourself. You were wrong about Dr. Lewis. Don't start hyperventilating.* She took several deep breaths and took her coffee to the lab.

Doctor Lewis greeted her. "Sheila, today you'll talk with a major player in the organization. Focus and put your best foot forward. Just tell the truth and you'll be fine."

She smiled as he squeezed her hand. *Doctor Lewis has been so nice to me. I can't imagine he would put me in danger. I wonder what this big shot wants.*

She was told to go into the next room and not be alarmed that the room would be dimly lit. *This is almost like when I was first captured.* She went to the chair by the table.

Sheila looked around and was startled by a man seated in a chair in the back of the room. She couldn't keep her eyes off him. The door opened and Arthur entered.

He sat with her at the table. "Miss Jones, we haven't met formally. I'm Arthur, one of Mr. Braun's staff. First, we appreciate your cooperation. As a result, we want to give you…"

He looked up from reading his document and noticed her staring off. "Miss Jones, have you heard anything I've said?"

He touched her hand and she jumped. "My God, you scared me half to death." She slapped at his hand. "Who is that man back there? Is he watching us?"

She pointed behind Arthur. "Can he hear what you're saying?"

Arthur dropped his head. "Miss Jones, pay attention to me. That person isn't important to you right now."

He continued to read and offered her an arrangement. "Since you've been very helpful, I've been authorized to give you an opportunity to amend some of your mistake."

Sheila heard the word amend and looked over at Arthur. "Is that his idea?"

Arthur frowned at her. "Whose idea?"

She pointed to the back of the room. "His idea!" When she looked, the figure was gone. She shook her head. "Where do I sign?"

Arthur glared at her. "You must listen to this proposal and have a clear understanding before you go signing your life away."

She stared back at him. "This is a no brainer. If I decline, you'll take my life."

Arthur shook his head. "Miss Jones!"

"Please call me Sheila."

Arthur put the paper in front of her. " Sheila, no one here is going to take your life. I'm trying to ask if you want to be our agent or spy. We feel the information you've given us has a connection to Mr. Braun's death and our main suspect would be Windsor."

Sheila sat back. "You mean you're going to let me out of here?"

Arthur pointed to the paper. "You need to read this. There're stipulations and you'll have to have a bit of surgery done."

"*Surgery!*" She tossed the pen on the table. "I get it; you're going to do something to my brain!" She put her head on the table. "Just kill me… Shoot me now! I'm not going to be one of those *zombies!*"

Arthur stiffened his lips to keep from laughing out loud. "Quiet down. Take a deep breath and read this paragraph." He put a mark next to the wording that she would have an implant in her ear, allowing her to hear Arthur and in turn would allow Arthur to hear her conversations.

"It would be for your protection. When this is all over, the device would be removed. It's not permanent and the incision will close up in a matter of time."

She sat up with surprise. "That's all it is? Do you have one?"

He nodded. She stared at him for a bit and grinned. "So that big shot in the back was talking to you... Right?"

He glared at her and nodded. *Dr. Lewis sure pegged her right. She's very smart. Bishop nailed it. We need her on the team. I can't force this on her. She has to join on her own.*

She smiled smugly at Arthur. He pushed the paper in front of her. "Well, what do you think?"

She hesitated. "If I help prove that Windsor killed Mr. Braun, will I be set free?"

Arthur frowned biting his lip. "No, I'm sorry."

He paused. "There still could be some prison time. You did steal for money and you did take the discs out of the country."

Arthur shrugged a bit. "You could be tried for international theft...At least it's not for murder."

"But...As long as I'm working with you that information could be held back?"

Arthur grinned and shook his head. *Now who's in charge?* "Sheila, are you going to sign or not? My superiors want to know."

She signed the paper and stared at him. "There...now what did he say?" She pointed to her ear and then to him nodding.

Robert, I think we may have met our match. She is quite the pistol. Arthur stared back at her. "He said...*Go to surgery!*"

᪶᪶

The next morning, Arthur, the Bishop and Martin met with Sheila in the same dimly lit lab room. "This is our team, Sheila. We'll be your contact twenty four seven."

She stared around Arthur to the back wall. "What about him. Won't he have a say in what I do?"

Wheels turned in the back of the room. Then in a very soft voice, Sheila heard from the implant. "Yes, Miss Jones, I'll be watching, and listening."

Her eyes lit up. "Wow, that is so ..."

Arthur grabbed her hand. "So very serious. Now, Sheila, we're running out of time. You need to pay attention!"

She saw the urgency in his remark and straightened up. "I'm listening."

Arthur pointed to Martin. "Martin is Mr. Braun's chauffeur, and..."

Sheila frowned and peeked to the rear, "Is... that would mean..." She pointed.

Arthur interrupted. "No, he was and now is for Kimberly. Martin, tell her what you've been doing."

"We have a detail watching your apartment and Windsor has been there twice. We need to get you back there tonight. We think he'll be back soon."

Sheila put her hand to her forehead. "Yeah, he wants those discs that I couldn't open."

Arthur handed her some paper work. "This is an assignment from my boss at the Studio. How'd you get this?"

"We've been in touch with your studio and asked that you do a photo shoot on the new CEO of R & K Plastics Co. Show this to Windsor and tell him you've been given the run of the place, which will allow you to get another disc. We'll then arrange for you to get a couple."

"You really got this assignment? So should I go in to work?"

Arthur looked at his watch. "Yes, and before we send you on your way, Bishop is going to take you to our practice range and give you a quick course on shooting and some tricks on self-defense."

Arthur looked to the back of the room. They all stood up.

Sheila hesitated, realizing she would be leaving her safe haven.

The boss spoke to her. "Miss Jones, you'll do fine. Remember, we hear everything you say and can direct you if you ask."

She grinned a little and waved to the back as she followed the Bishop.

Braun estate

Kimberly went in the back entrance used mostly by the staff. She needed to confront Arthur about the conversation he'd promised her. More than a week had passed and nothing had happened.

Okay, where is everyone? Duke isn't around either. She called on the house phone for Arthur and got no response. Then checked the monitoring room. *What, no one is here! I can't believe this…*She went back outdoors to ask Martin and noticed his bike was gone.

Back in the kitchen she found on the bulletin board a picture of Mark and his dad with the times of the viewing and funeral. *That's right, the viewing is today and the funeral is tomorrow. Okay, I get that but where's Duke?*

She whistled but couldn't hear a thumping or even a bark. Out in the main hall, it suddenly dawned on her. This is the first time I've been alone in this house and I don't like the feeling. *Come on Duke. Where are you?*

She ran to her uncle's room. The big window drapes were closed. Looking for the remote, she stepped on something near her uncle's bed.

A gold medallion. She studied it. *It isn't heavy. Looks like gold. There's not an eyelet for a chain. I can't imagine what it could be used for.* Kimberly started to put it on her uncle's dresser. *Think I'll keep it and will ask Arthur about it. That would be item two hundred on the list.* Then she found the remote and the huge bank of drapes slowly opened. *I wonder who keeps closing these. Uncle Robert loved waking up to the sun rise.*

She looked out the big bay window and couldn't see anyone. *This is so strange. I can't believe I've never been alone in this house, and now even in daylight it's unsettling. Maybe I could override the monitoring system to check inside the house.*

Kimberly left her uncle's room and started toward the main stairway. She passed his doorway and a little alcove and stopped abruptly. *Gosh what was that noise?* There wasn't a sound in the air and she could have heard a pin drop. She took a few steps forward passing the recessed wall. Nothing. *How about walking backward a few steps. There it is, click, clicks. I can hear scratching!* "Duke!"

A yelping sound came from behind the wall.

Her eyes got teary. Panicked, she tried to think. She brushed her hands through her hair. As she turned, the clicking sounded more intense in the wall. She put her hand in her pocket and pulled out the medallion. *My God, is this a key?* She moved it along the outside of the paneled wall. *Use it where a door lock would be.* She moved it on the wall at waist level and suddenly the wall moved.

Kimberly stood, mouth open in disbelief. "Duke" She knelt and hugged him tightly. "Gosh, I was so scared. I thought I'd never find you."

She looked over Duke's shoulder into the room. "Duke, what is all of this?" *It looks like a hallway. There's lighting and gosh, it is as clean as the house. Obviously, Duke didn't get lost...*

Duke's low growl jolted her train of thought. "What's the matter, boy?"

Kimberly stood up and listened. Someone was calling over the speaker at the front door. *That's Windsor's voice. I've got to close* this *up. He can't see any of this.* "Come on Duke. Go with me to the door."

Duke wouldn't move. He continued to growl and stepped back into the secret passage. *Why won't he come with me?*

"Duke! Come with me" She stared at him and nodded. "You're protecting him, aren't you?"

Duke barked at her, growled and then disappeared. *I've got to shut this somehow.* She moved the medallion and nothing. Then she turned it over and moved it and the wall closed.

She ran down the front staircase and heard Windsor kicking and beating on the front door. "Open this fuckin door before I ram it with my car!"

Kimberly went into the monitoring room to watch him. *The way he's swaying, he's got to be drunk.*

"I'll show you mother fuckers. No one tells me I have to make an appointment!"

As he wheeled, Arthur and Martin met him on their bikes.

Arthur grumbled. "Well, look who's here, little Fauntleroy, and he's not sober, surprise, surprise."

Windsor's eyes widened. "You're the first fuckin bastard I'll get rid of when I get back what is mine!"

The two men dismounted. "Well, I look forward to the day that happens. Now, you need to leave."

Windsor opened his car door and reached for a small gun in the side door pocket.

Kimberly saw this on the monitor and pressed the loudspeaker button and yelled, "Arthur, he's got a gun."

Arthur and Martin reacted quickly and disarmed him before a shot was fired. "Why you prick!"

"Martin, call security and have Windsor removed from the property."

Within minutes security arrived.

Arthur had Windsor in an arm lock.

Martin opened the car door for the guard. "Don't press charges. Just get him the hell out of here. Here, let me help you into the car."

Windsor spat in Martin's face. "You'll wish…"

The guards held Windsor but as they pushed him into the car, he squirmed free.

169

His eyes were bulging with hate. He drew a knife from his boot and went flying at Arthur. "I'll kill you if it's the last fuckin thing I do, you fuckin bastard!"

The knife had come too close for comfort. Arthur, a black belt martial artist, didn't even flinch. "Sorry, Windsor, this just isn't your lucky day." With Arthur's upward kick, the knife flew out of Windsor's hand.

Reaching up, Martin caught the knife and shook his head. "Bad boy, Windsor! You could get hurt playing with this."

Windsor, seething with hate, gritted his teeth, and jumped at Martin with his fists. Martin leaned back into a kicking position twirling Windsor around into Arthur's waiting arms.

It was a no win situation for Windsor. Martin pushed Windsor's head into the car creasing the top of the opening just enough to give him a good reminder bruise. "OOPS" Martin flinched. *I hope that hurt!*

Arthur showed Windsor the gun. "I'll keep this for you. Any time you want to come back for it, I'll be waiting."

Martin held up the knife. "Me too."

Windsor gritted his teeth and smirked. "You can bet on it."

Arthur motioned for the driver to leave.

☙❧

Kimberly met Arthur when he came into the main hallway. "After you clean up, I would like to see you in the library."

The stern look and sound of her voice required only one reply.

While she waited in the library, Kimberly looked for the button or latch in the bookcase that would open the bookcase for the safe. As Arthur entered the room, she found it.

"First, give me the combination for this safe."

Arthur studied her stare. *Her eyes are exactly like Robert's. This has gone too far.* He started to touch the dial and stopped. "Only three people can open this safe, me, Robert and you, Miss Kim."

She frowned. "How could I open it? I didn't know it was there until..."

Arthur nodded. "I know and I'm sorry. The commotion the other night with Lauren didn't allow me the chance to explain this to you. Anything of any importance is opened by voice recognition or hand print. If your hand just touches the dial on the safe, the tumblers will automatically roll into place."

He smiled a little. "Robert didn't like wasting time."

He stepped aside and she touched the dial. The safe door opened. She looked at him with a tilt of the head. "You also knew the microfilm wouldn't be there."

He closed the apparatus up. "It is in a safe place, Miss Kim."

Kimberly took him by the hand. "It's time we talk now."

She sat on the couch and Arthur took a chair across from her.

She was silent for several minutes. "You know, until a couple of hours ago, I had a lot of comments, a lot of questions I wanted to ask, and yet all I can say is I feel so very strongly that Uncle Robert is alive."

Arthur opened his mouth to speak.

"Let me finish, Arthur."

She leaned forward. "There have to be reasons why I'm being kept in the dark and I can appreciate that, but right now, all I want to know – is he alive and safe?"

Her eyes were already glassy and she didn't wait for an answer, pulling the medallion out of her pocket. "Arthur, I found this in uncle's room today."

He reached for it and she pulled it back.

She wiped her eyes. "I've come to realize that Uncle was right, everything... so far... has two sides to it. This does." She held it up to him. "Did you know that the coat of arms side will open a wall and the other side closes it?

Do you know I've never been in this mansion alone ever! When I couldn't find Duke, I felt so alone and scared. I called Duke and thought I heard him when I left uncle's room. Then I heard a clicking noise the closer I got to the wall. It was so still in the place. I ran the medallion all over the wall until the sounds got louder and finally I found Duke."

She put it back in her pocket. "Arthur, do you have two sides?"

171

Arthur dropped his head in despair. "Miss Kim, all I can say at this time is, we have sworn an oath to care for you and Robert, and that is what we are doing, as difficult as it is. The less you know, the safer you are, and that is all I'm at liberty to say."

Arthur stood to leave. "I know I can't stop you from following your sense of direction, but I truly hope you'll use the utmost discretion about what you do, or whom you talk to."

He opened the library door and hesitated. "In fact, Miss Kim, you know a lot more than you realize. My advice is to follow your highest sense of what is right, but be so very careful. I can't stress that enough."

As Arthur turned to go back to his duties, Kimberly touched his arm. "I think I understand. I'll try to be a help and not a burden."

He wanted to hug her as he could see how difficult this was. "You've a strong will like your uncle, and we know we can trust that. I can assure you, you'll know when you're needed."

Kimberly stopped on stairway. "Arthur, do you think Windsor will be back? I watched him on the monitor. He acted like a mad man at the front door. It's quite obvious he's got the same insane hatred for you as for me. The way he charged at you was so very frightening. Weren't you scared?"

Arthur smiled and shook his head. "No, Miss Kim. Don't get me wrong, he's not a pushover at all. Today, his mistake was his anger and the fact he was drunk. That's part of my point. We're concerned about Windsor. You must be aware of your surroundings if he should appear."

Kimberly smiled. "I get the distinct feeling that I'm the only one in the dark on all of these situations. You've continually said "we" in our conversation. May I ask, does the entire Braun staff know all about everything I don't?"

Arthur nodded shyly. "Yes they do. I regret the mishap today. We didn't think you'd return from London so soon. I thought it would be nice for the staff to pay their respects at Mark's viewing since they wouldn't be able to attend the funeral. Martin reported that you'd returned and we left immediately. This won't happen again."

Kimberly turned to leave. "I'm glad it did. I learned a lot!"

26

Scotland Yard

Ross and Bobbie couldn't say another word since the elevator was about full. Bobbie would be getting off last and Ross felt her squeeze his hand as he got off. *Hmm I wonder what she meant by that?* He smiled he turned toward Alex's office.

On the top floor, Bobbie went directly to the Chief Inspector's office. The secretary ignored the urgency of Bobbie's request to see the Chief Inspector. Instead, she checked credentials very deliberately. Eventually she went into the Inspector's office and returned after what seemed like an hour.

Bobbie glared when she motioned for her to enter. *To think I know her.*

The Chief was reading a report and motioned for her to sit. She didn't. Another minute he looked and she hadn't moved. He frowned and started to speak when she raised her finger to her lips, shaking her head motioning silence and showed him her paper.

Knowing Ross had asked for her to work with him, he motioned for her to hand him the note Ross had sent. She went around the desk and handed it to him and still didn't speak.

The note gave all of Ross's reasons for believing a serious security breach had occurred there. He needed to meet with all people concerned as soon as possible outside of the Yard. *'Please, give Bobbie your answer. I really think it would be a good idea if you'd put a tail on Alex until this case is finished.'*

The Chief Inspector looked at her and nodded. He wrote down an answer quickly and handed it to her. She smiled, nodded and then left his office to hurry three floors down to Alex McGraw's office.

Not knowing the scope of the breach, Chief O'Doul wrote another note to the Yard's security ordering a complete sweep of the entire building. He left his office to personally deliver the directive.

"As you can see, this must be done on the quiet. I suggest you rotate your intervals every fifteen minutes. This order is *not* to be discussed with anyone but me. If anyone should inquire, I want to know about it."

To have the Chief Inspector deliver the order meant total secrecy. "Yes sir, I'll personally handle this."

Chief Inspector O'Doul left the Yard and went directly to the American Embassy.

෴

As instructed, Bobbie went to Inspector McGraw's office to find her boss.

She approached the secretary. "Inspector Grantwood to see Dennis Ross."

"I'm sorry Inspector, Inspector McGraw isn't to be disturbed. He's in conference..."

"Could you let Inspector Ross know I'm here? He needs this information for this meeting. At least let him know I have it."

The secretary hesitated and then rang her boss. "I told you, I'm in conference...Well, tell her to leave it or she'll have to wait."

Alex hung up the phone, noticing a look of displeasure on his colleague. "Someone is here for you with some information you need...Would it be for this case?"

Ross felt cornered by the remark and noticed anger in Alex's eyes. "As a matter of fact, that could be the photographer I used at the scene. I wanted to know what the coroner's report is. After all, Robert Braun just died and this is his wife. A little ironic, wouldn't you say?"

Ross didn't wait for Alex to pick up the phone; he got up and opened the door. He motioned to Bobbie. He sighed seeing she had a folder with her. "Bobbie, I thought, it might be you. What have you got for me?"

She opened and handed the folder to Ross, with the chief's note clipped inside. She saw Ross read he was to meet the Chief and others at Westminster Cathedral at seven that night. As she gave him the report, she removed the Chief's reply.

Stepping back to the door, she pointed to the folder. "You'll see both parties were way over the alcohol limit. That's the conclusion."

She turned and looked at Alex. "Sorry to intrude. I thought you'd want this info." She smiled and left.

Alex was so taken back by Ross's action he waved her away in an annoyed manner.

Ross studied the report to gather his thoughts. She had altered it to read *accident. Bobbie is brilliant. She already knows more about this case based on her suspicions. The Chief must see she's needed on this case.*

He handed the report to Alex. "We can drive over there, if you like. We still have the area roped off."

Ross sat across from Alex's desk.

"What's with the frown? Aren't you satisfied with the report?"

Alex highlighted a paragraph and showed it to Ross. "What's this supposed to mean?"

Ross straightened. "What this means is we found several items around the car with no connection to either person."

Ross's face stiffened as he fell back into his chair. "And now we'll never know because someone didn't mark the evidence bag with the appropriate symbols and the bag never made it to the lab."

"So, that's really the reason you are upset. Would it have made a difference?"

Ross got up, signed off on the report, and threw the pen down on the desk. "No...The coroner's report says it all. I just get annoyed when procedures aren't followed to the letter. They'll probably find the damn bag six months from now in the back of one of the delivery trucks."

He took his coat off the hall tree and picked up his brief case. *I hope he accepted that.*

Alex looked at his watch. "Do you have time for a pint?"

Ross was startled. *This is like old times, yet I wonder now if he suspects something.* "Sure! Fish and chips are the best over at the Blue Boar...My treat."

Ross opened the door. *That answer surprised him.*

Windsor and Dr. Edse

The local police arrived and Windsor was turned over to them.

The police sergeant grinned. "Same old, same old. The only difference is we're usually bringing him here not taking him away."

The Braun security guards pulled him out of their car. "My boss said not to charge him with anything other than he's blitzed."

Windsor sneered at them as he got out of the car. "You've brought my car?" He looked at the police sergeant. "Should I call my attorney? I know my rights. You haven't stopped me for a driving violation. So, give me my keys!"

The sergeant nodded and motioned for his officer to give Windsor his keys.

Windsor blew a kiss to them, got in his car and drove off at a modest speed.

The sergeant bit his lip and shook his head. "What a demeaning piece he is. If that's what money does for you, you can bloody well keep it."

The security guard laughed. "He and his mother were the bad ones and they've moved out now. The niece lives here and she's very nice. I can assure you, you won't be making any more trips here. She's a tea totaler."

∂∼∽

As the estate disappeared in his rear view mirror, Windsor became crazed with anger and started to beat at his steering wheel. "You son of a bitch, Arthur, you mother fuckin bastard you're going to die!"

Mesmerized by his hatred for Arthur, Windsor almost missed the exit off the round-about taking him to his lover's home.

He came to a screeching halt in the driveway.

He pushed the front door so hard it bashed into a standing antique vase. It went crashing to the floor.

Edward Edse ran into the room. "What in God's name was that?" He threw the flowers he had just picked onto a center table and ran to the shattered vase. "Windsor, what have you done? You've broken my jewel."

"I'll show you what's broken. Look at my *face!*"

He lifted Eddie by the shoulders, glared in his face and shoved him against the wall.

The doctor was overcome with fear. *My God, I've never seen him like this! My bag is in the kitchen. I've got to give him a shot or he may hurt me.*

"Oh, my dear man, who did this to you? Let me get my bag. Better yet let's go upstairs and I'll take care of you."

He knew he couldn't subdue Windsor, who was much bigger. He talked very softly to calm him.

∂∼∽

The telephone awakened the doctor and Windsor. Windsor had hired several regulars from the local bar to watch Sheila's apartment. The first to call would get a bonus.

"Why don't you just wait until the morning? How can you be sure it really is Sheila? Those bar dwellers you hired aren't exactly trained for this."

"Money talks my sweet….As you well know."

The good doctor put his mask over his eyes and prepared to sleep. "That's not entirely true."

Windsor heard him chuckling. "No, I need to know where the fuck she's been all of this time. We were to meet three days ago. Before you drift off, are you going to be satisfied with those two discs she said she couldn't open? Then are we done with her? Should I hire someone to get rid of her? She said she has kept a record on us."

Windsor moved closer to the bed. He heard snoring. He shook Eddie's shoulder. "This is not the time to be funny. What should I tell her?"

Eddie sat up in bed and took off his mask. "At this hour, all you're to do is find out where she's been. She probably won't tell you anyway. Set up a meeting with her at a decent hour and we'll talk. Now go! Before I can't go back to sleep."

∾∾

Twenty minutes later, Windsor knocked on Sheila's door.

She opened the door with a little gasp and a step backward. "How did you get in without buzzing my suite? You realize Lauren lives down the hall!"

Windsor glared at her and walked in.

She frowned as he walked by and then grinned. "Whatever happened to your face?" *I must thank whoever it was for the face job on the prima donna.*

Windsor stared and bit his lip. "Never mind my face! Have you forgotten we had an appointment *three days ago*? Where in the fuck have you been? I truly hope for your sake, Sheila, you haven't done something very stupid."

Sheila walked past Windsor to her kitchenette, her heart pounding!

She heard Arthur's voice from the implant reassure her. "You're doing fine. Just be yourself and he'll back off."

She stood with her eyes closed for a moment and sighed with

relief. She plugged in the kettle and turned around. "Well, Mr. Big shot, I've been away on a photo shoot. You do remember I have a job!"

She didn't look at him, continued preparing her tea. "When my company sends me on an assignment, I can't refuse, that's unless you want to put me on your payroll."

Windsor lit up a cigarette and glanced out of the window. He saw one of the goons he hired to watch the place. *How effective is that, standing out in the open.* He shook his head. "I'm not here on a social visit. Do you have anything for me?"

She poured her tea. "I told you, you'd have to wait until I had access to her stuff. Lauren doesn't have set hours. A lot of times she works at home. You better hope she doesn't ask for my key to the apartment."

Sheila plumped down on her couch with a big smile. "Besides, I was going to call you, at a more appropriate hour, to tell you I've been assigned to do a photo shoot on the new CEO for the R & K Plastics Company."

Windsor stared at her with gritted teeth. *She should be doing it on me instead of that bitch.* "Is that supposed to impress me? Have you ever met that bitch?"

Sheila could see he was starting to lose his composure. She felt defenseless sitting down and got up. "Yeah, it should impress you, because I'll have full run of the place. They want pictures of her and the staff, in the lab, in the offices, everywhere."

She went to her little make-shift bar and poured some brandy into her tea. Windsor followed and poured his own drink. "Thanks for asking."

"I pour drinks for my... *friends!*" She walked to the door.

Windsor swallowed a shot and stopped as she opened the door. "Okay, I'll go along with this photo shoot, but, for your sake you better come up with the rest of those discs." He stared at her. "Sheila...Don't fuck with me. You won't like it."

She bit her lip and shook her head. *For once you've said something I can agree with.* She peeked into the hallway. She shut the door slightly. "The hall is clear. I start this job tomorrow. It will take time to get settled and organized as it was a last minute arrangement. Someone else had the assignment." She peeked again. "You're the one that will be fucked up if you do this again and are seen. *I'll call you. Now get out of here.*"

She shut the door and stood against it for a few minutes. "Thank God, that's over. I was so worried Lauren would stop in."

"You did a good job. See you tomorrow."

28

Braun estate

Their conversation finished, Kimberly and Arthur left the library and stopped in front of the main stairway.

"Arthur, it's been almost a month since the funeral. Do you have any idea why Windsor would come back here and be so belligerent about it?"

"He said something about getting things that belonged to his mother. Martin told him the movers had removed everything she asked for, but he wasn't going to accept that."

"Has anyone checked her place?" *I wonder if that secret passage leads to her suite. Could it be that Windsor knows about the passageways?*

They turned, hearing a thumping sound coming down the stairway.

"Well, look who's here."

Kimberly hugged Duke and looked at her watch. "Dinner won't be for another hour. I think I'll have a look around her place. It shouldn't take long." *I'm curious what Windsor could be looking for. If Arthur knows what I'm up to, he might ask for the medallion.*

Arthur tilted his head with a frown. *Darn her. She doesn't need to be in Lucille's rooms. If I say anything to put her off, she'll just be more curious.* "I was hoping you might be able to have a talk with…

ah… Herr Dietrich regarding his contract."

Kimberly stared wide-eyed at Arthur. "What are you talking about? His contract? You are pulling my leg…?"

Arthur stood stiff with a tightened face. "No, Miss Kim, he might want to leave your employment." *Now I must find Dietrich.* "I really think you should talk with him. He doesn't listen to me." *I have to get Gretchen to lock those rooms until we can seal everything off.*

Kimberly started up the stairway. "Let me change clothes and then I'll go see him."

On her way to her room she met Bertha and Gretchen coming from her aunt's wing of the house.

"Well, you saved me looking for you."

They stopped and smiled. "What can we do for you, Miss Kim?"

"Oh, I wondered if you had cleaned Aunt Lucille's wing yet or closed it up." *I know the monitors are off in the house until midnight. So maybe Herr Dietrich will have to wait until after dinner. I don't think Arthur wants me to go in those rooms and used the chef for an excuse.*

Bertha nodded and then frowned at Kimberly. "Do you need to go in there? It isn't locked anymore."

"I was just curious how it would look empty."

Gretchen grinned and shook her head. "It's not empty, Miss Kim. Mrs. Braun took her clothes and little else."

Kimberly stood for a moment with a frown. *Then, Windsor is looking for something. I wish I could ask them if they clean those secret passages. I'm sure they do but then Arthur would feel I had betrayed him.* "Thank you. I'll go up when I can."

Kimberly dashed back to her rooms and changed her clothes. She met Duke licking his mouth as she got to the center of the hall. She hesitated. "Duke, you come with me. You know more about this place than anyone." She could see he was going to talk to her and didn't want him to be heard. "Shush."

She took hold of his collar and whispered. "There are too many people upstairs to see us play around the wall opening next to uncle's room. We'll take the long way." *The women have finished in Aunt Lucille's wing. Nobody will know we're there and maybe we can find out what dear cousin was after.*

Kimberly and Duke climbed the flight of steps. Every other year, her aunt had a new theme for this section of the house and it took about a year to put it in.

"Duke, do you remember the theme about India?"

Duke looked up at her. He knew the word India and it made him growl. He slowed his walk. "Not to worry. No more tigers."

They got to the top step before the main entrance hallway. *Actually, I'm quite impressed. The hallway is very English. Wow, I wonder what came over her.*

The lighting came on in her aunt's suite. Gretchen was right. Nothing was changed. They walked around the living room.

She found a pick-up order from the moving company indicating all the items removed. *There're two pages here, and it doesn't look like anything has been disturbed. This would be a book if she'd taken everything.*

She and Duke walked through all ten rooms. "I bet Windsor wants to sell all of this for the money. There's got to be several million here."

They went into her aunt's bedroom and she stood aghast at the doorway. *I've not been in here since this was done. How could you ever fall asleep!* "Duke, look at this color scheme."

She walked over to the walls.

Duke stopped at the doorway. She chuckled, *Duke's not color blind.* "Thank god this is wallpaper. It would be pretty hard to remove black paint."

Kimberly stood at the steps that surrounded a king-size round bed. *Look at the drapes around the bed.*

She felt them. *I can't believe Gretchen hasn't said how awful this room is. Shocking pink silk with red and purple stripes!*

Convinced that Windsor wanted the remaining furnishings in his mother's rooms, Kimberly looked for Duke. *Now where's he gone?* "Duke!"

Duke came from the mammoth closet door and sat. He barked at her and then ran back inside. *I can't believe this. The closet is almost the size of her bedroom.* "Duke, do you know that these two rooms would make up my entire condominium in New York and I've a big apartment."

Duke ran back along an outside wall yelping. He stopped as if to wait for her. He threw his head back with another yelp.

"Okay, you want to show me something. What is it? Better not be a mouse."

He went to a wall-alcove. *Kimberly didn't need to have it spelled out. So that's the scheme. Very cagy! At least fifty of these alcoves are in the house.* She took the medallion out of her pocket and put the coat of arms side facing the wall and..."It's not so scary this time."

The wall, without a sound, opened into a lit hallway. Duke led the way. In the corner a figurine of a Viking Soldier had a shield that resembled her medallion. She put hers up to it and they were the same. *Interesting, I wonder why it's in here. I remember Viking Soldiers on the mover's list. Another Arthur question. I've a feeling he wouldn't be thrilled to know we're in here.*

Duke was anxious to follow the narrow hallway. She knew her uncle's room was on this side of the house and followed. She figured at each alcove there would be a monitor. *That makes sense. You wouldn't surprise anyone.*

After looking at six monitors, Kimberly thought they should be getting close to her uncle's room. She checked one monitor showing the inside of her uncle's bedroom. Arthur stood at the bathroom doorway. "I don't know how to operate this monitor. I can see he's talking to someone. Duke, he's stepping back as if... Oh my! Look at the carpeting!"

Kimberly's mouth dropped open. "Wheel marks! Someone is in there with Arthur. It has to be Uncle Robert! It just must be him!"

Kimberly pulled her medallion out of her pocket and tried to locate the spot to open the wall. Nothing happened; she turned it over and over. She tried to remain calm. Her heart pounded. "Duke, I know that's Uncle Robert with Arthur. It has to be him. Why won't this medallion work?"

Her eyes filled with tears as she watched Arthur and the invisible something leave the viewing area. *What has happened to him? Please, God, let me be with him!*

She slumped to the floor sobbing in her hands. Duke whimpered next to her and licked her hands. He then went to the wall and barked several times, and then went back to her. She quieted down and stroked him. "You're a good boy, Duke. I'll be all right."

After a few minutes, Arthur opened the wall and took her by the hand. "We can't put this off any longer." Kimberly heard him mutter under his breath. "He can fire me!"

"Be very quiet Kim and just follow me."

Arthur took her through her uncle's bathroom to the linen closet. He used his medallion and the shelves all slid to the side exposing a door. Kimberly gasped as Arthur opened the door and they walked in. "This is an elevator."

Her eyes couldn't get any larger. She mouthed "What?" and then felt them going down. She heard a beeping sound and figured this indicated the floor level.

Kimberly looked up at Arthur. "We're still going down."

"It's all right, Miss Kim. We're almost there."

The elevator came to a gentle stop and the doors opened. The guard greeted them with a scanning device which scared her a little. *This isn't happening to me. What is this down here?*

Arthur touched her arm. "You're doing fine. This is standard procedure, Kim."

She watched the guard scan Arthur's hands and eyes. Then he scanned hers. To relieve her anxiety, the guard showed her results on the scanner. He smiled. "It says you passed the test, Miss Braun. You may go on."

Arthur led her over to some chairs and motioned for her to sit. "I need to brief you."

She almost choked. "Brief me! Try, is this a dream? Has the world stopped? *What is all of this?"*

Arthur dropped his head and then looked at her with searching eyes. "This is all so complicated and I'm not the one to explain it to you. I promise you'll understand it all, but right now your only concern is to be with Robert."

Kimberly took a deep breath. "You mean it. He's alive?" She jumped up ready to follow.

"Kim, sit for a minute. You need to know something before you see him."

"What's wrong with him?" She scowled at Arthur. "What has happened to him?"

"You need to be strong, and in control! It won't do him any good if he thinks you can't cope with this situation. We can't afford a setback for him. Can you get a grip here?"

She shut her eyes and nodded. "I'm sorry I'm acting like a child...Tell me what is wrong and what can I do?"

"Some months back Robert made a major discovery in his work. About the same time he suddenly couldn't keep his food down and became very lethargic. After testing his project and himself, he realized he was having side effects from another source. He detected he was being poisoned."

Kimberly put her hand to her mouth. "You have arrested the poison?"

Arthur nodded. "It is a long story and we'll tell you but right now what's important for you to realize is that a reaction had already occurred in his body, and he's seriously disfigured."

Kimberly shut her eyes tight against the thought. "How awful. Is he in a lot of pain? Take me to him!"

"We're going now, but you *must understand that he doesn't want you to see him*. He is covered with gauze. He's improving every day. We have the very best care for him. I'll take you into his room. Promise me you'll abide by his wishes."

She had her head down. "I promise. I can do this. Thank you for letting me be with him, Arthur."

Arthur knocked on the door. The room was dimly lit. Her uncle sat in a wheel chair with his back to her. Arthur seated her and then checked on his boss and left.

It was quiet for a few moments. She heard him laboring for breath. "Kim, my dear child...I'm...sorry...I've put..."

"Uncle Robert, don't talk. I'm here with you and that's all that matters."

"Each day...gets better."

Ten minutes passed and Arthur returned. Robert whispered to

Arthur. "She's a strong girl. I should have listened to you. Let her come every day. You can explain the situation to her." Arthur repeated what her uncle said.

She smiled and nodded. "Thank you."

"I must get him back to his room. We'll see if you can't visit him there tomorrow and be able to stay longer."

Robert looked up at Arthur. Kimberly heard him whisper about his appearance.

"Uncle Robert, please let me be with you. I'm not afraid."

Arthur wheeled Robert out of the room. "Miss, Kim. I'll be back in a few minutes. The doctor doesn't want his skin covered for long periods."

Kim stood up and spoke sharply at Arthur. "Surely, you're not talking about Dr. Edse? I don't want that man near Uncle Robert!"

Robert's eyes smiled through slits in his bandages as Arthur replied. "No, Miss Kim, Dr. Edse is another person of interest. We have reason to believe that he is an associate of Windsor's."

The door closed and the full lighting came on. Kimberly sighed with great relief. *I knew he was alive. Thank you for proving it to me. I can be a team player. I can handle this and do whatever it takes to help uncle survive.*

Arthur returned to find Kimberly standing outside one of the labs watching a lab experiment being done.

She looked up and shook her head. "This is unbelievable!"

He grinned and nodded. "It's pretty amazing. Would you like to see it or would you like me to take you back to the house?"

"I would love to see the other side of my uncle's life, and … I don't mean that facetiously either."

He took her back toward the elevator and opened a door to a room filled with bicycles. "My word, how many people work here?"

"Here at the estate, about sixty-five. That's down here. With the house staff, it's close to a hundred."

They walked the bikes down the hall, while Arthur briefly explained the development of the underground facility. "Robert's brilliance in chemistry couldn't be shelved after the Korean War. He tried to step out of the picture. He changed his name, moved to

England but his attempt to be reclusive failed."

"What happened?"

Arthur beamed. "Well, one major occurrence –you came into his life. He had just started R & K Plastics and it wasn't making a lot of money at the beginning."

Kimberly frowned, "Uncle Robert told me a different version...but I guess...never mind...he was just protecting his secrets."

Arthur nodded. "Yes, he had to. Anyway, when he returned from Washington, he not only had a secret agreement to work for the two countries with an unlimited budget and very nice salary, but had custody of you."

Arthur swung his leg over the bike seat. "What you see down here didn't get developed until you were in the upper grades."

She shook her head. "I can't imagine how this was accomplished and no one knew about it." She shrugged her shoulders. "I lived here and played here and never once saw anything different... What's more, Windsor never said anything either and he of all people loved to sneak around."

"So...I'm going to guess Uncle Robert had something like this over at R & K until he needed more space."

"We still have a sub-level lab there. Yes, his creativity launched new directions and not only was more space needed but more highly skilled personnel."

"Does Lauren fall into that group?"

Arthur nodded and slowly pedaled along the corridor.

"Not going into a lot of detail, I can tell you that after a year of planning, he contrived a time table for the drilling, digging and removal." Arthur laughed. "You didn't want to be around him when the plan got interrupted."

Kimberly closed her eyes and nodded. "Perhaps when Aunt Lucille returned unexpectedly from one of her trips or Windsor came home from boarding school. If no one knew, how did they interrupt the work?"

"With all of you out of the place, Robert could have the crews working twenty-four seven. Plus, there was a definite noise factor. He put in a noise meter and it would blast a sound down here if the meter showed too many decibels."

They rode without a word for a few minutes. Arthur sensed Kimberly had a concern.

He saw her frown. "What's troubling you, Miss Kim?"

They came to wall and had to stop.

"No, it's not a concern. I was just thinking it's obvious all the secret government stuff is being done here. Yet, when I went over to R & K the other day for the first time in my new capacity, Lauren showed me a test she was running. Now that I know about all of this, I think a mistake has been made, and she's been given something very unusual, if not of a sensitive nature, to be tested...."

She stared at Arthur for a moment. "That's right! The upset we had over the safe in the library. That's when I solved the mystery about Uncle Robert's ring and the microfilm. You certainly remember sternly asking her about the test results."

Kimberly turned her bike around. "You do remember that incident! Vouching for you almost ruined my friendship with Lauren."

"Yes, I recall it very well, and I might add Robert was so pleased and relieved with her strong reply... He felt Lauren was protecting him even though she believed him to be dead...By the way, don't turn your bike around."

Arthur leaned against the wall. "I can explain the need for the test results. It wasn't a mistake that Lauren was asked to make those tests. Years ago, Gunther asked Robert if he would take Lauren under his wing as she had a real love for chemistry. She was in high school at the time. Robert let her work during the summer months. Anyway, the long and short of it is, he said she has a gift in the field. After she got her Ph.D., he made her his assistant."

"Didn't she ever question the use of a code always for identification?"

"Her respect for Robert was such that she never questioned him. Anyway Robert felt he needed to test her and did so using the code. He would give her tests from the company and then once in a while put one of his projects in for testing."

"You realize we both saw the difference in the code sheets."

Arthur grinned. "So she asked you what you thought."

Kimberly sat on the edge of her seat balancing her foot on the floor. "Am I not taking uncle's place? She had to have someone to confide in. That's only fair.... Arthur, what she showed me under that microscope is monstrous! She promised not to say anything to anyone until she can arrive at a conclusion....Why didn't Uncle Robert bring her here?"

Arthur reached into his pocket for his medallion.

"He almost did right after he made this discovery." He saw Kimberly's eye brows raise. "He didn't because he had a visit from his ex-commander from Korea who is now his liaison to the Pentagon. Admiral Benjamin told him that some of his formulas have surfaced on the Russian black market."

Kimberly's mouth dropped open. "Are you serious?"

"Dead serious."

Arthur looked at his watch. "We're going this way." He scanned the block wall and it moved exposing a ramp. On the inside wall, he switched on a monitor to check the area. As he pressed another switch, the stone vault her uncle's casket had been lowered into moved sideways.

Kimberly dropped her head and shook it. "Why am I no longer surprised?"

Arthur chuckled. "I know you are because your eyes are like saucers! Stay here, I'll come back for your bike, this ramp is a bit tricky."

Arthur rode up the ramp and barely got off his bike before she was right behind him.

Kimberly tried to mimic him. "I know you're surprised to see me here because your eyes are like saucers!"

He walked over to the wall in the crypt muttering. "She's his spitting image...I hope I don't have to work with these women at the same time." *First it was Lauren, then Sheila and now this one.*

"Are you talking to yourself?"

Arthur shook his head and pressed a button inside a fold out panel on the crypt wall. The vault moved slowly to its position. He pressed another panel and a phone appeared. "James, Miss Kimberly and I are in the crypt. We'll be leaving shortly. Yes, the meeting is at nine."

"James says we're clear to return to the house."

Kimberly glanced at her watch. "I take it these are standard procedures, checking the monitors, checking in with James."

"They are now, Miss Kim. You must learn to make it a practice. Robert will explain." He held the door open for her to take her bike out. "I've to get ready for a team meeting, so we must go."

"Is that the one at nine tonight? Aren't I a team player now?"

Arthur shook his head. "I can see it's a catch twenty-two with you." He nodded. "You can come."

"You didn't finish explaining about Lauren."

"You'll learn more about her at the meeting."

"Well, I'll never believe she would be the mole." She jumped on her bike "Last one in is..." and took off leaving Arthur locking up the gate.

Arthur could hear a chuckle from his implant.

29

Westminster Cathedral

It was almost seven thirty before Inspector McGraw called it a night with his partner.

Ross had determined to have a good meal and a few pints of lager and not give any indication of concern for what his colleague might be thinking.

Alex in fact tried to wheedle out some of the facts of the case to see if Dennis would hold back any information that Alex already knew existed.

"What was the evidence you found that you think was so important?" Alex never took his eyes off Ross.

I wondered when this question would be coming. I bet he knows what's in the bag. Ross took a bite of his fish and speedily took a drink of his beer. "Whoa, that was hot!"

He leaned back. "Actually, it was just some bits and pieces we found around the car. There was some broken glass not from windows, and ah, some pieces of broken plastic and an odd looking piece of jewelry."

Ross waved his fork as if it was nothing. "I don't even know if there was or could have been a connection. It was just that procedures hadn't been followed." He cautiously took another bite. "I've lodged a complaint about the courier."

Alex finished his drink and put a couple of notes on the table. Dennis motioned for him to put it away. "Remember, I said it was my treat. Wish you would have eaten something. This is really great. I'll take care of it. By the way, Kimberly Braun came in to identify the pictures of the bodies and pretty much supported the coroner's report, admitting her aunt had a drinking problem."

Alex put on his coat. "Isn't there a son?" *This was a waste of time.*

"Can't find him. Miss Braun made it very clear she has no relationship of any kind with her cousin." Dennis went on eating.

"Well, I'm sure when the aunt's money is given out, he'll show up. See you tomorrow." *Same old Dennis. Protocol. Boring.*

"Give my love to Jane."

Alex waved.

Ross hastily finished his dinner and hurried out. He walked to Westminster Cathedral, only four streets away. *I hope I didn't act too casual about the case. Too casual or not, Alex will sense when he's being duped. I gave it my best shot.*

Ross entered the side door of the rectory and apologized to the Chief Inspector and Admiral for being late. "I thought it best that Alex make the first move to leave. I just kept eating, hoping he wouldn't want to wait."

The Chief Inspector motioned for them to follow. "You did the right thing." He pointed to the boys' choir in the front and whispered, "My grandson is in the choir. We only have a few more minutes before they're done."

He showed them quickly to the back of the cathedral but within earshot of the choir.

"Dennis, the Admiral and I think you need to bring Bobbie on board. She's quick and correct. I was impressed how she handled your communication."

Dennis smiled warmly. "I'll attend to that first thing tomorrow, sir."

Dennis then brought the two men up to speed regarding the Braun accident, his curious meeting with Braun's staff member, Arthur, and his main concern, Alex. "That's all I have to report. It's not all good, but I would bet that Alex bugged my phone to get that information. Somehow he intercepted that courier's delivery, and that evidence is gone."

The Chief Inspector got up. He saw the choir practice was over. "I must leave now. John, I'll be in touch with you very soon. All we can do is hang tight. This case is evolving to another level. What Dennis has reported puts Alex in the mainstream of suspects and right now that's all we have."

The Admiral shook hands with the men. "I'm always available if you need another meeting or assistance."

The Admiral turned to leave by a different exit and stopped. "Inspector Ross, perhaps you could do me a favor."

Ross waited for him. *Whatever could I do for an Admiral?*

"I don't want you to make a special trip, but if you should go out to the Braun estate again, would you give my business card to Arthur?"

Ross glanced at the card and grinned. "Is this a signal of some kind?"

The Admiral stared at him. "You're quick."

Ross put the card in his wallet. *I was kidding the man. Now I need to know.* "Sir, is there something I should know about this? Does the Chief know? Or, is this a Navy seal situation..?"

The Admiral nodded. "You're right, it is a signal. Yes, the Chief knows about all of this and when it's convenient give the card... Tomorrow will do fine."

He didn't smile. He rotated on his heel and left.

30

Braun team meeting at the crypt

Nine o'clock sharp Kimberly arrived at the crypt. She rode her bike and Duke followed.

She sat down quickly. *Being the boss's niece makes it a bit awkward, but I don't have to worry about being the only woman. Gosh, Bertha and Gretchen are Seals?*

Arthur saw Kimberly's look of surprise. He called the meeting to order.

"First, we have a new member to our team, though we can't fault her for being the boss's daughter."

They all gasped at Arthur's remark. "Sorry, niece! The consolation is, we needn't worry about a slip of the tongue as she is one of us."

Kimberly heard a few chuckles and clapping, but didn't respond.

Arthur called on various people to report on the activities of people they were assigned to watch.

The Bishop returned from a day at the resort. "Robert wanted a full report about the latest information from our informant, Sheila Jones. It seems the resort has been and is still being used by Windsor and Edward Edse. The staff at the hotel confirmed a monthly reservation of one of the penthouse suites, in the doctor's name. When I asked how it was paid for, there wasn't a record of it. Not to upset the scheme, I advised the manager to be aware and keep in touch with us."

Kimberly relaxed when Arthur and the Bishop reported the capture of Sheila Jones. The results of her interrogation proved that Lauren Woodgrieves wasn't involved at all in the theft of the formulas being sold on the Russian black market.

The Bishop stood. "In addition to that summary, you need to know that Robert was quite impressed with this woman and is giving her an opportunity to amend her past performance by acting as a decoy to catch Windsor and Edward Edse. We've set up a photo shoot to be done by Sheila covering the new CEO of R & K Plastics. She'll lead Windsor and the doctor to believe she'll have access to Lauren's work. Hopefully the information she'll pass on to Windsor will satisfy all concerned that Robert's discovery died with him."

Arthur raised a copy of a folder. "You should all have a copy of the interrogation. Robert wants you all to become familiar with this information."

"For the benefit of Kimberly, we all know Mark's death wasn't an accident. We feel both his and Mike's death were orchestrated by the same person, Windsor. To be sure, we'll have to prove it." Arthur leaned against the wall.

Gretchen blurted out. "Arthur, that means Windsor murdered his mother!"

Arthur nodded. "That would be correct, but still has to be proven."

The room fell silent.

Martin walked to the front. He cleared his throat... "In the meantime, Robert is concerned about the rest of us, and has ordered, until this whole business is behind us, we operate under a red alert. We know from Sheila's testimony, Windsor is selling these formulas...If she is right, the formulas are being sold on the Black market and that means Windsor has a contact within the Russian Black Market."

Martin put his folder on the vault and shook his head. "Mind you, we have to substantiate all of this, but for now we assume the information is correct. What Windsor fails to realize is that he has stepped into a territory he's not at all equipped to handle. We know the man has an obsession about money. His shortsightedness is that the

Russian Mafia has and will always have the upper hand. They now own Windsor. In the meantime, he has inadvertently made the estate the target for the Russian Mafia…"

Puzzled, Kimberly frowned and raised her hand slightly. "I guess I don't understand the ramifications here."

Martin gave his copy of the Jones folder to Kimberly. "Sheila points out in one of her interviews with Doctor Lewis that Windsor thought the discs he was selling on various markets were designs for plastic car parts. On one occasion she had given Windsor a disc that couldn't be opened and he went ballistic. She returned it to Lauren's files thinking it was broken. Then she related that not more than a week passed and Windsor wanted that disc back and fast."

Martin walked back into the center of the room. "Well, in that interim Arthur and the Bishop caught her in the building and detained her in the parking lot."

The Austrian agent stood. "What do you think changed Windsor's mind?"

"Robert seems to think Windsor may have aligned himself with someone who knows Robert's background with the code."

Kimberly had been taking notes. She stared at Martin for a moment. She wrote down what Martin said, stared at it, then made a star next to it.

Gustov raised his hand again. "How do you propose to fool Windsor using the Jones woman?"

Arthur dropped his head for a moment. "You've raised a good question; however, this is what is being done. The lab has designed a disc that has a homing device and a lock down device so the moment it's put into play, it will immediately by satellite identify the user. The information on it will be a tease…to draw them in. The authorities will then be notified…"

Gustov, determined to hear more of what was going on, pushed. "Arthur, what makes you so sure that the disc the Jones woman will give to Windsor will do the trick? This all *sounds* good, but what do you really think?"

Kimberly looked at Arthur and Bishop abruptly.

Arthur stepped forward. "This is conjecture until we can verify. It would be premature to take any further action than to adhere to the red alert and protect our position, which is what Robert wants us to do. Just be alert, especially when you leave. Also be aware of the deliveries made. Most of you on the grounds know the people that come in and out. If that changes, make sure you report it to James."

Several raised their hands.

Arthur pointed. "Yes, James."

James stood. "Will any of these people be coming to the estate? We know what Windsor and Edse look like. Will you issue a picture of Sheila Jones?"

The Bishop held up the folder. "The last sheet in the folder is a picture of Sheila."

Arthur grinned. "While we were at Mark's viewing earlier, we had a surprise visit from Windsor who tried to get inside."

Arthur looked over at Kimberly. "And, we know that situation will never happen again… To further answer your question, James, as of now, the only people permitted inside the estate will be by appointment only.

Bertha raised her hand and stood. "How is Robert doing?"

"Robert is improving better than the doctor imagined. We feel it's because Kimberly is now able to spend time with him…"

The Bishop stepped forward next to Arthur. "Even though Kimberly is on board, we still must believe that Robert has died. I can't emphasize that too much. No one can know otherwise."

He held up a newspaper. "Because of Windsor's ignorance, we now have the Russian mafia to contend with. We all know Lucille's and Mark's death was no accident. The logical explanation is, Windsor has aligned with others. Robert feels we can prevent further escalation, if we can prove Windsor and the doctor planned and executed Robert's death. Once the media gets hold of this, we think the mafia will back off not wanting any exposure. Bringing this to trial, we can prove Windsor sold everything."

James stood up on a stone bench and whistled. "Before you leave, I'm instructed that all of you must be scanned twice a day, when you come to work and when you leave, especially if you live off the estate."

Kimberly frowned hearing that. "Do I have to do that as well?"

Arthur shook his head. "That's only for staff."

Arthur, the Bishop and Martin walked out of the crypt with Kimberly.

James brought Kimberly's bike. "I'm real glad you know about all of this, Miss Kim. I was so sure I'd be the one to goof."

She grinned and he took off on his bike to the house.

"Well, do you still want to be on the team?" Arthur walked around the corner to get his bike. He had the Bishop's and Martin's as well.

They walked in silence for a moment.

"Of course I want to be on the team! This meeting wasn't at all what I expected. You run a tight ship and I learned a lot..." She stopped. "I guess I'm still in a daze that all of these years have passed and I had no idea that Uncle Robert was-- is living a double life."

Arthur shrugged and nodded to the Bishop and Martin. "Have we not had this conversation with Robert many times, to tell Kimberly?"

The Bishop stopped walking with his bike and chuckled. "It almost became a weekly argument, especially if you'd be coming home soon."

Martin propped his bike against the wall that lined the path back to the mansion. He hopped on the wall to sit. "Yeah, and then our tunes changed when Robert got violently ill."

Kimberly gaped at them. "When did this happen? No one told me!" She leaned her bike against the wall and sat next to Martin. "You have to tell me."

Arthur fell silent... "It's been maybe five months or more, Admiral Benjamin came out here to tell Robert that some of Robert's formulas had been sold on the open market. Before the Admiral left, he told Robert he needed to slow down a bit, he thought he looked tired."

Kimberly admitted with a nod. "I know that name, and I think I met the Admiral on several occasions growing up."

"I can tell you Robert was devastated to find his formulas had been stolen. He had just given Lauren a phase of his discovery for testing. He really wanted to bring her here to work on the government projects and thought her results of this test would decide it for him. Needless to say, the thought she could be the thief tore him up. To make matters worse, he wasn't able to keep food down."

Kimberly dropped her head into her hands. "How awful...How did you find out about the poison?"

The three men chuckled. Martin scratched his head. "The way Robert found out was so amazing....His inquisitive mind never stops."

Martin grinned. "Well, you know the main beverage in this place is bottled water... aside from the occasional lager. Anyway, the three of us were having a little down time with Robert in Robert's office over at R & K. He was having a pretty good day. You were supposed to go on a ski trip together or something. That always made him happy.

While we were chatting, he took his feet off the desk and stared at his bottle of water."

Martin motioned to Arthur and the Bishop. "Do you remember, Bishop? He asked you to grab a bottle of water out of the refrigerator."

The Bishop sat on his bike with his leg on the wall. "I gave him two bottles to look at. He put them side by side and watched them. Then he pulled a magnifier out of desk drawer and surveyed the tops of each bottle. One of the bottles he opened and asked me to fill it up to the top."

Kimberly leaned forward to listen, "And? Then, what did you do.?"

"He told us to watch the bottles while he took the first bottle to the lab."

Arthur looked very sober. "Even though it all seemed crazy or like a game, he returned very distraught... we finally saw what he was so intrigued with. He saw a drip coming out of the bottle. The lab test showed it was poison."

Kimberly gasped with shock. "I can't believe this! Was this accidental? No, it couldn't be if he found punctures in the plastic bottles."

"I can tell you Miss Kim., every bottle at the company and here at the estate was tested."

"What were the results or should I guess? It was positive."

Arthur shook his head. "No, only the bottles that Robert would normally have access to."

She put her hand up. "Is that why you grabbed those two bottles of water I was going to open in the game room the other day? You weren't sure about them."

Arthur glanced at his watch. "Yes, you're right. I couldn't take a chance. Listen, I've got to leave. Robert wants to see me. You can finish telling her."

Kimberly frowned. "Just like that you know Uncle Robert wants to see you?"

The men chuckled. Arthur pointed to his ear. "We're not being rude laughing, Miss Kim...We all have ear implants allowing us to communicate with Robert or with each other. Robert wants to see me before he retires for the night."

Arthur rolled his bike back to the crypt. "This will be quicker."

Kimberly sat with her arms resting on her knees. "Okay, what happened after the water was tested." She ran her hands through her hair. "Why didn't any of you get sick?"

Martin chuckled. "Robert was always on our case about drinking water. We preferred juice or pop."

He looked at her sadly. "I guess you could say lucky for us."

"Are there any other extraordinary things going on I need to know about?"

She saw from their expressions there was more. Bishop smiled sheepishly. "Robert will tell you about his discovery...Now where were we."

The Bishop could see Kimberly was going to burst. "Miss Kim, we did find out who did this.

At the time, this was no laughing matter, we're just so grateful Robert has such a tenacious mind. A day or two later, Robert had another severe bout of heaving. Arthur called Dr. Edse. The doctor left some medication for Robert to take as soon as he was able."

The Bishop continued. "Another lucky moment occurred, if you want to call it that. James almost ordered Arthur and Robert to stop whatever they were doing and look at a series of pictures taken on the monitor."

Kimberly jumped off the wall. "How did James get in on this? He's in the monitoring room."

"That's it exactly! The main gate is required to let the MRoom know all entries. They called and said Windsor had just arrived. The doctor had just left. Windsor must have seen him driving around the end of the circular drive and chased after him. The pictures showed Windsor talking with the doctor and reaching through the window to ruffle the doctor's hair."

Kimberly put her hand to her mouth. "Collusion?"

"No one had a clue that Windsor and Edse knew one another let alone were intimate. That scene was enough to do some digging. The first step was to analyze the medication Edse left. We weren't surprised to find traces of the poison in the pills."

"So you're saying Windsor and the doctor planned this whole scheme so he..." She thought for a moment... "He thought he would inherit all of this. But wouldn't an autopsy prove otherwise?"

"If you remember, Doctor Edse signed the death certificate. It is pretty much a standard practice in the western world that if the presiding doctor signs a death certificate marking natural causes as the cause of death, then no autopsy would be required. It was obvious that was their plan.

"Aside from that, our biggest threat was an antidote couldn't be found. Robert called a friend of his in the Navy, Dr. Mathews, to come to the estate. Alarmed by what he saw, Dr. Mathews had Martin and me take samples of Robert's skin to a botanist friend at the London Botanical Gardens. Arthur also ran an in depth background check on Edse. The results were quite interesting and the information was passed on to Dr. Brokaw over at the Garden's institute."

Kimberly propped herself against her bike. "I'm getting confused with all the names here. I'm glad you can keep them together. How did a background check on Dr. Edse help?"

The Bishop shifted his position. "It led Dr. Brokaw to quickly find the correct poison. We were amazed to learn how many hundreds of poisons there are. Arthur found Edse never attended school here in the UK nor was he born here. His parents are South African and they were botanists at a South African university. With that information, Dr. Brokaw directed her attention to African plants. Within a few hours, she found a match on the poison and by the end of the next day, we had the antidote. The poison came from a South African plant that has a very long name, but she explained in laymen's terms, it would cause a cardiac seizure. The plant was used to make poison darts and from what Dr. Brokaw said, elephant poachers use it today so the game wardens don't hear the guns."

Martin added. "That wasn't enough; Robert tested his new development on his body. He never guessed a reaction like this could happen."

Arthur reappeared as they got on their bikes. "Have they filled you in with most of the details?"

The Bishop turned his bike around. "It's pretty late. We haven't told her about faking Robert's death." His eyes opened wide and he shook his head. "I don't want to ever go through that again. I'll let you tell her about it. Good night."

Kimberly looked at them and shivered. "That sounded rather scary."

"What happened?" Kimberly got off her bike to walk next to Martin and Arthur.

Martin looked over to Arthur. "Robert improved almost immediately after the first shot was given."

Kimberly smiled. "That's wonderful!"

Arthur shook his head. "Yes it was relief to know Robert would survive, but then we realized we had another problem."

Kimberly stopped walking. "I think I see where you're going with this. You had asked Bishop if he told me about faking uncle's death. I'm assuming you thought Windsor would continue to try, so if he thought he succeeded..."

Arthur grinned. "That's exactly right. Dr. Mathews pointed this out and told Robert that his body had been impaired and needed time to heal. So with Mathew's help, we orchestrated Robert's death to coincide with Windsor's plan. I can tell you this was the hardest thing Robert has ever done. He was tormented more what the event would do to you, than what he'd have to endure physically."

Martin shook his head. "I agree with Bishop. We all went through hell over this."

Kimberly frowned. "What all did you have to do?"

"For Mathews to monitor Robert's heart, we secretly arranged a mattress similar to a sling, with compartment doors under it. These allowed Mathews almost complete access to Robert's body. Plus the fabric we used gave Bishop and Mathews a good view around Robert.

"You see, Kim, we had to stop Robert's heart long enough for Edse to do his thing, and then jump start his heart to revive him."

She gasped. "How awful is that? You had to be scared witless!"

Arthur pointed at Martin. "Bishop and the doctor would give me the amount of time left before he had to restart Robert's heart. Robert's hands were tied downward so that when the jumpstart injection was given, he wouldn't be able to flinch. "

Kimberly's eyes widened. "Yes, but then wouldn't his eyes flash open?"

Martin shook his head. "I still sweat over the thought of that day. As soon as Edse listened for a heartbeat and signaled Robert's death, Arthur was supposed to cover Robert with his sheet. We never dreamed Lucille would carry on as she did."

Arthur continued. "Edse saw you were upset with Lucille's actions, and probably feared you'd leave before he had a chance to ask you to handle the funeral arrangements. When he asked to speak with you, we took that opportunity to break up the bedside crying scene and clear the room. "

Kimberly relaxed a little. "My gosh, that had to be frightening. Here I thought I was showing weakness by leaving the room."

"Do you think she knew Windsor poisoned Uncle Robert?"

Martin slowed his step. "We really don't know. And I guess we never will know."

"Poor man, he should have divorced her."

"And lose custody of you? No way, child."

She looked up at the full moon. *I wish I could share their thinking. Why did Uncle Robert raise me this way? Thirty years loving books.*

Kimberly looked at her watch. "Well, he should have divorced her after I was of legal age. I know it's getting late but I have one last

205

question. Was Uncle Robert really in the casket?"

Arthur smiled a little. "No, he wasn't." And started to walk along the dimly lit path toward the mansion.

Kimberly hesitated—reluctant to break the companionable silence that had fallen on their little group but needing one more answer… "Weren't you concerned that Windsor could have opened the casket in the crypt to get the rings and watch? "

Martin shook his head. "We thought he might pull a stunt like that, so the casket was locked….I think it's noted in the Will that it be closed."

Kimberly nodded. "It was… Wait a minute, and then you had the mortuary involved as well. Because, Gunthie said to me as we were leaving he was surprised the director didn't ask if we wanted a few moments with Robert. Actually, I think he felt bad we weren't asked. In my heart I knew Uncle Robert was alive and I couldn't look at a body."

Martin nodded. "To avoid all those concerns and the possibility that Windsor would show up at the mortuary on his own, Robert decided to buy the place under another name."

She stared at them thinking. "Poor Gunthie…He was so sure Uncle Robert had made arrangements with the one in London. So you did change the wording of the will.

Then…The mortuary director was really another retired navy seal."

Arthur put his watch in his vest pocket and chuckled. "Yes, I did alter the Will and no, that was Doctor Mathews that spoke with you and Gunther…Now it's past *my* bed time."

In her room, Kimberly's answering machine flashed. Lauren asked if she'd call her back that night.

"Hi, sorry it's so late; I hope I didn't wake you."

"No, not at all. Sheila was just telling me about the photo shoot at the company. Sounds wonderful, good PR. Maybe I could come and watch."

Kimberly paused. She couldn't let on this was news to her. "I wish I could be more enthused, but having my picture taken is last on my list of things to do. We can talk about it tomorrow. Have a good night."

31

Lauren's Apartment

Lauren hung up. *She seemed rather cool. I wonder if she thinks Sheila and I've made up.*

"Is everything all right? You look worried?"

Lauren plopped down on the couch. "Not really, I just thought Kim would sound a little more enthusiastic about the photo shoot... She did sound very tired."

Sheila looked at her watch just as a clock started to chime. "Wow, it's getting late. Can't handle the hours like I used to."

She reached into her blazer pocket for an envelope and handed it to Lauren. "The next couple of weeks are going to be pretty hectic. I wonder if you could hold onto this for me."

Lauren looked at the bold writing, *DO NOT OPEN UNLESS NOTIFIED.* "What the heck is this? Are you in trouble?"

Sheila stared at Lauren. The reality of her situation emerged. *I can't get weepy over this. Not now.*

She smiled, finished her drink and chuckled. "No, don't be stupid. The other day I almost was sideswiped by some ass hole. Anyway, I mentioned it at work and one of the guys asked if I had life and accidental death insurance. I realized that all my family is in New Zealand and you're about the only one I'd trust with the key to my security box at the bank, in case of an emergency. So that's all that's about."

Sheila moved slowly to the door. "By the way, I'm really glad for you and Kimberly. You seem to make a good match. Not the opposite poles like you and me." She cleared her throat. *Time to leave. Don't push your luck.*

"Thanks, but I think this is going to take some time. Kimberly is far from worldly. She's led a very sheltered life."

Sheila laughed. "Not like some of us."

Lauren grinned. "I would say so! Best just to let things take their course. This is so new to her I don't want to jeopardize what could be."

Sheila hugged Lauren. "Thanks for keeping my envelope."

"Not to worry. It will be here for you whenever you need it back."

Lauren picked up their wine glasses. *Something is bothering her. Sheila's never been so caring. She even hugged me differently.* She tidied up the kitchen and went to bed.

Windsor goes back to Edse's house

After leaving Sheila's apartment, Windsor was angry that he again let her have the upper hand. He got into his car and beat on the steering wheel. *God, I hate her...she's got to go.* He sat for a moment, his head on the steering wheel.

As he was ready to turn into the Eddie's drive, a black car very slowly stopped in front of the drive, blocking it.

Windsor stopped short. "What the fuck is this?"

Windsor parked his car on the street and started to get out when Alex McGraw approached from the other car.

Windsor scowled at McGraw. "Are you following me? You've got a lot of fuckin nerve."

He tried to strike a blow at McGraw, who gave him a sucker punch to the groin doubling him over. "Windsor, if I were you, I wouldn't try to play with the big boys. You're out of your league. Now let's go in and have a nice conversation with your partner, Dr. Edse."

Windsor held his side. "How do you know about him?"

McGraw pushed Windsor toward the house. "Oh, you'll be surprised just how much I do know. Now I think your lover is waiting for us."

Windsor straightened his back and pulled his arm away. "Just fuck off!" He shook his head. "What do you mean, he's waiting?"

Alex quite irritated. "Oh, I've had a little chat with your Eddie and he's quite interested to know how we know each other."

The door opened quickly as Windsor tried his key.

The doctor stood in his doorway. "Would you like to explain who the fuck this person is... Windsor! I don't exactly appreciate being awakened in the middle of the night."

McGraw shook his head. *These damn queens.* He pushed Windsor past the doctor. "Now is not the time for you to have a hissy fit!"

The three went into a solarium off the main hall, filled with exotic plants and several bird cages with covers on.

Windsor sat in the chair nearest to the bar and said nothing.

Doctor Edse poured a cup of tea he had made while waiting for their arrival.

He offered a cup to Alex and motioned with his hand. "You'll have to excuse me, but at this hour of the morning, it is rather difficult to be pleasant...Mr.?"

Alex took the cup. "Alex McGraw."

Eddie looked over at Windsor who sat tightlipped. "And, Mr. McGraw you're here to...?"

Alex chuckled. "Obviously, you don't know jack about what your lover boy has been up to. He hired me to get rid of several people. I'm here to collect on one of them."

"And, how much does he owe you?"

Alex motioned to Windsor. "Hey, Mr. Big Shot, tell the man, what you're paying for each hit."

Windsor continued staring at the floor. *If I had a gun I would shoot this man in the face.*

Alex laughed heartily. "Your pathetic friend here owes me five thousand pounds. Half down and the other half at completion. Well, his mother is completed...So where's my money?"

The doctor stared at Windsor. "When were you going to tell me about this?" Eddie got up to fill his cup. "Windsor, pay the man. Now!"

Knowing he couldn't physically subdue Alex, Windsor bit his lip and clenched his fists.

He thrust the money at Alex. "There! You crooked fuckin cop."

The doctor choked on his tea. "You're a cop?"

Eddie put his cup down, crossed his legs, folded his hands in his lap and glared at Alex. "Mr. McGraw, you've been paid. Now I think it's time for you to leave... I hope you realize there won't be any more hits."

Windsor jumped up and wiped some blood off his mouth. "No! Eddie. I want what is mine! He agreed to do this. All he cares about is the money."

Alex put his money away and stood up. "That is a wise decision under the circumstances."

Edse didn't move and ignored Windsor's rambling. "Circumstances? When you called, you said your help would be needed to complete our mission?" Eddie smirked at Alex. "Just what is our mission?"

Alex closed his eyes with his head down. *This is getting all too complicated. These queens are pissing me off. Windsor is right. I do want the money.* "You know, my better sense tells me to leave now, but before I go, let me show you something and ask you a few questions. Then if you don't get my drift, we'll part company and you're on your own." He grinned. "Fair enough?"

The doctor nodded and motioned for Alex to sit. "Tell me, Inspector McGraw, what made you become a bad cop?"

Alex glared at Eddie. "I believe there's a cliché of not mixing business with pleasure. For your information, Doctor Edse, I'm an excellent policeman for Scotland Yard which is my business, and I take great pleasure, for money of course, in killing people, especially those that become a nuisance." He continued to stare as he gave his cup to be filled.

"Now before we get all the cards on the table, be aware that Windsor is considered to be a person of interest, and because you've travelled together to Austria frequently, you've been added to the list."

Windsor sneered. "I suppose I'm to feel threatened."

Alex cocked his head with a frown and glanced at the doctor. "I'm going to overlook that remark. I want to make something very clear to you. Industrial espionage is as serious a crime as murder, and it is international. Therefore, once you're on a list, you haven't anywhere to run. You're in Windsor's terms... *fucked up.* So, yes, Mr. Braun, I'd be very concerned. According to my sources at Interpol, some of Dr. Braun's formulas have showed up on the open market."

Alex frowned and rubbed his chin. "What would an obvious answer be to the obvious question of who would have access and who would benefit?"

Windsor went to the bar. "Just because I'm related to the fuckin bastard, that makes me the person of interest? What other bullshit do you have for us to swallow?"

Alex shook his head and opened his brief case. He tossed some pictures on the coffee table. "Will this help?" Then he pulled out copies of an Interpol profile and tossed it too.

Windsor chugged down two shots. The doctor glared at him as he handed him pictures of him being arrested at the airport for drunkenness.

Windsor threw the pictures back. "So, this proves I stole formulas!"

The doctor read the profile. "No, you ass." He waved it at him. "For someone who has never had a job, expelled from six schools for student endangerment?" Eddie sent a chilling glare at Windsor.

"Very wealthy, travels biweekly to Austria, arrested five times for disorderly conduct, and... and is related to the man would tweak some interest...and with all of this, my name has been added to this Person of Interest List."

The doctor stared off. *There's got to be a solution. We're so close to making a fortune. Windsor, why do you have to be such a fool?* Eddie shut his eyes. *I can't give him up yet.*

Windsor watched the doctor's face shift from anger to concern and slumped into a chair.

Eddie looked back at Alex. "Now, I suppose, this is when you give us our options?"

Alex nodded. *The doctor is a smart man. Windsor is such a waste but...needed.* "You do have an option, but first, have either of you seen this brass medallion?" Alex pulled it out of his brief case and handed it to Windsor.

Windsor handled it. He saw the coat of arms on the one side. "Where did you get this?"

Windsor handed it to the doctor. "I know I've seen this somewhere."

Alex's eyes enlarged. "The day I put your mother down, the chauffeur showed up unexpectedly. I had no other choice but to kill him. This meant a change of plan."

Windsor grinned. "The paper showed the car in the ravine and said two bodies were found. I wondered if you had a problem. I owe you more money."

Alex and the doctor raised their brows. "What? Why?"

"I don't know what was more disgusting, my mother slurring her words and falling all over that kid or his obnoxious remarks to me. I had a feeling he was trying to come on to me, but I wasn't going to have anything to do with him. I'm glad he's dead."

Alex studied the doctor. *I'll bet Eddie is thinking that Windsor made a pass at that chauffeur and may have gotten a kick in the ass.*

Windsor straightened his back. "His dad was a fuckin bastard too. He tried to lure me into a garden shed once. We tested the poi…"

"Windsor! That's enough!"

"This medallion was in his pocket. I tried to get him to tell me what it is, but, the poison I injected into his neck tortured him to death."

Alex continued. "I ran some tests and it's real gold with a strong magnet in the center. This leads me to think it's a key of some sort."

The doctor rolled it across the coffee table toward Alex.

Windsor watched it roll and slapped his knees. "I remember one time when I was a kid that I got into some big trouble with Robert and Arthur. That's when I saw this medallion. It rolled…"

"What do you mean it rolled, by itself?"

"No, I was playing in the library with Robert's first dog, Duchess. I found one just like this piece on the desk. I held it next to my chest like an award. When Arthur and Robert came in, Robert yelled at me for touching his stuff. He frightened me so the medallion dropped out of my hand and rolled on the floor. It came to a stop standing on its side in front of the book case."

Windsor shut his eyes to recapture the scene. "I remember Robert and Arthur making a dash for that medallion like it was a bomb or something."

Windsor opened his eyes and stared at Alex. "Something happened they didn't want me to see. I can't remember. I know I was banned from the room forever."

"Could the wall have opened?"

"I don't know. Maybe. The two of them stood in front of the medallion and Robert kept yelling at me to get the fuck out of the room and never come back into it. He was so angry. I just ran like crazy. Mother and I took a trip soon after that."

Alex put the medallion into his pocket. "I want to show you again this K code."

He handed each a copy. Windsor put it on the table. "I told you at that cemetery that I've never seen this."

The doctor studied the sheet. "Some of these letters and numbers are on the two discs that Sheila gave us."

Alex frowned. "Sheila? You've got someone else working with you?"

While Eddie got the discs, Windsor explained the relationship he'd arranged between Robert's assistant Lauren Woodgrieves and Sheila Jones. "After a few months, Sheila moved in with Lauren. The idea came to me when I was having lunch with Sheila, who was moaning about her finances. I just tossed out the idea to her. As far as she knew, she was getting me copies of plastic car parts. Things were going along great until Kimberly came into the picture... I was at Sheila's tonight because I was pissed that she missed a drop off."

"Did she have anything?"

"No, she just cried about them breaking up but did say she had been given an assignment to do a photo shoot on Kimberly at the company."

Eddie came back with the two discs and put them on the table. Alex looked at the markings on each and nodded his head. "These markings are from Braun's K Code."

Alex rubbed his hands together. "You're looking at a billion dollars!"

Windsor put his glass down. "Are you fuckin with me?"

"No, I'm dead serious. Robert must have developed something top secret to use this code. These discs are useless, unless we have the translator. The translator will interpret the code, opening the formulas, and I'll bet my soul it is in a vault at that estate."

Eddie sat on the edge of his chair. "Why do you think that?"

Alex looked sternly at them. "Have you noticed the security system there? It's probably better than the Tower of London where the royal jewels are guarded. When my partner and I were there on an inquiry, we were shown the security system. Every inch of the hundred twenty five acres is covered."

Alex didn't miss the quick look Eddie and Windsor gave one another. *Seems there have been some indiscretions like a quickie in one of the back halls.* "Miss Braun told us during the day the monitoring was only of outside entrances."

Alex fell back in his chair holding one of the discs. "I wonder if this project is finished or did it die with him?"

Windsor took the disc from Alex. "According to Sheila, there are more like this. She brought me several her last drop and we got into quite an argument over the fact they couldn't be opened. That's when she told me Lauren had dumped her and she raised her price for any future drops."

Alex folded his hands. "I'm sure you graciously accepted her demands."

Eddie glanced at Windsor. *McGraw is agitating Windsor on purpose.* "Okay, so Windsor screwed up. We all do at some time. We'll get her back."

Alex nodded his head and stared at Windsor.

"Why are you staring at me?"

"I was staring at you, because…you've unknowingly uncovered a potential mega fortune to be made. The problem is, do I want to get involved? I can say with a hundred percent accuracy, your temper and your alcoholic dependency will get you killed or caught, and with those odds, I think I'll pass."

Alex leaned forward to gather his stuff into his brief case. *I'll bet before I get to the front door the doctor will want my help.* "Thank you for the tea. I'll report to the Yard that I came to inform you of your mother's passing."

Eddie walked Alex to the door. "Inspector, if I could guarantee Windsor's cooperation, would you reconsider joining forces with us?"

Alex stood in the doorway and shook his head. "This is a chance of a lifetime. That translator is worth more than the discs.*" I had it once before until one of Braunstein's teammates caught me in Korea. Am I getting another chance to have it or to get caught again?*

He stared at Eddie. "I don't know if you really understand the scope of what you're getting into. This will be a life or death situation. It will require a lot of planning and many hours of training and practice. Frankly, I don't know that there's enough time to do all of this. Plus,..."

Windsor, carrying his glass, stalked in and blurted. "What is so fuckin worrisome? We got rid of the bastard. Why should you worry about time?"

Alex shook his head. *His brain is no bigger than his...not even worth saying.* "I'm sorry, Eddie. It's just too risky."

Alex gritted his teeth. "You probably have three weeks max to get that translator before the Americans will be asking your cousin for all of her uncle's stuff related to the code."

He smirked at Windsor. "I'm sure you know all that."

Windsor went back to the solarium. "Just fuck off, McGraw."

Eddie stood in front of the door. "Wait! Do you think it could be pulled off?"

Alex stopped. "My greatest concern is disarming the security system. That's the big question. How can we get inside? It's a fort!"

Walking toward the gate, Eddie took hold of Alex's arm. "McGraw, wait a minute. Didn't Windsor tell us earlier that Sheila is doing a photo shoot on Kim? Why couldn't she do one at the estate?"

Alex opened the gate at the hedge and leaned on it. "You know, this Sheila just might provide the cover we need."

He handed Eddie his card. "This is my private business card. You've given me some ideas I need to check out. Call me tonight after six and Eddie … make sure you call from a pay phone away from the house."

Alex started to leave and turned. "One other point. If I need to talk to you, I'll ring your phone twice. Then you'll have to go to the call box at the corner and call this number."

Edse glowered. "Is my phone being tapped?"

"I'll find out today. Is this the only number you have?"

The doctor gave Alex a business card. "This number Sheila uses to call Windsor. It's under an assumed name. I don't think they can trace it."

33

Early morning at Ross's house

About six a.m., Inspector Ross stood at his dresser fumbling with his tie in front of the mirror. His fingers refused to cooperate as his mind jumped from the Braun case to Bobby to Alex to Bobby and... He had to focus!

Finally dressed, he rinsed out his cup in the kitchen sink. *Dennis, you know this is total nonsense to have a crush...* He shook his head, grabbed his brief case ready to leave. When he opened the door, Bobbie sat in her car out at the front gate, not more than twenty steps away. He was so startled seeing her there he didn't know what to say.

Her smile only increased his loss of concentration. "Ah, you did say six fifteen, right?"

I forget why she's driving today. That's right, the Braun estate. Save me backtracking. He looked at his pocket watch. "It's six sixteen."

She laughed. "Sorry boss, I'll do better....Well, are you going to get in?"

Embarrassed, Ross got in the car. "Did you have trouble with the traffic? It can get crazy around here. I think everyone who works in London lives in this burg."

I wonder why he isn't looking at me. He's just staring out the front. Something's going on. "Dennis, are you feeling all right? You look like you're ready to burst."

Ross looked around and saw a little dirt path ahead. "Could you pull in over there?"

She stopped the car and frowned at him. "What's the matter, Dennis? Have I done something wrong?"

He got out of the car and lit his pipe. Without looking at her, he suddenly felt warm almost hot in his face. "Bobbie... I just can't work this way...because you're..."

Bobbie smiled and walked around the car to stand next to him. "Because..."

Ross puffed on his pipe looking off at the landscape. *There's no way she could be interested in me.* He looked down at her tenderly. "Because..."

Bobbie saw love in his eyes and felt his struggle. She put her arms around his neck. "Because...you want to tell me how much you like me and feel you can't?"

He smiled. "I just can't imagine you'd be interested in an old geezer like..."

Bobbie's eyes sparkled with joy. "You mean a handsome, older man whom I've been attracted to since the first day we met....Now, kiss me before I make a fool of myself."

After a few moments, they collected their emotions and continued to the Braun estate.

Arthur met them at the front door. "Inspector Ross, I'm sorry but Miss Kimberly is at the company today. You can see her there if you like, or I can call her for you."

"We appreciate that but we're actually here to see you."

Arthur drew in a breath and frowned. "Me, why?"

Ross handed him the Admiral's card. "Admiral Benjamin asked me to give this to you. He said you'd know what to do." *Whatever is he thinking? I've never seen anyone who shows no attitude, emotion, nothing.*

Arthur put the card in his vest pocket. "The Admiral is a good friend of the Brauns. I'm sure he's concerned about Kimberly."

Arthur stepped back to close the door. "I'll tell Miss Kimberly that you called in."

Ross handed Arthur his card. He hesitated. "One other item… If, ah… Inspector McGraw comes out here… or should call…would you call me? and right away."

Arthur nodded. "Sounds like an interesting request. Yes, I can do that."

Ross, all of six foot three, still had to look up at Arthur. He shrugged his shoulders. "Trust has to begin somewhere, and we feel you need to know he could come out here, and we need to know if he does."

Walking back to the car, Bobbie grimaced at Ross. "Do I dare ask what that was all about or is this on a need to know thing?"

Ross opened his door and chuckled. "Your perception is so quick, I doubt if I'll be telling you anything new."

The drive to Scotland Yard gave Ross time to bring Bobbie up to speed and answer her questions.

"So your giving Arthur the Admiral's card is a sign of some sort."

"According to the Admiral, there's a lot of history between Braun and his team. I've concluded that being a navy seal is a commitment to one another never to be broken. Anyway, this code that Braun developed is only associated with his discoveries. The Admiral didn't say, but I think his card is alerting the team to danger."

Ross stared out the window. *If we only knew what all this is about, we could have a more definite plan. All we can do…*

Bobbie glanced over. "I see that look in your eyes. What's brewing?"

Ross caught that special look from her. "Just drive…"

34

Alex makes a decision

A s Alex got into his car, he made a visual sweep of the area. It had just gone four in the morning. He was pretty keyed up. *That car wasn't here when I arrived. Looks like someone sitting in it.* He stood for a moment looking at the car parked across the street. The car started and drove past him. *Maybe he just got in the car, but for the hell of it I'll run that license number through registration.* Before he got into his car, he scribbled down the number. Soon Alex came up behind the car at a traffic light. The car made a left hand turn. *Can't see his face real good, I don't recognize him. Anyway, why would I be followed? More likely Windsor or Edse. That might be a good thing. There's the tube station. Think I'll leave my car and ride into work.*

He had time to make some calls before the train arrived. From the call box he could watch the trains. "Charlie...I know, it's...early, but you'll be wide awake when you hear this. I'm almost sure the K code and translator have surfaced...we are talking over a billion. This time it won't get away. Money is no object. Our benefactor is Braunstein's so called son. I'll explain that later. By the way, he changed his name to Braun after he left the navy, so it's Robert Braun, who lived outside of Burlington, Berkshire County. I need as much information you can

222

get on his family, staff, and property. Don't overlook one item no matter what it is."

He hung up as his train stopped at the platform. *No one is more thorough than Charlie. My plan for him to work at Interpol has paid off more times than I can count. His information will either make or break the deal with Edse and Windsor.*

The train arrived around six in the morning at the London station. He drank some coffee waiting for a call box to become available.

He started to dial the doctor. *I can't take a chance. I have to find out.* He called the Yard. "This is Alex McGraw, let me have security. Tony, Alex. I know we have a tap on Windsor Braun, but has one been issued for Edward Edse? I'll be in to sign the paper for it and will talk to the Chief...Okay, thanks."

He called the Doctor. "I just checked, Windsor's line is tapped and yours will be by the end of the day. My sources tell me it will cost fifty thousand pounds or more just to conduct a search on Braun, especially that property and that security system."

The doctor was silent. Alex chuckled. "Are you still there?"

Eddie cleared his throat. "My God, that's a lot with no guarantees?"

"No guarantees. People have to be paid off to talk. We'll never get through to any of the staff there, but I'm sure the locals have seen a lot over the years. We need any and all information about that place. There's no point forming a plan if the security system can't be disarmed or destroyed. Right now the question is, are you willing to pay this?"

"That won't be a problem. We can handle that. Should I still call tonight? Will do."

Thirty minutes later, Alex got to his office. He sat at his desk for some time looking at Lucille Braun's file stamped with bold letters ACCIDENTAL DEATH. *Why is this bothering me so? I should be happy the file went through. It's because Ross is as thorough as me. I'd have had that courier fired. I can't open a can of worms. Not now.*

He opened the file, signed it, and took it out to his secretary who had just come in. "Mrs. Logan, could you send this for processing?"

He handed her the file. He paused at the door. "By the way, can we access the license registration of our vehicles? I saw a car in the garage with the plate hanging. Thought I'd give the owner a head's up."

Mrs. Logan smiled as she typed a few words. "You can access the registration either by name or plate number. Do you want me to check it out for you?"

"No, you've got enough to do. Give me the wording and I can do it."

In a few minutes he had exactly what he wanted on the screen. He leaned back studying a cross reference of one of the new agents and his own vehicle. *It would make sense to use a new agent that I wouldn't recognize to follow me, but why would they follow Windsor? Something doesn't smell right. Dennis!*

He slipped by his secretary's desk. "I'll be back in a few minutes."

He rushed over to his partner's office hoping to find him in. Ross was just hanging up his coat when Alex knocked.

Dennis smiled. "I was going to light my pipe and give you a call."

Alex saw a beam of happiness in his colleague's face which stopped him cold. "Wow, it certainly has been awhile since I've seen that kind of smile. I can tell you're a man in love."

Just as he got the words out, Bobbie came in, saw Alex, and did a one eighty.... "Talk with you later."

Alex laughed heartily. "How many guesses do I get?"

For the first time since his wife's death, Dennis felt the closeness he once had with his friend. "You're right and I'm just as surprised... I wanted you and Jane to be the first to know. The four of us could have dinner out so Jane could meet Bobbie."

Dennis lit his pipe and sat at his desk. Alex sat across from him. "That would be great, but Jane had to go to Ireland to help her sister, who isn't very well. I've no idea when she'll be back, but I'll pass the good news to her."

Dennis grinned. "That's a shame. I hope it's not too serious... I'm sorry. You've come to ask me something. What can I do for you?"

"I saw you'd called my office. Also, I wanted you to know that I got the Lucille Braun file back stamped Case Closed, Accidental Death. Since Windsor Braun hadn't been notified, I did some checking and found that he travels a lot with Edward Edse. I went to Edse's place last night and found Windsor. I informed him of the accident and asked him a few questions about his mother. The man is definitely off the charts. He showed zero emotion and wasn't at all surprised about the chauffeur. He made some comment his mother paid the guy to be her escort."

Alex took his inhaler out for a shot. Dennis jumped in his seat. "I'm terribly sorry, I forgot about your allergy."

Dennis put his pipe out and laid it next to Alex's inhaler.

Alex fastened his eyes on Dennis. *He's looking at the end of my inhaler. That's right, when we put the chauffeur's body in the car; he came to and tried to fight me... the end piece must have broken off ... The plastic in the evidence bag! Then...Could he be suspecting, but why? Over the plastic? He knows something that I don't!* He scratched his arm and took up his inhaler. "When I left, I saw you had an agent watching the place."

Ross dropped his head. "The Chief called a meeting yesterday. I called your office. Mrs. Logan told me you were gone for the day. A lab report on the car indicated a chance of foul play on the wheel tie rods. The Chief thought it enough to watch him for a while, and do some checking. The amount of money and properties this guy will be inheriting is staggering and the Chief thinks maybe this Windsor fellow didn't want to wait for his mother to die of old age."

Alex grinned a little, tilting his head. *That makes sense.* "So, the case isn't closed? What do I do with the file I just received?"

Dennis leaned forward. "Believe me, I was surprised, but O'Doul didn't like the shade of gray in that lab report, even though everything else checked out ... Seems he met the son and the mother at an arraignment over one of the arrests at Heathrow, and it wasn't very pleasant."

Dennis chuckled. "Chief said he'd like to screw the bastard, the way he talked to his mother and his attorney."

Alex laughed. "That's a first for him!"

He got up. "So we're watching Windsor as a formality and I can go on with my other work."

Dennis walked with him to the outer office. "So it appears."

Alex smiled and patted him on the shoulder. "Got to go. Take good care of that photographer. She's a keeper."

Alex's office

A lex was in his office when his secretary buzzed him. "Inspector, you've a call on line one and the man won't give his name. He says it is very important."

Frowning, Alex thanked her and pressed line one. "Inspector McGraw here."

"Alex, it's…"

Alex's eyes flashed wide. "The usual spot." He hung up. *Son of a bitch, I hope a telephone scanning wasn't going on. I really didn't think Charlie would call here. Damn, I've got to warn him.* Alex grabbed his coat, brief case and left the office. "Mrs. Logan, I'll be gone until after lunch. I'll call you later."

When the elevator opened at the garage level, Alex almost bumped into Dennis and Bobbie.

"Shit, son of a bitch."

Dennis laughed. "I hope that wasn't our greeting."

Startled, Alex glanced up and shrugged his shoulders. "No, no. I'm sorry. It just dawned on me I'd taken the tube in to work because my car broke down last night. I just remembered."

"Here, take my car. I won't need it."

Dennis tossed his keys to Alex.

"I won't be long, thanks," and he scooted.

Dennis and Bobbie got on the elevator. *He's in an awful big rush. I hope the agent who's tailing him isn't sitting watching his car. I better check in with the Chief.*

Alex adjusted the seat and mirrors and then took off. *I need to talk to Dennis. It's time he gets another car...this is slower than a mule. That photographer has a car almost like mine. This is God awful...*

Alex still made it to his rendezvous point within twenty minutes. Alex honked several times at Charlie, who saw a different car and started to walk away from the grave site.

Charlie walked over to the car. "Where'd you ever get this pile of junk? Are you in disguise?"

Alex got out of the car. "Long story, not important. Do you have information already? I about died hearing your voice. Sorry to cut you off, but that device you gave me had indicated security was scanning the lines."

Charlie chuckled. "Don't worry, they won't be able to trace anything. For the amount of money you say we're going to make, I figured you needed this stuff as quick as we could find it."

"You're the best, Charlie." Alex read through some of the pages and looked over at his friend. "That security system is vulnerable. Unless there's a generator, they haven't a backup. I didn't see one when Ross and I were there. We drove all over the place." *This looks like we have an opportunity.*

Alex smiled handing Charlie two envelopes. "I'm sure Peter helped you get all this great information. We might have a last hurrah in our grasp. Don't take any vacation time; we may get that translator after all."

They shook hands. "Oh, I've got a little bonus for you. No charge, but, one of our informants over at the Yard told me this morning that several of the Yard pictures show a Yankee Admiral visiting frequently. I had him check the register. You're going to crap when you hear this..."

Alex stared at his friend. "Are you fuckin serious?"

Charlie laughed and shook his head. "When I heard him tell me it was Admiral Benjamin, it was like yesterday back in Korea. I don't know which one you hated the most, Braunstein or Benjamin. It seems he's a good friend of the Chief Inspector, but I'm wondering in light of Braunstein's death if there's a connection. What do you think?"

Alex reached into his brief case for the cash Windsor had given him. He handed it to Charlie.

Charlie backed off raising his hands. "No, I knew this would make your day. It's my treat. We're with you on this all the way."

Alex beamed with excitement. "Oh, most definitely, there's got to be a connection. The Admiral will contact the Braun estate and ask if he can have not only the translator for the code but also any formulas that are protected by the code."

"Let me get a plan together and then we'll meet to fine tune it. Do you still have all your outlets for equipment?"

Charlie smiled. "I can get almost anything now."

Alex patted Charlie on the shoulder. "I'll call you later. This'll have to be planned to the last minute..."

They walked back to their cars. Alex bent down and burst into laughter making Charlie jump to a dead stop. "My God, are you all right?"

"Yes! For some reason I just remembered what you said to me before... You asked if I was in disguise and that has given me an incredible idea....I've to check this out. I'll talk to you later..."

Alex heard a bell chime in the distance. He looked at his watch. *Time flies when you need more of it. Wait a minute, Charlie.* He ran back to Charlie's car.

He motioned for him to roll down his window. "Charlie, do you still have surveillance camera stuff?"

Charlie frowned. "Do birds fly? Of course I do—day or night."

Alex leaned back on the car and used his inhaler. "That's good...I need you to make a detailed film and voice track by the hour, if you can of the Admiral's activities. I'm looking for any mannerisms -- how he walks, gestures, speaks. Can you do that? Thing is I need it ASAP."

Charlie gave him thumbs up and rolled up the window.

Alex followed Charlie out of the cemetery. *I need to call Edse before I go back. There's a call box.*

"Eddie, it's almost nine o'clock. Can you arrange a meeting with Sheila tonight? I've just gotten some very positive information and your idea for a photo shoot at the estate will be the ticket. Don't meet with her anywhere you'll be seen. You'll need to entice her with money and a lot of it. Windsor may have to swallow his pride and apologize. Whatever it takes, you've got to get her on board for a photo shoot at the estate."

"I've got a piece of property in Burlington, which is between where each of us lives. Not too much is around it. I think everything is empty. I quit renting it out--- too much of a hassle. We could meet her there."

"That'll work. When you're done, call this number from the tube station in Burlington. I'll let you know what train to take and which stop. Oh, and Eddie? Windsor better be sober or the deal's off."

Alex drove back to the Yard. *The doors are starting to open.*

The Photo Shoot at R & K

Eight o'clock sharp the door opened at R & K Plastics, and Kimberly appeared at the front counter to sign in.

"You just hang the chain and badge around your neck, Miss Braun. This gets left here when you sign out. Remember your thumb is your key to open any room in the building."

Kimberly smiled and nodded. "So far so good. Thank you!"

She entered her new office alone. As she swiped her thumb on the screen by the door, the door opened enough for her to push on it. *Even though I know he's alive this still is so strange.* As she looked for a directory, there was a knock on the door.

"Come in...come in" She opened the door and beamed to see Lauren. "Didn't you hear me?"

Lauren chuckled. "I thought I better come over and give you a quick rundown of all the gadgets and whatnots."

She breezed by Kimberly and took on the role of a hotel concierge. "The office door is explosion proof, fire proof, and sound proof. So you can press this first button to unlock the door....or..."

Lauren slid a panel on the desk and an array of buttons appeared. "Now if you sit in the boss's chair, I'll show you what each button does."

Kimberly's grin disappeared. "I think I'll pass on that for now."

Lauren saw anguish in Kimberly's eyes. She put her arms around her. "Kim, don't do this to yourself. Your uncle wouldn't have left this for you had he thought you couldn't handle it."

Kimberly looked down at Lauren. "You're still having to save me." *Her smile just lights up the room and chases all the darkness out.*

Lauren blushed, and continued to show her the popup monitor. "This isn't a TV. If someone knocks on your door, you can see who it is by pressing this button."

Kimberly leaned forward and frowned. *Don't these look familiar?* She pressed a button on the side of the screen and another panel opened with more buttons to press. She pressed the top button and they were watching two of the chemists in the lab, another tap and they were watching the activity in the library. *Don't think I should have done that.*

Lauren gasped. "So much for privacy. Wow!"

Kimberly went back to the original screen. "That's all there is on the monitor." *I'm sure this whole place is on that screen. This is ridiculous. She'll feel he didn't trust her.*

Almost a half hour had passed when Lauren showed her the last button in the panel. "Interesting isn't it?"

Kimberly chuckled. "Or sheer laziness...I guess I still like opening and closing a window."

Lauren looked at her watch. "I better get to work; I've got a test scheduled. Gee, I almost forgot the most important item, the bathroom."

Kimberly giggled. "I found it the other day."

"Don't forget Sheila will be here today around ten. Oh, are you still wanting to interview for a secretary? Uncle Charles asked if they should send you someone from the main office, or do you want to stick with the people from the seal team?"

Kimberly nodded. "The seal team will be fine...How are the tests coming? Have you found anymore add-ons?"

"No, it seems it was just those two. Maybe I did miscount...We are making progress. You'll have to come and see."

Lauren opened the door. "Maybe lunch later?"

She didn't wait for an answer, just waved and left.

༄༅

About ten o'clock Sheila arrived. She was given a security badge allowing her full run of the facility, and a grand tour of all the key areas before she met with Kimberly.

During the morning hours, Kimberly had interviewed two men and a woman to be her secretary.

When Sheila arrived, Kimberly was standing at the conference table. "What a way to start a day, not knowing which one to pick."

Kimberly studied the pictures and resumes. "I like all three. What do you think? They're more than qualified."

Sheila first snapped some pictures of the scene. "Well..." She hesitated with a cagey smile. "I guess I would want to enjoy the scenery each day, so I would pick the chick...but that's just me...I guess."

Her camera clicked away catching Kimberly's reaction.

With her hand on her hip and the other waving the picture at Sheila, "You mean to say, you would hire someone on looks only!"

"As rich as you are, I doubt very much if a good looking nerd would be sent for an interview.... Gosh, look at you! Are you a dumb blond?...Wow, that was a great shot!"

Sheila teased Kimberly and got some candid shots as a result of her prodding.

She busied herself taking pictures of the whole office, while Kimberly confirmed her choice of secretary.

"Yes, Marion Atwell will do fine. She can start this afternoon." She leaned forward and saw Sheila's smile of approval.

"It's almost lunch time. I'll call Lauren and have her meet us in the cafeteria."

Sheila nodded as she took photos of the gorgeous, huge bathroom. *Cafeteria, I know that place very well.*

"Ready?"

The phone rang. "I better answer it... No secretary yet."

Kimberly picked up the receiver on the third ring. "Yes, she is."

She turned and motioned to Sheila. "It's for you."

Sheila frowned and took the phone. "Yes, what time? Where?"

She wrote something on the note pad and put it in her pocket."

She hung up the phone in total disgust. Under her breath she muttered, "That fuckin prick."

Kimberly's eyes flashed. "Did you just say what I think you said?"

Sheila grinned, gritting her teeth. "Sorry, but there are times when it's impossible to make a photo look good, especially when the subject is uglier than sin." She put her camera strap around her neck. "You should see the before and after. I'll meet him tonight and try to explain to him." *Windsor sure has balls calling here. I hope Arthur...oh that's right!*

She smiled. "Well, I hope you got that."

Kimberly glanced at her abruptly. "Got what?"

"Nothing, I was just talking to myself. I do it a lot." Sheila nodded as she passed by Kimberly holding the door.

Lauren had a test set up for them in the main lab, the next floor down.

Sheila told them to act natural. "Pretend I'm not here."

After ten minutes of constant clicking, Kimberly frowned at Sheila. "Has anyone ever told you how annoying your clicking is?"

Sheila nodded, and continued until Kimberly motioned to Lauren. "It's lunch time."

She sternly stared at Sheila. "That means no more pictures until tomorrow. We are done for today. I'm leaving after lunch for a meeting, and you can't come."

Sheila chuckled and looked at Lauren. "That tough look doesn't work, does it? She's too good looking."

After lunch, Sheila signed out and turned in her badge when Arthur appeared and she followed him to the elevator. "We need to brief you about this meeting."

She went into the lab and took a seat at the table. She looked to see if the older man sat in the back of the room, and was disappointed he wasn't there. *I'm sure he's the one in the wheel chair. I know he talked to me. He was nice.*

Arthur and the Bishop came in and sat with her.

"Where's the man in the wheel chair? Is he okay?"

Arthur grinned. "Yes, he's fine. He couldn't make it today."

Sheila frowned. "That's too bad because I wanted to tell him something."

"We can tell him for you."

She thought for a moment. *I can't believe he's not here.* "No, this is a conversation I need to have with him because I think I've figured out who he is."

Out of nowhere, a voice said, "Oh, and who am I, Miss Jones?"

She smiled even though his voice made her jump. "I was right. You're the invisible person. So... that makes you Mr. Braun. I'm right, aren't I?"

She looked at Arthur and the Bishop who both nodded.

"Miss Jones, the address you were given for this meeting tonight, have you ever been there?"

Sheila's head turned to follow the voice and she smiled. "No, sir, I'll have to find it on a street map first."

Arthur frowned. "Why are you smiling?"

Sheila frowned back at him. "I don't hear the wheels on the chair and unless you got him a better chair, I would guess he's walking because... his voice is almost by the door. So, isn't that good?"

The men nodded and smiled. "Miss Jones, you're quite observant and yes, I'm walking now and very much on the mend...We do have a satellite view of the terrain and a large map of the area. Arthur, put it up on the screen."

A large screen appeared on the back wall. Arthur took a pointer. "Sheila, as you can see this is a dead-end street. We have no lead time to get in place any real protective measures for you. We're going to see if we can get a mobile unit on the next street over."

Arthur pointed to the picture from the satellite. "There is, in this area, a patch of woods where we can have a few of our seals listen and watch over you. We're hoping we won't have to tip our hand."

Sheila's eyes flashed. "Are you saying I could be in danger with Windsor?"

The Bishop leaned back in his chair and looked toward the door. "Robert, she can handle Windsor, physically. I've taught her some good moves and she shoots a gun well too."

Sheila sat up straight and smiled.

"It's not Windsor I'm worried about. This meeting idea is not Windsor's. The location is not at all Windsor. It doesn't display the rich and flashy. He's joined up with someone else. All the more reason for her to meet him or whoever else is with him. I have to leave now. Arthur, give her the ear rings and show her a picture of Edse. You've got a good head on you, young lady. You won't be alone."

The door opened. "Miss Jones, you realize all of our lives are at risk now that you know that I'm alive. That includes you as well." And then the door closed.

Arthur handed her a box. She put the earrings on. Arthur turned on a monitor. "Okay, turn slowly and watch the screen."

"Wow, you'll be able to see everything I do. Arthur, now's your chance to smile while I'm filming you!"

The Bishop laughed. "That'll never happen."

Arthur cleared his throat. "Quit the clowning, you two. Those earrings may not work at all if the mobile unit can't get close enough. We didn't have time to link with a satellite."

She leaned back in her chair. "You have a satellite?"

"No, we can borrow one. Anyway, Robert wants you to get to the address fifteen or twenty minutes early so we can check out the video and audio."

The Bishop opened the door. "Come on, Missy, I'll walk you to your car."

"Bishop, I think I'm starting to get a picture here about…"

The Bishop opened her car door. He smiled and shook his head. "Sheila, there's too much for you to understand and to even try to explain this whole business would take months. Your main concern is to focus on the task at hand. Forget trying to uncover secrets. It will only lead to bloodshed."

She got into the car. "Bishop, I hope you know I wouldn't ever do that."

He closed the door. "Then keep focused and believe that Robert Braun is dead."

He gave her thumbs up and smiled. "Talk to you later."

Kimberly's problem

After lunch Kimberly returned to her office. She needed to freshen up and get her questions together for the afternoon meeting at the main office. *I felt awkward watching Sheila and Lauren. They're both so gregarious and I'm not. I don't fit into this scene.*

She stood at her desk looking at what Lauren called gadgets. *These aren't toys, these are defenses. What is Uncle Robert so afraid of? I can't live this way and expect to share a life with someone.*

Kimberly picked up the phone and called the security office. "I'll be leaving for the day. Before I come in tomorrow, I'd like my monitor to show only the halls and shut down everything else. Thank you."

Then she called the main office in London. "Gunthie, I've got so much on my plate here, I think I'll come over tomorrow after lunch."

"We do have two new clients to meet with. That might be good for you to sit in on the negotiations. We have one in the morning and one in the afternoon. Either one or both is fine…Have you had a chance to talk with Lauren?"

"I can be there by one thirty… Please don't worry about us. We're doing just fine." *I knew that was coming and that's why I don't want to go over there. Relationships are too complicated.*

A knock at a door broke the trance. The secretary's office door opened. "Good afternoon, Miss Braun. I just wanted to thank you for choosing me and ask if you need anything done."

Kimberly stopped day dreaming. "You'll have to thank the photographer. I'd like you to become familiar with the clients and I'll need a breakdown of the various types of analysis we do. Perhaps a chart would help."

She got her coat. "I'll be leaving for the day. We can start looking at your findings in the morning."

Her secretary's eyes bulged with anxiety. She nodded as Kimberly left. *I thought this was going to be a cushy job. The others are right; she's just like her uncle.*

Kimberly went to the elevator. She pressed Lauren's floor and found her in the lab.

"Well, this is a surprise." Lauren looked around. "We can go into my office if you like. You won't have to whisper."

They crossed the hall and Lauren shut the door. "This is better." *Maybe for her first day she wants to go out for dinner to celebrate.*

She pushed out two chairs from her conference table.

"No, I really can't stay"...*Now what. If I tell her how foolish I felt at lunch she's going to think I'm jealous of Sheila...I probably am. God, I feel so stupid.*

Kimberly looked around the office and then at Lauren. "I wondered how that test came out you ran this morning."

Lauren noticed some blushing and frowned. "You could have watched, from the comfort of your desk, and...until we see what's on that microfilm you entrusted to Arthur, I don't know that I can evaluate what I've got." *Well so much for romance.*

Kimberly put her head down. "I've had those units shut down. And they will be removed. Maybe Uncle Robert's age was a factor, or he might have been suffering from paranoia. I'm truly sorry."

Lauren's hopes were deflated, and Kimberly saw the letdown.

She opened the door. "I'm going home now and ask for the microfilm. Could we have dinner tonight?"

"Aunt Harriett called. She's making my favorite meal so I'll be there tonight."

Kimberly hesitated. "There wouldn't be enough for one more, would there?"

Lauren shrugged her shoulders. "I don't know."

Opening the car door, Martin didn't see a smile as Kimberly got into the car. *Looks like her first day didn't go very well.* "Will you be going into London?"

He could see she was deep in thought or not happy. He cleared his throat. "Miss Kimberly, will we be going into London?"

"No, Martin, I need to go home."

Either way, it would be a twenty minute ride but in opposite directions. Martin spoke softly as he drove to alert Arthur that Kimberly appeared upset about something.

"Martin, would you let me out at the front entrance."

Arthur met her. "You had a good day, Miss Kim?"

She nodded. "Arthur, can Uncle Robert see me?"

"He's very anxious to hear about the day."

Kimberly headed for the elevator she knew about. "No, Miss Kim. This way. There's an elevator on every floor."

She shook her head. *Why am I not surprised.* "What happens if an elevator fails? Is there a staircase?"

"There is a backup generator and no staircase." *She didn't hear a word I said.*

She followed him to the kitchen pantry. He brushed his medallion waist high across a shelf and the wall moved exposing the elevator door. Arthur tried to talk to her but she didn't respond. *I can't imagine what has upset her so.*

They rode bikes to her uncle's rooms. Arthur knocked and entered. Her uncle's wheelchair was there. Kimberly gasped. "Arthur, he hasn't had a set back?"

She dashed from room to room. "Uncle Robert!"

She returned to the living room and grabbed the phone. "Wouldn't security or his doctor call you, Arthur?" As she picked it up the door opened. She sank down on the arm of the couch.

Robert walked in slowly. "I wanted to surprise you."

"You surprised me. I was sick with worry." She went to him and stopped. She wanted so much for him to hold her.

"Let me put my arm around you. Soon this gauze will be gone. You needn't worry anymore."

They walked slowly to the couch. She helped him sit and Arthur had a special pillow to support his back. "You see, I'm almost back to normal."

Kimberly nodded with a frown. "You're much better but not normal yet."

Arthur had relayed Martin's observation to Robert. "Well, now, how was your first day on the job?"

Kimberly looked down. "Oh, it was interesting. Lauren wanted to show me how to work all the gadgets on your desk and we found out, to my embarrassment, your monitor does in fact watch over every inch of that place. Oh, yes, I did hire a secretary, had my picture taken a zillion times."

She shut her eyes and nodded and then looked at both of them, "But you already know all of that, don't you?"

She sat down next to Robert. "I can't live with paranoia. What are you doing or have done to make this life style necessary?"

Robert squeezed her hand. "I've been so torn over this. Arthur and the others kept telling me years ago I should trust you to know of my activities. Each time I developed a new device for warfare, I envisioned you would be taken from me. I tried to quit but the ideas just kept coming. I had to keep you safe. I'm so, so very sorry."

Kimberly held his hand. "The fact you've staged your death, does that mean you're done, finished, retired?"

"Arthur, bring me glasses for Kim."

She sat up straight. "Whatever for?"

Robert said, "Duke, speak."

Kimberly glanced around. "Duke isn't here, Uncle Robert."

He smiled when Duke barked. "Yes, he is. Arthur."

Arthur gave Kimberly a pair of glasses to put on. "Look around the room."

Kimberly stood and scanned the room. She shook her head. "I don't believe it." She tilted the glasses and the spot was blank. Back on again, she smiled. "Duke, come here."

Duke came to her. She took off her glasses and her mouth fell open as she petted him but couldn't see him. "Whatever this is can't hurt Duke, can it? After all that you've gone through."

Robert leaned back and sighed. "No, no... This formula has been tested so many times before I used it on myself and many more times before I put it on Duke. This skin problem was a reaction from the poison in my system to the formula. I didn't know about the poison when I used it."

Kimberly sat again. "How long have you been working on this idea?"

She still couldn't see her uncle's face behind the gauze. She frowned. "Would this be the test that Lauren showed me?"

Robert nodded his head. She heard him chuckle. "I was in the lab the night she showed you the results. I sat in my wheelchair almost next to you."

Kimberly shut her eyes. "The wheel noise...And we were gullible to believe that noise came from the heat ducts... I'm sorry Uncle Robert, but that isn't funny. Now, I feel I'm being watched. That's not right."

"Actually, Windsor gave me the idea years ago. Mike and the others told me they saw Windsor hiding in places. They didn't make much of it as he was a kid, until, one day you were playing in the upstairs hall near the stairway. We had just put in the first monitor and Arthur saw Windsor hiding near you. It was clear he planned to hurt you."

Kimberly stared at him. "Was that the day a big horn went off in the house. I remember that!"

Arthur stood by the couch. "I couldn't think how I could stop him or save you if he had carried out his plan to push you down the staircase. The noise scared the crap out him and he ran. I showed the tape we made to Robert."

"That's when I wondered if I could become invisible. About a year ago, I made a breakthrough. The formula isn't finished yet and now I feel it should be destroyed. I can't see any good coming from its use. I can assure you the navy wasn't real happy to hear my decision after they witnessed a demonstration."

Kimberly squeezed his hand. "Yes, Uncle. I agree. You must destroy the formula. This whole situation now is allowing you to step back and quietly live out your life. Please, promise me you'll stop saving the world. Your nightmare may come true if you continue to work on these secret projects."

Her uncle felt her hand shaking as she spoke. "I promise, Kim. Now I think I'd like to rest a bit."

She and Arthur made him comfortable. As she kissed him on the forehead, she saw an imprint made at the end of the couch. "Looks like Duke needs a rest too."

As they walked to the elevator, they heard over the intercom that Kimberly had a phone call.

"Miss Kim, any of the wall phones have outside lines. Just press line four."

"Hello…Harriett." She laughed. "Are you sure?…Would love to."

Arthur whispered. "I'll be upstairs. You know your way around."

Kimberly hung up and glanced at the wall clock. *I can't remember if there's a florist on the way to their house. I better hurry. Lauren must have said something.*

An hour had passed as she walked before her mirror to check out her outfit. She liked looking smart in her tailored clothes. *Burgundy is cheerful!*

She hadn't said anything to Arthur about going to Gunthers for dinner, and didn't see anyone in the kitchen. *Maybe Arthur is feeding Uncle Robert. I don't have time to set up a time table for Martin. Besides he probably would like an evening to himself. I'll just take the Jaguar. It's fast and I think I can still make it to a florist on my way.*

At the main gate, she surprised the gate keeper. "Miss Kimberly, Martin isn't with you? You do remember the red alert."

Kimberly almost did a double take with his question. "Good observation, John! That red alert applies to the seals. I'm not a seal, am I? Now open the gate so I won't be late for a dinner engagement."

She had a remote in the car and while the keeper went to his phone, she pressed it and the gate opened. *I feel like I just broke out of prison. This is insanity.* "Sorry, John!"

By the time she got to the Gunthers, her mood had softened. *There's Lauren's car.*

Harriet met her at the door. "Oh, those are beautiful lilacs, Kimberly. We're so glad you could make it." She took the flowers and smelled them. "The fragrance is wonderful."

She hugged Kimberly. "Now you've got a choice, Charles is probably napping watching a cricket match or you can help us in the kitchen."

Kimberly smiled. "Two things I've never done....I think the kitchen."

Harriet took her by the hand. "Good choice."

The Gunthers lived in a very old cottage. They had renovated it to the twentieth century for gas and electricity. Otherwise, it still had the charming original wall coverings, wood floors that squeaked and wood burning fireplaces in each room including the kitchen.

Lauren beamed. "Hi, I guess Aunt Harriet made enough for one more."

Harriet handed Lauren the flowers. "Would you put these in a vase in the dining room? Tell your uncle we'll be sitting down in five minutes."

&ⁿ&

Kimberly put her napkin on the table. "I don't dare tell Herr Dietrich, but Harriet that was the best meal. I can understand why Lauren calls it her favorite."

Harriet blushed when Gunther took hold of her hand. "Now, you can understand why I'm so fat. Almost fifty years of a wonderful life with her." He turned to Lauren. "And, you see we want..."

Harriet knew her husband wanted to play cupid. "Charles wants to help me get dessert. Why don't you girls go in the family room? We'll call when it's ready."

Gunther got up. "It's a beautiful evening. Why don't you go out and sit on the swing? I think the moon is out."

Lauren blushed getting up from the table. "Uncle Charles...."

Kimberly stood. "That sounds like a wonderful idea."

Lauren led the way from the dining room to a side porch through the family room. *I hope Kim doesn't think I put Uncle Charles up to this.*

She grabbed her sweater and they walked along the stone porch wall. Lauren put her arm around Kimberly's arm. "It is a perfect night. There's not a cloud to be seen."

Kimberly glowed. "I agree. This feels comfortable. I don't feel the pressure." *To be on guard, have eyes around my head.*

Lauren stopped and gazed up at Kimberly. "I was hoping that might be the reason you seemed distant."

Kimberly shut her eyes. *Distant out of embarrassment.* "I think it's pretty obvious I'm not good at multitasking." Kimberly looked out over the wall. "This business is far more than what I expected...I don't know that I'm equipped to handle it. Each day another door opens and I'm flooded with decisions to make. Maybe that is why my uncle became so paranoid, but that's not living."

Kimberly took Lauren's hand into hers. "Then, I look at you and my world changes. Lauren, I've never had these feelings before. Everything is so foreign to me. I'm overwhelmed."

Lauren touched Kimberly's mouth. "Don't...beat yourself up, Kim. You need time....we both need time. I'm not going anywhere. Each day is a learning experience...Okay?"

Standing on her tip toes, Lauren kissed Kimberly on the cheek. Enchanted by the moment, Kimberly embraced Lauren and they kissed.

Very shortly, Harriet came out on the porch. "We can have dessert now." She laughed. "Mark that spot, your uncle can't see it from any of the windows."

Lauren and Kimberly giggled as they followed.

The grandfather clock chimed nine times as Kimberly said goodnight. Lauren walked her to the car.

Kimberly took Lauren's hand. "Thank you, I'm so glad there was enough for one more. I'll see you tomorrow." They kissed.

Still in a state of total happiness, Kimberly drove slowly out of the drive. Out of nowhere car lights appeared in her rear view mirror. She slowed at a roundabout and saw a car door open from her side view mirror. Then a shadow appeared and a man tried her door handle. *This is not good.*

Heart pumping, she down shifted gears, took the turn, sped around to the second exit, down shifted again and then hurtled down a very dark country road. *My heart feels like it's going to jump out...Thank goodness Lauren didn't come back with me. How would I explain this?*

Worried about animals running into the road, Kimberly strained to watch ahead with the bright lights on. *Please don't cross tonight.*

Not more than ten minutes into her twenty minute drive back to the estate, a car suddenly appeared behind her. *Wow, where did this come from?* The lights flashed at her. *Fat chance, if you think I'm stopping.* She floored the accelerator! She didn't slow down until she saw the estate gate opening. *I wonder if my car has a monitor in it.* She sped through the gate, only to look back and see the other car do the same.

She came to a screeching halt! It was Martin following her. She jumped out and stomped to his car.

"Do you know you scared the life out of me?"

Martin got out of his car sporting a black eye. "Oh, and you didn't worry any of us!"

John and another guard came running. Martin had radioed in asking for the police to be called. He opened his trunk and there was a man, much younger than Martin, tied up. "This is the guy who tried to get in your car."

Her eyes wide as saucers. "When I saw that car door open, I knew I had to get out of there. Do you know who he is?"

"No he has no id on him. I was behind them when I saw this guy get out of his car."

Martin helped the police lift the man out of the trunk.

"I saw him get out of his car and run to your side of the car. After you took off, I jumped out and tackled him before he was able to get back in. For a moment he was able to pin me down and yelled to the driver, in Russian, to go after you. The guy driving changed his mind when he saw me flip this little shit and took off in another direction."

"I'm so sorry. I've caused you a lot of pain." Kimberly pointed to his eye.

Martin chuckled. "This…was his lucky punch.

Then he cracked a little smile. "That was some mighty good driving. I guess I taught you pretty good. I wasn't sure if I'd be able to catch up to you."

He put his arm around her. "Kimberly, you've got to follow the rules. Robert would die if anything happened to you."

They walked to the house.

Sheila's meeting with Windsor

It was just getting dark when Sheila found the street. It looked abandoned. There were a couple of houses and three buildings, but no cars or trucks anywhere. The address she wanted was a building with three floors and set further back from the street than the others. She pulled into the parking lot next to the building.

"Well, I'm twenty minutes early like you said."

"We know. We were able to get our mobile truck on a vacant lot on the next street over. We have very good reception...."

Sheila smoked several cigarettes trying to calm her nerves.

"Okay, Sheila, a black Jaguar is coming down the street. I want you to get out and lean against your car. We have the place surrounded, but we really don't want to show our hand if at all possible...We know you can do this."

The car pulled in next to her car.

Windsor introduced the doctor to her. "Why don't we go inside and talk. Windsor tells me you're a photographer, doing a photo shoot with the Braun woman."

Sheila followed them to the back of the building. "You know, I think we can talk just fine right here."

A street light came on and gave them some lighting.

She backed up as Windsor and the doctor walked toward her.

Sheila had her hand in her pocket and motioned. "That's good, now what is it you want?"

The two men stopped. "Sheila, why do you need a gun?"

Sheila grinned. "Too much booze, Windsor. Are you forgetting our last meeting? As I recall…you made some comments that seemed pretty threatening."

Windsor bit on his lip. "Okay, okay."

Sheila looked at the doctor. "I hope you're not tightly involved with this bastard."

She glanced over at Windsor. "He thinks you'll forget all of his threats and come across as the nice guy. Those days are gone, ass hole."

The doctor put his hands up. "Okay, we've got the picture, and I can assure you that Windsor is trying to make changes." The doctor stared at Windsor.

"He has you fooled. I told him *not* to call me and what happens? He has the balls to call me on my photo shoot. That would have been great had Kimberly Braun recognized his voice."

"Well, she didn't. I made the call, because we needed this meeting and you're not the easiest person to get a hold of. Can we stop the name calling and get to the point?"

"I'm listening."

Windsor stared at Sheila the whole time Eddie Edse explained to her their findings. "You, see, Sheila, we've recently found out the locked disc you gave Windsor is worth a fortune if it has the decoder. We think it's on a piece of microfilm and it's either at the company or the Braun estate."

Sheila glared back at Windsor. "You… piece of shit. You told me I was taking insignificant formulas for car parts used for toys. Now you want me to steal a piece of microfilm that is a decoder! That's more than toys! What the fuck are you getting me into? How did you find this out?"

Windsor flinched and gritted his teeth. "She's fuckin with me…"

Sheila pulled her gun out.

The doctor stood in front of Windsor. "Please, listen. We really need your help. This is a deal that will make us all very rich forever. This photo shoot idea is the key element of this plan. It'll allow us to get inside the estate if you find out the microfilm is there. Sheila, we have it on good authority the disc and decoder have a value of over a billion dollars! Just think what your share would be!"

Sheila smiled and then started to laugh. "My share, you must be joking! No one is tighter than a duck's ass than your friend here."

Windsor pushed the doctor to the side. "Listen, you fuckin bitch, are you going to help or not?"

She heard Arthur whisper to back off. "Sheila, Robert said to accept the caper and get out of there before Windsor flips."

Sheila nodded her head. "For the right price, I might be interested."

The doctor leaned against his car door. "We figure each person will get at least a hundred million if not more."

Her eyes flashed at them. "There's a lot of hundred million in a billion. How many more people are involved?"

The doctor ignored her. "Sheila, there are time constraints. We have to know where the microfilm is no later than tomorrow."

Her eyes widened. *"Tomorrow!"*

Windsor opened his car door. "Yes, that's why we called. We were told tomorrow."

Eddie stared at Windsor and turned to her. "No. You're only dealing with us. But, we have some people to work with us if we need them."

Sheila put her gun in her pocket, still holding on to it. "This afternoon, I took a lot of pictures in the main lab and Lauren showed Kimberly the vault. I overheard her say that since the passing of Dr. Braun, she was the only one to have the combination to the vault. She wouldn't let me take pictures inside the vault, but I was able to walk in."

The doctor offered her a cigarette. "Could you see anything?"

Arthur whispered quickly. "Pull out your own cigarettes. Don't take one of his... Tell them you've got a miniature camera."

Sheila frowned and then grinned. "It was light enough to take a picture. Are you asking if I knew what I was looking at? No, it was just a bunch of tests on shelves."

She puffed on her cigarette. "You know, if I used some really fast film, I know I can rig something up to...get some ..."

Edse's hands went up. "Sheila, we'll wait for your call."

Sheila stepped on her cigarette. "I'll call on that number I used before. Now you leave first."

She stood and watched them leave before she got in her car.

"Holy fu ...sorry, I don't feel I can breathe. God, I was scared. I just couldn't go into that building, I was afraid to be with that crazy bastard. I felt I had a better chance..."

"Sheila, you did fine. Just go home; we'll talk with you tomorrow morning."

"Wait a minute; you're not leaving me alone are you? Wonder if..."

She heard another voice. "We've got you covered, Sheila. You won't be alone."

Inspector Ross's house

The sun appeared at six fifteen as inspectors Ross and Bobbie Grantwood got into the inspector's car. Ross beamed at Bobbie. *Life sure has many wonderful surprises. She makes me feel like a new man.* They arrived early at the Yard. Neither could get past the night before. Before getting out, Bobbie leaned over and kissed him. After sometime she opened her eyes and saw several people gawking.

She grimaced! "I think we better go in. We're being watched."

Ross jumped and bumped his head getting out so quickly. "Lord, I hope that doesn't leave a bruise I don't want to explain."

Bobbie laughed over his comedy of errors. As they rushed to the elevator, they were followed by cheers and clapping.

"Hey, you've got a reputation. It's obvious they like you a lot."

When the door shut, Ross frowned at her. "No, they're all thinking I'm robbing the cradle."

"Dennis, stop that right now! There's ten years difference in our age. I'm not bothered by it and if they are, which I'm sure they aren't, then they aren't very good friends."

She leaned up to kiss him. "Now, this matter is over! Got it?"

As they kissed, the door opened and this time they were both embarrassed when they were greeted with the jolly good fellow song. They got off and went directly to the Chief's office.

Chief Inspector O'Doul chuckled. "Congratulations, I could see this coming."

Nervous and blushing, Ross corrected him. "Sir we're just dating."

The chief motioned for them to sit. "The Admiral told me he asked you to take his card out to Arthur. How'd that go?"

Ross shook his head. "Arthur is a strange man. He shows no emotion. You haven't a notion what he's thinking. I almost asked the Admiral to clue Arthur in that we are on his side."

O'Doul shook his head. "That bunch live by a different set of rules. You earn their trust. We just have to be ready for his call."

The Chief handed Ross a folder. "Here's what the new operative has come up with about Alex."

Ross shook his head. "You're not going to fool Alex. Even with a new agent. Yesterday, before I could get my coat off, Alex showed up to tell me he spotted an agent watching the doctor's house."

The Chief frowned. "Why was he there?"

Ross waved the folder. "He said Windsor had not been officially informed of his mother's death. He tracked him down, finding he travelled a lot with Dr. Edse, and went to the doctor's house where he saw the agent parked on the street...Actually it was good he spotted the tail there. It gave me an out. I told him you suspected Windsor of speeding up his inheritance and put a tail on him."

O'Doul wrote down what Ross said. "I'll send out a memo to support what you've said. Hopefully that will convince him."

The Chief leaned back and lit his pipe. "Well, I do have something positive to show you."

He handed Ross and Bobbie three pictures. Ross's eyes opened wide. "Who are these men standing with Alex?"

Bobbie pointed to one of the pictures. "I saw this man at the accident scene for Mrs. Braun...One of the policemen called him Charlie."

The Chief stood to get a file out of a cabinet. "Ross, she's right. His name is Charlie."

Ross frowned at her. "Why was he there?"

"After you left to go to the Braun estate, I finished taking pictures. You had asked me to take the evidence bag with me. I climbed up the hill and this man gave me a hand up. I asked one of the policemen about him as he wasn't wearing any ID. He called him Charlie from Interpol. He told me he would show up at accidents to make sure no foreigner was involved."

"His name is Charles Donahue. He's an agent with Interpol and his friend's name is Peter Ghent, who also is on the staff at Interpol. What's interesting about these men is that they both served in the British armed services." He grinned. "In Korea."

Ross handed the pictures back. "How were you able to get these?"

The Chief showed them another picture. "This is our latest surveillance unit. The three of us are the only ones, beside the drivers, who know about this at this time."

"A tow truck?" Ross leaned back and laughed. "How many cameras?"

Bobbie's eyes widened as she nodded her head toward the Chief. "That's why you showed so much interest in film speed, and types of cameras?" She laughed. "What a sneak!"

Ross did a double take. "That's not very nice."

The Chief chuckled. "She's right. About a month ago I went to her lab and kind of grilled her about cameras."

"Yes, I believe you wanted one for your son's birthday. Well, seems I recommended for what all you said he'd be doing, combination digital and movie using high speed film a thousand or better. That had to be custom made for you."

The Chief nodded. "You're right. We had ten of these cameras made to the tune of twelve thousand pounds each. They're mounted on all four sides of the truck. Monitors in the truck allow the operator to view what each camera is seeing. They can change the angles and zoom the lens in and out and never have to look out the window. For a first time shooting, I think they did very well."

Ross frowned. "Sir, you wouldn't have a magnifier glass in your desk? I'm curious about one of the pictures."

He stood over the three pictures. "I thought they were shaking hands. Look, Alex is either giving an envelope or receiving it."

He handed the magnifier to the Chief. "Something is going on and I've a gut feeling it has to do with Braun's K Code."

Chief O'Doul sat quietly. "Bobbie, would you be able to handle the cataloging of these cameras if we set up a watch on these men? I really don't want to get more people involved in this until we know that the Yard is clean. From the phone sweeps, we're finding, sadly, information is leaking out."

He puffed on his pipe. "I'm afraid money is more powerful than God and country."

Bobbie looked at Ross. "Do you mind? It'll be a lot of overtime."

Ross swallowed and adjusted a cuff before he said quietly, "You have to do what is best for you. Besides, we know how passionate you are in your field as I am in mine. You know you want to. I think it's great."

The Chief stood up and got his coat. "For the time being, you need to show you're working on other cases. The lab is preparing another vehicle for the camera use. It's obvious; we aren't going to tail Alex using agents. I've petitioned for more cameras so we're not wasting time changing out vehicles."

Walking to the outer office, the Chief whispered, "If anyone should ask, I invited you in to congratulate you on your... your engagement."

Ross's mouth fell open. "Engagement! Sir..."

The Chief motioned to Bobbie smiling. "You deal with it."

Alex's rendezvous with Windsor and the doctor

Having left Sheila in the parking lot of Eddie's property, the doctor and Windsor arrived at the tube station about nine fifteen.

Eddie took some coins out of the ashtray. "Are you coming or are you going to stay here and pout?"

Windsor shrugged his shoulders. "You're always looking for something better."

"Windsor, what are you talking about?"

"Do I have to pour out more money to impress you?" *Getting the discs is my idea and he goes running off to that fuckin stud.*

Eddie got out of the car shaking his head. "Sometimes, I just don't understand you." He threw his arms up and then on his hips. "Please, tell me what this is all about? We've just met with Sheila and now… Oh, I get it. You think I'm interested in that detective guy."

"Well, aren't you? I saw how you sized him up."

Eddie shook his head. They walked to the call box outside of the station area. Windsor stood outside.

Eddie left the door open as he dialed the number Alex had given. "The next train won't be for another twenty minutes. We'll be there."

He closed the call box door looking around. *Surprising. This place is dead and it's early.* Smiling inside, the doctor looked around. *Why does this big lug turn me on when he acts so rejected? Ah...just the place for a quick f...*

Eddie pulled Windsor by the arm. "What are you doing?"

"Shush..." He pulled him behind a shed almost hidden by the dark and forced his body against Windsor. He whispered in his ear as he groped at Windsor's clothes. "Your size will do just fine. I don't need another."

ॐ

"Oh fuck! Look at the time! Get yourself together. We have to hurry!"

Eddie zipped his pants, combed his hair and whispered. "You better hurry; I think I hear the train. I'll run and get the tickets."

Windsor couldn't move or utter a word, making Eddie laugh as he ran off. "This will be your fault if we miss the train."

Alex met their train at ten thirty. *Well, something's happened between these two. I don't want to know. As long as Windsor's sober.*

"We don't have much time. My train will be coming very soon. Tell me about your meeting with that girl."

They walked away from the tracks. Windsor whispered to Eddie, "You tell him. I'm going to the men's room."

Eddie grinned. "On your way back, bring three coffees....please."

Alex found them a bench at the end of the platform. "Did you take his bottle away? He's almost lethargic."

Eddie shrugged his shoulders. "He'll be fine. He just gets a little jealous at times, needs some reassuring."

Alex frowned and nodded... *I think I'll pass on that.* "Were you able to get her back on board?"

Windsor returned with coffee as the doctor finished giving a summary of their meeting with Sheila.

"The bitch had the balls to pull a gun on us."

Alex flashed his eyes at Eddie. "*A gun?*"

"Windsor, don't go there. Knowing your temper, I'd probably do the same."

"As soon as we find out where that microfilm is, I want to watch her die."

Alex watched the area as they talked. He frowned at Windsor. "I'm afraid it's not that easy. We do need her as I tend to think the microfilm probably is at the estate. I'm glad you gave her the go ahead to set up a photo shoot."

He got up to look around the corner of the building. He threw his coffee cup in the trash. "Doctor, I'm working on several plans and one of them would require making a mask."

Alex hesitated. "By chance did you do any masking in medical school?"

The doctor pressed his lips together and nodded. "I almost went into rhytidoplasty. I took all the courses. If that's what you mean."

Alex and Windsor both looked at him with frowns.

He grinned. "Sorry, that's the medical term for the study of plastic surgery."

Alex continued looking around. "So, you could make *a very* believable mask?"

The doctor raised his eye brows and nodded finishing his coffee. "I've done both, surgery and masking."

He gave Windsor his cup. "Not from a picture of course. To be totally perfect you'd need the body. The mask is better made from a live body or one that has just expired before rigor mortis. Once the decomposition occurs, it's difficult. Why do you ask?"

Alex stopped and stared off. "Masking, does it require a lot of equipment or supplies,"

"Alex, it would be nice to know what you're thinking or planning. You're being evasive so I can't give you any real answers."

Alex continued pacing, watching every movement people were making. "Eddie, humor me, just answer the question."

Eddie frowned at Windsor and shrugged his shoulders. "Everyone is different. It would help to know beforehand, blood type, skin texture, but on the whole there wouldn't be a lot of supplies."

Alex crouched in front of Eddie and stared. "Then you're saying you don't need a refresher course. Right? I could have a body, say in two days, and you could make the mask, and it would be perfect."

Eddie glared back at Alex. "You want proof? I'll be in my office tomorrow. Then, Mr. McGraw, I'll tell you the right way to capture this person so you don't fuck up my work."

Alex's eyes beamed. "I'll be there. Say around ten?"

Alex walked by the corner of the building. "One last question, the place you met Sheila, you said you own the property?"

"Yes, it's run down now. At one time it was a nice area but the job market left and so did my tenants. I keep it for a tax write off now. It's been empty for years. It has water and electricity too... Very secluded."

Alex heard a train whistle. "What's the address of your place? I want to check it out tonight on my way home."

The doctor wrote it down. "It's 420 Sheldon, that's in Burlington. It's not easy to find. Here's my key."

Alex took out his ticket. "I'll see you in the morning, doctor."

ക്ക

Alex hadn't mentioned he had left his car at the Burlington stop the night before. To avoid being seen with them, he made several additional train stops before returning to his car and going to the address.

He walked around the building. The street light at the corner shed enough light to give him a view. *The back entrance has a ramp. That's perfect. Nothing will be too heavy.*

He shined a flashlight in a basement window and tried the key. *At least I don't have to move a lot of stuff. Better add a broom to the list. The doctor will need at least a dust free space.*

He nodded and smiled as he got into his car. *We have a plan.*

ക്ക

Sleep didn't come easily. Alex heard every ticking minute. This plan is perfect. I can't let this opportunity get past me.

Seven o'clock he walked into his office and locked the door behind him. He went to the hidden panel in the closet and took out a small case containing his stash of neuromuscular-blocking drug and two small syringes. *The first step in the demise of Admiral Benjamin.*

Unlocking his office door, he went to his desk, took out his laundry list, and crossed off the first item–AJB drug.

Next he called Charlie. He attached the voice scrambler to the phone. "Charlie, can you meet? Same place? One hour." *That doesn't leave me much time. I need to go to the lab first.*

Checking off his third and last item, he wrote a note to his secretary telling her he would be taking the rest of the week off for vacation with his wife in Scotland. He put the note on her desk and left the office.

A short time later, Alex shut his car door. "I hate being late."

Charlie nodded. "Ah, all of thirty seconds," and handed Alex a video cartridge.

He sat on a head stone. "The Admiral gave a speech at a luncheon yesterday. We filmed the whole thing with all the sound too. Our camera when it zooms in gets the sound as well."

Alex handed him an envelope. "That's exactly what I need. Was the luncheon some official event?"

Charlie put the envelope in his coat and jumped off the head stone. "Oh, yeah, O'Doul was there and I think I saw the Defense Minister. There were a lot of people, at least fifty. A couple of times the Admiral and O'Doul talked but they had their backs to us. We only had the one camera and their conversation was muffled. You'll see what I mean, but I'm sure you've got what you wanted."

Charlie frowned at Alex. "I know you hate the man, but, why is this tape so important. Usually I can guess what the plan is, but you've got me stumped this time."

They strolled back to the cars. "Here's the address of the doctor's property. If you can, bring Peter with you tonight and we'll go over my ideas."

Alex turned around at his car. "Charlie, just so you don't think you're at the wrong place, I won't have this car tonight. I'll have my little van. I don't want you to be spooked."

❧

The receptionist escorted Alex to Eddie's office. Eddie, dressed in his white coat, handed him an album filled with before and after pictures.

"Interesting, you've done more than a hundred surgeries on people. How come they're all men?"

Eddie sat down at his desk. "That's the first album I made when I interned during the Viet Nam War. Some of those were done out in the field, and I can tell you the surgeries were done under the worst conditions."

Alex closed the album. "I don't understand. Why did you change fields? You're listed as a heart surgeon."

Eddie leaned back into his very plush all leather chair. "I guess you could say plastic surgery hadn't made the top ten on the money tree compared to the demand for heart specialists. I do what I call "Identity Surgery," on the side."

He leaned forward. "Now, do you suppose you can tell me why my being able to make a mask for you is so important to this project?"

Alex smiled and nodded. *I'm beginning to like this man.* "I must admit I'm impressed and can see a plan is evolving. The key elements have fallen into place and you, Doctor Edse, are the final element."

Alex got up to leave. "Two of my associates will be meeting me at your property tonight around nine o'clock. If you can be there, we'll discuss my plan. I know you want to bring Windsor, only if …"

"He's got to be sober… He will be." *I'll just tell him his surprise fucks are over if he gets drunk another time.*

Alex shrugged his shoulders as he opened the door. "I don't have to tell you how important details are to any project, and Windsor's sobriety is one of them."

Eddie leaned against the front of his desk and smirked. "Exactly why I want to make sure you understand there're two ways of masking and I'd need to know what procedure you're wanting. Though I would guess you wouldn't want anything permanent."

Alex raised his eye brows and shut the door. "For the project I would not, but for leaving the country afterwards, yes, I would." *This just gets better and better.*

He grinned at the doctor. "We're meeting at nine o'clock. The plan will be ready for discussion and your input. See you then."

Doctor Edse opened the door. "We'll be there."

Alex stopped the door from opening. "You haven't forgotten you're still being watched. My last communication with my partner is that the department still suspects Windsor of having some involvement in his mother's death. Never...never take the same route to go anywhere. Never make a turn on the street you want if a car is behind you. I always allow an hour for travel."

The doctor frowned, studying him.

Alex smiled. "Doctor, I've been diagnosed with a phobic disorder. I know all about them. Without my phobias I would have been caught or killed a long time ago. Trust me! Having a phobic disorder in my work is a good thing. Just follow my directions and you'll be fine."

Ross is mystified

Ross got on the elevator to go down to the third floor. Bobbie had left a message she had been called out on an emergency that needed pictures. He wanted to set up a dinner date since they missed lunch together. Her department shared the floor with the equipment lab.

He had never been to her office. His eyes bulged. "What a mess!" He walked around the room. *I'd have to apologize if she were here. This is very organized. She's overwhelmed with cases and needs more room.*

There's no paper around to leave her a note. He saw the blackboard was clean. *Hmm, I could leave a note on it.* "Dinner at the pub, tonight 7:00 pm. My treat....xxDR."

He saw the light on in the equipment lab. *I wonder if she's over there checking out those new cameras.*

He was surprised to find her department ran the equipment room as well. "Good afternoon, I'm Dennis..."

The young fellow behind the counter smiled and nodded. "Inspector Ross, I believe. What can I do for you?"

With that look it's obvious we have no secret here. "I wondered if Bobbie was over here."

The phone rang; the attendant excused himself to answer it. Ross stood looking around, amused by the outdated layout of the room. The ledger for signing out equipment still was on the counter that swiveled. *I wonder why they haven't computerized all of this.*

He spun the big book around. *What is this? Alex was here this morning! He signed out a video screen analyzer. What is that?*

Ross brushed his hand through his hair. "I have to go. Just tell Bobbie I was here. Bye."

He pressed on the elevator buttons several times. *Finally! I can't believe these things are so slow.*

Ross ran into the Chief Inspector's office, out of breath, and blurted, "I've got to see him, right *now!*"

The secretary was startled. "He's on the phone Inspector. Have a seat..."

Ross ignored her and dashed through. "Chief, Alex has signed out a..."

The Chief stood at his desk on the phone. He motioned for Dennis to sit down.

Dennis first paced around and then quickly sat. *He was my best friend. What has happened to him?*

"That was the lab." The Chief frowned at Alex. "What on earth are you in a state about?"

"Sir! I'm sorry to interrupt but Alex has signed out some sort of analyzing equipment."

The Chief took up his pipe. "Interesting, I wonder if your discovery works in with my phone call?"

He struck a match and began puffing. "They've just finished downloading the cameras from the tow truck. Seems they've gotten more interesting pictures. They're faxing them over."

"Since we know Alex has connections at Interpol, I added Interpol to the call alert. We had two numbers come up this morning. One was from Alex's office. The call was jammed but the number still showed. On a hunch I sent the tow truck out to that cemetery. Sure enough, it must be a rendezvous point for Alex."

The Chief's secretary knocked and handed him a folder. "That was fast."

He viewed the pictures and nodded his head. "My hunch was right. Here're the shots we got."

O'Doul handed Ross the folder. "Looks to me like they're making an exchange. I think Alex is handing him an envelope of money."

Ross dropped his head. "Yes, but what's the guy from Interpol giving in return?"

Chief O'Doul sat on the edge of his desk. "It must be important if he's paying for it… "

Ross handed the folder back shaking his head. "There's nothing worse than feeling helpless."

"What did you say Alex took from the equipment room?"

"I went to see if Bobbie was…" Ross blushed. "Anyway, the light in the equipment lab was on. The counter guy had a phone call and I looked around. The sign out book indicated Alex had taken out a video analyzer this morning. Chief, let me look at that picture again. Do you have your magnifier?"

They both looked at the picture of Charlie from Interpol handing Alex something. Ross nodded. "It could be a video. What of?"

There was a knock at the door.

"Chief O'Doul, it's five o'clock. Remember I've a class tonight. You've had several messages, including one from your wife reminding you to take your grandson for his choir practice." His secretary gave him a sheet. "Sir, you better leave or you'll be late. Goodnight."

Ross got up quickly. "I think we're stuck. Everything is circumstantial, unsupported and I'm tormented by the whole thing because Alex was a good friend. I'm sorry sir for bursting out."

"I feel the same way, Ross, but as you said, we're stuck and Alex knows it. And when you ask the question, has he broken the law, we have to conclude, he hasn't. We have nothing to connect him with either Braun's deaths. Those two exchanges, can we prove stolen materials, conspiracy?"

The Chief donned his coat and they walked out of the office. "If Alex knew the Yard's activities, we're the ones that could be held culpable. Having a gut feeling doesn't go over big in a court of law."

Ross put on his coat. "Did you ever find out if the Admiral made contact with the Braun estate?"

At the elevator, the Chief pressed the button. "I saw him yesterday at a luncheon at the Embassy and he did say that Arthur called him to set up a date next week when all of Dr. Braun's formulas relating to the government would be handed over."

Ross frowned and nodded. "I hope he'll take an armored truck and have an escort. If the Braun estate is being watched, that kind of attention would certainly end any outside interest, especially the Russian mafia." *Alex wouldn't have gotten involved with the Russians.*

〰

Ross got to the pub early. He asked for a table tucked away from the noise. *Hope she went back to her office or I'll be having dinner by myself tonight.* He looked at his watch. *It's after seven; bet she went straight home.* He finished his lager and started to get up when he was suddenly surrounded by Bobbie and her team. The noise of chairs and tables moving around him startled him. They all sang out "What a great idea this is! Thanks for the treat!"

Ross saw and heard Bobbie's camera clicking away at his state of shock. It suddenly dawned on him, his message on the blackboard.

He put his hands up and laughed. "You got me... I did say it was my treat."

Bobbie sat down with a big smile and kissed him on the cheek. "Wait till you see the pictures. You won't be able to deny this was a surprise."

The team stayed just long enough to have a beer with them. When they left, Ross's snug atmosphere returned.

Ross took her hand and looked at Bobbie shyly. "Would it destroy the moment if I ask you to explain a piece of equipment?"

Bobbie stared at him. *How can I get upset? He's as dedicated to his work as I am.* "Poor planning skills. The morning wouldn't have worked?" She squeezed his arm. "I'm teasing you. What's the piece you need explained?"

Ross gazed into her eyes. "I never noticed your eyes are so blue."

She sat up in her chair and folded her hands. "Too late, I'm in my work mode. What's the piece?"

Ross sat back in his chair grinning. "What is a video analyzer? When I came looking for you, I noticed in the ledger that Alex checked one out this morning."

She frowned. "Well…We use it to scan footage for detail, running it at a very slow speed. It can document tone qualities in speech, body movement, mannerisms. Then we can run next to the original a secondary film for comparison, with the equipment pointing out discrepancies. We would know, for example, if someone was impersonating another. The banks that have voice recognition for safety boxes sometime will ask for an analysis. It's very accurate."

She sat back with her drink. *Something is going on. He's so torn up with this Alex stuff. Somehow I think it has to do with the closeness they shared with their wives. So much for romance tonight.*

Ross paid the check and walked Bobbie to her car.

Alex prepares his strategy

After an hour of driving, Alex arrived at the doctor's property on Sheldon Street in the little burg of Burlington. *I couldn't have timed this more perfectly. In another couple of hours it should be dark. Plenty of time to set the security.*

He backed his van down the ramp and unloaded all of his gear. *Put this fold out table in the center of the basement for the doctor. Have sleeping bag, cots, fold up chairs for later, food, propane, guns, detonators, pe-4 plastic explosives with timers. Now for the security. Need to put black curtains on the windows. Staple gun should do that.*

He busied himself putting fifty sensors on the building, as well as on trees, starting with trees almost a hundred feet away.

Alex finished stapling the last curtain, turned on the lights, and went outdoors to check his work. *Perfect! I hope Charlie can see my van. That slope hides it pretty good.*

After he swept and prepared the entire basement, he carried in the video analyzer. He ate some sandwiches while he watched Charlie's video of the Admiral.

He clapped his hands. *Charlie, if you were here I'd kiss you. You're a genius! Wait a minute! I can hear what the Chief and Admiral are saying. This machine is something else. I can adjust the speed to clear up the distortion of their backs to the camera. I was right! The Americans are going to retrieve Braunstein's formulas.*

Alex turned off the machine and paced back and forth. *Holy shit, next week. Son of a bitch, Dennis knows the Admiral. He must be working this case. Then do I assume he knows of my relationship with Braunstein and the Admiral? How could he, my records were destroyed? It soon won't matter. I won't be returning to work.*

Alex went to his brief case and looked at the photos Charlie had given him of the Admiral and Braunstein and of the K Code. He took a knife and stabbed the pictures several times pinning them into the bench. *This Code will be mine! Now practice! Just run the tape in slow motion and ...begin.*

After several hours, Alex finished running a test of his voice mimic of the Admiral when one of the sensor lights flashed. Without batting an eye, he drew his gun, put on his night vision goggles, turned out the lights and quietly opened the door, easing out by his van.

He nodded. *I almost forgot Charlie and the doctor were coming. Shit...The Street light hasn't come on yet, where is he? ...* He whistled like a bird. With that two men appeared from the corner of the building. "Charlie, move to your right or you'll trip on a stone."

Alex no more said that and the street light came on. He checked his watch. *A timer or sensor is fucked up.*

Charlie and Peter walked over. "Jesus, it's so fuckin dark here. I'm glad you told me not to look for your car. Damn, I couldn't even see my hand."

Alex chuckled. "Wait here. I'll turn the lights on inside. The other two should be coming any minute."

࿇

The introductions were made and Alex got right into his plan. "I'm handing out my ideas for how this all should go down. I need to know first if you all can picture this and second if you have any suggestions."

"I want to go over every step of the plan with you, whether or not it pertains to you."

The doctor looked at Windsor. "Do you think Sheila can arrange for a Friday photo shoot?"

Windsor shrugged his shoulders to Alex. "There isn't much lead time in this plan. I suppose a photo shoot could be planned for Friday. This gives Sheila one day to make the arrangement. What if she needs more people, equipment? That place is enormous."

Alex went to the analyzer. "I agree, but, we have a problem. Let me show you." He turned to Charlie. "Remember when you gave me this tape? You said there was a part that was muffled because the Admiral and the Chief Inspector had their backs to you. Well, this wonderful piece of equipment un muffled it for you...Listen."

The tape showed the two men talking. "John, have you talked with Arthur? Ross wondered if your request to give Arthur your card did any good. Did he call you?"

The Admiral leaned over to the Inspector and whispered. "Yes, giving Arthur my card was a signal to Robert's staff to call me. I've arranged a pickup of all the government related materials that Robert developed, including his decoder, this coming Monday. Now that Robert is gone, the Pentagon feels those formulas need to be back in their possession. Arthur told me Robert's niece knows nothing about this work and he and his team are concerned about her safety."

Alex turned it off and glared at them. "What choice do we have? It's this week-end or fuck the whole idea...It's up to you.

In light of this new information, are you still in full agreement to go forward with this project?" Alex saw four hands raised and smiled.

"I need to know your thoughts...Windsor, do you really think Sheila can arrange a photo shoot at the estate in two days?"

Windsor nodded. "I sure hope so... Though I think it'd be better on Saturday or Sunday. There are fewer staff on hand at the estate. Plus, local police response would be slower."

Alex furrowed his brows. *He does make sense when he's sober.*

Alex noted what Windsor said. "What do you think, Doctor?"

The doctor, too, was surprised with Windsor's cooperative spirit. "I agree with Windsor from the standpoint that I'll need time to make a lot of masks."

The men shrugged their shoulders, wondering what he meant.

Eddie explained. "I assume you'll want an identity change to leave the country as soon as possible. Windsor and I certainly will. So that's five masks. I'll have to have them ready beforehand."

The doctor took the knife out of the three pictures stuck to the bench. He studied each one for a minute and waved one of them to Alex. "So you're going to impersonate this Admiral?"

Alex nodded. "I'm the same build. I've studied all his moves. The mask will do the rest."

Alex turned to Charlie. "You're going to like this," and turned on the machine. "Watch and listen to this segment of your video."

He pushed the play button and they heard and watched the Admiral say, "Yes, giving him my card."

Alex shut his eyes for a moment, then pressed record, and spoke the same words into the microphone. "Now watch the meter." Alex switched to the analyzer and it showed the voice segment approved.

Charlie clapped his hands. "Brilliant! We go a day early and Arthur will happily let you in! Alex, that is brilliant! He'll just hand over the whole fuckin thing."

Alex frowned and shook his head. "I wish it were that easy. I'll get in the door, but we have a lot more to plan."

Windsor blurted out. "You'll get in. Don't count on Arthur handing over anything. That fuckin bastard wouldn't trust his own mother. He'll watch you like a hawk and so will that monitoring room. What are you going to do about that? Those mother fuckers, I'm sure, watch you take a crap."

Alex chuckled. "Calm down, Windsor. I know that is the main strong hold of the estate. It has to be eliminated, and I've an explosive I can put in the lining of my coat. When Ross and I were there, one of the men in that room took our coats and put them in there. I'm assuming that's standard procedure."

Windsor smirked and nodded. "That's standard all right. I'm sure they scan everything."

Alex stared at Windsor. "I'm glad you said that. I know just what to use now, and still use a remote."

Charlie raised his hand. "You can line any of our jackets. I was just thinking, how about using Peter and me to make up the crew for the photographer? We both are good in the field and she doesn't have to know more than Windsor suggested it."

Alex grinned and nodded. "That's true. She can't know about anyone outside of Windsor and Edse. You want to get rid of her after this is over, anyway. So, she doesn't need to know anything more than her part."

Alex looked at his watch. "It's getting late. You know what to do. We'll meet back here tomorrow night around seven."

Eddie walked over to the bench. "You're bringing the body here? When are you planning this?"

"Tomorrow night I'll have the Admiral here in an unconscious state. You'll need to bring your stuff here. I would have extra in case..." Alex shrugged his shoulders and raised his hands a little. "It happens, no matter how good you are."

"Charlie, you'll need to make up your list of all the equipment you'll need to handle any adverse situations that could arise. Windsor, play it cool with Sheila...don't piss her off. Let her know you have a couple of guys that will be able to help her. Actually, let Charlie pick her up and that way we can control the getaway."

Charlie smiled. "My truck is bullet proof and loaded with lots of special equipment for the chase!"

The doctor raised his hand. "How will Windsor and I get in? The guards will never let us in, and for sure that would alert everyone if we showed up."

Alex put his hand on Windsor's shoulder. "The two of you will come with me. I have that all worked out. We'll go over it tomorrow night. I'd rather not have to call anyone. Can you all be here at seven? I know I'm being overly cautious but, don't use your phones."

Charlie tilted his head. "I've got an idea. Let me use your goggles. I'll be right back."

The doctor saw Alex's syringe kit on the bench. "Alex, what drug are you using? I meant to ask you this earlier at my office."

Alex showed him the vial of neuromuscular block. He frowned and pointed. "That's okay... if... you don't care what state of mind he's in. Let me explain. We want him in a normal frame of mind without any sense of fear, because, if he fears for his life, then that's almost frozen into his body and it will show up in the mask I'm duplicating."

He handed Alex another vial. "Use this. He'll be a happy camper and more cooperative. It's almost instantaneous and you needn't worry you'll overdose. You're killing him after this?"

Alex's eye widened as he stared at the doctor. "Oh, yes, I've a special ending for the Admiral all worked out, so please don't finish him off."

Alex smiled. *If all goes well, the doctor and I may have found the makings of a new business. The Identity Crisis.*

Charlie returned. He handed each person a pager. "Write this number down…331-8223. All the pagers act as one. So when Alex calls, this number will show on the pager and we'll know he's back. Alex, if you call us as soon as you have the Admiral, we can be here to help you move him in."

Alex grinned. "I can do that."

Charlie showed his pager. "By the way, this number is blocked and it will take hours to be routed…"

Charlie put his hand on Alex's shoulder. "You never did say how you plan to capture the Admiral. Are you sure you won't need any help?"

Alex stopped putting on the night vision goggles and explained. "You've given me his daily routine. He leaves for the day at four thirty. I plan to pose as a navy officer and bump into him."

Charlie chuckled. "The old standby injection- and- then- lead-them- away plan. You realize the area has surveillance cameras."

Alex nodded. "Yes, but if I play it right, it won't appear anything more than a mishap. Besides, how many hours will pass before he'd be considered missing? I'm really looking forward to this meeting. Just in case, I stole some license plates off a car out where I live, then tomorrow night while the good doctor is making the mask, you, Peter, and I'll paint my van another color."

Charlie laughed. "That sounds like a plan."

Wearing his night vision goggles, Alex led them from the dark ramp to where the streetlight would show them to their vehicles.

A brighter day begins at the Braun estate

At six thirty sharp, Kimberly sat at the dining room table at her usual spot, going over some reports Gunther had sent her. *That sounds like Duke coming.*

She looked up. "It is Duke…" She stood up in time to have two paws on her shoulders. "What a wonderful surprise, but…" *Duke wouldn't be here without Uncle Robert.*

She heard more footsteps. Duke barked for Kimberly to follow.

She wrapped her arms around her uncle as he slowly entered. "This is the best day! No wheel chair, no cane and no more bandages." She clapped her hands together. "Oh, I'm so happy." Her eyes glazed with tears. She hugged him and walked him to his chair at the head of the table.

Arthur followed behind to assist. Robert sat holding Kimberly's hand. "I don't mind working down there but living underground is not living."

Kimberly squeezed his hand. "It seems like an eternity you've been gone. Almost two months since Gunthie called me."

She put her napkin on her lap as a staff member brought in Robert Braun's favorite breakfast. "Apricot crepes and omelet! I'm so ready for this! Tell Herr Dietrich of my splendid approval."

Kimberly watched and shook her head. "No calories in any of that." The maid then put a bowl of oatmeal and cranberries for her.

"Uncle, I hope all of this mystery will be ending soon. When will you detach from the government?"

Arthur poured Robert's coffee and nudged him. Robert motioned for Arthur to sit.

"I need to discuss the last twenty-four hours with you."

Kimberly frowned putting her cup down. "What's happened? Does it have anything to do with my scary drive home from Gunther's last night? I now know I was in the wrong. Martin showed me the guy in his trunk and gave me a lecture."

Robert stared at her. "No...but—you realize *now*, just how serious and dangerous the next few days are going to be."

Kimberly looked at Arthur. "I'm missing something."

Arthur chuckled. "Your midnight chase is at the bottom of his *Items for Discussion list...* The first item is, we want to discuss Sheila's meeting last night with Windsor and Doctor Edse....She'll be asking you if a photo shoot can be set up in the next week."

Robert leaned forward. "We learned this last night, but then this morning Windsor went to her flat around five-thirty and told her she needed to set it up for either Saturday or Sunday."

"I can't imagine the urgency to tell her this at five thirty in the morning. She called you that early?"

Arthur pointed to his ear. "She has one also."

Kimberly shook her head. "I know it's helping you and protecting her, but, I sure couldn't live a life of constant scrutiny...I'll be so happy when this is over."

Robert started to eat and motioned to Arthur to continue. "We think Edse and Windsor have joined up with someone or maybe several others."

Kimberly finished her breakfast and sat with her coffee cup. "I've heard you say this before but you never gave any reasons, or names. Have you reached out to Scotland Yard for help?"

Arthur poured them more coffee. "No, but we did have a surprise visit two days ago from that Inspector Ross."

"I liked him. I went to his office to identify Aunt Lucille's body and I had the feeling he is dedicated to his work. Not at all like his partner. I can't remember his name... Alex something. When they were here for that briefing, this man went crazy over seeing ..."

Kimberly's raised her eyebrows and stared at her uncle. "He about flipped when Lauren showed all of us how she processed her findings, using the code sheets. Didn't you see that?"

Putting his napkin on the table, he frowned. "We weren't aware of that. Arthur wasn't in the room. Remember, the monitors are off in the house during the day, allowing privacy."

"Arthur, why did Inspector Ross come out?"

Arthur sat at the table. "He was with another partner, a woman inspector. They were sent to give me, personally, the Admiral's card. I found that odd in that we had no idea the Admiral had any involvement with Scotland Yard. When they left, Ross hesitated at the front door and asked if I should see Alex McGraw around the estate to call him...Then he handed me his card."

"Obviously you've talked to the Admiral. What did he say about all of this?"

Robert put his cup down. "Our team decided not to let the Admiral know of my fake demise, so Arthur called him. John was matter- of –fact and told Arthur the pentagon ordered him to recover all of my formulas, the decoder, anything pertinent to my military work."

Arthur stood behind his chair at the table. "I never had a one on one relationship with him like Robert. I didn't feel comfortable quizzing him why Ross brought it and so forth. He mentioned something about seeing the Chief Inspector at an Embassy luncheon. Maybe that's the connection."

Kimberly contemplated Arthur's comments. "The urgency of Windsor's early morning visit to Sheila has to be he found out the Admiral is coming out here next week...therefore the need for an early photo-shoot. The Inspector's request to be informed about McGraw's whereabouts makes me wonder – is Ross holding something back?"

Robert smiled at Arthur. "Your intuition is spot on. The Admiral's coming out this Monday. Now you know as much as we do."

Kimberly stared at her uncle. "But how did Windsor find this out?"

"It has to be someone in a position to know the Admiral's activities. But who?"

Arthur frowned pursing his lips. "Could Ross be suggesting McGraw is a rogue cop?"

Kimberly leaned back. "Now that you mention it, at the meeting McGraw did ask questions about Windsor's position in the company and asked why he wasn't present."

Arthur shrugged. "We'd know more if I hadn't been so closed mouthed with Ross. He's wanted to establish a rapport since the first time he came out about Lucille's death. He asked me about the medallion they found in the car, and I wouldn't give him an inch."

Kimberly frowned. "Did you ever get the medallion back?"

Arthur raised his brow. "Miss Kim, you're right. We never got any personal effects of Lucille's or Mark's! I bet his piece hasn't been turned off!... I'll be right back."

A few minutes later, a chagrinned Arthur returned. "That was a serious oversight. It's off now."

Robert nodded. "Arthur, I've set the rules around here which you were following. No-one's to blame. We'll assume we're dealing with more than Edse and Windsor. We know something will happen before Monday. Now my next concern is…"

She grinned at them. "You want to know if I can handle this. Obviously, I need to let Sheila know where we'll do the shoot. We've already done R & K, so I'm assuming you want the photo shoot here. Right?"

Duke's ears perked up and he trotted to the hall. He escorted Martin and the Bishop to the table. "We need to wear tennis shoes."

Arthur poured coffee for everyone. "That dog can hear anything. We already have a game we play. I lose all the time."

Robert folded his hands together on the table. "We're in full agreement the photo shoot should be on Saturday. If we needed outside help, fewer people would be around on Sunday, an advantage Windsor may be counting on."

Martin chuckled. "Yes, but, I'm surprised he would even contemplate coming back here after the last time he left with quite a bruise."

Arthur stood by Robert's chair. "He's got a vendetta against us and I would bet he's aligned with whomever with the sole purpose of having his revenge. I mean with everyone at this table. Remember...he and the doctor think they've killed Robert."

Kimberly nodded with a frown. "The reading of your Will is still fresh in memory. He and Lucille left making it quite clear I wouldn't have my inheritance for long as it belonged to Windsor. I think you're right in having the photo shoot here. I don't like exposing innocent people to this situation either."

Robert took her hand. "You're thinking we need to protect Lauren."

Kimberly blushed and nodded.

"Uncle Robert, why... Why keep Sheila in the dark?"

Robert studied each of them. "One of the biggest threats to loyalty is money, lots of it. The other night, Windsor and the doctor promised her at least a hundred million dollars to help them in this caper... The conscience can play a lot of tricks on us. Does she really believe Windsor will pay? We don't know, and as a result, the less she knows, the less she can tell. I think Windsor's biggest tool with this photo shoot is to take you hostage, knowing full well I'd give up anything to save you. In this case, Sheila would be the means to the end."

"I see what you mean... Now, I'm the target. Great feeling that is. It's getting late, I better get going."

Robert took hold of her arm. "Kim, that's been my greatest fear all along, because you've always been the target."

She stared at Arthur a moment trying to grasp this and then looked sternly at her uncle . "Will that stop Monday, after the Admiral's been here?"

Robert clenched his hands. "God, I pray it will. Knowing you'd be the target to get to me, we devised a protection plan for every conceivable situation that could arise."

She looked at each one of them. "This has been going on all my life?"

The Bishop tapped her on the shoulder. "Do you remember our little chat at the crypt?"

Kimberly nodded. "Yes, I do... I got upset that you knew all about me, and I'd never seen you before. As you left on your bike, you told me I was never out of your sight."

She squeezed the Bishop's hand. "I hope I wasn't a problem."

Martin piped up. "It's been routine up until two nights ago!"

Kimberly hugged her uncle. "You're not to worry. We'll get through all of this."

She gathered her papers. "I just remembered I was to have dinner with Lauren Saturday night." Kimberly scribbled *Lauren no dinner* on the report she had been reading.

She got up and looked coyly at Martin. "You finish your breakfast; I'll take the Jag coupe?"

Robert shook his head. "Martin, she's playing with us. You've my permission to spank her."

ॐॐ

Kimberly got out of the car. "Martin, go back to the estate. I'll be fine. My God, there are ten seals here."

"I trained them, too. Okay, but you know it'll be all our heads if you ..."

She reached up and patted him on the shoulder. "I know. I promise to be a good girl."

ॐॐ

Around ten o'clock the secretary, Marion Atwell, buzzed to say that Sheila had arrived. Kimberly was on the phone with Lauren.

Lauren heard her and started to laugh. "Kim, ask her how long Sheila's been there? My bet is Sheila's been flirting with her for fifteen minutes, probably knows her entire history and has a date with her tonight."

Kimberly chuckled. "No, I can't do that. I'm trying to set an example of a business atmosphere. Asking her would only encourage her. I won't even ask how you managed to get anything done with her around."

"It wasn't easy and…after a while very ……..wearing."

Kimberly squirmed in her chair. *This isn't a phone subject.* "Ah, I'd like to see your progress on that test you showed me…What's so funny?"

"Nothing, boss! I'll have the test ready to show you closer to lunch." *I bet she's as red as a beet.*

Kimberly buzzed her secretary. Clearly Lauren knew Sheila all too well as she entered the office beaming from ear to ear with a look of conquest on her face. "Good morning, Miss Braun. I must say you served yourself well taking my advice."

Kimberly looked up and frowned. "Your advice?" *It just occurred to me, Arthur or whoever, is listening to all of this, with that implant in her ear. I can't say anything, but I know she's going to feel like a jerk when Arthur tells her to focus on the job. Then again a reality check or embarrassment might do her good.*

Sheila put her camera strap over her head and motioned to the secretary's office door. "You know. Your new secretary." Sheila's eyes and smile got really big. "She's really got big….."

Kimberly interrupted. "Ah… Sheila! What other photos do you need now? I've got several appointments today and if it's all right with you, I'd like to get things rolling."

Unknown to Kimberly, Sheila had taken two pictures of Kimberly's blushing as she talked about the secretary. *That was perfect. Having the shutter remote in my pocket really catches everyone off guard. Being the same height, I don't need to adjust the lens.*

"Well, do you have an answer or are you still …?"

A knock at the door changed the moment. The secretary came in and handed Kimberly some messages. "Miss Braun, you've a call from the American Embassy on line one."

Sheila had her camera in hand and clicked away catching every gesture and movement.

Kimberly shook her head as she answered the call. "Yes Admiral, I do recall meeting you years ago. Arthur mentioned you the other day. I would be very grateful if you would come and get all of Uncle Robert's formulas. We have them at the estate. Monday would be fine. I'll make sure Arthur has everything ready."

Kimberly stared at Sheila as she hung up the phone. "Now can we get down to business? I need to go to the lab to watch a test. Do you need any more pictures?"

Sheila put her camera in her case. "You know, I just had an idea. It would be really cool to have the article showing your two lives, the business versus the personal. Would that be allowed, to have another photo shoot? This time at your estate? I know its short notice, but perhaps we could wrap this all up over the week-end? Say Sunday?"

Kimberly looked at her planner. "No, I'm having dinner guests on Sunday. Saturday afternoon around two or three. How much time do you need?"

Sheila shrugged. "Hey, I'll take what I can get. I'll bring my crew and we'll see you on Saturday at two. It will take about an hour to set up the lighting."

Sheila scribbled on a paper. "The magazine will want a photo from the listed rooms if possible."

Kimberly looked at the list and shook her head. "No pictures above the first floor. Outdoors is fine. I'll give this to Arthur and he'll direct your crew. I'm not the kind of celebrity your magazine would like me to be."

Sheila stared at Kimberly as she put on her coat. "Too bad... ." *Windsor will be pleased. Thank God for that. A hundred million bucks for her...Interesting.*

Kimberly opened the door. "Are you leaving? Sheila! I'm going down to the lab."

Caught in her day dream, Sheila nodded. "Ah...no...I've...got to return Miss Atwell's pen to her."

Kimberly shook her head and chuckled. "Any excuse will do. Don't scare the poor girl. Oh, you can tell her I'll be back after lunch."

Sheila waved her hand. "I've got the situation under control, go." She checked herself in the mirror, gave a wink with a smile and then opened the outer office door, only to hear Arthur. "Sorry, no time for dates. Report to the bottom floor."

Sheila gritted her teeth and shut her eyes. *Oh, fuck, tonight would have been perfect.* "I'm sorry, I've to cancel our date tonight."

The secretary teased her a bit by looking sad.

"Sheila! We are waiting!"

Sheila rubbed her ear. *How do you turn this thing off.* "And...Kimberly said to tell you she is going to have Lauren for lunch. You know what I mean. I'll call you later."

~∽

The elevator door opened at the bottom level. Sheila stared at Arthur. "Kill joy!"

Arthur frowned. "You'd better switch gears before you go in that room. The team is in there."

Prompted what to say, Sheila called Windsor. "The best I could do is to set the shoot for Saturday at two o'clock..."

Arthur turned on the speaker for the rest to hear Windsor. "Well done. We have two people to help you with the shoot. Their names are Charlie and Peter. They both have a background in photography and should be very helpful. You said everything was in the library safe so we would want you to use that room for your last set of pictures."

Arthur gave a note to her to read. "So when will you be there? How will you get in?"

Windsor said nothing. "Sheila, just take the fuckin pictures. Charlie and Peter have a large van and will pick you up at one-thirty. Be ready!"

She shrugged. *"Well, you have a nice day too. Can't wait to see you!"* She slammed the phone down.

Martin grinned. "Surely, he didn't hear that."

She shook her head. "That man is brain dead after he's pissed off. He'll go and drink now until he passes out."

The men almost said in unison. "Like mother like son."

Arthur handed her a large folder. "This is your homework until Saturday...Sheila, I hope you're paying attention. You'll find pictures of all the rooms on the first floor. Each picture has the sequence you had on your sheet you gave to Kimberly."

Sheila frowned at Arthur. "I just gave that to her." She smiled. "Business before pleasure... hmm Atwell sent that."

The Bishop grinned. "Remember, she's a navy seal and knows all the moves."

Sheila sat down. "The world I know and loved is coming to an end."

Arthur sat next to her. "Those words could be close to the truth if you don't listen and study all of this." He opened the folder. "You can take this with you. Or, you can stay here as long as you like. *But study this!* We're concerned about the two men who will be picking you up. See if you can get a last name. Remember to wear your ear rings to give us a chance to see what they look like and research our files if they've got backgrounds. You're good at idle chat and wasting time. See what you can find out."

The Bishop stopped at the door. "Sheila, I'll be in the gym for another hour if you want to go over the defensive moves I taught you."

She nodded. "Yes, I would like that."

They saw reality had set in.

Arthur and Martin followed the Bishop to the elevator. "Bishop, do you really think she can pull this off? She acts so goofy at times."

"She's very aware of what's going on and that goofiness, as you call it, is nothing more than she's covering up being scared. It's a safety mechanism for her... I'll give her a good work out."

Inspector Ross has an idea

Friday morning Inspector Ross went through his usual routine at six o'clock, standing in front of the dresser tying his tie in the mirror. His thoughts were mostly on Bobbie; however, this time his look in the mirror went past his tie to a picture on the chest of drawers behind him. He stopped tying and picked up the picture. It was the four of them, Alex, Jane, his wife Elizabeth and him. *Those were such wonderful years we had.* He took a deep breath. *I still can't believe Alex has jumped the line.* He put the picture back and stared for a moment. *He idolized Jane. I can't imagine he would jeopardize their relationship.*

Ross carried his tea cup to the kitchen. *What would cause me to break the law? When Lizzy was failing, the doctors wanted to do that procedure.* Ross stood at the kitchen sink and shut his eyes. *That would have cost the earth. Had she not died, would I have taken a bribe to save her? Maybe that's what's going on. He said Jane was taking care of her sister to cover up that she's ill!*

Ross dialed Bobbie's number. "Hi, it's too long of a story to go into, but I'm going to take the morning off. No I'm fine."

"Something is bothering you. I can hear it in your voice. Dennis, it has to do with Alex, doesn't it?"

Lizzy always knew when I was troubled. Maybe this is a sign I need to go forward. But… She's ten years younger. He pursed his lips.

"Dennis, let me help. My docket is clear until this afternoon. We can talk about it over breakfast."

Before he could say anything, Bobbie hung up.

❧◦❧

Ross knocked and heard Bobbie yell to come in. He smelled bacon. "You didn't need to make breakfast."

Bobbie turned. "The eggs and tomatoes are almost done, would you pop the bread in the toaster, and pour the coffee. I'll be just another minute."

After they sat, Bobbie took a deep breath. She raised her glass of orange juice. "Cheers, it should be edible."

Ross beamed. "It has been years since I've had a home cooked breakfast."

"Well, it's quiet and easier to talk. Now, tell me where we're going this morning?"

Ross pointed to his full mouth.

"I was right; this has to do with Alex?" She scooted a piece of tomato, egg and toast on her fork and took a bite.

Ross mumbled a few words and nodded as he kept eating.

"Sorry. That was delicious. Worth a king's ransom." He wiped his mouth and finished his coffee. "Yes, you're right about Alex. I've a picture of the four of us and looked at it this morning. You couldn't ask for a more devoted husband. He adores Jane. I couldn't imagine what could send him or me over the top. Then I recalled a time when the doctor told us about a procedure that had no guarantees and would cost a fortune. My wife died before we could make the decision, but…I couldn't help but think maybe Jane isn't well and he can't afford her care."

Bobbie finished clearing the dishes and got her coat. "So, we're going out to see them, or Jane."

Ross smiled and nodded. "Alex told me Jane was helping her

284

sister, who lives in Ireland. He said his sister-in-law had been ill and needed help with the children. Now I'm wondering if that's a cover-up. He lives outside of Woking not far from here in a little burg called Epsham."

૭∾৩

Bobbie studied Ross while he drove. *For his sake I hope he can help his friend. The four of them must have been very close. Dennis is such a loving soul.* "Well, I can tell we're getting close. You're recognizing old haunts."

"I've very fond memories of this place and haven't been back since Elizabeth passed away. She's buried here. She and Jane loved walking in the woods. We almost moved here, but she got ill and... I tried to visit her grave, but just couldn't handle it. Instead I buried myself in my work."

He pulled up in front of the McGraw cottage. "Dennis, there's an old man walking in the back yard."

"You ring the doorbell and I'll see what he's up to."

Ross walked around a hedge to get to the back of the cottage. "Excuse me, my friend and I are here to see Alex and Jane and who might you be?"

The old man took a pipe out of his mouth. "Well, sir, I'm the owner of this place. Alex moved out years ago."

"What are you saying?" Ross stepped back and sat on a tree stump.

Bobbie came around the hedge. "Dennis, what's wrong?"

The old man frowned. "Looks to me like he's bit upset. I just said Alex moved out years ago."

Ross stared at the old man. "What about Jane, his wife?"

The old man took several puffs. "I never met no Jane... It was just Alex. He moved to an old place down this path. You can't drive it. Alex always leaves his car and van out there on that path and then walks. His van is gone. He must be on a trip."

He tapped his pipe out in his hand. "Strange man he is. Not at all pleasant. You could say it's a beautiful day, and he'd tell you to mind your own business."

Bobbie stood behind Ross. "You're absolutely sure his wife wasn't with him?"

The old man shook his head while he filled his pipe with tobacco. "I was new to the area when I bought the place. Can't be any more help to you."

Bobbie patted Ross on the shoulder. "This is beyond weird. We have to see where he lives…"

They walked down the lane and Ross stopped and looked around. "My God, this is a shambles. I can't believe this. This can't be Alex's. He's an avid gardener. His office is filled with books about every flower in the world. This place is…mud."

"Bobbie, where'd you go?" He stood alone in his trance.

Bobbie had gone around the back of the house where he found her prying open a window. "What are you doing?"

"Well, we need answers and the only way to get them is to look." She had one of her cameras around her neck.

She opened the window. "Come on! Give me a boost…Dennis!"

He rushed over to her. "You know this is…"

"And, by the time you get a search warrant and for what reason? He's gone off the deep end."

Dennis wiped his head. "Whatever you do, don't touch anything. Just look around."

Bobbie walked gingerly to the back door. Ross was looking through the window he helped her through. "Do I need to come in?"

She used the zoom lens to look around. "Dennis, don't go on the porch. From where I'm standing, it looks like the back door is booby trapped. There's a waste paper basket with a lot of train tickets in it."

"Can you read any without touching it?"

"I can see three of them have Burlington on them." She snapped several pictures from where she was standing.

Ross felt his heart pumping. "Bobbie, get out of there. Now! We have to report this to the Chief. Just turn around and come back the same way. We need to leave."

He got the window shut and they hurried to the side of the house. Both were surprised when they were met by the old man and someone else.

"I brought my neighbor."

Dennis shook hands with the other old man. "Did you know Alex and his wife Jane?"

The old timer nodded. "Yep, I knew them." He started to walk back up the dirt road toward his cottage.

Ross followed him. "Sir, I need to ask you questions."

"I told you I knew them. Mrs. Jane was so sweet. We loved her. She had a best friend. We liked her too. Mrs. Jane called her Lizzy. They would go for walks two maybe three times a week over there."

Ross frowned and took hold of the old man's arm to stop him. "Just a minute. Are you saying you saw Jane and Lizzy walking in the woods?"

The old timer stopped and looked up at Ross with glassy eyes. "No, not always. Sometimes they'd work in the flower beds. Sometimes the two of them would come over and help my Mrs. In her vegetable garden... Say, you almost look like the man she sometimes came with to have dinner here." The old man stepped back to study Ross and nodded.

Bobbie stood next to Ross. "We realize it's been a long time ago, but do you remember anything else about Jane?"

He lit his pipe and resumed his slow gait. "When they went off into the woods they'd leave about this time and not come back for several hours. Sometimes, they would bring my wife back the prettiest wild flowers. Lots of times they would have tea on the front porch and invite my Mrs. to join them."

The old man stopped to wipe his eyes with an old rag-like handkerchief. "Then, Mrs. Jane's friend didn't come anymore and we heard her crying, sobbing for days. We heard her call out Lizzy's name. Sometimes she'd sit on the porch in the swing they'd enjoyed. My Mrs. took her soup and she just stared at her, crying....It was so sad. We asked Mr. Alex if we could help her, but he was very mean and he wouldn't talk to us."

He wiped his eyes again. "The crying stopped." He snapped his fingers. "Just like that! And we didn't see her again."

Bobbie raised her brow. "Did you ask Alex about her?"

"Never saw him. He would leave early and come home late."

Ross stared at the ground. His lips were pursed. "When did you last see her or hear her crying?"

The old man wiped his brow. "Gosh, fellow. My Mrs. died two years ago and it was way before that. Maybe four, five years."

Ross kicked a little pebble. "Lizzy's been gone now about eight years...Poor Jane. She wanted children so badly. Lizzy told me once that Jane had had several miscarriages. Their friendship probably kept her from going over the edge...Then, when Lizzy died, it must have been too much for her. I remember at the cemetery, Alex looked a bit embarrassed when Jane broke down sobbing." *You lose your sensitivity in this job. Lizzy asked me once if a crime scene ever made me cry.*

Bobbie pointed to the cottage next door. "Is that your cottage?"

The old man pointed. "Them are the bedroom windows."

She walked over to the side and snapped some pictures showing the short distance between the two cottages.

Ross stared at Bobbie, who clutched his hand. She turned to the man. "Thank you, very much. You've been a big help..."

She showed the two men her badge and handed each her card. "Both of us are with Scotland Yard. If you should see Alex, please call the department. Also we must ask you to stay away from that shanty in the back. A team will be out today."

Bobbie took hold of Ross's arm as he walked to the car. "Dennis, whatever you're thinking–stop! You've got to call the chief and report all of this now!"

They left the two old men. Bobbie drove while Ross talked to the Chief Inspector, "Yes sir, I'm convinced now Alex has gone rogue and you'll need to send a unit out to this town. The back door is booby trapped...The neighbors haven't seen his wife in a very long time...It's difficult to explain right now, but, there's that possibility he killed her. Bobbie's taken pictures of the shack he's supposedly living in."

Ross reported all they had learned, ending with the train receipts for Burlington. "That's within a radius of the Braun estate and where that Doctor Edse lives, too…

Yes, sir, I would canvas the Burlington area. That's not going to be easy if you send agents. If he's around, he'll surely spot them."

Bobbie pulled off to the side of the road. "Tell the Chief to call out the Dream Team."

Ross frowned at her. "What is the Dream Team?" He handed her the phone.

"Chief Inspector, call Inspector Carroll. Yes, sir. She just finished training an elite woman's task force. She calls it her Dream Team. I photographed the skill development for an in-house recruiting advertisement. She has a list of what they can do…Here's Dennis."

Bobbie checked her side mirror and pulled out into the highway.

Dennis still frowning. "Yes sir, I'm still trying to visualize Inspector Carroll in a…"

Bobbie poked him. "Not fair, Dennis. They're really good."

"Yes sir, we're on our way back now. It's about a forty minute drive."

Ross put the hand held microphone down. "He wants us to go directly to his office. Seems Alex left a note for his secretary that he'd be on vacation with his wife in Scotland for the rest of the week. He said to thank you for your idea to use the Dream Team."

Bobbie saw Ross staring out the window. "Dennis, don't jump to conclusions over what those old timers said. Alex may have put Jane into a rest home until she could cope."

Ross continued to stare. *Alex and I worked eighty to a hundred hour weeks for long periods of time. The girls were wonderful friends. Why shouldn't they spend time together.* He shut his eyes. *My God, they could have been seeing other men. That would have been horrible.*

The Admiral is kidnapped

Att three thirty five, Alex finished tying his spotless black shoes. *The show begins.* He put on his navy captain's uniform coat. *Now to go over my check list. Both syringes are in my pocket. Folder with my speech. Where's that name tag Charlie made for me?*

He panicked a little looking in his brief case. "This is not the time to fuck-up. Just cool down…"

He used his inhaler and stood for a moment. *Check your pockets. Here it is in the breast pocket. What's my name this time?* He pinned his tag in place. "Dr. Robert Turnbull at your service." He frowned. *I'm a Scotsman in the Royal Navy? It's time to go.*

❧

Thirty minutes later Alex parked his van near the American Embassy. He hung a parking permit from the mirror. *Time to roll. No turning back now. Just killing this man alone gives me great pleasure. I wish I could have been in on Robert's with Windsor.*

Alex got out of his car. *Charlie said he comes out around the time the Tower strikes four thirty. I probably should have practiced this movement. Too late now, Benjamin is coming my way now. The first syringe is ready. Steady Alex. One, two…three…go!*

He stood looking at the papers in his folder watching for the Admiral to get within five yards of Alex's van and then very abruptly with his head down, Alex walked right into the Admiral dropping his papers to the ground. The Admiral, taken by surprise, offered to help gather the papers.

Alex saluted to the Admiral. "Admiral, please, I'm so sorry!... I'm to give a speech, and..." Alex stooped and with all activity going on, the Admiral never felt the prick made to his leg.

Alex stood up with his papers. "Are you alright, sir?"

The Admiral was smiling. "Young man, you should watch where... you're... going."

Alex grinned. *Edse knows his stuff.* "Admiral, if you just walk over here, I'll take you home."

The Admiral stared at Alex and then smiled. "That would be very kind of you. Seems I've misplaced my driver."

Alex shut the Admiral's door. "That you have, sir. That you have." Laughing, he nonchalantly walked around the van and got in. *That was a piece of cake. The Admiral is having a good time too.* "Sir, can you buckle your seat belt? Very good."

As soon as Alex was out of sight of the Embassy's cameras, he turned into a side street. "Benjamin, how about another shot of this great stuff?"

The Admiral opened his eyes and smiled. He mouthed a few words. Alex chuckled, then stabbed the Admiral's leg and emptied the syringe. "We'll give that a few minutes to reach you and then I'll call Charlie's number. Isn't that a good idea?"

The Admiral's head slumped forward. Alex reclined the Admiral's seat to make sure he wouldn't cut off any circulation. "Happy dreams, Benjamin. You'll soon be dreaming permanently. It's certainly turned out to be a beautiful day for a drive in the country."

೧ೲ

Thirty minutes later, he backed his van down the ramp. Charlie opened the Admiral's door. "Haven't seen you smile like that in a long time."

Alex got out. "Right you are. Is the doctor here?"

Charlie whistled and Peter opened the basement door. "The

291

package is here. Need some help to move it."

The three of them came out. The doctor stood off to the side as the four men very carefully carried the Admiral to the operating table in the middle of the room.

Windsor smacked the Admiral's arm. "Your fuckin shoulder bar pad broke one of my nails."

Charlie and Peter stared at Alex with raised brows. Alex raised his hands a little and shook his head to them and mouthed, "Forget it."

Alex beamed with his conquest. "Well, doctor, what do you think?"

Eddie Edse stood over the Admiral's body. He studied the face, rolling it from side to side. "Hmm." He nodded his head. Then he stood behind the Admiral's head and held his cheeks, squatted a bit to look down the face as if to check the alignment.

Eddie looked over to Alex and smiled. "This man's features are almost perfect."

The doctor had brought his own swivel stool. "Alex, sit on the stool for a minute."

He took a caliper and a six inch rule out of his bag. He measured the Admiral's forehead, from his ear to his nose, nose to his lips, eyes to his nose until he had completed all the entries in his little book.

The doctor looked at the Admiral's hands. "Windsor, you wouldn't know if that monitoring system checks finger prints?"

Windsor walked over to the table. "Those fuckin bastards know everything about you before you get past the gate."

He watched his lover examine the Admiral's fingers and burst out laughing. "It's funny, but I don't think I've ever gone through that gate sober. I do know everyone has to sign in."

Charlie heard Windsor's remarks. "Alex, the sign-in pen could be part of the security system. Dr. Edse, if you've got a way of lifting prints, do it! It can't hurt."

Edse smiled and stared at Alex. "Now, it's your turn. I'll wager I won't need to make more than a centimeter adjustment on any of the Admiral's measurements to match yours. I can't get over the symmetry between your facial structures."

Alex frowned. "So, what's the big deal?"

Eddie shook his head. "Nothing, other than he's a good ten years older than you…and he's in *great shape*. No face lifts either…" *Those Americans must live well.*

After a few hours of silence in the basement, Eddie backed away from the work bench and sat hard on his stool. *Done, finally.* He sat up straight to stretch his back muscles. *I'll do the finger prints tomorrow. I must be out of shape, I'm dead…. I wonder where everyone is.* "Windsor!" *That's strange…*Raising his brows he jumped off the stool. "Oh Fuck! I hope he didn't piss Alex off or sneak out for some Scotch."

The doctor rushed to the basement door and opened it. It was dark out. He stood for a moment to adjust his vision and saw a shadow moving about fifty feet away. *I can't call out. Wonder if that isn't Windsor or any of them. They must have painted the van. I can smell paint. I'm not walking out there. Better to stay inside.*

He turned the door handle and heard Alex behind him. "Hold the door. We're coming in."

The four men, wearing night vision goggles, marched in carrying bags, as Eddie held the door. *What on earth is all this?*

Charlie walked by him and smiled. "Thought you might be getting hungry cause we're starved!"

Eddie motioned a kiss when Windsor walked past.

Alex stood at the work bench looking at the finished product. "Superb!" He put his arm around Eddie. "I've waited a long time for this opportunity. You'll never know how I've dreamed of this day…this is fabulous." He shook his head. "Just Outstanding." *Doctor, if this job goes off the way I think it will, we'll start a new world.*

Out of the corner of his eye, the doctor saw Windsor coming and backed away. "I finished my work and called out to you. Where did you go?"

Before Windsor could respond, Eddie took his lover by the arm and they went outside of the building. "Carry on… don't wait for us, but leave some."

Alex turned quickly to Charlie and Peter, putting his finger to his lips. He whispered, "Whatever you do, don't make fun of them. They

293

may be Puffs, but we need them. Windsor has more than one screw loose. He would kill you as soon as look at you. The doctor can't live without him. So, for now that's how it has to be."

While Windsor and Eddie ate the left overs, Alex handed out a sketch of what he remembered of the first floor main entrance. "Windsor, is this accurate?"

Windsor swallowed quickly. "Just remember how big that main hall is. You said last night about disarming the monitoring station." He held up his sketch and pointed. "You've got at least two hundred steps from the front door to the library."

Alex nodded. "That's a good point. Charlie, I guess we'll use the remote instead of a timer. I would like to be in the library when that goes off."

Charlie looked over at Peter and chuckled. "Holy shit! That hall is like a soccer field. How big is this place?"

Windsor put his cup down. "Probably sixty rooms or better. When the weather was bad, Robert would let the staff use the hall to exercise or play games there. After so many nights of noise, mother had her suite of rooms moved to the back of the mansion."

Alex saw the Admiral move and motioned to the doctor. "I think our guest is coming to."

Eddie took his vitals. The Admiral tried to wrench out of the restraints. "Who are you? What do you want?"

Alex walked over to the table. "You're here, *Benjamin*, because I want your face! You better give him something to settle down."

Eddie studied the Admiral. "You know, I'm thinking it would be a nifty idea to use his face as a base and alter it slightly five times." He smiled at the Admiral as he gave him a small amount of his secret potion. "Nighty, night, Sir."

Alex turned from the table. "Okay, here's the deal. I don't want any of you going back to your homes. Peter, you probably could, but certainly Windsor and Eddie can't. I saw a motel in town or you can use my van or sleep in here. I brought some cots."

Charlie and Peter walked to the door. "Alex, I can stay with Peter. We've got stuff to pick up and I want to see where this Sheila lives before Saturday."

Alex picked up his list. "Oh, that data you gave me about the Admiral-- did you get, by chance, any of the names of his staff? I had an idea to call his office in the morning and tell him he was going fishing until Monday."

Charlie nodded. "Yes, I did. It should be on the last page…"

Charlie shut the door. "Alex, I'm concerned how big that estate is. Sixty rooms mean a lot of staff. Think about it. There are really three of us."

Windsor overheard Charlie. "I wouldn't be too sure about that! I can match your shooting skill any day of the week, buddy."

Charlie smirked. "Well, you're hearing isn't impaired." He bit his lip. "No, I'm sorry…that was out of line. I'm just thinking we need more advantage."

Alex stared off. "Yes, I see what you're getting at. My idea is to cripple the place by destroying that main station. If I'm in the library where Kimberly is, then she becomes our ticket out of there."

Charlie opened the door. "Okay, but I want to roll this around tonight. I know something isn't right and it'll come to me. When should we be back? Around dinner? We'll bring it."

◌◦◌

Alex returned from calling the Admiral's office. The doctor and Windsor had already showered and were having a cup of tea when Alex opened the basement door.

"That went especially well." He walked over to the Admiral who was a bit conscious.

"Benjamin, you're taking a few days off to go fishing."

Windsor nodded. "So his aide fell for it?"

Alex clapped his hands. "He did! He reminded me of my schedule for Monday morning at the Braun estate. I thanked him and said it was duly noted…Now, Doctor what is the plan for today?"

"First we have to get some nutrients into the Admiral. I brought some fluids to put in his veins. While I take care of the Admiral, you need to shower and shave."

Alex frowned. "Where do you propose I do that?"

295

"Upstairs in the first unit the shower is still useable. I want to put your mask on and it will be a lot more comfortable if you're clean shaven. You need to get used to it as you'll feel a weight difference. Then, I'll spend the rest of the day making masks for the others. I should be done by the time Charlie and Peter get here."

❧❧

Alex met Charlie at the door. "What do you think?"

Charlie and Peter stared at him. "Wow, you can't tell the difference. Doctor, you're a genius."

"Thank you, I've prepared a mask for each of you. I'll show you after we eat. I'm famished."

"Alex, I think I've resolved my concern about the largeness of the estate." Charlie opened a box he'd set on the work bench.

"I thought we could each wear a wireless hearing aid with a voice activator on our jacket or shirt. It's very small as you can see. It's got a high frequency and should work throughout that place. These would allow us to keep each other informed until we're all together in the library."

Alex shook his head. " Charlie, what don't you know?"

Windsor put the aid in his ear. "You're not going to give one to Sheila, are you? I want to keep her in the dark as much as I can. When this is over, I personally want to deal with her. She's a fuckin bitch. Eddie has a special treat for her."

"Show us how to use them. Then we need to go over the plans for tomorrow."

Charlie adjusted each unit making sure they all worked. "That's better. It gives us more control of our surroundings... Alex, that box is filled with all the explosives you wanted. You realize you have enough there to blow up half the UK."

Alex grinned. "That's my intention. Since we're within fifteen maybe twenty minutes of the Braun mansion, blowing up this building would create quite a diversion. I plan on having it go off about the same time I figure we'll be taking the niece hostage."

Windsor tightened his lips. "Then we'll take Sheila as well. That would make for a great visual." He started to laugh.

Charlie frowned at Alex. Alex shook his head and motioned to him not to say anything.

Alex looked inside the box. "There're fifteen set ups. I asked you for twenty-five."

"Alex, look at the size of them! How big a crater do you want?"

Alex laughed. "Here's the schedule. Charlie and Peter, pick up Sheila at noon. You'll get to the Braun place just before one. Start shooting pictures by two o'clock, if not before. Kid around, do whatever you need to do to make everyone at ease. I should get there no later than three. So you've got to be in the library by that time. If all goes well, we should be able to get out of there with the stuff by four. If we need to take the niece, then add a few more minutes."

Eddie raised his hand. "How will Windsor and I get in?"

Alex stared at him. "You'll ride with me. I've made an area in the back of the van where you'll hide. As soon as the main station blows, that will be your signal to come in the front door. You'll have guns and can eliminate anyone you want."

Windsor chuckled. "Have you forgotten the fuckin guards at the main gate?"

"Since the Admiral is a close friend of the Brauns and high in rank, I think the guard will be accommodating."

Charlie raised his brow. "I do have some smaller explosives if you wanted to cripple the gate house."

"That's a good idea."

Eddie frowned. "Yes, but if the guard wants to look over your van?"

Windsor nudged him. "We'll shoot the bastard, put him in the guard house and then blow it up."

Peter whispered to Charlie. "That guy sure likes to party."

Charlie put his hand over his mouth. "Shush, he'll hear you."

Charlie raised his hand. "The getaway. Are we leaving together in my van? Six people. Right? Where are we going?"

Alex looked at Eddie. "Didn't you say you owned another empty property?"

Eddie nodded. "Just north of the Braun estate is an old airstrip used during the war. I bought it. There's still one building on it. I figured we can change all our identities there. A friend of ours keeps his plane there. He'll take us wherever we want."

"Time to go."

Windsor raised his hand. "Wait a minute. I think you've forgotten something? My car!"

 Alex nodded. "You're right. You'll be with me."

He looked at Charlie. "What do you think?"

Eddie put a towel down on the bench. "I've an idea. We could take it to the air strip and leave it in the hanger. That way, Charlie will know exactly how to get there."

He looked at Charlie. "What do you think?"

Charlie nodded. "Good idea."

"I'll stay with the Admiral. You and Windsor take the car. Charlie will bring you back."

Peter opened the door. Alex yelled to them. "No stopping for drinks on the way back! We'll celebrate tomorrow night."

Chief Inspector's Office

"Chief, Inspector Carroll is here."

The Chief twirled around in his chair. "By all means send her in."

Chief O'Doul stood up and motioned for her to sit. "I appreciate your coming in on such short notice. I'll get right to the point. We've a situation that is urgent and…must be kept quiet. Only two other people in the whole yard have any knowledge of this – Ross and Bobbie, who sing your praises." *She's a handsome woman and from her build I would imagine she can take care of herself.*

The Inspector stared at him. "I'm glad for the opportunity to prove the uniqueness of my team."

After a half hour of discussion, the Chief Inspector handed Inspector Carroll a folder. "These are our most recent photos of Alex McGraw. We think he may be hiding for some reason in the Burlington area, because again, we're assuming he has an affiliation with Windsor Braun and Dr. Edward Edse. These names you should be aware of as they are on our Persons of Interest List."

"Are there pictures of these men in this folder?"

He nodded. "Have you ever been to Burlington?"

Carroll shook her head. "No, I can't say I have. I know it's been in the news recently. Seems they've had a problem with a priest or something in the church there."

She cocked her head. "That gives me an idea. Because of that news item, I could have my team dress as nuns and go door to door acting as bearers of good tidings. I bet that priest would be grateful for the help."

The Chief Inspector's brow rose. "That sounds very good. How soon can you get started? We really don't have much time."

Then he frowned. "I don't know, Carroll. This man is very dangerous. I'm hesitant about giving you such a challenge for your first time."

She stood up. "Sir, we're up to the task. Now, I don't want to sound rude, but we're wasting time." She extended her hand to him. "We'll start today."

Five minutes later, the secretary announced, "Chief, Inspectors Ross and Bobbie are here."

O'Doul motioned for them to sit. "Well, I've just met your Dream Team leader."

Bobbie smiled. "Yes, she rather flew by us in the hall. She was smiling so I assumed you approved using her team."

O'Doul chuckled. "One of us did. Haven't quite accepted having women agents assigned to dangerous tasks."

Bobbie looked over at Ross and grinned. "You're not alone sir."

The Chief sat down and cleared his throat. "I've sent an investigative team and the bomb squad out to Woking. How were you able to detect the back door was booby trapped?"

Ross frowned shrugging his shoulders. "Bobbie..."

"I climbed through the kitchen window and saw it when I looked around."

The Chief shook his head. He mumbled to himself. "Another Dream Team... Twice in one day."

"Chief, if it's all right with you, I'd like to ask the Admiral to go out to the Braun estate with us and have an open conversation with Arthur, putting our cards on the table, letting him know all of our concerns."

The Chief sat back tapping the tobacco in his pipe. He lit his pipe and nodded. "You might have a good idea."

He leaned forward and picked up the phone. "I've his private number. Admiral Benjamin, please. Yes, this is."

O'Doul frowned and shook his head. "Hmm. When will he return? Have him call as soon as possible. Thank you."

He hung up. "That's very strange. The Admiral called this morning and told his aide that he would be on vacation until Monday. I know he loves to fish, but, in light of this Braun business..."

Ross and Bobbie rose together. Firmly Ross said, "I'm not going to call for an appointment; I still think it best just to go out there. We'll go tomorrow ...We'll stay in touch."

The two inspectors got to the door when the Chief stood up. "Ross, tomorrow is Saturday! What are you investigating to warrant the intrusion? Or, are you letting your emotions lead?"

Ross stopped and dropped his head. "Chief, I'm sure my emotions have a lot to do with this. I won't deny that! I have to say, all we saw this morning has put a different light on this hypothetical situation. All that I heard from you and the Admiral on this matter, and the drastic change in Alex's behavior, a man I've known for many years, leads me to feel that something awful is about to happen and I really think Arthur knows more than he's telling us."

Ross turned. "Sir, with all due respect to you and the Yard, don't tell me I can't go out there. I realize this is a sensitive matter and a lot of embarrassment could come of it if I make a fool out of myself. I just want to let Arthur know what we know. If it helps avert a nasty situation, then I've done my job. If nothing happens, then Arthur will think I'm a nutter."

Chief O'Doul stared at Ross. *Maybe he's right. It would be a worse embarrassment if we didn't follow through and something did happen. I'd feel better if Benjamin were there. Damn, why would ...*

"Chief, I'll be there too."

The Chief shook his head grinning. "If they don't answer the door, you'll not climb through any windows!" He raised his brows to her.

Bobbie shrugged her shoulders and smiled. "Yes, sir."

"Now, go and keep me informed. Use an official car. There's a phone in it. Here's my number at home."

Bobbie grabbed the Chief's card and almost pushed Ross out the door.

The end is in sight

Sheila poured a cup of tea. It had gone on eleven in the morning.
"Do I hear you rattling your cup and saucer?"

She sat down at her kitchen table. "Bishop, I'm scared! This whole situation has just hit me and now I don't know if I can go through with it. Are you still there?"

"I'm here. You know we've told you, you can quit at any time. Problem is, you'll have to tell Windsor you can't go through it."

"Someone's at my door."

She opened the door and there stood Lauren with a big grin. "I worked at home this morning and before I leave for work, I wanted to wish you good luck on your shoot. Hope it gives you a boost at your job."

"Come on in. I'm just having a cup of tea."

Lauren got a cup and poured her own. "I was wondering what time you think you'll be wrapping up today. It would be fun to come out and watch."

Sheila's insecurity evaporated. *That can't happen. No Way!* She shook her head. "Sorry, you'll have to come out after we've left... The magazine had a hard enough time getting a window of two hours for this shooting from the Braun regime, let alone have observers. What's more, the Princess Kimberly isn't at all amenable to being photographed. In actual fact, she's a bitch."

302

Sheila could hear chuckling in her ear plant.

"Sheila! She isn't! You're just putting me on."

"Well...someone has laid down a lot of rules of what we can and can't do. So I would definitely call before you come."

The phone rang. "Hello, oh, you're here! I'll buzz you in."

She hung up and looked at Lauren. "Sorry, I have to cut our visit short."

She pressed the buzzer. "Two of my crew are here to go over the plans and pick me up."

Lauren put her cup down. *This really must be a major job for her. She's hardly herself.* "Are you okay?"

Sheila opened the door. "Yeah, I'm fine. I just haven't worked with these guys before and you know most men don't like having a woman for a boss...Don't worry..."

Sheila walked Lauren out the door. She could hear noise coming from the stairway. "You'll call first?"

Lauren passed Charlie and Peter on the stairwell. *These must be the men Sheila hasn't met yet. They look good. I should be done around three. I promised I would call.*

ॐॐ

Sheila opened the door. "You must be Charlie... and Peter. Please come in."

As they walked by, Sheila felt a noise in her ear and it hurt. She heard "earrings" *Son of a bitch, I almost forgot them. What the fuck was that! That hurt.*

Charlie frowned at her. "Are you okay?"

Sheila stood still and the pain left. They sat down. She moved a little toward them and felt this pain again.

She nodded her head. "If you'll excuse me I'm just finishing dressing and need to get my earrings. I left them in the bathroom. There's tea in the kitchen. Help yourself. Have a scone. They're delicious."

She dashed into the bathroom and shut the door. *I need to be able to talk to Bishop. Need a diversion.* She flushed the toilet and turned on the tap. She went into the far corner of the bathroom and whispered. " Bishop, I had a piercing pain in my ear when these guys walked past me. What's happened? Is my ear thing broken?"

"No, we felt it too. It's called frequency override. Which means, those men must be wearing listening devices similar to yours. Here's what we have to do. We have to find another frequency that is compatible. So for a short time we'll have to unplug you."

"You should have put in an implant for my heart because this one has just left the apartment!"

"You're fine. Sheila, these men need you. They aren't going to hurt you. So put your earrings on and get out there. There are ten seals around the apartment watching. Now do your stuff!"

She felt the disconnection. *Look in the mirror. You can do this. Go!*

Sheila left the bathroom abruptly, thinking she had been in there a long time. Charlie and Peter had just taken a bite of scone when she returned.

"Sorry, one of my earrings fell off the dresser under the tub. Did you find everything?"

They both nodded with mouths full.

"Here's the schedule Kimberly Braun's secretary gave me. They're allowing four sittings and that's it. Obviously we'll do the outdoor stuff first and then inside. I've only been to the mansion once and that was years ago, but, I do remember the library would make an excellent background."

Charlie put his cup down. "That'll work. Four sittings will give you at least fifty cuts per."

He handed her a photo album. "Peter and I can handle the camera as well as the lighting. Hope you won't mind us making suggestions."

She looked through the pages. *A little on the grotesque side but the shading is great.* She frowned at Charlie. "Do you work at the morgue?"

Charlie grinned. "No, we're ambulance chasers for an insurance company. Those were used for advertisement." *She's a good photographer. Shame this is her last gig.*

Sheila looked at her watch. "I think we'd better go."

The Show begins

Putting on the Admiral's uniform jacket, Alex turned from the mirror to Windsor and the doctor, mimicking the Admiral's voice. "What do you think?"

Windsor put his arm around Eddie. "This is amazing!"

He walked up to Alex and studied his face and around the neck. "You can't see any transition. Perfect. Just perfect."

Alex looked at his watch. "It's one o'clock." He took the suit coat off and hung it up and then put on an apron. "I'm going to set the explosives. You need to pack up all of your stuff and put it in the van."

Eddie smiled at Windsor and then looked at Alex. "Will you be on the first floor? I think we have time to shower."

Alex shrugged his shoulders. "God, how many times do you guys...."

Windsor chuckled. "As many times as we can. You should try it. With someone else of course."

Eddie sashayed to the stairway. "It helps me keep focused."

Alex shook his head. *I'm sure. I need to focus on where I need to place these.*

❧✦❧

After all the pins were in place, Alex took the box of explosives outdoors and put most of them around the perimeter of the building. He came in and stared at the table the Admiral was on. *I've got one left. It seems only fitting to put it under the table. Maybe I should set the timer to go off ten seconds before the others.* "You'll lead the pack. You're set to go off at three twenty nine!"

Alex looked at his watch. *Where are those two?* He opened the door and yelled up the stairs. "We have to leave in ten minutes!"

He set the timer and placed it on the lower shelf of the table. As he stood up the Admiral's hand grabbed his apron. "Why are you doing this?"

Alex pulled the Admiral's hand off of his apron and stood up. He mimicked him, "Well, look who's awake."

He stared in the Admiral's face. "Feel like you're looking in the mirror?"

Eddie and Windsor appeared. "Should I give him a final dose?"

Alex grinned and shook his head. "No, we want the Admiral to enjoy his very own explosion. He will be the first to fly!"

The Admiral tried to fight against the restraints. "Who are you? At least tell me why?"

Alex took off his apron. "Who am I and Why am I doing this?...Hmm. ah, the first time I did this it was for money. The job got screwed up by one of Braunstein's men. Now this time, it's still for money, but I'm going to let you pick up the prize."

The Admiral's eyes opened wide. "Wyndgate!"

Alex smirked. "Wow, you do remember. I'd loved to stay and reminisce but we have a date with your buddy's niece. We decided to change your schedule and you're going to pick up all Robert's stuff today."

He motioned to Eddie and Windsor. "Shut off the lights and we'll leave the Admiral in peace."

Windsor yelled over the noise of the van engine. "So, who's Wyndgate?"

"Turn on your voice activator so we don't have to shout."

306

The estate photo shoot

It was one forty-five when Charlie stopped at the main gate, and the guard met them. "Miss Jones, you're on the guest list. May I see some identification from your crew members?"

Charlie and Peter handed the guard some fake driver's licenses. "Thank you, enjoy your day."

Arthur met them at the door. "Miss Jones, Miss Kimberly's in the library waiting for you."

Here we go with all the formal stuff. "Charlie, why don't you bring in all the lights and I'll get the subject."

Charlie and Peter stared at the vaulted ceiling as they walked back to the front door. "How'd you like to wake up in a joint like this every day?"

Peter stopped to look at a huge Fresco and whispered, "Can you hear me okay? Perhaps when this is over, we should come back and buy this place."

Charlie chuckled and whispered. "Who'd be the Seller? That's right, our friend Windsor."

Arthur frowned. *They do have devices. I wonder why they didn't give one to Sheila, unless...she's not a part of this plan. Robert needs to know this.*

He started to go toward the kitchen when he felt a hand on his shoulder. " Jesus, Robert, that is so unnerving without my glasses and the implants working. I can understand how Sheila felt."

"Sorry…Have those two left?"

Arthur nodded. "They went out to their van for the lighting equipment. Did you see them talking? I was coming to tell you Sheila wasn't given a device."

Arthur kept watching the front door while they talked.

"Then she is nothing more than a way to get into the house. I still haven't solved the time span of the formula. I have to leave. Another batch won't be ready for another hour. You're going to have to run the show until I can get back.."

"The front door is opening. You better go."

Arthur watched as Charlie and Peter set up the lighting standards in the hall.

A few minutes later Sheila, Kimberly and Duke came in the front door. "Well, I took all the pictures of Miss Braun outdoors. There's a gorgeous balcony off the library and got some nice shots of her and her dog, Duke."

Duke had been trained to be intimidating, but in a friendly way.

Charlie turned his back to the others and whispered to Peter. "That dog is trained to protect the niece. When this goes down, shoot the dog first."

Sheila introduced Charlie and Peter to Kimberly. "We still have forty-five minutes. I'd like to get a series of pics here in the hall. One of you and Duke coming down the main staircase would look very stately."

Kimberly stared at Sheila as she knew Sheila's request was to impress and nothing more.

Sheila gave her a silly grin. "Miss Braun… Just walk down like…you're going out with the love of your life! When the bachelors see these pictures, you'll be the talk of London!"

Kimberly gave her a deadly look. "Thank you so much. Just what I've been wanting."

"That's it. A regal look now."

James, the head of the monitoring station, came to Arthur and whispered. "When are the implants going to be activated? I'm not supposed to leave my post. The gate just called and Admiral Benjamin is here!"

Arthur turned his back to the others and spoke softly. "What? Are you sure? Benjamin?"

"I have to get back. Do I approve? We can't keep him waiting."

"Tell the gate..." and Arthur sighed. "Finally! The implants have come back on...Tell them you've got to get my approval."

He and James walked to the monitoring room. "Robert, thank God, Richard found another frequency. Now, James just told me Benjamin is at the main gate. What are we to do? "

James heard the conversation. "Yes, sir, the Admiral's voice passed the test and when he signed in, his fingerprints on the pen came up as a match.

"Okay, take the Admiral to the library. Make the introductions. The photo shoot is almost over. If those two men are a part of Windsor's plan to get the microfilm, then maybe Benjamin being in there will chicken them out. JB is very good in martial arts, and likes to look the part, especially when women are around. After they leave, you can give him the case and we're done."

Arthur agreed. "I'll be in there too... Plus, Kimberly and Sheila won't just stand there screaming."

"No, but remember they could take her hostage. Make sure they aren't near her. I'll turn on Sheila's implant and tell her. You take care of the rest."

Arthur opened the front door to greet the Admiral. "Good afternoon sir, we weren't expecting you until Monday. May I have your coat?"

Alex smiled within and outwardly and in the Admiral's voice carried on. "Well, I'm sorry for the short notice, but something has come up and I've been called back to the Pentagon. I'm to leave Monday morning. You see, this would work out for all concerned."

The guard took the Admiral's coat into the monitoring room as Windsor said he would. The Admiral fingered his remote in his pocket as he watched.

He turned to Arthur. "I saw a van out front and wondered if you had something going on."

Arthur motioned for him to follow. "One of the magazines asked to do a feature on Miss Kimberly's new position as head of her uncle's company. The photographers are just finishing up…"

The Admiral raised his brows. "That sounds interesting. Photography happens to be one of my hobbies, next to fishing of course."

Arthur opened the library door for the Admiral. *I wonder when he took up that hobby. Robert told us Benjamin spent whatever time he had fishing. Hmm, his wife divorced him because of it.*

The shooting stopped. Kimberly stood up from the chair she was posing in.

"Miss Kimberly, this is your uncle's good friend and former commander, Admiral John Benjamin."

"Yes, I do remember meeting you. I was just a little girl at the time."

They shook hands. The Admiral just smiled and nodded. "Please, carry on. I'd love to watch."

Kimberly was puzzled. *I wonder why he doesn't chat on like he did the other day on the phone. Maybe because there're strangers in the room.*

Sheila had some background music going to set the mood for Kimberly. Arthur stood by the door. "Boom!" Even over the music Arthur felt something. He frowned and opened the door. *What the hell was that noise? I smell smoke!*

Closing the door behind him, Arthur went out into the hall. Smoke poured from the monitoring room. *Now what has happened?*

He ran and whispered, "Robert, James, Martin! Can you hear me?"

He found James and his other guards slumped over. The screens were shattered. He felt for a pulse. *Thank God, they aren't dead.* He pressed the main alarm and nothing. *I hope the silent alarm has a backup! Kimberly! I've got to get back to her. How did a bomb get in here? The last person was…*

As Arthur ran from the room, a crashing blow from behind knocked him to the floor. Dazed and in pain, Arthur tried to get up.

310

Windsor kicked him in the stomach as Arthur turned over. "Not going to happen, you mother fucker." He then knelt down and grabbed him by the shirt and kissed him hard on the lips. "That is your kiss of death. I told you I'd be back."

Windsor spit in Arthur's face.

Eddie shook his head. *Oh God, he's got that look on his face.* "Jesus, Windsor. How dramatic is that!"

Windsor got up and took out his gun. "Drama? I've just begun."

" Windsor, stick with the program. You'll get your chance."

Eddie shook Windsor's arm hard. "Snap out of it, Windsor! You can't lose control! *Not now!* You'll get us killed!" The doctor got into Windsor's face. "All of this will be for nothing but your vengeance."

Windsor's eyes were glued to Arthur as he stepped back.

The unexpected happens

Inspectors Ross and Bobbie arrived at the main gate. Ross honked his horn. "That's strange. Why isn't the gate opening? I'm sure they can see the emblem on the car."

The walk-through gate opened and the guard came out. Ross rolled down his window.

"Is there a problem with your system?"

He and Bobbie showed their badges. "We've been here before."

The guard nodded. "You're names are on our list of repeat visitors. I can let you in but you'll have to give me a moment to release the control to manual."

Ross jumped out. "I can help. Release it and I'll push the gate open."

Bobbie scooted into the driver's seat and drove through.

Ross got back in. "Has this happened before?"

"No sir, the silent alarm has gone off and the power is gone from the gate and monitor. I'm not supposed to leave my post. I can't get anyone to respond. We have been training for emergencies this past week, but I don't know if this is a drill."

"We'll tell Arthur."

Ross started up. Bobbie put her hand on his. "Why don't we take him with us? He can lock the gate. His name is John. If you didn't see his tag."

Ross backed up a bit. "John!"

The guard came out of the gatehouse and walked over to the car. "Yes, inspector."

Bobbie leaned across Ross. "To save time. Why don't you ride with us and then you can tell Arthur yourself."

The guard frowned. "Thank you, but my orders say I can't leave my post under any circumstance."

"Okay, just thought we could save you some time."

The guard walked half way back to the guardhouse when an explosion knocked him to the ground.

Ross screeched to a halt looking in his rear view mirror. "Oh! My God. That guardhouse has blown up."

They got out of the car and ran back to the guard lying in the grass.

Ross put his coat over the young man. "Is he alive?"

Bobbie nodded. "His pulse is strong. He's breathing. Thank God you called to him!"

She took her coat off, rolled it up and put it under his head. "Dennis, you better call the Chief."

Just then John, the guard, opened his eyes and tried to get up. "Stay down. Give yourself a minute."

He did what he was told. "I don't think anything is broken, mum."

"Can you explain any of this? Has anyone been around today?"

"I came on duty at two o'clock. A magazine photographer for a photo shoot arrived earlier. They were expected. Then around three something, Admiral Benjamin arrived. He wasn't on the expected list so I had to call it in for approval. He had to wait for about five minutes and wasn't too happy about it."

Ross frowned at Bobbie. "Didn't the Chief say Benjamin had gone fishing."

"There's a large pond in the back of the estate. He was driving and not in any official car either. Maybe he wanted the privacy. Though.."

Bobbie stopped Ross from asking another question. "Though what, John?"

John sat up and brushed his hands through his hair. "I'm okay now. I can get up."

Ross helped him. "What were you going to say about the Admiral?"

John stood up and adjusted his jacket. "Well, it just seemed strange for him to come in a van and be dressed in full uniform."

Ross looked at his watch. "It's almost four. We'll take you up to the house."

"Dennis, before we go, maybe we should check in with the Chief. Blowing up a guardhouse doesn't seem like a training exercise."

John got into the back seat. "Inspector Ross. There's another road we can take to the mansion and you won't be seen. It'll be dark soon."

Bobbie motioned to him. "How do we get there? We still have a long way to the house."

"A quarter of a mile, mum. At the fork take the road on the right. That will go to the rear of the estate. There's an area of trees and bushes you can stop at if you want to look around."

Ross drove around a corner.

"On the left about fifty yards, you can hide your car, sir."

Before Ross came to a full stop, Bobbie was out of the car.

She had found a pair of binoculars in the glove box. "Someone has just come out of the house."

"Dennis, that's that Charlie from Interpol!"

"Are you sure?"

She handed him the binoculars. "Look!" She stood back for him.

"You're right, it is..."

"You've got to call the Chief, now!"

They hurried back to car.

Bobbie paced in front of him. "Alex is in there with those guys. He's got everyone hostage to get to the formulas! What else could it be?"

While Ross called in his report to his superior, Bobbie and the guard watched for any other activity. "John, how far are we from the back? Aren't those garages over there?"

"Yes they are. We're at least fifty yards from them. Can you run that far?"

She glared at him. "I'm not that much older than you!"

In a matter of minutes, Ross concluded his conversation. "Yes sir, one of us will call. You can send back-up but we can't wait another minute. Something is happening in there. My idea of going to the front door will give them a good chance of not being seen going to a back entrance. The line is breaking up... Have you heard from Carroll's team? ..."

Bobbie met Ross as he got out of the car. She nodded with lips pressed together. "You don't think the three of us can get across the grass so you're going to be a decoy?" She put her hands on her hips. "Dennis, why not wait a little longer? A storm must be coming, the sky is darkening. Besides, you've got such a great rapport with Arthur, you're going to go to the front door and say you were just passing by and thought you'd stop for a cup of tea!"

Ross held back a smile. *She is so beautiful even when she's madder than a...* "Bobbie, we don't have time to discuss this. I'm just going to the door; I'll see if Arthur can talk and if not I'll leave. You and John run as soon as I get to the door. We don't know how many people Alex has working with him. By the time the Chief gets here, it could be too late... Now go on. You know this is the only way we have."

Ross rolled down the window. "Wait until you see the front door open."

Bobbie held up a little flashlight to him. "Can you read Morse code?"

Ross frowned at her. "What do you mean?"

" I've got a red indicator light on this. If you see it flash, it will be me. Can you read it?"

He turned the car around. "Yes, I can. Be careful!"

315

51

The Dream Team in Burlington

At two-forty five p.m., Inspector Carroll's Dream team pulled into a gas depot.

Kitty Carroll took out her notebook. "Hennessy, it's your turn to fill us up. No smoking either. Remember you're a nun today."

She looked in the rear mirror and saw how tired her team was. "Sorry, I've had to push you hard the last two days. We really have to do a good job; I want the Chief to realize what an asset we can be."

Theresa leaned forward. "Couldn't you have come up with a better idea than posing as nuns? These clothes are so stiff, I've got a rash and my one foot hurts in these shoes."

Linda Severance and her sister Karen laughed. "Her foot hurts because I knew she was going to let out with the F bomb at one of the houses and I stepped on her."

"Well that ass hole gave me the finger when I told him the church missed seeing him."

They all leaned back laughing. Hennessy got back in the car. "Filled up and ready to go...home! Right?"

Carroll looked over to her newest recruit, Linda Burr. "Well, you've got the map, are we done?"

"Say, yes" came the call from the back seat.

"In actual fact there are two more streets, back to back. The first one is across from us, Sheldon Street. We would've missed it had we not stopped for petrol."

Carroll drove across the road and down a little hill. "What's this? Three houses and two buildings! We still have to check them out." She pulled into the first building's parking lot.

They all piled out of the car. Carroll glanced around. "You can take part of the habits off now. I don't think you need them in this area. It's five after three; I told the Chief I would give him a report by four."

Inspectors Crough and Severance shed their stuff and headed to the building to look around.

Theresa Crough waved her arm. "Heads up over here."

The group walked over to where she had squatted down looking at some tire tracks.

"What did you find?"

She looked up and pointed. "These tracks are fresh. I'd say within the last twenty-four hours. Plus, there are some cigarettes butts, Dunhill, right next to them. Those ciggys aren't cheap."

Crough squatted next to her. "Must have rained. These are good tracks. My guess is, they are from a sports car. Rather new at that."

Karen looked. "Terry, are you pulling our legs?"

Crough glared at Karen, "You know, I'm not just a pretty face! My father was a mechanic, my uncle …."

Severance piped in. "Trust me, she's right. I had a summer job at her uncle's place. I met her way back then."

Carroll pulled off her head gear and tossed it in the car. "Okay, we better split up in partners. Linda, you and Theresa look around the front. Karen and Burr check the sides of the building and I'll take Hennessy. We'll check the back. Have your guns ready. You know the drill."

They split up and headed to their areas. Severance turned the front door knob. "This door is open." She stepped inside. "This is strange; the light works in the hall."

Inspector Crough put her hand on her partner's shoulder. "Don't take another step!"

Severance froze. "Why? What's the matter?"

"Just step back two steps!"

"Now, look down at the floor and follow that string that's across the entrance."

Severance's mouth dropped open. "Holy crap. There's a bomb by the wall!"

Crough pointed her flashlight. "This is an easy one. Give me your pocket knife and then go tell the others to be looking for more. Wait a minute! "

She knelt down. "Oh fuck! Linda, this has a timer on it. It set for three thirty!"

Severance looked at her watch. "Holy shit, Terry, it's three-fifteen!"

"Just run and tell the others. I'll defuse this."

Crough found two more outside and then ran to the back carrying one of the explosives. "Look, this is what you do. Before you pull the timer out, cut the blue wire, *not* the white one. *Then* pull the timer out."

Before long, they had fourteen explosives on the grass away from the building.

"Where are Carroll and Hennessy?"

Karen put her explosive down. "I saw them go in that basement door."

Burr looked at her watch. "It's twenty-three after. We still don't know if we're in the clear. Why would anyone want to blow up this property? What are they hiding?"

Severance, Burr and Crough headed to the basement door. "All good questions, Burr, but we still need to find Carroll. Let's go in. Karen, stay out here by the door and keep track of the time. Give us a countdown."

With flashlights shining, the three went in.

Karen yelled in. "It's twenty-four after"

Severance yelled. "Carroll, Hennessy!"

They came to the main basement room and opened the door. The light was on.

They saw Carroll and Hennessy trying to hold up a man who was almost lifeless. They had cut his restraints and had him sitting up.

"We found this man. He's too big for us to move. Give us a hand!"

They heard Karen. "Guys, it's twenty-five after!"

The man tried to talk. "Bomb!....Bomb under!"

Crough frowned and stared at the table. *Under...of course under the table.*

Crough helped him off the table. "Come on mister, give us some help here. Stand on your fuckin legs!"

He opened his eyes. "Bomb, under... table." And passed out.

Crough tore the sheet off and looked. "It's in a deep box!"

Karen yelled. "It's three twenty eight!"

Crough couldn't pick up the box nor the explosive. "Severance, this won't pull out, and I can't see to cut the wire!"

Severance fell to the floor with her flashlight. "It's been duct taped! Put one arm in and I'll guide you...slowly to the right. Okay, cut it!"

"It's three twenty nine!"

Crough pulled out the timer and they sunk to the floor looking at it. It had three twenty nine on it.

She took a deep breath and looked over at Severance. "That was too fuckin close!"

Hennessy yelled, "Could use a hand here!"

They rushed to get the man up the ramp. Carroll ran to the car.

Burr pulled off her coat. "The concrete is too cold. We can make a nest out of our coats to put him in."

∾∾

Out of breath, she called the Chief Inspector. "Sir, we're at 420 Sheldon Road in Burlington. We need an ambulance ASAP. We've found a man tied in restraints. My team has defused fifteen timed explosives....yes, sir he's at least six feet, trim. Just a minute."

Carroll yelled. "Severance, are there any markings on the back of his left shoulder?"

Karen waved. "Can you bring the car?"

Carroll waved. "Sir, I'll have to call you back! Ah, yes, a helicopter could get in here."

She backed the car up to the ramp, opened the trunk and pulled out blankets and the first aid case. "The best we can do is keep him warm. Chief is sending a rescue helicopter…Oh were there any markings?"

Burr took his pulse. "He's got a good pulse, and it looks like a scar from a gunshot wound on his back shoulder."

The basement door opened. Crough turned quickly, pulling her gun. "Holy…"

Severance raised her brows and motioned that Carroll was standing there.

Crough smiled, "Holy gosh!...Hennessy! You darn near got a bullet. What happened to your outfit?"

Hennessy almost dropped the vials in her hand. "Sorry! Oh gosh! That would've been awful…" She squinted at Crough pursing her lips. She had pulled the bottom of her dress through her legs and tucked the end in her belt giving her a pair of pants. "You're just jealous of my designer talents!"

"Boss, I found these on the bench. It's some kind of drug." Hennessy handed them to Carroll. "I'd forgotten my flashlight, and saw these. There're several bags of stuff and a big mixing bowl too."

Within a few minutes, the helicopter whirled to a landing.

Carroll gave the rescue team the vials and they rushed the man into the side door of the chopper and lifted off.

"Yes sir, they just took off. By the way, one of my team is a nurse and said the mark on the man's shoulder looked like an old wound. Next week. Yes sir. Thank you."

Carroll hung up. Turned to her team radiating a huge smile. "Well, we are now an official task force for Scotland Yard! Yes! Thank you, you performed brilliantly."

52

Ross and Bobbie gain entrance

John, the guard, moved to the side of the end bush. "We should run from here, inspector. You'll be able to see his car from here...He's coming now."

Ross was half way to the front door when he heard the car phone ringing. *Damn, it can only be the Chief. Wonder if he orders me not to go in. Should I ignore it? Oh, hell.*

He went back to the car. "Yes sir, I... What? "

"Thank God you answered. That dream team found a man I think is Admiral Benjamin, in a basement at Sheldon St. Burlington. We've checked the address and that Doctor Edse owns it...Ross, my guess is Alex is impersonating the Admiral, and has partnered up with Windsor and Edse. You're walking into a trap!"

Ross looked at the ground and shut his eyes. "Someone has surely seen me from the house. I've got to go in. At least I'll be ready for them."

Ross knocked on the front door.

Eddie looked out the monitoring room window. "Windsor, there's an official car from Scotland Yard out front! Looks like an inspector at the door and he's alone."

Windsor put the barrel of his gun in Arthur's neck. "Friend of yours? Why would Scotland Yard come out here?"

Arthur fought the pain. "It must be Inspector Ross. He suspects you had something to do with Lucille's death."

Ross pounded on the door harder.

" Smart guy. Obviously, your friend isn't going to leave."

Eddie rushed over to Windsor. "I told Alex about this man at the door. He said to tell Arthur to answer. If it's Inspector Ross, capture him as well."

Windsor glared at Eddie and then at Arthur. "Why not have a fuckin party, while we're at it."

Windsor and Eddie got Arthur up and pushed him to the door. Windsor got into Arthur's face. "May I remind you, three people in the library are ready to kill Kimberly the minute I say her name."

Arthur straightened his jacket, brushed his hands through his hair and opened the door. "Inspector Ross, come in." He flashed his eyes and jerked his head a little.

The Inspector smiled and nodded. "I have some more information for you."

Arthur stepped aside, wincing in pain. "I'll take your coat and hat."

Windsor and Eddie came out from the monitoring room. "Inspector Ross, I believe you want to talk to me. I'm Windsor Braun and this is my associate Doctor Edward Edse. Under the circumstances, this ends our pleasantries. Sorry!"

Windsor and Eddie pointed their guns at them and motioned to move to the library.

Sheila and Kimberly were working on the last pose at the big desk when out of the corner of her eye, Kimberly saw someone approaching.

"*Windsor!.. Edse!* Arthur, how did they get in?"

She gasped at the sight of Windsor's gun in Arthur's back.

Windsor saw Arthur flinch and grit his teeth. "Charlie, Peter? I think it's time you get involved here."

The two men in the back of the room pulled out automatic weapons. "We're ready!"

ॐℭ

Bobbie and John reached the garages. Out of breath and scared, Bobbie took a moment looking at the two vans. "John, do you have a knife?"

John stared at her. "Yes, but for what?"

"Come on! Puncture the tires! Will the hoods open? Let's get rid of the distributor caps."

They ran back to the side entrance of the garage. "Inspector, we can go in here. It's going to be dark. Just hold onto the back of my jacket."

She watched him put on some glasses. "Are those night vision?"

"A bit more than that, but, we can still see in the dark." He felt her knocking into the fender of one of the cars. "Put them on and you can see what I mean."

"Wow, it's like being in daylight. Should we disable these cars too?'

A deep voice behind her said. "It's already been done."

Bobbie drew her gun and wheeled around. "Who the…"

"Inspector! It's okay, it's Martin , one of the staff!"

Bobbie put her gun down and sighed. "Oh, my gosh. You scared me to death." *I've never shot anyone before. To think I almost did! To think I almost did!*

Her heart pounded. She bent down to catch her breath while Martin and John whispered.

John took his glasses back and led her to another door. He swiped the door with his medallion. A light came on in a chamber.

Her mouth opened, he laughed. "Come on. We're okay now. Wait here."

Bobbie turned around. *That big door closed and I didn't hear it. I can't be dreaming all this!* She walked up to it with a frown. *That's not a door! It's….it's a wall!*

John came back with two bikes. "We have to hurry."

"John, where are we? That was a wall you opened! We need to get inside the house to help Ross."

John pumped on the pedals. "That's what we're doing. Hurry!"

They rode swiftly down a long ramp to the Braun lab in about three minutes, what would have been a fast ten minute walk.

Bobbie got off her bike almost breathless. "No one will ever believe this!"

"You sit out here, and I'll be right back."

Five minutes later, John gave her a pair of glasses like he was wearing. He got right in her face and stared at her. "Inspector, you have to trust me. I don't have time to explain any of this to you because you probably wouldn't believe it. Just keep these on and you'll be able to see everyone!"

Bobbie frowned. "What do you mean see..."

"Shush, just listen and follow directions. Everyone's life depends on it, including Inspector Ross...No questions...Okay?"

She nodded. "As long as you promise a full explanation later."

"Deal! Come on. We're going in here to find out the plan."

Robert Braun commenced the meeting. "We know the main body of our communications for the estate is destroyed. Your implants for one on one communication are useless. The backup system is working giving electricity. This is about all we have at this time. At least the medallions can be used."

The door opened and Martin went to the front of the room. Robert stepped aside.

Martin picked up a pointer stick. "Could you project a first floor plan of the house? Thanks...."

He pointed to the library. "We have five people in harm's way. Kimberly, Arthur, the Admiral, hopefully Sheila, and an Inspector from Scotland Yard. We've four targets, Windsor, Edse and Sheila's two crew men. At this time, we can't rule out Sheila so you must keep her in your sights."

Robert stepped forward. "Speak up if any of you have an idea. Since we can't talk to either Sheila or Arthur, we can't hear what's going on in the room. We know they're here to get my code."

Bobbie flinched. "What! That's..."

John stared at her. "Shush!"

"We have to act fast. Every minute counts. Windsor is a time bomb and will go off if he doesn't get what he wants."

Bobbie's head was down when the door opened and Richard, one of the lab engineers, rushed up to Robert. She peered out over the glasses. Her eyes got huge and her mouth fell open. *That man is talking and facing to a blank space! Holy mother that's what this is all about! Braun's formula is... She pushed her glasses back on. That's better. There's a dog too!*

Richard showed a paper. "Robert, I think I've come up with a back handed way to communicate with Arthur."

Robert's eyes widened. "How?"

"We can do it by relay. To use the ear implants I've had to restructure the frequencies. It dawned on me to go back to the primitive basic levels! We can't possibly create any disturbance at those levels! The downside is, I can only have one or two people on a frequency load. I'd need three levels, but still that wouldn't interfere with the levels Windsor is using."

Richard turned around looking at the key players. "It sounds difficult, but it'll work."

The Bishop raised his hand. "Robert, the space behind the wall safe. We could put someone in there. They can see what's going on and tell Richard."

Richard nodded. "That would work. That person will tell me what's going on in the library. Then I'll tell you and the others. It'll take longer, but..." He shrugged. "It'll work and really it's all you have now."

Bobbie nudged John. "Tell him we'll do that. I can signal Ross."

John raised his hand. "Sir, Inspector Ross's partner is with us and she has a signaling light she feels would work too."

Martin and Bishop stepped in front of Robert. "How much time do we have left in this invisible state?"

Robert shook his head. "Not much, maybe forty minutes at the most. You realize, we're the only ones to get in there."

Martin rubbed his head. "Is that back entrance wall still operating? The one back by the conference table? You'd talked about closing it off for more space."

"I'd forgotten about that wall. That's a great idea, but we first need to see what's going on in there."

They turned around. "John, good idea. You and the inspector go now with Richard and get what you need. Martin will let you know when you can cross the main hall."

Robert put his hands on the shoulder of Martin and Bishop. "Listen, you know you can…"

The two faced their boss and good friend. Bishop put his hand on Robert's shoulder. "Robert, we know that, but after all these years we're a family and we take care of our own. Come on."

Robert held his arm. "Bishop, this is a do or die situation!"

Martin stared at Robert tilting his head. "Oh, and Korea wasn't?" He rushed out to meet John and the Inspector.

"Duke, time to go!"

᪥

Martin waited for John and Bobbie to come up to the kitchen. "Shush, keep your voices down."

He chuckled at the old fashioned headset and mouthpiece John had. "That is pretty primitive stuff you've got there. Damn good thing Richard kept all that equipment."

John whispered back. "Richard said it all had to be compatible."

Martin handed them some booties. "I'll check the hall while you put these on."

Martin came back in the kitchen. "I've another idea. I'm going to stand by the wall that opens. When I signal, run straight across the hall from this doorway to me. When you get within range of the room, I'll open the wall."

Bobbie blurted. "But you'll be…" She blushed. "Never mind, I forgot these glasses."

"That's okay. The room is very small. You'll find about four port doors. They're one way so you won't be seen. Call Richard as soon as you get in. Are you ready?"

They both nodded.

Martin scooted across and stopped where the wall would open. Just as he lifted his arm the library door opened. *Holy shit, now what!* He immediately signaled to stay put. Bobbie stood in the doorway

326

ready to run, but John grabbed her up and pulled her back into the kitchen.

Peter stopped to shut the door behind him. He spoke to Charlie. "I've got to take a leak. How long is Alex going to let that ass hole have his revenge? He's going to kill him before the safe is opened…I'll be quick."

When the bathroom door shut, Martin waved and mouthed. "Run!"

John took Bobbie by the hand and they ran straight for Martin. The wall closed as the bathroom door opened.

Martin took a deep breath. *Shit! Not even another second!*

He waited for Peter to go back into the library and then went to join Robert and the Bishop.

Windsor exceeds the plan

Windsor and Edse escorted everyone away from the desk. Windsor ordered the Admiral to sit near the couch where he had Sheila and Kimberly.

"Ross and Arthur, sit in those club chairs." He sneered. "I don't want you too far from this wall. The safe is still in there, isn't it?"

"Charlie, give Sheila the plastic ties. She can tie their hands behind them."

Charlie handed her the plastic ties and then moved to the back wall near the library door. Sheila tied each man up, with her hand inside the tie, yanked on it giving Windsor the impression she'd done it well.

The Admiral, playing his role to bluff Arthur, asked, "Who are you and why are you here?"

Windsor smirked. "I'm the real master of this house! Am I not, Arthur?" With the butt of his gun, Windsor whipped across Arthur's face, knocking him violently back into his chair.

Kimberly jumped to her feet. "Windsor, *are you insane!"*

When she rushed to help Arthur, Windsor grabbed her face. "If he doesn't tell me the combination to this safe, you'll be the next to feel my insanity, cousin!" Sneering, Windsor pushed her back onto the couch.

Sheila, breaking Kimberly's fall, whispered. "Just wait, he'll do something stupid."

"You see, Admiral, we happen to want what you're here to pick up. So, Arthur, are you going to unlock this fuckin safe or ..."

Windsor rushed over to the fireplace and grabbed the poker. "Do you need some coaxing?"

He stabbed Arthur in the leg. Arthur wrenched back and forth, not uttering a sound.

Ross dropped his head and shut his eyes. *God, I felt that!*

He saw the blood flowing from Arthur's pant leg.

Windsor yanked Arthur's head back by his hair and whispered. "Do you know what a cock sucker is?" He turned Arthur's head to face Kimberly, and whispered again. "You've got five minutes to give me the combination, or... before you die, you're going to watch!"

Windsor grinned. "Hey, what do you think? Great idea isn't it, *Arthur?*" He let go of Arthur's head and it dropped. Arthur lost consciousness.

Sheila and Kimberly shut their eyes. Sheila held Kimberly tight and whispered, "Somebody called Richard just said in my ear to get Windsor's attention. Don't look at me. I'll make the first move and then you follow. Squeeze my hand if you can handle this."

Kimberly responded with a vice-like grip!

Ross looked over at the Admiral. *His lips moved. That's Alex all right and no one knows but me and these thugs. He's got to be giving orders to Windsor or all of them. I wonder if Bobbie and John made it inside. If I say anything, they'll kill me before I can help.*

৯৵৩

John and Bobbie quickly opened the four ports.

"Richard, can you hear me? It's John. I'm afraid to talk too loud. We can see the whole area. Windsor has practically maimed Arthur. He looks to be unconscious. Kimberly and Sheila are okay. The Inspector's head is down. Can't tell if he's been hurt. The Admiral is sitting by himself. It looks like he's being guarded by one of the thugs. Windsor and Edse are standing next to Arthur's chair by the safe."

"That's dreadful...I'll pass that on to Robert... I've given a message to Arthur and Sheila, but now from what you've said, I doubt if Arthur heard it... By now, Robert, Martin and Bishop should be in the back of the room near the conference table. Can you see them?"

John checked the last port. "Yes, I see them. There're no lights on in that portion of the room so they can move freely. The rest of the library is lit up."

" Okay, Robert said their footprints will show in the carpeting, so they'll need a distraction to move. We're running out of time. They have twenty minutes before they become visible."

John looked flushed. "Gosh, what can we do? I feel so helpless, watching this horror!"

Bobbie found a slit in the wall. When she saw Windsor talking to Edse, she flashed her red beam on Ross's shoe. *Can see you. Each time you see light make a distraction!* "Dennis read my message! His head's down. He turned a little, and smiled."

John nudged Bobbie. "Richard's talking to Robert. He must've forgotten to shut me off. He told him Scotland Yard is out front."

Wide-eyed, Bobbie stared at John and shook her head. "Tell Richard they can't come in or let it be known they're here. My God, this place will be a blood bath. Those two guys in the back have automatics!"

"Richard, they're at the desk now."

"Sheila, Robert is by the desk. We need to move Bishop past the fireplace to the back of the room. Can you do something?"

Sheila whispered to Kimberly. "Get hysterical. I'm going to hit you."

Kimberly jumped up screaming at Windsor. "You can't let Arthur die. Let me stop the bleeding!"

Windsor gritted his teeth with rage. Sheila slapped Kimberly in the face knocking her back on the couch.

Sheila glared at Windsor. "Let me help Arthur. You kill him and we'll never get out of here with anything!"

Edse took Windsor's arm and whispered. "Alex is getting upset. You've ignored his orders. *Please,* don't screw this up!"

"Sheila, crack one of these by Arthur's nose." The doctor tossed her a smelling salt.

Arthur's head jerked back. She loosened his hands. "Arthur, give me the combination and I'll get the stuff out of the safe."

Arthur heard in his ear. "Arthur, Robert said to open the safe. They're in the room."

He whispered to Sheila with effort. Sheila relayed his message to Windsor. "He has to touch the knob or it won't open."

With that the phone rang. Sheila put her head down. *That's got to be Lauren.* She glared at Windsor. "Lauren wanted to watch and I told her we'd be done around four. I've got to answer it or you'll have another one to handle."

She walked to the desk and heard Richard. "Answer the phone from the back of the desk. Robert and Martin are standing in the front. We've got fifteen minutes before they will be visible! You've got to hurry!"

"Hi Lauren. Yes, we're just wrapping things up. Kimberly has gone to her room to change. I told her you might call. She said she wanted to have dinner out tonight and would meet you at the Pub where you ate the other night. She said it was your favorite. Have to go. Bye." *God I hope that sounded sincere.*

Lauren frowned as she put the phone down. *The other night we ate with Uncle Charles and Aunt Harriet. Favorite pub? It's only after four. I'll go pick her up.*

Sheila rushed back to Arthur. "Put your arm around me."

She eased him toward the safe.

Windsor stepped quickly away from Arthur's movement. Arthur glared over his shoulder at Windsor with satisfaction. *That weasel is still afraid of me.*

Sheila helped him sit after the safe door had opened. Arthur felt a hand on his shoulder and knew the end of the nightmare neared.

Windsor yelled at Sheila! "Tie his fuckin hands behind him!"

She frowned. "Yeah, he's going to leap out of this chair and tackle you." She tied his hands and glared at Windsor. "Okay, now are the odds even?"

Windsor smirked at her. "Tie Kimberly's hands and the Admiral!

We're taking them with us for insurance." He reached into the safe and took out the envelope. "Eddie, we've finally beaten that bastard."

Eddie grabbed Windsor's arm. "No more violence. Let's just go."

All the commotion allowed Robert to move by the wall safe, behind Windsor and Edse. The Bishop moved behind the Admiral ready to handle Charlie. Martin moved within arm's reach of Peter.

Richard spoke to Robert. "Robert, you've got five minutes! It's now or never!"

Robert put his thumb up and showed a finger countdown. Three, two, one.

Robert's voice rang out. "You haven't beaten me yet, Windsor!"

Windsor's shoulder wheeled around and out of nowhere he felt a blow to his stomach knocking him to the floor.

"And for you, Edward, a small pay back." Robert hit Edse square in the face knocking him out cold. The doctor slumped to the floor next to Windsor's body.

Charlie and Peter, flabbergasted, cocked their guns. "What the fuck was that?"

The Bishop touched Charlie. "Your name Charlie?"

He grabbed Charlie's gun and wheeled him around with his arm around Charlie's neck. He tightened his grip until he heard the crunch of bones. Charlie went limp, slipping out of the Bishop's relaxed hold, and fell to the floor.

When Peter turned to shoot at a blank spot, Martin repeated the act, letting Peter's body slump to the floor.

Suddenly – their time up – the three men became visible.

"John, the five minutes is up! Did they do it?

John wiped his brow. "Just! Not a minute to spare!"

Bobbie poked John to turn. "Look!"

As Kimberly rushed to her uncle, the Admiral drew his gun, grabbing her. "This isn't over yet!" pointing the gun at her head. "Sheila, bring me that envelope, Now!"

He backed Kimberly up to the fireplace away from the Bishop and Martin, motioning them to move over by Robert.

Ross freed his hands and as Sheila passed by him, he jumped up, pushing her away. "Alex, you won't get away with this. *Give it up! It's over!*"

Alex turned his gun on Ross. Kimberly shoved her elbow into his stomach and rolled her body away from him. Alex fired, hitting Ross in the leg.

He recovered from her blow and caught her arm, aiming his gun right at her back. "Not so fast. You're going with me."

Duke, still invisible, didn't need a command. He knew his mistress was in danger. He leaped on Alex, sunk his teeth into the arm holding the gun, and swung his head back forth ravaging the flesh. Blood spurted and then burst as Duke tore out a large piece of flesh.

The gun flew out of Alex's hand and he fell to the floor screaming. "*Call him off! Call him off!*"

His fall didn't dislodge Duke, who was now visible. He'd been trained to protect his family. Duke yanked and shook deepening his grip until Alex lay still.

Robert blocked Kimberly from seeing that Duke had almost torn the arm off. "Sitz dich hin! Platz!"

Blood all over his face, Duke immediately stopped and sat, still staring at Alex.

Bobbie yelled at John. "Open the wall! *Now John!*"

She drew her gun and flew out of the room with John right behind. "John, go down and let the police in and bring the paramedics to the library."

Martin met her at the door. "Inspector, Ross is okay. We've put a tourniquet on his leg and he's resting by the bookcase."

Bobbie crouched by Ross and kissed him on the forehead. He opened his eyes and smiled.

She took his hand. "It's over now. Just relax."

"Is Alex alive?"

She nodded. "Martin told me the dog tore Alex's arm badly. He looks unconscious."

Robert came over to them. "How are you doing? We'll have you out of here in a few more minutes."

Ross muttered. "Doctor Braun…will Arthur make it?"

Robert smiled faintly. "I can tell you he's sustained worse than this."

Robert put his hand on Ross's arm. "You called that man Alex. But he looks like the Admiral, whom I know. Is the Admiral alive?"

"I believe so. Chief Inspector O'Doul can explain it."

Robert stepped back to let the paramedics roll Ross out of the room. Bobbie met the Chief Inspector at the door.

He frowned at the paramedics. "How's he doing?"

They put an IV into Ross's arm and laid the bag on his chest. "We need to get him to surgery."

The Chief followed the gurney with Bobbie. "Sir, if it's alright with you."

"Just go and keep in touch."

☙❧

No one had checked on Windsor and Edse still slumped to the floor.

Windsor regained consciousness but didn't move. He cracked his eyes. *Is Eddie alive? The envelope is next to him. His gun is under him. Bastard took mine. He's talking to someone. That fucker's been alive all along. If I can get Eddie's gun...maybe I can still pull this off.*

Eddie's body had fallen within five inches of Windsor. *The voices sound far enough away I can get his gun if I move slowly.*

Sheila saw Arthur trying to move and went to help. "Hold on. What do you need?"

He whispered. "We never switched the microfilm, where's the envelope?"

She looked over at Windsor's body and saw him move with the gun. "I think it's by...oh my God."

Sheila leaped up and screamed. "*Gun, Windsor, Gun!*"

Windsor saw Robert and pointed the gun at him. Sheila threw herself in front of Robert as Windsor shot.

The Bishop and Martin wheeled and opened fire, hitting Windsor multiple times, slamming his body into the wall of bookcases.

☙❧

Outside the front door, the Chief Inspector turned abruptly. *"Were those gun shots?"*

Inside, Robert and Kimberly caught Sheila as she fell. Blood spurted from her chest. *"Don't* let that ambulance go!"

The paramedic ran back into the room with his bag. "We've got another ambulance on the way!"

He knelt next to Sheila. "Dr. Braun, she won't make it if we don't take her now."

Bishop shook his head. "No, she's not going to die...Martin bring the Land Rover to the front. When you come back, bring a board for a stretcher."

He ordered the paramedic. "Get your adhesive tape out. Kimberly, see if there's any superglue, fast acting glue in the desk."

Robert pointed to the desk. "Kim, in the bottom drawer there's a red box. Just bring it; you don't want to open it."

Bishop grinned. "Is that the stuff you made for us?"

Robert handed him the box. "Yes, it worked so well, I keep making it … for special occasions. Move your hands or you'll be a Siamese twin."

He put on a pair of gloves and opened a bottle. "I made this up for the medics when we were in Korea. It's a form of liquid skin but more powerful. It's like cauterizing an open wound with a hot iron."

Bishop nodded. "Yes... and less painful. It saved me when Robert carried..."

Robert gave Bishop a sharp look, and the conversation ended.

The paramedic's mouth dropped. "I don't believe it! You've stopped the bleeding and I know the bullet hit her heart."

Martin ran into the room. "Car's out front. No board though."

Robert pushed some chairs. "Use this oriental rug. We'll make a sling."

The four men and Kimberly put Sheila in the middle of the rug. Just as they laid her down, her eyes flashed opened. Sheila grabbed Kimberly's hand. She tried to say something.

Kimberly nodded. "You're going to live, Sheila."

Kimberly tried to stand but Sheila pulled her. "F..m...."

Robert knelt down. "Sheila, we have to get you..."

Sheila's eyes flashed at him. "En...velp" and she passed out.

Kimberly rushed to open the library doors. "Roll the carpet down on each side. It'll tighten up better."

They got to the hall. "Put her down on the floor and pull the rug. It'll be quicker and you won't knock her about."

The paramedic rode with Sheila in the back as Kimberly shut the hatchback door. "Uncle Robert, what do you suppose she was trying to tell us?"

Robert shook his head frowning. "Whatever...it must be very important. Go with them and check up on the others. I'll handle Scotland Yard. You ride back with Martin and Bishop."

She nodded and jumped into the front seat with them.

Robert wearily faced the chaos inside. *What a God awful mess!* "John, I want some guards at the front gate. No one gets in without my say-so, especially the press. Now, have you seen the Chief Inspector?"

John nodded. "When we heard the gun shots, he and his men were outside. They ran across the balcony to the library doors.

Robert looked inside the monitoring room. *Looks like a war zone.* "Did James and the other two go to the hospital?"

"Yes sir, they went in the first ambulance. One of the paramedics said the guard closest to the bomb didn't make it....I don't know who it was."

Robert paused outside of the library. *Arthur handled everything and now I've got to get a plan going.* "John, you'll have to fill in for Arthur. Bishop and Martin will guide you. Until they get back from the hospital, you might set up a command post outside the monitoring room. I want a list of all the injuries. You'll need to set up a guard duty roster for the grounds until we get a new system. Martin will unearth the jeeps. Get a crew up here to clean the room and find out from Richard about our communications."

He opened the library door. "Oh, one other item." He pointed. "Duke needs a bath!"

Robert looked around and saw a man about his age standing in front of the fireplace. "I'm guessing, you must be the Chief Inspector?" He extended his hand. "I'm Robert Braun."

The Chief Inspector took his pipe out of his mouth, raised his brows, and shook Robert's hand. "It's good to know you're alive after all. I must say this whole situation is a first for me and I'm dumbfounded."

Robert pointed to the gurney leaving the room. "Well, for openers, who the heck is that man posing as Admiral Benjamin! My God, it looks just like him. Not only that, his voice and prints passed our security checks."

Robert turned to watch Windsor be zipped into a body bag. "You realize none of this can be given to the media, and because of my diplomatic immunity, this entire mess will have to be sorted out by the American Embassy and the Pentagon."

Chief O'Doul tapped his pipe out in the fireplace. "Our information is scanty as yet, but we think Benjamin was kidnapped by this group and Doctor Edse made up a mask for Alex, who happens to be a rogue agent for Scotland Yard. From what we gathered, he was the man who tried to steal your code in Korea."

Robert bristled, glaring at the Chief. "Alex Wyndgate! I tried to track that man down for over a year and couldn't find a trace of him anywhere. He murdered one of my men. He shot him in the back."

Robert shook his head. "I think it's time for a break… Could I interest you in a cup of tea? Or, better yet a drink of…?"

The Chief smiled. "Brandy or Cognac perhaps?"

O'Doul went to one of his men. "None of this information leaves this room. I'll be with Dr. Braun in another part of the house. Don't leave without me."

"Lead the way, Dr. Braun."

They started to walk out when a policeman passed them with Eddie Edse in handcuffs.

Edse tugged away and got into Robert's face. "You'll pay for taking Windsor away from me! You ruined his life, you fucking bastard!" He spit at him.

Robert glared. He grabbed Edse by his suit coat and banged him against the wall. "You, son of a bitch! You belong in that body bag next to that bastard! Where you're going, I'm sure you'll find someone to take his place. Prisons are filled with losers." He shoved Edse back to the policeman. "Please, get this piece of …out of my house!"

Robert wiped his face. "Chief, follow me please."

He watched the police pull Edse out of the room. He heard the doctor snap at the policeman. "That's my stuff in that bag! That belongs to me!"

"Envelp" had been going over in Robert's mind. He yelled at the policeman. "Wait! Officer!" The two policemen with Edse stopped.

Robert and the Chief hurried to them. Robert stared at the Chief and whispered. "That bag can't leave this house! There's an envelope in it that belongs to the Pentagon. *National security.*"

The Chief nodded. "Officer, open the bag and empty it." He handed the small yellow envelope to Robert. "Does this belong to you?"

Edse tried to jerk away from the officers. "You Bastard, fuckin bastard! That's my stuff you've taken. I'll sue you! I've witnesses!"

Finally, when it was quiet, Robert shrugged and sighed. "Now, I'm ready for a drink!"

They walked across the hall to the Game Room. Robert motioned for the Chief to sit wherever he'd be comfortable while he brought two glasses and two bottles.

O'Doul couldn't resist the wing back chairs in front of a beautiful fire blazing in the fireplace. *I've never had such luxury. Have to have a taste.*

Robert poured the drinks and put the Cognac bottle on a side table next to the chief. Hmm. *The admiration on the man's face! And I take all this for granted. I need to be more aware.*

Robert poured his drink and stoked the fire. "You didn't finish. Have you found Benjamin?"

The Chief took a sip and his eyes gleamed. *I can't remember the last time I had this luscious drink.* He paused…enjoying the warmth as it slipped down his throat.

"We think so." He repeated all the information he had given to Ross about the Dream Team's findings.

"The helicopter flew him to one of your carriers, USS. Bainbridge, which happens to be in the North Sea. I'm waiting to hear from the ship's doctor."

One of Robert's staff knocked at the door to report that Martin called and they'd be returning with Arthur. The bullet was removed from Sheila's chest. It did knick her heart. The doctor didn't want her moved until she was stabilized.

Robert sighed and nodded. *I'm grateful for that.* "Good news… Call Martin back. Sheila is to be brought here when she's able to travel. Also, have John contact the USS. Bainbridge. Ask for the data on the rescue of Admiral Benjamin."

Lauren's revelations!

Lauren left her office at R & K and got into her car. *Sheila must have gotten Kim's message all screwed up. I wonder if a maid caught her eye. That girl will never change. She wore me out that's for sure. Whatever, I can be there in plenty of time before Kim would start to go wherever we're to meet. Plus, she won't believe the surprise I've got to show her.*

At the estate, she was shocked to see the gate house scattered on the ground. She hurried to the gate. "What has happened? Is Kimberly all right?" Three guards blocked the entrance, manually operating the entrance gate.

She showed them her R & K Badge. "I'm Lauren Woodgrieves."

The guard shook his head. "I'm sorry, Miss Woodgrieves, your name's not on our list. You'll have to come in and turn around and then leave."

Outside the gate many vehicles from Scotland Yard and local police were parked along the roadside. The guards pushed the gate back and motioned for her to enter.

As she made the turn, another guard she recognized arrived on his bicycle. She stopped short and jumped out to catch him.

The guard got off his bike. "Miss Woodgrieves…I can see you've not heard anything about this disturbance."

"No…I haven't! Miss Kimberly! Is she okay?"

The guard used a hand-held radio. "John, Miss Woodgrieves is here. Her name's not on the list. Can I still send her in?"

"Just a minute, let me ask the boss."

Lauren paced a few steps anxiously. *Who's the boss? Since when is Arthur the boss. They shouldn't be referring to Kimberly that way either.*

The guard called to her. "Boss says it's okay. Before you go we have to scan you."

"Stand away from the car and put your arms out."

Lauren pulled her hand out of her coat pocket with a gauze wrapping around the fingers."

The guard waved the wand around her. "That must have hurt."

She frowned. "Oh, you mean my hand! No, I got a rash from somewhere; the gauze keeps me from scratching it."

He smiled. "You're okay. Go on up to the house!"

Lauren jumped into her car. "Thanks so much!"

慢慤

My God, more cars everywhere! She ran toward the front door. *There's been an explosion! The windows are blown out in that monitoring room Kim showed me. Boarding the windows.* She ran up to the house to look in. *This is dreadful. There's nothing left of the monitors. Part of the wall is gone. What has happened! Sheila! Never so much as gave a clue. She didn't want me out here.*

A voice behind her startled her. "Miss Woodgrieves, you're in an unauthorized area. Please proceed to the front door."

Lauren nodded with a shrug. "I'm sorry."

The guard looked at her badge and opened the door.

"I'm sorry, Miss Woodgrieves; you'll have to wait here until we can take you to the boss. It may be a while. There's a chair over there."

She watched the crew remove the debris. *Something awful has happened. I wish someone would at least tell me if Kim is okay. Sheila's with her too. Maybe I should call Uncle Charles. At least he'd have some clout.*

She walked to the table. "Excuse me. May I use the phone?"

"I'm sorry, Miss Woodgrieves, you may not."

She heard voices and looked up the hall. *Who are those men? That laugh!* She stared as they came closer. *Kim was so right! My god, he is alive!*

Lauren walked very fast toward the men. Robert stopped with the Chief Inspector.

She wiped her eyes as she put her arms around Robert. "Doctor Braun! Doctor Braun! Kim was so right. You're alive!"

Robert nodded to the Chief. "I'll be in touch."

Robert stopped short as she slid her hand back into her pocket. "Have you hurt yourself?" He stared at her. "You didn't get a chemical burn, did you?"

Lauren tucked her hand away quickly. "No sir, just a rash. Really."

He put his arm around her. "We need to talk. Come with me."

Almost an hour went by before Robert finished explaining to Lauren all that had led up to the day's tragedy.

Holding her hand to her mouth, listening in disbelief, Lauren blurted. "Sheila and Arthur! They are alive?..."

Robert nodded. "But they've been injured. Kim, Bishop and Martin took Sheila to the hospital. She saved our lives by leaping in front of Kim and me. They should be back soon with Arthur. Seems he's determined not to stay there. Sheila will be there for a few days."

She sank in her seat. *That's why Sheila gave me that envelope. She knew this would be dangerous. She wanted to protect me.*

"Lauren, I hope you can understand I felt it was in your best interests to keep you out of the loop. What happened today confirms my decision. Windsor would have mutilated you to get the information he thought you knew."

Lauren sat back in her chair and sighed. "You mean, sir, what I do know."

Robert stared at her. "What do you mean?...I was just going to ask if you'd like to work with me on other projects....like..."

Lauren leaned forward. "Like transfiguration?"

Robert grinned shaking his head. "How did you know?"

"On the plane, coming back from our ski trip, Kim and I studied the differences in the code sheets you'd given me for various tests. Uncle Charles used my lap top at a conference you'd sent him to and neglected to take out your disc. I showed it to Kim as I couldn't understand it. She recognized you'd used the program she developed for her dissertation, and.."

Robert smiled. "You needn't say any more ...I've already been raked over the coals for using it!"

She raised her brow. "So...I spent several days going over every code piece. My suspicions were confirmed when I came to the last test you wanted before you die...well, before you left the scene. I'd showed it to Kim. We both knew this wasn't the typical kind of results, something *blank but there*!"

She got up and walked to the wall switches. "Of all the tests, only three had different code sheets attached....and Dr. Braun, that last test was one of them. I need more light to show you something."

He frowned. "Go ahead, third switch in from the left."

She turned on a pendant light over the table where they sat. "At first I was torn by my curiosity versus the requested test parameters. So...I did the test as prescribed, but then, I remembered you telling me that a good chemist always let curiosity lead."

Robert studied Lauren's expression. *What is this girl up to? She knows something.* He nodded his head. "Yes, that's always been what's driven me."

"Lauren, what is it you want to show me?"

She sat on one leg, leaned forward on the table, unwrapping the gauze that covered her left hand.

He frowned. "How did you really hurt your hand?"

"I had to wrap it because... I had an accident with that last test, Dr. Braun."

She smiled looking up at her boss and mentor.

Robert's mouth dropped open. "How long has it been?" He took her hand and felt the fingers. Then put on his special glasses to examine them.

She gleamed. "My fingers have been invisible for two days!"

Robert beamed with excitement. "My God, I hope you took down all your findings!"

"Yes, sir, I have it all recorded."

"How did this happen? What prompted you to look deeper?"

Lauren sat back in her chair putting the gauze on her hand. "I showed the results of the first stage of your last test to Kim."

"Yes, I know, I was in the room that night."

She squinted. "Were you in a wheel chair?"

He stared at her. "I'll explain later...go on with your story."

"We decided not to tell anyone about the test. Then we attended the meeting that Scotland Yard had set up and I, unknowingly at the time, handed everyone the code sheets I would fill out after each test. To make a long story short, I was stunned by the reaction one of the inspectors had when he saw the papers. The second code sheet, actually."

Robert sat back. "That second page went with the last test you ran. Right?"

Lauren sat back excited. "Yes it did! I knew I couldn't figure out the code, but I could break down the chemicals and come up with the formula or close to it. So, I spent many a long night breaking down the chemicals involved. I put a drop of the solution on small items and they'd disappear for an hour. Then one of the fellas offered me a piece of fried chicken. I don't care for the skin and laid it on the plate when I wondered if a different form of matter would be affected."

"That's when you realized I wanted to be invisible and not the object."

"Yes, but I also realized that sixty minutes wouldn't be enough to accomplish whatever you wanted to do."

"That's when you had the accident."

Lauren nodded slowly. "I made up a vial of each chemical and they were lined up on the table. Something spooked me and when I turned, my lab coat cuff caused a domino effect, knocking over the vials in order except the last one didn't pour out completely. It fell resting on one of the others and only half came out....Causing this to happen."

The game room door opened. Duke led Kimberly, Martin and the Bishop into the room. Martin went to the bar. "I hope we're done for the day, because I'm having a lager. Bishop?" He slid a bottle down the bar to his comrade.

Robert and Lauren turned to watch. "What's the report?"

Bishop grinned. "The hospital was very grateful we took Arthur. He's not at all the ideal patient."

Robert chuckled. "Where's the surprise in that truth?"

Kimberly sat next to Lauren. "Hi, you missed a great party today."

"Uncle, did any of Sheila's jabber mean anything to you. She never said anything else and they took her right into surgery."

Robert grinned and put his arm around Kimberly. "Sheila was trying to say envelope. When the guards took Edse out he gave it away that he had the envelope. He snarled at the officer so wickedly when they took his belongings, I realized he had to have it. I'm very relieved to say the microfilm is back in the vault."

Lauren tried to wrap her hand quickly with the gauze. Kimberly raised her brow. "What did you do to your hand?"

Kimberly reached for Lauren's hand

She took hold of Lauren's hand and looked at her uncle's jubilant smile. *Why is Uncle Robert looking ecstatic? After all, Lauren has an ...injury or is missing...* "Uncle Robert, where are her fingers?"

Kimberly put Lauren's hand down, staring at her uncle. "She's developed more of your formula, hasn't she?"

Lauren grabbed Kimberly's arm. "No, Kim, it was accident. Let me explain."

Kimberly stood, her face drained of life. "Today wasn't enough entertainment for all of you? You have no intention of retiring do you? You're not going to destroy this formula, nor give your stuff to the Pentagon?"

She glared at them. "Time to start yet another episode. But... sorry, not with me."

She shook her head sadly and hurried from the room.

Robert's head dropped and he slumped forward. "I broke my

promise to her."

Lauren dashed out of the room to the stairway. "Kim, please don't go. Let me explain."

Kimberly slumped on the top step. "Lauren, there's nothing to explain. Whatever you discovered has added twenty years to his life. I can't fault that. All that happened today is trivial compared to what you've found. This is his life. Unfortunately, not mine."

Lauren took Kim's hand. "Please don't leave. I need you."

Tears ran down both their faces. Kim sniffled and took a deep breath. "I care for you too. But I'm sorry, I must have time to think."

She covered her face with her hands. "This cloak and dagger life he has created has turned into a monster. He barely leaves this place. It's a damned fortress. You're watched constantly. At least in New York, I can walk freely everywhere. I don't have to be concerned that I'm being watched."

Lauren stared tenderly into Kimberly's eyes. "Grab a coat and stay with me tonight. We can talk."

Kimberly squeezed Lauren's hands and nodded.

Classified

S everal weeks later, Chief Inspector O'Doul put his pen down and shut his notebook. "Well, Dr. Braun, Miss Kimberly and the rest of your staff, I think we've got the complete picture here for our department. Ross, do you have anything more to add or ask?"

Ross nodded and looked at Arthur. "I'm sorry the military trials for Alex and Edse didn't turn out the way we expected. Because the whole incident has been classified, much of the information has been excluded. As a result, Alex got a life sentence rather than the death penalty."

Robert frowned and closed his copy of the report. "Edse had some of the best lawyers. I'm amazed they used his foreign extraction to allow him to serve his sentence in his home country." *He can run as far as he wants but we'll be there.*

The Defense Minister O'Bryan gathered his papers. "I agree. Edse's father is very much involved in the South African government. A team of attorneys from that government handled the case for the two of them. They certainly convoluted our legal system to their advantage. Unfortunately, it was brilliant. Using Windsor's insanity as a strategy for Edse's defense was a bit much."

Arthur muttered under his breath. "We shall see who has the last laugh."

Chief Inspector raised his brows. "I do have one question, though I think I know the answer… The name Sheila Jones was on the list of friendly witnesses for the prosecution and the defense. Then the name disappeared. Can anyone explain this to us?"

Robert cleared his throat. "Yes, I can see you'd have a question about that."

Kimberly interrupted. "I can explain. She happens to be our photographer for the business. Uncle Robert suspected Windsor of stealing formulas from him and asked Sheila to take pictures where ever she could to prove his whereabouts at the times of the thefts. Since Sheila saved our lives, our attorneys didn't feel she needed to testify in her frail condition. They removed her name from both lists."

The Chief Inspector stared at Kimberly. "That's very interesting." He frowned at each member of the Braun staff including Robert Braun. "Not exactly the story I'd been given by Doctor Edse."

Robert stared back at the Chief. "If you recall, when the police took Edse out, he blamed me for killing Windsor."

O'Doul nodded his head and chuckled. "That was a bit excessive…. Anyway, he's already been extradited to the South African embassy waiting for deportation; I think we can drop this issue."

The Chief gathered his papers and saw Ross standing near the fireplace reliving the nightmare. O'Doul stood next to him. "Are you okay?"

Ross nodded.

O'Doul sat in one of the chairs. "Have you talked to Alex?"

Ross, still using a cane, pointed to where Alex had fallen. "Not a day goes by that I don't ask if he'll see me…The guard returns with the same answer, Alex won't see anyone."

Ross leaned against the mantel. "Chief, I know my job; I've a degree in criminal psychology. How could I not see all those years were a sham?"

He dropped his head. "I can't believe –won't believe he didn't love his wife, Jane."

O'Doul frowned. "For some reason he's torturing you, Ross. You must get to the bottom of this. When we get back to the yard, we need to look into this again."

The others started to leave the library. "I can assure you, you will have that meeting with Alex."

Before they left the estate, Robert showed his guests the rebuilt monitoring room. "We are now connected to a satellite. This is a fail-safe system now, with back-ups."

Kimberly and Lauren heard her uncle's remarks. "He's so proud and happy again." She gazed sweetly at Lauren as they strolled out the front door. "I just hope you can maintain a life separate from his as I have."

Kimberly opened Lauren's car door. "Promise me you will, or at least try."

56

Kimberly makes a decision

Martin looked in the rearview mirror. *Kimberly looks troubled. I wonder if she's decided to return to the States.* "Miss Kim, which entrance would you like?"

He had taken the back drive to the estate. She looked out the window and saw her uncle in her favorite garden. "Stop, Martin. I can get out here. Uncle Robert is in the garden."

She didn't wait for him to open her door. She popped out and jogged over to where he sat. Duke sprawled under the tree next to the bench and didn't move.

Robert's head was bowed as he pushed her little swing. "You're leaving, aren't you?"

Kimberly sat next to him. "How did you know?"

He avoided looking at her. "I knew the minute I let you down it would be just a matter of time before you'd leave."

Kimberly gasped. "No, no Uncle Robert. You've not let me down!"

She put her arms around him and held him tight. "I love you with all my heart. You've made me the person I am....but I....Please understand...I can't live in your world."

She cried on his shoulder. Robert turned to hold her. He wiped the tears flowing down her face. "Kim, my darling child, you're the daughter I've always wanted. It wasn't my intention to hurt you in anyway. I'm so sorry. I'll close up everything ..."

"Uncle Robert,...please don't say that. I'm only one part of your love. You have a gift and that is your other love. You mustn't give that up. You've led two lives to keep from sacrificing this gift for humanity. I realize that now....But...you see..."

The tears gates opened. She buried her head on his shoulder and whispered. "You raised me to live a different way from the world you live in....The thought I'm being watched every minute of the day is more than I can take. I don't want to have an ear implant, have my conversations heard by all. I want my private times, my intimate moments..."

She clasped her hands around his. "I want to surprise you with my efforts, my friends, my problems, my whatever. Uncle Robert, I need my freedom to be my own person."

Robert held her firmly in his arms. He closed his eyes as a tear ran down his cheek. "Kim, we can work this out. I understand and you're right in wanting this."

They sat quietly for some time.

Robert pushed the little swing. "I can't believe thirty years has passed. I look out here and visualize all the little and big moments we shared."

Kimberly took hold of his hand. "Those memories never stop, Uncle. No matter where I am, we still have them and create more."

He forced a weak smile. "This won't be my favorite."

Kimberly straightened up wiping her eyes. "Nor mine... Can we go for a walk?"

They strolled into the garden arm in arm. Kimberly pointed to the pond. "Do you remember when you gave me this garden?"

His eyes glowed. "It was on your first birthday living here. You'd turned four years old. You were so smart for your age. I feared I wouldn't be able to nurture your innate abilities. You had such an insatiable awareness!"

Kimberly looked into his eyes. "Do you remember what you told me when you gave this to me?"

He chuckled. "You surely don't remember what I said...You were only four."

She beamed at him. "Yes I do...You told me...to take care of my garden and love it. It will always be beautiful."

Kimberly walked a few steps from him. "I realized later on that was a metaphor and you were comparing the garden to one's consciousness."

He beamed looking at her. "You've become a very beautiful woman. I'm so very proud of you."

☞❦

They sauntered back to the house. "Uncle, you remember you're having the Gunthers and Gabriels for dinner tonight."

Robert stopped. "I feel dreadful I still haven't talked with any of them since before...my funeral." He bit his lip and paced a few steps. "You and Lauren broke the news to them gently?"

Kimberly grinned. "As I remember, we had the hardest time telling them. Lauren kept asking her Uncle Charles a lot of what ifs. Like, what if Robert's ghost was here with us, what you would say to him."

Robert chuckled. "He'd probably tell me to slow down and go visit you."

She laughed out loud. "That's exactly what he said. After so many of our hypothetical questions, her Aunt Harriet frowned, looked quizzically at us, and asked what we were up to. She paused for a moment, gasped a little, and then asked if we were telling them you're alive."

Robert bit his lip. "I hope that didn't shake Charles too badly. He's like an older brother, a dear friend. One of the few I have outside of my *secret world*."

"He cried, but they were tears of joy. Harriet called to say the news of Robert being alive has given Gunthie renewed energy."

Robert stopped to look around. "I'm so relieved about that. I know they'll want an explanation and as hard as it will be, I won't be able to go into a lot of detail."

"Uncle Robert, rather than beat around the bush, just tell them the whole story. I'm sure they've pieced some of this together ever since the meeting with Scotland Yard. They certainly aren't clueless! They wouldn't be working for you."

∾∾

Kimberly stooped to pick up one of Duke's toys. Robert put his hand out to stop her. "Duke, you didn't get all your toys."

Duke barked at him and grabbed up the ball. They grinned. "He doesn't like being corrected, does he?"

Kimberly knelt next to Duke. "Uncle? Is Duke too old to father a litter?"

Robert frowned. "What's up your sleeve?"

Kimberly hugged Duke. "Until I found out you hadn't died, I was prepared to take Duke home with me. Now, I won't be able to, but, I thought maybe I could have one of his offspring. What do you think?"

Robert opened the kitchen entrance door. "I don't see why not. I'll talk to the vet tomorrow. When are you leaving?" *Now I've to look shocked. Damn it!*

Kimberly didn't look at him. "In two days."

Arthur met them in the kitchen. "Robert, here's the guest list for tonight's dinner and the menu."

"Kim, are you and Lauren coming tonight?"

She shook her head. "Lauren's playing Chef."

He crossed off the orange sorbet and handed the menu back to Arthur.

Robert cleared his throat. "Kim, before you run, would you consider a suggestion?"

She frowned, squinting one eye. *Something's going on.......* "Yes...what are you planning?"

Robert smiled and put his arm around her. "No...no.. I just thought you might consider taking Bertha with you."

She stared at him for a moment as her mind raced. *"NO!* Uncle Robert. I love her dearly, but....I've got to find out for myself what I need." She looked at both of them and shook her head. "No way.

The worst in New York is the vagrant on the street. You've trained me for that. Are you wanting her to go to work with me? Walk with me? You can have all the mystery, spy stuff here....Bertha would be your eyes and ears, and you know it!"

Kimberly stood back from him. "Can't you see how ridiculous this is? A thirty-two year old having her *Nanny* with her twenty-four seven!"

She glared at both of them. *"NO!"*

Arthur turned as he didn't want her to see his grin. *Robert's twin!*

Robert, wide eyed, backed away and put his hands up. "Okay!" *Now we have to go to plan B.*

᚛ळ᚜

An hour later, Kimberly pulled up at Lauren's. She got out of the car and waved to the headlights behind her that moved slowly to a stop. *There's no point saying anything. If I stay the night, Arthur will send a replacement.*

Lauren opened the door, noted annoyance in Kim's face, and frowned. "Is it that bad coming over here?"

Kimberly stepped back and pointed to the cars. "Nothing changes. I still have an escort..."

Lauren shut the door and put her arm through Kimberly's. "I hope this hasn't ruined our evening together."

Kimberly turned and put her arms around Lauren. "Gosh no!" *Leaving is the hardest thing I've had to do. Now especially.*

This time Kimberly really kissed Lauren for some time in the hallway.

Lauren studied Kimberly. "Maybe you should travel more often!"

She led Kimberly into the kitchen and handed her an apron. "You look weary. You've had the big conversation with your uncle."

Kimberly tied the apron string behind her. "Yes, it was very difficult, but I'm relieved Uncle Robert understands now and is willing to let me find my own way."

Kimberly lifted the lid on the roaster. "This smells delicious..."

She leaned against the cupboard. "Am I being selfish or hurting myself by leaving?"

Lauren frowned. "What makes you feel that way?"

Kimberly snatched a carrot from Lauren's dishing up. "I've never cried so hard and so much as today. I felt like I crushed Uncle Robert to have my own way. I can't understand why I can't be satisfied with his world."

Lauren saw tears welling up. She put her spoon down and turned off the stove.

She looked at Kimberly wistfully. "We can eat later. Let's sit by the fire."

Lauren cuddled up inside Kimberly's arms. "Kim, my darling. This is not a matter of right or wrong. Of course there's conflict between you."

Lauren beamed in Kim's face. "Your character and personalities are identical. He told me his biggest mistake was hiding his intrigue from you. He thought he was protecting you...Now that you know, he feels you should jump on board. You have to do what is best for you. Behind all of that control and paranoia, he knows you're making the right move...."

Lauren reached for a blanket robe from the top of the couch. She kissed Kimberly tenderly. "If it's right for us to be together, it will happen. Regardless, I'll always be your friend. I've never been as comfortable as I am right now."

Lauren kissed Kimberly on the cheek. "Do you feel the same?"

Kimberly shut her eyes and held Lauren. *She's so wonderful. The weight has fallen off. She's so right.* Kimberly looked into Lauren's beautiful eyes and smiled. "Thank you, I was afraid you wouldn't understand and I'd lose you."

They kissed and...

ॐ∽ॐ

The Braun limo pulled into a private gate at the airport. Robert wore a hat and sunglasses to avoid recognition. He got out of the car with Kimberly, Arthur, and the Bishop. Martin parked the car.

Inside, Robert looked at Kimberly. "You could have flown in the company jet, and then…"

Kimberly shook her head. "Uncle Robert…I'm following my plan…"

He shrugged. "Okay, I'm sorry."

He turned and winked at Arthur and the Bishop.

The flight attendant announced the flight. "Third class tickets please enter the plane now."

Robert turned to Kimberly, "You did get first class tickets, I hope! That looks like a full plane."

Kimberly nodded. "That's strange. When I first called, I was told that flying during the week the business class would be available. Then yesterday Continental called to ask if I'd take first class at no extra charge. They had a team of business men they wanted to keep together for some company. Well, it's time for me to go."

She hugged her uncle. "I don't want to cry so I'm going to leave you all quickly."

Robert whispered. "I love you my daughter. Come back to me when you can. I'll always miss you."

She wiped her eyes and nodded as she squeezed the Bishop's hands. "Kimberly, you're doing the right thing."

She hugged him. "You'll take care of him?"

He smiled and nodded. "With all my heart."

She hugged Arthur, and Martin, and then rushed to the door.

Arthur stared at the gate door frowning, and then turned to the others. "Did you see that woman race to the door?"

Martin zipped up his jacket. "Before or after Kim went through?"

"After! I could swear it was Sheila."

The three men turned to Robert. "What have you done?"

They walked to where Martin had the car. "Robert!"

"Well, it took some doing, but I bought out the plane and gave the tickets to any of service men at the Embassy who had leave coming up."

The Bishop stopped. "Was that Sheila?"

Then with a laugh, "It was, wasn't it?"

Robert ducked his head and got into the car. "Well, it seemed there's an apartment available in Kim's building and…a friend of mine in New York needs a photographer and…"

The other three piled in and slammed the door. Arthur blurted, "So you bought the apartment for Sheila and she will accidentally run into Kimberly. Did you send Kimberly's secretary as well. Sheila's pretty stuck on her."

Bishop nudged Martin. "Any bets half of the Navy live in that building."

Robert hesitated and put on a hurt look. "That's very unkind. I would never do that. Kim is making her way on her own!"

Robert's colleagues heartily laughed and looked at one another. The Bishop leaned forward from the backseat. " Have either of you ever heard Robert say that before?"

Martin looked at Robert in the rear view mirror and laughed. "Maybe once a week for the last thirty years"

Arthur gleamed. "And, it always sounds so…"

"You're all fired."

"Heard that one too!…"

I need to remind Charles not to mention the properties I own in New York……nor who lives in them…….in front of these three. I'll never hear the end of it.

THE END

About the Author

The author lives in Rocky River, Ohio, and is a graduate of Ohio State. She taught school for six years and then entered the business world where she still keeps her day job.

61453857R00200

Made in the USA
Columbia, SC
23 June 2019